PRAISE FOR T[...] NNER OF THE
ALL ABOUT R[...] [...]EST EROTICA

"An intensely sexual love story."   —*Kirkus Reviews*

"Addictive, delectable reading."   —*USA Today*

"Wicked good storytelling."
                    —Jaci Burton, *New York Times* bestselling author

"Holy hell HAWT."   —Under the Covers Book Blog

"Suspenseful . . . hella sexy and hot. [The hero and heroine's]
erotic relationship is good enough to make one's toes curl."
                                              —*RT Book Reviews*

"One of the sexiest, most erotic love stories that I have read in a
long time."   —Affaire de Coeur

"A sleek, sexy thrill ride."   —Jo Davis, national bestselling author

"One of the best erotic romances I've ever read."
                                              —All About Romance

"Nearly singed my eyebrows."   —Dear Author

"Fabulous, sizzling hot."
                    —Julie James, *New York Times* bestselling author

"Action and sex and plenty of spins and twists."
                                      —Genre Go Round Reviews

"Intoxicating and exhilarating."   —Fresh Fiction

"Some of the sexiest love scenes I have read this year."
                                              —Romance Junkies

"Scorching hot! I was held spellbound."   —Wild on Books

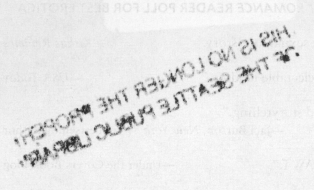

LOOKING INSIDE

BETH KERY

BERKLEY
NEW YORK

BERKLEY
An imprint of Penguin Random House LLC
375 Hudson Street, New York, New York 10014

Library of Congress Cataloging-in-Publication Data

Names: Kery, Beth, author.
Title: Looking inside / Beth Kery.
Description: First edition. | New York : Berkley, [2016]
Identifiers: LCCN 2016026199 (print) | LCCN 2016032233 (ebook) | ISBN
9780399583698 (softcover) | ISBN 9780399583704
Subjects: | BISAC: FICTION / Romance / Contemporary. | FICTION / Romance /
General. | FICTION / Contemporary Women. | GSAFD: Romantic suspense
fiction. | Erotic fiction.
Classification: LCC PS3611.E79 L66 2016 (print) | LCC PS3611.E79 (ebook) |
DDC 813/.6—dc23
LC record available at https://lccn.loc.gov/2016026199

First Edition: November 2016

Printed in the United States of America
3   5   7   9   10   8   6   4   2

Cover photo © plainpicture / Cédric Roulliat;
back cover photo: Chicago Skyline © MaxyM / Shutterstock
Cover design by Sarah Oberrender
Book design by Laura K. Corless

In deepest gratitude to my husband,
who is the continual source of my romantic
inspiration and support

PROLOGUE

Eleanor awakened at two thirty a.m. from a deep sleep. Had she sensed a light going on outside the bedroom window?

Maybe your voyeuristic instincts are sharpening.

She smirked at the thought. Common sense made her hesitate for a moment. Eleanor was known for being even-keeled and rational, after all. But it wasn't logic that made her throw off the covers and glide through the dark room, drawn to the window irrevocably.

Not a sound could be heard in Caddy's condominium. She and her sister had stayed up late, putting up Caddy's Christmas tree and drinking hot chocolate. It was an annual tradition. Undoubtedly Caddy slept deeply in the master bedroom suite down the hall, unsuspecting of her sister's compulsion. If Caddy ever found out why Eleanor had grown to love staying in her guest bedroom so much, she'd be stunned at first, and then burst out with incredulous laughter.

No one would ever suspect practical, bookish Eleanor of such salacious behavior.

She stood at the corner of the window and peered furtively out to the adjacent high-rise. Her entire body quickened.

He's there. I can see him.

It had happened rarely enough in the past several months, either that he happened to leave his curtains open or that she stayed over in the guest room at Caddy's. Tonight, the stars had aligned. She looked into a lit, luxurious bedroom, and onto a scene of vibrant, bold sensuality.

She spied into another world.

He came down over the naked woman on the bed. It was a different woman than she'd seen him with before. He had a new lover. His big, lean body and golden-brown coloring created a stunning contrast to the female's pale ivory skin, jet-black hair and petite proportions. He'd restrained her arms to the bed, but her legs were free. The woman clamped her thighs together and wriggled her hips in response to his mouth trailing across her skin. The man opened his hand on the woman's pelvis and kept her in place while his mouth fixed on a breast. Eleanor didn't even know his name, but she sensed something about him at that moment. He didn't like a woman to twist and writhe while he made love to her. He wanted her to take every ounce of pleasure he gave . . .

. . . And he gave plenty.

His burnished brown head moved subtly, and Eleanor vividly imagined his wet, lashing tongue, his taut sucking. The woman's back arched off the bed, as if she offered more of herself to him. Eleanor touched the tip of her own breast, wincing as arousal stabbed at her. He'd taken off his shirt but still wore a pair of black pants. His back muscles and powerful arms bunched and flexed as his head moved lower on the woman's body. His mouth grazed down her sides while his large hands bracketed her tiny waist. One hand detailed the curve of her hip. Whatever he was doing with his mouth made the woman squirm. He held her hips down firmly, continuing his explorations with his mouth. When she writhed against his hold, one hand slid down to her buttock and flexed in a deliberate, greedy gesture. He spanked the flesh—

not hard, but briskly—and then squeezed again. Eleanor started and moaned softly. His lover turned her hip on the bed, again offering more of her flesh to him . . . no, *begging* him to take more.

What would it be like, to be the focus of his pointed hunger? She'd only seen him make love once before, but he always took and gave with such precision. It had been shocking to her upon first viewing it: his masterful, confident handling of a woman's body. It wasn't something she'd ever witnessed before, let alone experienced.

The man's hand coasted up the woman's thigh and slid between her legs. His mouth continued to caress her belly, waist and hip while his hand moved knowingly.

Eleanor left the shadows like a sleepwalker and pressed her hands to the frigid windowpane, her entire being vibrating with lust and desperate, hopeless longing.

ONE

One year later

Eleanor Briggs thought it fitting that she'd chosen a reading event to make her debut as a sexually confident, "I take what I want *when* I want it" female. Her entire job revolved around books, after all. Well . . . the part that didn't involve conserving historical documents, costumes and artifacts, or doing research that would bore most people out of their minds.

In books, whole new worlds were born and new identities created, all through the power of the imagination. What better venue for her to transform herself into a sexual force of nature and worthy bedmate for her obsession, Trey Riordan? If it weren't for her imagination, the fuel of distilled longing, and perhaps the cruel eye-opening she'd had after the abrupt loss of her sister, she'd never have the nerve to go after an unobtainable dream like him.

Tonight, she moved out of the shadows and officially into the spotlight.

"Are you here for the reading event?" Stacy Moffitt asked her in a bored tone as she slipped an iPad and phone in a manila envelope and wound a numbered string around the enclosure.

Eleanor took heart from Stacy's lack of attention. Maybe Stacy wouldn't notice who she was. Stacy worked under Jimmy Garcia. Jimmy was the director of special events at the Illinois Historical

Museum, and Eleanor's longtime friend. Eleanor worked for the museum too, as the conservation and preservation librarian. Jimmy had been called out of town unexpectedly yesterday, which was a good thing for Eleanor. Jimmy was the only other person on earth who knew about her obsession with Trey Riordan. He didn't, however, know about her aggressive plan for finally getting his attention.

"That's what I'm here for," Eleanor told Stacy.

"There's a strictly enforced 'no talking' policy during reading hours. I need you to turn in all cell phones, tablets and computers. This is a technology-free zone. We only want you focusing on your book for the next two hours," Stacy said in a preachy voice.

"Ah, I get it now. Thus the name of the event: Leave Everything Behind but a Book. Clever," Eleanor said under her breath as she dug in the Italian designer bag that used to belong to her sister, Caddy. Stacy glanced up at her sarcastic tone. The way Jimmy's assistant gaped at her disbelievingly was *not* flattering.

"Eleanor. Is that *you*?"

"None other," Eleanor replied grimly, placing her cell phone on the counter. With a furious effort, she held the young woman's stare. She would *not* be cowed a mere minute into her performance.

Stacy's gaze dropped down over her snug suede bodice and the fitted, conservative blazer paired with it. As far as Eleanor knew, her sister Caddy had only worn the outfit once. Eleanor had practically achieved photosynthesis, she'd been so green with envy when she'd watched her sister leave her condo in it. The occasion had been an Odesza concert given by Chicago socialite Sasha Allen Severnsen exclusively for her closest friends in honor of Caddy's thirty-third birthday. Caddy was always having awesome, glamorous parties thrown for her. Along with the short skirt, dark brown tights and the soft, fitted, beige thigh-high Rockerchick boots, the outfit screamed money, good times, boldness and sex. In other words, it had Caddy stamped all over it.

Stacy's stare lingered on the tops of Eleanor's breasts. The suede bodice had cupped them softly in a seduction that was somehow both tasteful and flagrant at once. It wasn't just a sensual invitation to Trey Riordan either. Eleanor herself was being seduced by the feeling of the suede against her bare breasts.

"That's quite an outfit," Stacy finally said disbelievingly as she held out a claim ticket for Eleanor's phone. "Not your typical work wardrobe, that's for sure. What's the occasion?"

Eleanor shrugged, reached into her bag and withdrew her reading choice for the evening. "I'm reading a very sexy book."

Normally, she wouldn't have the nerve. It was Caddy's outfit that made her say it. Ignoring Stacy's openmouthed shock at her book choice for what was supposed to be a serious, highbrow literary event, Eleanor plucked the claim ticket out of Stacy's hand and strode into the quickly filling Historic Grounds Coffee Shop. The thigh-high boots she wore were the equivalent of sexual jet fuel. They weren't "fuck me" boots, necessarily. They had only a half-inch flat heel, but they hugged her legs tightly, showing off their shape. Eleanor would more describe them as "fuck *you*" boots . . . and *maybe* "me," if you've got some major balls.

Trey Riordan did. Her fingers were crossed.

It was surprising how easy it was to play the part while wearing Caddy's clothing. Eleanor suspected this was how all understudies felt when they first donned the star's wardrobe and felt the rush of an enraptured audience.

Not that she was interested in the audience in general, Eleanor acknowledged as she scanned the crowd and several men's stares landed on her and stuck. It was flattering, of course. A month ago, she would have grown giddy at the idea of men going glassy-eyed when they looked at her. That was before she'd sampled a couple of the outfits she'd inherited from Caddy and noticed their effect on people.

She should skip ordering coffee, knowing it wasn't a good idea to add caffeine to her nervous excitement. Her jitters only amplified when she couldn't locate her target audience. Jimmy had told her Trey Riordan's name had been the second one on the list when he'd signed up for the Historical Society reading event a month ago. Surely such eagerness implied he wasn't likely to change his mind? Just as her heart began to sink in disappointment, she saw the back of his golden-brown hair and those edible shoulders beneath a light blue shirt.

How could she have missed him? He was only ten feet away from her. She was used to seeing him from the distance between the two adjacent buildings, that was the problem. Plus, he'd grown even leaner in the past month. His waist appeared especially narrow in comparison to his powerful back and shoulders. Even though he probably had lost negligible weight, his muscles were even more pronounced than they'd been in the past. Eleanor wondered what had him appearing so wiry and fighting lean.

He bent and withdrew a leather-bound book from his briefcase. His close proximity struck her as surreal.

Her heartbeat started to drum in her ears, but whether the rhythm was a death march or a sexual tattoo, Eleanor couldn't say. *I'm going to make a hot mess of this.* For a charged few seconds, she experienced a strong urge to run. Sure, she'd dressed in Caddy's clothes a few times, but only Jimmy and her parents had ever really seen her in them. And with *them*, it was impossible to thoroughly disguise bookish, distracted Eleanor, whom they knew all too well.

There was still time to run home, cuddle up on her couch with a bag of Cheetos and watch the latest episode of *The Librarians*.

But as a dazed state of fear descended upon her, she found her vision narrowing on Trey's riot of burnished brown waves of hair. It wasn't long, but it wasn't close-clipped either. It symbolized his irreverent, carelessly sexy style: the hallmark of a corporate rebel. It looked so soft, especially in comparison to those wide, very solid shoulders. What she wouldn't dare, to sink her fingers into that thick, tousled hair and dig her nails into that muscular, rippling back, urging him on while he drove his cock into her body.

God, I hope this works.

She had good reason to worry. For more than a month now, he'd typically been alone when he'd entered the penthouse late at night. He watched television alone, ate alone and slept alone. He pleasured himself alone. *That* memory would burn her until her dying day, it'd been scorched so deep in her brain.

Still, Trey Riordan wasn't the type of man to stay solitary for long. He was the brilliant bad-boy entrepreneur. He'd been at the center of the Scarpetti twin controversy after being photographed with the heiress sisters in flagrante delicto behind the curtain of an upscale club in Rome. Trey wasn't anywhere near as famous as the Scarpetti twins. Yet a recent survey had calculated that the seminude, viral photo of him and the gorgeous twin sisters was unique, because it was prized equally among males and females across the globe.

No, a man like Trey didn't stay partnerless for long. Her entire performance tonight was solely to encourage him to abandon his flirtation with celibacy and indulge in the delights of the flesh once again.

With her.

She hoped she was one of those rare females who made it to Trey Riordan's bed more than once, but she wasn't holding her breath. Surely one ride on that man-coaster would be enough to silence this uncustomary, uncontrollable hunger of hers. One thing was for certain: he'd never have a more appreciative lover.

For over a year now, Eleanor's obsession with him had taken root and flourished. But to this day, she'd never looked into his eyes. That simple fact festered.

She inhaled, breathing in determination.

The boots seemed to strut *her* instead of her strutting in *them*. She jogged up two stairs and slid into a window seat at a small table just eight or so feet in front of Riordan. Unfortunately, all of the lounging chairs were taken, but maybe that was for the best. A puffy armchair might block her performance from her target audience in a way that an armless wooden one wouldn't.

She swung her bag onto the back of the chair, her heart fluttering uncomfortably in her chest. As if she had all the time in the world, she smoothed her long, loose curls over her shoulder in seeming distraction, pausing over the sensation of the strands' texture. It'd been part of her act, but she was surprised to feel just how soft and sexy her hair felt sliding against her fingertips.

She knew the precise moment when Trey's stare landed on her. It was the moment her cheek tickled in awareness and her breasts suddenly felt obvious and swollen in the suede cradle of the bodice. She suppressed a strong urge to finally look point-blank into his eyes. *Don't blow it, Eleanor. Trey Riordan cut his teeth on some of the boldest femme fatales in the world. You've only got one first time.*

Slowly, she crossed her legs, feeling her skirt ride higher on her thigh. When she felt air brush against the strip of skin at the top of her thigh-high tights, she ran her fingertips across it in a seemingly distracted gesture. Her bare skin felt smooth and warm. Her clit prickled. She instinctively clamped her thighs tight to alleviate that pinch of excitement. Perhaps it was that she knew Trey's stare was on her at that moment, or maybe it was because for the first time in her life she wasn't wearing any underwear in public, but the sexual charge she experienced was shockingly strong.

Keeping her stare demurely lowered, she reached into her bag and pulled out the coup de grace: her newly purchased copy of the hugest source of derisive jokes, critical outrage and horniness in recent history, the cultural phenomenon *Born to Submit*. Due to her voyeurism, she knew firsthand the topic might capture Trey's attention. Again, she ran her fingertips over the strip of silky skin between the hem of her skirt and the top of her thigh-highs.

Making sure that Trey could see the cover, she opened the book to page one.

It is a truth universally acknowledged, that a single man in possession of a good fortune, must be in want of a wife.

Trey Riordan read the first line of *Pride and Prejudice* and smirked. He hadn't realized Jane Austen had a sense of humor. Maybe that's why ninety percent of the women he'd ever known adored this book. No, that wasn't it. It was because of the romance that women loved it. When women talked about *Pride and Prejudice*, they did so with a faraway look and a little Mona Lisa smile. It wasn't an expression he much associated with himself or his relationships. There was *nothing* mysterious about what he typically inspired in a woman.

Not that he was complaining, of course. What kind of idiot would whine over the fact that the most common reaction he drew from women was hunger? A hunger to screw, sure, but also apparently a hunger to monopolize, to control all of his time and his attention, to trap him into something he wasn't interested in . . . to squash his very spirit.

Clearly, he was not attracting the right kind of female.

It was either that, or his problems were *far* more serious. There was a very good possibility that he just wasn't meant for the long term.

That's why he'd made a conscious effort a month ago to step back from women and dating and examine what the hell he was doing with his life. Because the sad truth was he *was* complaining, wasn't he? He'd grown frustrated and listless in regard to smoking-hot but brittle, unsatisfying relationships. His dating life had grown as stale as week-old pizza . . . and about as nutritive to his well-being.

For more than a decade, the success ran just as thick as the stream of women and easy sex. He'd come into money and a kind of minor fame as a carefree, partying twenty-one-year-old when he first created BandBook, a mixture of a social and career Internet platform that hosted pages for musicians and bands. The site became popular for its original customers: people looking to book a band or musician for an event. But with its sophisticated search options, videos and the audience rating and comments feature, BandBook quickly earned a reputation as being a pulse-taker of popular culture. His start-up company became a go-to site for talent scouts looking for the next hot thing. It'd taken off like a rocket, and Trey had soon expanded the applications to other groups, like actors, artists and filmmakers. Since then, his newly consolidated company, TalentNet, had gone global. Today, Trey was proud to say that dozens of bands, musicians and other artists credited TalentNet with their first big break into celebrity status.

But he wasn't that smart-mouthed, cocky, oversexed kid who had unexpectedly discovered entrepreneurial gold anymore. After losing two friends recently, along with a couple of ugly, messy breakups in a row, it had started to dawn on him how empty and unsatisfied his relationships with women were leaving him.

So he'd vowed to take a sexual sabbatical.

Almost five weeks without sex. It'd been hard, of course, but he'd kept his eye on the prize. If he wasn't cut out to be in a serious relationship, best he figured that out now. And if he was? Well, he wasn't ever going to achieve the gratification of a meaningful relationship until he broke his old patterns and figured out what he wanted . . .

And what women wanted, of course.

Romance. That was what he suspected they wanted. He wasn't entirely sure what the meaning of the word was. He couldn't help but feel that he'd never really appreciated the inner workings of the female mind. He'd certainly never been in a relationship that resembled anything close to what his father and mother, or what his sister and her husband, shared. Like his perennially single but never alone older brother, Kevin, Trey worried he'd missed out on the meaningful relationship gene.

It was time to do a serious self-examination and personal overhaul. So far, that had involved working out for an extra hour every day at the gym, because it was *hell* being a celibate thirty-three-year-old healthy man. He had a shitload of sexual energy to burn.

Self-improvement also meant taking a class on degenerate art at the Art Institute and enrolling in an advanced tai chi class that emphasized the meditative aspects. It included daily practice on his guitar and focusing again on writing music, another thing he had abandoned by the wayside in the energy-sucking process of developing, expanding and steering TalentNet for more than a decade. He'd reapplied himself to his massive music collection too, relearning the medium that he loved and that had originally made his career.

Trey also possessed a respectable personal library in his home. That library had started to represent everything he'd begun to resent about his life. Recently he'd realized that he hadn't actually *read* anything of significance in almost a year. The library had become a decoration, a novelty talking point when he gave a guest a tour of the penthouse. When he'd started BandBook twelve years ago, he used to regularly inhale three or four books a week: great works of philosophy, literature and history, and biographies of the world's movers and shakers.

Now, the only action his library was getting was his maid's weekly dusting. God, it was lame. *He* was.

That's why when he'd seen the ad for Leave Everything Behind but a Book, he'd signed up immediately. It was the prod he needed. The concept was that while people might want to get around to reading that one particular book collecting shelf dust, it was hard to do so in this busy, technology-ridden world, especially during the frantic holiday season, which was just around the corner. The museum came up with a simple idea: grab that book you've been meaning to read forever, check your technology at the door, sit your ass down in a chair and pledge to read for two hours, two nights a week for two weeks in the company of like-minded, committed readers.

With his commitment not only to self-improvement, but to understanding the mysteries of the female mind a little better, Trey had chosen *Pride and Prejudice* as his book for the event. He'd never read it in his life, despite all the cultural references to it. He didn't get its appeal; he often didn't get women; women loved *Pride and Prejudice*.

It couldn't be more obvious he should be reading this damn book.

By the end of the short first chapter, Trey was feeling mildly optimistic. He hadn't encountered the adored Lizzy yet, let alone any of the famed romance, but it was entertaining watching Mr. Bennet verbally dance circles around his stupid wife. He flipped the page to Chapter Two, and that's when it happened.

His attention fractured at movement: a purse swinging at the very top of his vision. He glanced up distractedly and did a double take.

Oh no.

No, no, *no*. This was *not* good. What had he done to deserve *this*?

Realizing he was gaping, he lowered his head back to the book, but his gaze shot back up over his reading glasses. He watched, his mouth going dry. The newly arrived bombshell who sat just feet away from him pushed a sexy mane of loose chestnut brown curls behind her shoulder. A rebellious, glossy tendril remained. She slid her fingers down the smooth length distractedly and let it fall on the upper curve of a mouthwatering breast. Lust poured through him, the strength of it surprising him a little.

Sweet Jesus. She wore some kind of tight suede vest under her blazer, like a modernized, chic version of those lace-up bustiers women used to wear on the covers of those old-fashioned bodice-ripper romance novels. She crossed her legs. He went rigid.

Everywhere.

Her legs were slender and about a mile long. She wore a pair of tight, supple suede boots that rose several inches past her knees. When she crossed her legs, the tops of her thigh-high stockings eased into view . . . along with a strip of golden, gleaming skin. She distractedly glided her fingers across the tops of her thigh-highs. His cock jumped higher to attention.

Realizing he was staring, he lowered his head and covertly traced the profile of her face from beneath a lowered brow. She wasn't your standard beauty, but that made her even more of a knockout. Unique. Exotic. Off the charts on the sexy factor: Those were a few descriptors that came to his mind. Her neck was slender and graceful, her facial features delicate and finely wrought. He couldn't get over the color and quality of her skin. It was a feature meant to be flaunted. She looked like she'd tan easily, but refrained from roasting in the sun. The result was a smooth, satiny texture and a pale gold, dewy glow. His gaze stuck on the expanse of skin at her chest and the incredible tease of the upper swells of her breasts in that suede lace-up vest-thingy she wore. She'd be so soft there, her curving flesh firm and velvety against his lips and tongue. He imagined unlacing that vest and exposing the treasure of her breasts, cradling them in his hands and then—

He abruptly became aware of his runaway fantasizing. Was this some kind of a joke? How was he supposed to concentrate on reading a book with *this* goddess just feet away? It'd be torture enough if he hadn't sworn off sex for the past month, but considering the circumstances, this was nothing less than downright cruelty.

He glanced aside, half expecting someone to be filming his lechery. Unfortunately, he wasn't unfamiliar with the possibility. Some joker to the left of him stared at the woman in slack-jawed wonder, his book forgotten in his lap: *The Iliad*. Trey suppressed a strong urge to laugh. And he'd thought *he* had it bad trying to comprehend a word of *Pride and Prejudice* with sex personified sitting just feet away. A quick survey of the room told him that the woman was having a similar effect on more than half a dozen other helpless saps.

Forget it. Forget about her. You came here to read. Remember, the self-improvement campaign?

Right. Focus.

Mr. Bennet was among the earliest of those who waited on Mr. Bingley.

What? Who was Mr. Bingley, and who was this waiter, Mr. Bennet? Why should Trey care? He read the line again, but apparently, his brain had been turned to sex mush.

Sometimes, it was just plain shit being a guy.

Movement caught his eye again and he glanced up against his will. The goddess was pulling her book out of an expensive handbag. (He'd bought enough designer purses as gifts for girlfriends over the years to know that the woman's bag did *not* come cheap.)

His stare got stuck on her legs. She must be pretty tall to have legs that long. Five foot eight or nine? At six three, he liked a tall woman . . . liked the feeling of long, strong legs wrapped around him, pulling him deep. He liked seeing them spread-eagled and tied to his bed too. He'd love to see this woman in that position. The boots? Hell *yeah*, he'd keep those on, right along with those stockings.

She settled into the wooden chair, shifting her hips ever so slightly. Ever so *distractingly.* The stockings she wore weren't lacy lingerie; they were opaque. In combination with the boots, short skirt and legs that seemed to extend all the way up to her armpits, they struck him as ridiculously sexy. His gaze locked on the juncture of smooth, toned thighs. His mind zeroed in on what was snuggled in that dark, tight crevice. She shifted her hips again slightly, as if she was getting friction on her pussy, stimulating herself ever so subtly.

Not that she *was* getting off on exhibiting herself so enticingly, of course. That was just his filthy man brain pulsing with hormones and going into overdrive.

Wasn't it?

She set her book on the top of her thigh and opened it, the cover facing him. He immediately recognized what was quickly becoming an iconic cover. *Born to Submit.*

You have got to be fucking kidding me.

He started to sweat. He hadn't read it, any more than he'd read *Pride and Prejudice.* Both the book he held in his hands and the one she held in hers were considered women's reading, even if they were drastically different in content. Of course, he, along with every other salivating schmo in this coffee shop, knew that *Born to Submit* was about sex. Raw, hardcore BDSM. Trey didn't consider himself to be some kind of card-carrying BDSM master, but he enjoyed being the dominant in the bedroom.

He was aware of the cultural buzz about the book, the massive sales figures, the talk shows, the *Saturday Night Live* and YouTube spoofs, the snarky newspaper and magazine articles. But he'd never thought about it much until tonight, seeing it in this woman's hands. Surely *she* knew what the book involved too. Yet she'd brought it to a high-minded reading event at a museum.

Well, she *was* wearing that sexy, sophisticated outfit, wasn't she? This was no naïve little girl.

Then she began to read, and Trey found himself doubting. He had the bizarre thought that the somber, endearing expression she wore while she focused on the page was a completely natural one for her. This was how she looked often: sweet and sexy and utterly absorbed in her task, her succulent, full mouth pursed ever so slightly, her brow wrinkled with the innocent hunger of curiosity.

Suddenly, she looked up and met his stare dead on. He started slightly at being caught red-handed at gawping. Huge greenish gold eyes—cat's eyes—held him in their hypnotic trap, making it impossible to look away. Then she smiled, slow and sexy, the widening of her pink lips corresponding with the swelling of his erection.

And he wondered how the hell he could have ever thought she seemed innocent.

TWO

*B*lue.

Trey Riordan possessed the most amazing pair of clear, cobalt blue eyes. They seemed to see straight through her.

Eleanor had been dubbed shy as a child. As an adult, she preferred to call herself reserved, or possibly just extremely discerning about to whom she opened up. Whatever her excuse du jour, the truth was that self-consciousness usually overwhelmed her when she met an attractive man's stare. At twenty-eight years old, this particular trait had grown beyond annoying, but she couldn't seem to prevent it. Her gaze typically skipped off a man's interested glance like a nervous twitch.

Miraculously, that didn't happen with Trey. Instead, she sunk into his direct stare.

His dark-rimmed glasses were swoonworthy. He didn't wear them in his bedroom that she'd ever seen, or when he was making love to a woman. She'd seen photos of him before, once in *Rolling Stone* magazine and another time in *Forbes* in an article entitled "Trey Riordan and TalentNet, Rocking the Online Artist Scene." But she'd never seen him wear glasses. She couldn't have guessed at the impact of his eyes, either from those photos or her bouts of voyeurism into his bedroom window. She sensed his intelligence in his gaze, the crystal-clear acuity of his mind. Her smile came naturally, along with a rush of warmth that suffused her limbs and chest.

Her sex.

Before she knew how far she'd sunk into his eyes, they suddenly turned smoky. *Hot.* It hit her that she was sharing a steamy stare with *Trey Riordan.* As if he'd experienced a similar shock to the flesh, he started slightly. Her gaze popped off his face before she could stop it. *Damn it, stop being so jumpy.* She was supposed to be a bold, experienced woman, not a skittish virgin. Not that she was a virgin, of course. Even if she *did* sometimes feel like she was the next closest thing to one.

Forcing herself not to look away from him entirely, her gaze slid down his mouthwatering, cut torso to the book he held on one long, jean-covered thigh. He abruptly moved the open book a few inches so that it blocked his crotch. She caught the title.

Pride and Prejudice?

You've got to be kidding me.

She'd pegged him for committing to reading a book on technology and its interface with art and creativity, a weighty history or maybe even a Hemingway novel that he'd always wanted to finish. But *Pride and Prejudice*, that beacon of feminine escape and pleasure, not to mention Eleanor's favorite book of all time? It was disorienting, almost as if *he'd* been the one to arrive here tonight with the explicit purpose of seducing *her* versus the other way around.

She glanced back up at his face again. His brow knitted slightly in consternation above his glasses. She realized belatedly he'd noticed her amazed expression upon seeing his book choice. Worried she'd exposed her hand yet again, Eleanor forced her attention back to page one of her book.

Have you ever met a person that completely altered you, to such a degree that you left your everyday self behind and did something outrageous? Exciting?

Forbidden?

That's what happened to me when I first laid eyes on my boss, Xander MacKenna. I took one look into eyes as black and deep as the devil's own, and in the seconds it took me to catch my breath, I'd become his slave. Mock me if you will. Call me spineless or a naïve young fool. Label me a sick nymphomaniac if it makes you feel better. But know this. I'm free now, thanks to his touch and his punishments, his harsh commands and his epic tenderness.

And after you hear my true story, I dare you not to envy me.

She resisted rolling her eyes and smirking. Well, Ms. Andora St. Honore certainly knew how to set a stage, Eleanor thought wryly. Maybe it was a cliché, but it was an arousing one. Even though she was amused by the introduction, she was also titillated. Still, she was more focused on Trey than the book. Her awareness was like iron, and he was a powerful magnet. It was like his gaze tied it all together: him, her, the book. Every cell in her body seemed to orient itself in his direction.

She glanced up cautiously and saw that he was staring directly at her crossed thighs and crotch. She read pure male hunger in his expression.

He wanted her.

Her clit pinched in arousal. She wiggled her hips slightly to alleviate the ache, and suddenly his gaze shot to her face.

You are the most beautiful, exciting man I've ever seen. I just want to bite you all over.

The force behind her thought was so precise, so powerful, Eleanor felt like she'd just yelled the truth of her lechery out loud to the whole room. Her eyes widened in alarm. Trey Riordan *knew* what she was thinking. He had to, given the potency of her desire. She stared at her book, seeing nothing. Overwhelmed by mixed self-consciousness and excitement, she flipped a thin section of pages, trying to even her erratic breathing. She read nervously.

> *"I'm not trying to humiliate you, Katherine. But a woman who makes such obvious mistakes repeatedly is searching for an obvious consequence."*
>
> *I held my ground in front of his desk, but Xander's midnight eyes burned me deep. I knew what was about to happen. I craved it as much as I feared it.*
>
> *"What consequence is that?" I asked, my head held high.*
>
> *"I'm going to punish you. I'm going to lay you across my lap and spank you."*
>
> *Lust bit at me. I wanted to put my hand between my thighs and rub myself to silence that horrible wanting. But I couldn't. I was too proud.*
>
> *"Like hell you are."*
>
> *"Like hell I am," he said, standing behind his desk. I was reminded of how tall he was. How intimidating . . . how beautiful. "Come here." He put out his hand, beckoning me to him. I stood there, wild with wanting, but afraid to commit to my secret desire.*
>
> *Suddenly, his hard, unyielding expression altered. Was that compassion that glowed in his amazing eyes?*
>
> *"You can walk away, of course," he said, his deep, rough voice caressing my prickling skin. "But you have courage, Katya. I saw that in you from the first. Take a deep breath." I inhaled shakily. "Good. Now come to me."*

*Something inside me had awakened when he called me
by what became his pet name for me for the first time. Katya.
It sounded a little like my name, but it was different, like
he'd recognized a woman inside me that I hadn't, as if he'd
seen a secret woman hiding beneath my skin, a more exciting one. The syllables rolling off his tongue were a call . . .
a spell, licking some deep, secret place in my soul, melting
my fear. I found myself walking around his desk, unable to
look away from his dark, compelling stare.*

"Lift your skirt to your waist," he said.

Someone coughed loudly, fracturing Eleanor's attention. She
looked up and saw a bearded man's face in the crowded coffee
house, his stare on her eager . . . a little manic, the truth be told.
He'd been the one to cough in order to get her attention. Her gaze
darted to Trey. He was turned in profile, but he looked at her at
the same moment she looked at him. He too had glanced up from
his reading when the guy had coughed. She rolled her eyes slightly
and smiled. He smiled back.

Incredulous euphoria shot through her.

The book had been steamy, but the quick, nonverbal exchange
with Trey was much hotter. Maybe it was because although he
was a stranger, she knew so many private things about him. Once,
she'd watched, her heart in her throat, while Trey had positioned
a naked, curvaceous blonde bent over his bed. Then he'd spanked
her while he'd pleasured her with a vibrator.

Afterward, he'd taken her hard and thoroughly. Eleanor still
recalled the woman's openmouthed expression of unbearable bliss.
It had excited her beyond belief.

He had. He had a way in the bedroom, there was no doubt
about it.

Presently, Trey's gaze remained steady on her. He had an

easygoing, laidback manner that was about a hair's-breadth thick. At least that's how it seemed to her. Beneath that golden, bad-boy persona, she sensed his simmering focus. She realized the insides of her naked thighs were damp with a layer of perspiration . . . and arousal.

His glance flickered down to her book. She read curiosity in his gaze . . . a little amusement. Or was it a silent question? She looked down at *his* book pointedly—he was still holding it on his thighs, blocking the view of his crotch from her. She arched her eyebrows. His smile widened, and she knew he'd read her amused counter query about *his* reading choice for the event.

Hiding her grin, she determinedly turned her attention to her book. He was definitely nibbling at the hook. Reeling him in at the right moment was the delicate part.

It was quite a challenge, reading the erotic scene where Xander had Katya lie in his lap and spanked her bare bottom while she writhed around in mounting excitement, all the while knowing Trey Riordan was watching her. Part of her was triumphant, though, as mean as that was. All those times she'd watched him while he made those other women scream, and she'd been forced to watch.

And suffer.

Now the tables had been turned, hadn't they?

By the time she'd almost finished the spanking scene, her cheeks were hot from arousal. Xander finally gave Katya what she needed by bringing her to climax with his hand at the end of her punishment.

At the end of the chapter, she found herself biting down on her lower lip. Did she think she'd cry out in ecstasy, like Katya did as she exploded with pleasure? Maybe so, because her sex was on fire.

She glanced up furtively, still biting down on her lower lip. Vaguely, she was aware that several men's faces were turned her way, but she only had eyes for Trey. His stare on her was unguarded now . . . even hotter and sharper than before.

She reacted purely on instinct. Entranced by what she read in his gaze, she slowly uncrossed her legs and swiveled slightly in her chair, so that she directly faced Trey. There was nothing obstructing *his* view, even if there was plenty keeping others from witnessing her outrageous behavior.

She opened her thighs several inches, feeling the cool air tickle her aching, naked sex.

He pulsed with lust. Thank God for this otherwise worthless book, because it was the only thing partially shielding the huge tent in his jeans. Had he *ever* had such a raging erection in public? He didn't think so. Because in the past, he would have *done* something about it. But presently, he couldn't move. He was a complete hostage to her. *God* he hurt, watching in enthralled fascination as the woman submersed herself in the pages. At first, her fingers played with that curl that fell distractingly across the swell of her breast. After a minute, however, she gripped both sides of the book tightly, like she was steadying herself for a bumpy ride.

He knew she was reading an erotic scene, of course. He knew it from the way her cheeks, lips and chest flushed with color and her breathing grew slightly erratic. When she bit down on her lower lip with small white teeth and tensed her thighs, he thought for a frantic moment he was going to come in his pants like some kind of horny, thwarted teenager.

He couldn't believe how quickly she'd turned him into a rutting pig, when his intentions in coming here had been so pure. For a few seconds, his irritation at her for making him want her so much cut through his intense lust.

Until she looked up and met his stare, and he saw that her heat equaled his.

Until she slowly turned in her chair, as though she were in a trance, and spread her thighs. Her skirt eased up her legs another inch higher. His heart seized. His cock jumped eagerly.

The little tease wasn't wearing any underwear.

The cleft between her thighs was shadowy. He strained to see, all the while holding his breath. *Jesus.* He wiped the perspiration off his upper lip, his brain and body buzzing in furious arousal. Not only was she not wearing underwear, she was shaved. He could just make out the shape of her smooth labia. He tried to peer through the shadows, desperate, but he couldn't make out any more detail. Just the glimpse was enough, though. It was *more* than enough, the state she'd put him in. Was it his sex-revved imagination, or were those delicate folds of flesh glistening from arousal? She resituated her book on her upper thigh, shifting her hips slightly. Air popped out of his lungs. His cock raged.

He glanced up at her face. She wore a small, smug smile.

He snarled slightly. Her grin vanished.

She had him on a goddamned hook, and she knew it. He'd like to turn her over his knee, and then give her what she deserved.

Every blessed inch of it.

She's turning me into a sex-crazed lunatic, right here in the midst of a hushed reading event.

He blinked in surprise when he recognized anxiety flashing across her face. Abruptly, his personal view of heaven was gone. She'd turned stiffly in her chair. Now she shoved her book into her purse. He started at her jerky movement, guilt sweeping through him.

Had he scared her? He *had* been snarling at her like he was about to eat her up in one bite. Her averted face and furtive movements as she dug around in her purse alarmed him. He started to get up—he wasn't sure what he planned to say or do, as this was a no-talking zone. A middle-aged woman to the left of him glanced up from her book. Her gaze slid down his body to the giant bulge in his jeans. Her eyes widened.

He plopped back down into his chair, opening his book on his thighs rapidly to block her view of his crotch. The woman noticed the title on his book. She gave him that disgusted female glare reserved solely for perverts.

Great, he seethed. Now he was the pond slime who dared to read this revered feminine homage to romance and get a chubby from it.

He saw the gorgeous woman stand abruptly. She slung her bag over her shoulder. *Shit.* She was leaving early. And all he could do was sit here and hide his raging erection. *She's coming this way.* He'd stop her as she passed. No way he was going to let her get away. Not a chance. But as she came within feet of him, those long legs motoring, he realized she was pointedly avoiding looking at him. She was just in front of him.

Do something, idiot.

She dropped her arm as she swept past him. He glanced over his shoulder, stunned by the quickness of her departure, not to mention the tongue-tying rear view of strutting long legs and a twitching, tight ass.

Planning to rush after her, he leaned down to shove his book in his briefcase, outraged female onlooker be damned. He paused in a bent-over position when he noticed the folded piece of paper on the low coffee table in front of him. It hadn't been there before. Slowly, he straightened and picked it up, opening the note. There was only one sentence written in a hasty but elegant hand.

Look out your bedroom window at eleven o'clock tonight and you'll see everything that you only caught a glimpse of just now.

His bedroom *window*? What the hell did *that* mean?

He glanced up in bemusement just in time to see the woman

snatch the envelope that stored her personal technology from the female attendant. In the time it took him to grab his briefcase and coat off the back of the chair, she was out of the coffee shop.

He headed straight for the exit, telling himself he'd come back for his tablet and phone. He was cut off in his pursuit just outside the door when a youngish, black-haired bearded guy bumped into him roughly and jogged ahead of him without an apology.

"Take it easy," Trey remonstrated, recognizing him as the coughing man who'd been salivating over Sexy Boots just minutes ago. The man continued on his mission unfazed, however, running through the museum's circular lobby and making a beeline for a bank of glass doors leading to LaSalle Street. Trey glimpsed a long mane of brown hair and scissoring boots rushing out the doors just feet ahead of him.

Sure, he empathized with any guy's enthusiasm to catch up to her. Who better? But he *didn't* like the dude's rabid, aggressive pursuit, especially when the woman didn't look like she wanted to be caught.

"Hey. I'm *talking* to you," Trey shouted. He sprinted and caught the guy's arm just as he plowed through the glass doors after the female. The man whipped his head around, frowning furiously at being interrupted while on the hunt. His foot stuck at the bottom of the door, keeping it propped open. "Just let her go, man."

"Let go, asshole," the guy seethed. Trey held on to his flailing arm securely, however, glancing behind him onto the street. He saw a cab fly up to the curb. The woman flung open the back door.

Trey only let go of the man once she was in the cab and the door was shut. He transferred his hand to the handle on the door. The guy staggered a few steps toward the street, only to see the cab pull away from the curb. He turned to Trey, his mouth opening to spew accusations at him, no doubt.

"She didn't want to be caught. That wasn't part of her game,"

Trey interrupted. He waited tensely while the guy's gaze lowered over him, probably assessing his chances in a fight. Black Beard exhaled, wilting a little.

"How the hell do you know what she wanted?" the guy muttered resentfully under his breath before he reentered the door. He stalked away through the lobby. Trey gritted his teeth, tamping down his irritation. He stood there in the opened door for several seconds, letting the cold November air cool off both his lust and his stupid flash of aggression.

Maybe the guy had been right. Who knew what a woman like that wanted? She'd been teasing not just him, but the entire room, mercilessly. She was just another manipulative man-eater, exactly the type of woman he was trying to avoid at all costs.

He was sick of playing conniving females' games. He was tired of letting his cock dictate his life. At eleven o'clock tonight, his curtains were going to be drawn tight. As penance for his idiocy, maybe he'd force himself to read *Pride and Prejudice* again.

The vision of the woman reading that racy book with that open, almost innocent expression of curiosity crossed his brain, as did the potent recollection of her obvious mounting arousal as she flipped the pages. Christ, she'd been sexy.

She may have held all the cocks in that room at her mercy, but she gave the note to you.

His thought sobered him. It signified that he wasn't entirely free of her hook.

Not by a long shot.

Eleanor paced back and forth while she bit at her thumbnail, the Rockerchick boots beating a path on the wood floor of her kitchen.

"Just because I felt like I was in over my head all of a sudden doesn't mean *Trey* knew it. All he knows is that I walked out early from the event. But I left the note. Everyone always says I think too much. That's all that's happening, right?" she muttered under her breath and abruptly turned to retrace her path.

She scowled, because silence wasn't much of an answer.

It was an uncomfortable recent realization that she'd started talking to herself more and more. That hadn't stopped Eleanor from doing it regularly ever since she'd moved into Caddy's place.

The big condominium often made her feel very alone.

"It doesn't matter, does it?" she continued shakily. The fact of the matter was she knew next to nothing about Trey Riordan other than she lusted after him with an obsessive focus. Guessing his motivations was a pointless exercise. "Either he'll look out his bedroom window at eleven o'clock because he's interested, or he won't. And I will have blown it from the first."

She glanced at the kitchen clock and saw that it was ten forty-five. Anxiety boiled in her belly.

He'd definitely been interested. True, Eleanor had quite an imagination at times. It helped to have the ability to dream a little when she was down in the museum's basement all alone in the cataloguing or storage rooms, her only company her beloved photographs, costumes, ephemera and books. But she hadn't imagined Trey Riordan's attention and arousal. *Yes*. Arousal. His stare on her had seemed to burn a hole straight down to her core.

She took a step back on the shining wood floor, glancing down the length of the glamorous condominium. Caddy had married young and been divorced by the time she was twenty-four. Her husband, Clarke Green, had been a good deal older than Caddy, not to mention a hell of a lot wealthier. He'd let go of his young bride with a sad sense of fatalism and provided well for her in the divorce. Caddy had gotten the condo in the agreement along with a healthy alimony.

Eleanor still couldn't get over the fact that the posh playgirl condo was *hers*. Would she always feel like a guest here? Would it always seem like Caddy was just away on a business trip or luxurious vacation and would return any minute to entertain Eleanor with a story about someone famous she'd met or some new club or restaurant she'd tried?

Somehow, being the wallflower librarian little sister hadn't been so bad when Caddy was alive. Sure, she'd envied her sister, but she'd been crazy proud of her too. They were very close. It was impossible not to love Caddy. Everyone said so. Even Clarke Green had seemed to come to the sad realization that his vibrant young wife shouldn't be caged up like a rare, beautiful bird. Caddy was so full of warmth and sensuality, joy and fun. She was meant to fly free.

"What would you do if you were me, Caddy?" she whispered to the empty condominium.

"I'd go shake my ass off. Go for it, Nora. Turn on the music and let loose. Have some fun. *Make Trey Riordan sweat."*

She could perfectly imagine Caddy's dark brown eyes sparkling with mischief at the last, see the curve of her naughty smile.

How could someone so full of life possibly be *gone*? Vanished, like some kind of cruel magic trick? Once the ovarian cancer was diagnosed, it had taken its toll with shocking rapidity. After only three months, Eleanor and her parents had been left stunned and empty-handed, wondering what the hell had just happened to them.

She recalled vividly what Caddy had said to her in the week before she died, before her limbs had started to go cold and she grew so sleepy and confused it was as if she were sampling the death state before committing to it completely.

"We all only have so much time here on this planet," she'd said to Eleanor. "Problem is, we don't know when our last days will be. I have no regrets. Well, at least very few," she'd added, laughing with effort. "I lived every day to its fullest."

Their clasped hands had been lying on top of the hospital bed. When Caddy'd squeezed her, Eleanor knew she wanted her to look at her face. Eleanor had kept her eyes downcast, however. They were full of tears, and she hadn't wanted Caddy to see her crying. She didn't want her sister to witness her lack of courage.

"You have so much to offer, Nora. Why don't you leave that underworld of your job? Live in the sunlight a little, sweetie. Look life full in the face and never blink. Take a bite out of it while you have the chance, and think of me while you're doing it."

Presently, Eleanor noticed the glass of wine she'd poured herself upon arriving at the condo. She'd left it untouched until now. Slowly, she picked it up.

"Here's to you, Caddy," she whispered.

She took a deep draw on the wine and walked out of the kitchen, her pace picking up when she reached the living room. She punched a button on the stereo, and the condo was filled with the pulse of a driving dance beat. It was the music to which she'd been practicing her aerobics routine.

Her *strip* aerobics routine.

She took another drink of wine. *I hope you're there, Trey. Because I'm going to be.*

She marched to the bathroom to apply the finishing touches for her performance.

When she left the bathroom at a minute before eleven o'clock she was still nervous, but excited by her daring plan as well. A half glass of wine and the music had fortified her.

She went to the living room and started the music again at the beginning. The dance beat throbbed in her head . . . seemingly in her very blood. She inhaled for strength and started down the hallway. Her hair had been brushed and fluffed, and she'd reapplied her makeup. She'd spritzed her perfume on her neck, even though Trey would never know what she smelled like from his penthouse in the high-rise next door. She'd applied the perfume after another remembered tip from Caddy: *"Every detail about your presentation when you go out, including your perfume, should be for your pleasure, and yours alone. If you think you're beautiful and sexy, so will everyone else."*

She definitely felt sexy at the moment. If Trey Riordan didn't think so, it was his damn problem.

Right.

She ignored the sarcastic voice in her head. The music goaded her on.

She'd made some wardrobe alterations. Her jacket was gone, leaving her chest, arms and shoulders bare above the snug suede lace-up bodice. Instead of the dark brown thigh-highs, she now wore a pair of sheer white ones. She'd practiced in them before, and knew they'd stay put during her dance routine. Plus, Trey would be in the high-rise next door to her building. The paler hose on her legs would project across the distance better than a dark pair. She'd replaced the boots with a sexy pair of suede pumps that included ankle straps. She thought of them as her dancing shoes, because they definitely put her in the right mood for strip aerobics.

It was just one of the many eye-opening discoveries she'd made after inheriting Caddy's Gold Coast condominium and everything in it following her death. She'd found several of Caddy's workout routines cued up on her television in her workout room. As kids, their mother had herded Caddy and Eleanor into dance lessons. She and her sister occasionally took a dance exercise class together at the gym or worked out with a dance aerobics video. But Eleanor had never done *these* workouts with Caddy.

At first, Eleanor had just watched the strip aerobics routines in fascination. It wasn't long before she was giving it a try, examining her progress closely in the mirrored wall beneath the television screen. She'd practiced her dance every night for a month now . . . ever since she'd heard from Jimmy down at the museum that Trey Riordan had signed up for the book event. That had been when she'd first hatched her plan.

Opening night had finally arrived.

Her heart in her throat, she entered the guest room and switched on the light, then dimmed it to an intimate glow. When Caddy had been alive, she'd stayed in the master suite, a spacious, beautiful room that faced Lake Michigan. Eleanor slept in that room now. But *this* room, the second bedroom, had been Eleanor's when she'd house-sat or spent the night over at Caddy's. This is the room where she'd first glimpsed Trey Riordan and where she'd watched him, even before she knew his name.

The high-rises along Lake Shore Drive crowded close. Trey's building was only about twenty-five feet or so from the guest bedroom window. His was one of those modernistic, smooth, steel and plate-glass buildings that had typified Chicago architecture in the forties and fifties. His unit was the penthouse on the top two floors. It was because of the prominence of his unit that Eleanor had been able to get his name from Harry, the doorman, who was buddies with the doorman at Trey's building. Caddy's tower was thirty-six stories high, but Caddy's unit was on the nineteenth floor. From the guest bedroom, there was a straight line of sight into the intimate, exciting territory of Trey's bedroom.

Caddy had never stayed in the guest room and seemed entirely unaware of the forbidden displays Trey himself, or Trey and his lovers, put on in that penthouse. Eleanor only stayed at Caddy's two or three nights a month, on average. Therefore, Caddy's guest bedroom was usually dark and seemingly unoccupied. Eleanor figured the lack of light and movement in the adjacent condo had never alerted Trey for vigilance about privacy. And in truth, his drapes *were* more often than not closed in his bedroom, much to

Eleanor's disappointment. He wasn't an exhibitionist. He was just a man, and therefore often careless or too preoccupied to care about details. Such as whether or not the curtains were drawn completely when he walked naked out of the bathroom from his shower, for instance. Or what was happening outside the window when he laid a woman down on his bed and proceeded to own not only her, but Eleanor in the building next door as she looked on in anguished longing and lust.

Presently, she walked boldly around the bed, but her glance out the window was anxiously skittish.

Shit. Trey's bedroom was dark. He'd refused her invitation. She could see her reflection in the window. Her face looked pale and disappointed.

But wait . . . the room wasn't entirely black, was it?

His bedroom door was open, she realized as she neared the window. There was a light on somewhere down the hallway. As her eyes accustomed to the interior darkness of his bedroom, her breath hitched. She saw *him*.

She saw *part* of him, anyway, around the edge of an opened floor-to-ceiling curtain. He stood very still about a foot or two from the window. Only half of his body was dimly visible, as if he hadn't fully committed to his action. Neither the distant light nor the glow of the city lights reached him completely. Part of him still remained cloaked in the shadows, poised for a departure.

The music swelled and pounded into the familiar opening to her routine. She raised her arms over her head, parted her thighs and placed her hands on the cool glass. She leaned into the window in a sinuous motion, gyrating her hips.

You're not going anywhere, Trey Riordan.

THREE

Knowing he was out there in combination with the sexy dance brought it all back to her: how aroused she'd felt reading that spanking scene in her book, all the while knowing Trey was watching her. Wanting her. She *liked* having him watch her. His desire went to her head like an intoxicant.

Staring directly at his distant figure, but still highly aware of the image she made in the window's reflection, she undulated her hips, imagining her sex drawing invisible circles. The air itself seemed to tickle and lick at her naked flesh. She lifted one hand from the window in a subtle beckoning gesture, and then touched the side of her neck, feeling the throb of her pounding heart. Slowly, still swinging her hips to the driving beat of the music, she glided her hand down her bare chest and over the soft suede of the camisole. She cupped the side of her breast, feeling its weight and firmness in her palm, before her hand coasted down to her waist. Her head fell back, her hair caressing her shoulders, back and bare waist beneath the bodice. She opened her hand on her hip, feeling the sensual movement of her body.

The music seemed to unfurl her. The heat it generated made her blossom. Her hand trailed down to the bottom of her short skirt, her fingertips touching the smooth skin of her thigh. She lifted the fabric higher, feeling the hem brush ever so lightly against her naked labia. She ground her hips forward, instinctively craving more of the fabric's light touch on her sex.

When she lowered her head and opened her eyelids a slit, she saw Trey's curtain flutter. His shadowed figure stepped around it. With the added ambience of the city lights, she saw that he placed one hand against the glass.

He'd taken a step closer.

It was working.

Her confidence swelled. She spun rapidly, her hands above her head, the knowledge of his observation pulsing in her blood. She blatantly seduced him with her swiveling hips, sliding hair and popping ass, calling him with a siren dance. Her back to him, she strutted several feet over to the edge of the bed. She didn't need to look to know she had his full attention.

She bent and planted her hands on the mattress and slid onto it belly down, ass elevated in a sensual, sinful glide. The bed portion of the routine was her favorite. It was decadently sexy, but also required some skill. After her initial awkwardness, Eleanor had taken to it like a high-priced call girl. She'd loved practicing it and imagining Trey watching her.

Right here, right now, it was no longer a fantasy. His gaze was glued to her undulating, swiveling ass, and that knowledge was a power unlike anything she'd ever known.

She rolled over onto her back and lifted her stocking-covered legs high in the air. Her skirt had ridden down so that it now barely covered her ass and sex. Legs straight, she opened her thighs.

Wide.

She was nearly doing sideways splits midair. She closed, opened and closed them again. With her legs together and straightened in the air, she bent her knees and rolled her sexy shoes in the air, flirting shamelessly. The movements to the dance were precise, but she made them into a gliding, sensual tease. She knew his gaze was glued to her legs, most especially to what was between them. She sensed his focused attention on her, felt his stare burning her sex. Her pussy ached in response. It was a delicious tease for her as much as it was for him.

Still scissoring and posing her legs in midair, she caressed the back of one thigh. This wasn't part of the official strip exercise routine, but it certainly felt right. She cupped the bottom of one buttock and slowly circled her hand, causing her skirt to lower and then rise in rhythm to the music, up and down . . . just a fraction of an inch. She was flashing her pussy at him, and it was a potent intoxicant.

She kept the skirt in place, just covering her sex from him. One finger strayed over the edge of her skirt to her pussy. She sunk it into her snug, liquid channel, only letting him see the movement of her hand, but not her sex itself, as she stimulated herself.

Her moan sounded over the loud music.

For a stretched moment, she lost herself. The idea entered her brain that she should fully expose what she was doing. It was such a strong, precise prod that she couldn't help but wonder if it was *him* thinking it at that moment . . . if it was Trey demanding it silently, projecting his command across the distance. But that wasn't part of her routine.

Not yet it wasn't, anyway.

She lowered her legs and slid off the bed. She stood facing him, fully exposed. Her heart leapt into overtime as she danced to the music, caressing her body all the while, falling victim to her own seduction. He'd stepped even closer to the window. She could make out his form better. He wore nothing but a pair of jeans, leaving the magnificent landscape of his lean, cut torso exposed.

The jeans rode low on his narrow hips. God, what it would be like to touch all that hard male flesh?

Heaven.

She sensed the coiled tension in his muscles. She saw the rigidness of his rugged, handsome face. Like he had for a moment there in the coffee shop, he looked positively fierce. Both of his hands pressed against the windowpane now, only adding to the impression of a caged animal poised to spring. And Jesus . . . she didn't think it was her imagination. Things looked very *full* behind the fly of his jeans.

Still pulsing her hips to the driving beat, she cupped one sensitive breast through the suede bodice. With her other hand, she drew on the lace. His elbows bent slightly, making him lean in closer to the window, arm muscles bulging. His attention on her was absolute and cuttingly sharp. It stole her breath.

She worked a finger beneath the lace and drew it out of the first holes on the camisole. She proceeded downward teasingly, drawing out the laces while she danced. As she undressed, she shaped her breast to her palm, plumping the flesh into the widening opening. When she was entirely unlaced, she cupped both of her breasts, squeezing them into the inch-wide opening while keeping the fabric over her nipples.

She saw his teeth flash as his mouth curled into a snarl. She'd been intimidated by his fierceness in the coffee shop. Now she understood him better. Now she shared in his fever.

She opened the bodice, but almost immediately covered her bare breasts again with her hands. Her head went back and she moaned. She played with herself to entice Trey, of course. But she'd been unprepared for how *good* it felt. Her nipples were diamond hard against her palms. She massaged her breasts sensually while she danced to the music.

Show them to me, you little tease.

Her eyelids snapped open. The sharp demand had just popped into her head. Gasping softly, she stared at Trey in the distance. Was his focus so intent that she was reading his mind?

It didn't matter, because her desire matched his perfectly.

Gyrating her hips, she slowly lowered her hands, caressing her ribs. Then she sinuously pushed the bodice off her body. Now topless, she stalked toward the window, swinging her hips boldly. She lifted her breasts in a shameless invitation, massaging the firm flesh with her hands while her thumb and forefinger pinched lightly at her excited nipples.

He cupped his cock in one hand. Heat rushed through her at his matter-of-fact, lewd action. She continued to pound her hips to the music and massage her breasts, but for an electric moment, she switched from being in the glare of the spotlight to being the captive audience. He moved his big hand, his thumb and forefinger pinching hard at the thick shaft of his erection through the fabric of his jeans.

She'd seen his cock from a distance before. She'd salivated over his beautiful shape and his blatant virility. But she'd never longed for him like she did in that moment. Would she ever see him up close? Would she ever touch him? Taste him?

His hand moved faster now, jerking at his cock through his jeans. It suddenly came to her that she'd stopped dancing. She stood stock still a few feet away from the windows, her breasts lifted and displayed in her hands. She existed in a haze of heat and lust. Without telling herself to do it, she lowered one hand over her bare, heaving rib cage and down over her skirt. She lifted the hem, exposing her outer sex to him.

She slid a finger between her slippery labia. Moaning hoarsely, she closed her eyes and began to move again, dancing against the pressure of her rubbing, pressing fingers. It was like Trey himself was touching her . . . his blazing gaze on her working her into a frenzy. She *felt* him, even if she couldn't bring herself to meet his stare in those seconds. The tension in her built faster than she would have expected. She was going to come. She was going to break in pleasure while standing here nearly nude in this window.

Trey was going to watch it all.

The idea was unbearably exciting, and yet . . . her hand lowered to her naked thigh, her fingers trailing her juices across her skin. She lowered her head. The intimacy of the moment suddenly overwhelmed her.

Open your eyes, stupid. See what he's doing. Meet his stare and do this thing with eyes wide open.

Instead, she found herself strutting back to the bed, her flash of self-consciousness not entirely erasing her sexual boldness. She did her favorite sinuous move, going belly down on the mattress. Her skirt had been jacked up higher this time. The bottom of her ass was showing as she undulated her hips several inches off the bedspread.

Lift up that skirt all the way. Now.

This time, she didn't bother to tease out whether it was his desire or hers, his demand or her own. She was too far gone, about to explode into flame. She lifted her skirt to her waist, fully exposing her ass. Pressing her hot cheek and breasts against the cool duvet, she drew her knees up under her, still pulsing her hips and ass to the driving beat of the music.

She spread her thighs wider. She'd crossed the boundary. There was no going back.

His stare pierced her, even when she couldn't bring herself to meet it. He saw all of her now. She reached between her thighs and cupped her sex. Her finger slid between her labia onto her simmering clit. Another plunged into her slit.

Trey.

Her undulating hips wavered. Her body seized.

Pleasure splintered her awareness.

She came back to herself at the sound of her own sharp cries. They segued into breathy moans.

The reality of what she'd just done entered her awareness sluggishly, even while she still rippled and vibrated in pleasure. Despite the unwanted return of her self-consciousness, she still swam in hot, sticky pleasure. She continued to shamelessly rub herself, groaning as aftershocks pulsed through her body. She was drenched . . . wetter than she'd ever experienced herself to be.

She lay facedown on the mattress with her ass raised the air, her legs spread apart, her pussy exposed and wet. Trey Riordan's stare bore right through just like it had that first time in the coffee shop tonight.

Except this time, it did it from the rear view and sliced right up to her heart.

It shocked her, how intimate it'd all felt. Shouldn't their exchange have been as distant as the space that separated them? It scared her a little. She'd thought she'd be safe, that space between them like the zone between audience and performer.

True, she'd held him in the palm of her hand. It was as though he'd been right there with her in the moment. But as every second passed, she felt more and more alone. She'd just brought herself off in front of an absolute stranger.

Mixed mortification and renewed arousal swept through her. Yes, arousal, because she'd *loved* having the power to hold every ounce of his attention at her mercy.

She pulled her hand away from her sex. It dropped to the mattress near her face. For a tense moment, she just listened to the ragged sound of her breathing while her ass and sex tingled and burned. She'd exposed herself to him minutes ago, but she hadn't actually felt *naked* until now.

Her sexual confidence evaporated with the speed of her cooling body. It stunned her, what she'd just done . . . how far she'd lost herself to the moment. God, what was Trey doing now? Was he masturbating, like she had been doing for him? If so, was he *finished*?

Was he even still *there*?

Maybe her own single-minded lust had caused her to imagine his stare on her like a burning touch.

Overwhelmed by a wave of anxiety, she abruptly pushed herself off the bed. With her back to the window, she shoved her skirt down, covering her ass. For a moment, she just stood there with her head lowered, her fingers clutching at the bottom of her skirt, her mind awash with uncertainty.

She may have walked the walk. She may have played the part. But the role had abandoned her like an unfaithful lover. She was left standing there clutching her skirt like a little girl caught red-handed, her cheeks and eyelids burning, feeling foolish and ashamed of her impulsivity . . .

Of her gargantuan need for a man she didn't even know.

Her lungs hitched uncomfortably when she tried to inhale.

It was regular, boring Eleanor who enacted the anticlimactic finale to her performance. She hurried out of the bedroom, too cowardly to turn and look Trey Riordan directly in the face, too timid to take that full, greedy bite out of life that she so longed to taste.

FOUR

On Tuesday night, Eleanor put on the finishing touches to her "costume." She'd been too nervous to enter the guest bedroom since her infamous window dance last night, too afraid to look out the window. She didn't know which would be worse, to see his empty bedroom or to see *him*.

Despite her uncertainty, she *had* slowly rebuilt her defenses last night and today at work. She'd willfully quashed her mortification at her shameless, hedonistic display. It *hadn't* been embarrassing (or so she tried to convince herself). It had been confident and sensual, to seduce what she'd wanted so badly for so long. She wanted one glorious night of no-holds-barred passion with the most beautiful, desirable man she'd ever seen.

There was *nothing* wrong with knowing what you wanted and going for it.

The memories of those heart-pounding moments of the dance increasingly took center stage in her mind while she toiled away in the library's basement all day, helping to convince her. She recalled how excited she'd been, how powerful she'd felt witnessing Trey's blatant, honest male arousal and absolute focus on her. She still cringed when she thought about facing him tonight at the museum's reading event. Nevertheless, she *was* preparing to go.

Maybe it was because the idea of *him* not showing, of him avoiding *her* because he'd found her display embarrassing in the aftermath, pained her even more than giving up. How else could she reassure herself on that count unless she went to the coffee shop tonight, book in hand, and saw firsthand if he was willing to face her or not?

She'd chosen her outfit for the evening from Caddy's wardrobe—a sexy black romper with opaque black thigh-highs and boots. The romper had a darling, oversized white schoolgirl-like collar, its modesty in direct contrast to the garment's short length and the provocative way the knit tightly fitted her breasts, waist and rib cage. The boots she chose went several inches above her knee and were made of black leather with a three-inch chunky heel. Panties and bra remained in her drawer. The white collar cleverly dipped down to obscure her nipples, while the clinging knit suggested—strongly—the truth about her braless state. It was a wardrobe tease, one of those features that got you thinking . . . *Is she, or isn't she?* Eleanor loved it. Besides, she'd already showed Trey everything. No need to grow modest now.

The romper's fabric hung loose around her hips and thighs. When she stood with her legs slightly parted, she could feel the air caressing her sex. The sensation aroused her, maybe even more so than it had the first night she'd gone into public without underwear.

She was transforming into a shameless exhibitionist, no doubt about it.

She'd just donned a short black suede trench coat and was finger-combing her long, loosely curled hair over the faux-fur collar when the house phone rang. As she lifted the receiver, she had a sinking feeling. Only Harry, the doorman, typically called on the house phone, and Harry called only when she had a delivery or a visitor. It was too late for a delivery. She had a pretty good suspicion whom the visitor would be.

"Hello?"

"Caddy, it's Harry downstairs. Your gorgeous mama is here to see you," Harry Carver boomed warmly into the receiver.

Eleanor heard a sharp female voice in the background. She didn't reply at first, too stunned at unexpectedly being called her sister's name. There was an uncomfortable pause on the line.

"Oh, *Jesus*, I'm so sorry, Eleanor," Harry apologized rapidly. He sounded very upset. Eleanor's heart went out to him.

"It's okay, Harry," she assured.

"I dialed the number and was looking at your mom, and it just came out—"

"I understand. Really. My mom came to visit Caddy here hundreds of times. It's only natural."

She glanced down at her sexy outfit, frowning. She wouldn't have time to change if she wanted to actually make the event. Her mother was a professor of psychology. As a psychologist's daughter, Eleanor had an uncomfortable suspicion about her mother's theory on why Eleanor was dressing up in her big sister's clothes.

"You can go ahead and send my mom up, Harry," she finally said resignedly.

"Will do. And again, I'm sorry about that . . . before."

Eleanor closed her eyes. She knew how much Harry had doted on Caddy.

"It's okay, Harry," she said softly. "I consider it a compliment, to be accidentally called her name."

She heard Harry's gruff, uncomfortable laugh before she hung up the phone.

Catherine Briggs was always certain to bring two things with her on her surprise visits to her daughters: a sumptuous Russian delicacy and unwanted motherly advice. For Caddy and Eleanor, the former had always gone a long way in helping them endure the latter, a fact they expected their mother knew and for which she planned.

Her parents lived in Evanston, where her father was a professor of physics at Northwestern University. Her mother commuted downtown to her job in the psychology department at Loyola University. This meant that Caddy and Eleanor had long been subject to her unannounced drop-ins.

"Are you going out?" Catherine Briggs asked bluntly when Eleanor opened the door a minute later. Eleanor was putting on her gloves, making it abundantly clear to her mother she *definitely* was going out. She felt her mother's sharp gaze drop down over her. The outfit was toned down with the coat closed and belted, but Eleanor immediately knew her mother wasn't fooled. She still looked dressed to kill in Caddy's sleek, expensive clothing.

"I have an event at the museum," Eleanor said, reaching to take the glass-lidded casserole dish her mother held clutched against her practical, wool winter coat.

"You're going to the museum dressed like that?" her mother asked disapprovingly as she stepped over the threshold and Eleanor shut the door behind her. Eleanor turned to hide her eye roll.

"That's the idea, yes," she said with forced breeziness as she walked toward the kitchen, casserole dish in hand. "I was just on my way out the door. What'd you bring me? Beef pirog? Yum. I'll never become a ballerina if you keep feeding me like this."

"You and your sister were marvelous dancers. I always said it was a pity to waste such talent."

It was a long-standing, scripted exchange between Eleanor, Caddy and their mom upon being presented with one of her delicious, rich dishes. Eleanor and Caddy were kidding saying it, of course. But somehow, their mom always had seemed to genuinely believe her daughters had come *this close* to becoming prima ballerinas, while she fed them diets suitable for a professional Russian weight lifter.

"Why are you in the city so late?" Eleanor asked as she popped the casserole dish inside the refrigerator.

"Late faculty meeting." Eleanor turned to see her mom shrewdly peering at her over her professorial glasses. "I was hoping we'd have time to talk this evening."

Eleanor checked her watch. "I'm sorry. I'm already running late. We can talk tomorrow when I come to the house? We're still planning on cooking for Thanksgiving tomorrow night, right?"

"Of course. But your father will be there. I think we should talk about *this* now, woman to woman," her mother said while waving her hand, indicating Eleanor's outfit.

"*This?*" Eleanor asked, feigning confusion. She refused to willingly go down this path with her mother. No, she'd kick and scream the whole way.

"Yes, *this*." Her mom made a stabbing motion in the direction of Eleanor's person. "The way you've been wearing Cad's clothes recently, the way you're doing your hair and wearing your makeup. It's not *you*, Eleanor."

"Mom, I don't have time for this right now—"

"I'm concerned about you, honey. So is your dad."

"Then how come you don't want Dad to hear you talking to me about it?"

Her mom ignored her, which was typical if a comment strayed from the point she was determined to make.

"We never thought it was a good idea for you to move right into the condo so soon after Caddy . . ." Her mother's still-pretty face creased with anguish as she faded off. Despite her annoyance, Eleanor's heart squeezed in her chest. Her mother could be bossy and overbearing, but Caddy had been the apple of her eye, the princess who was destined to become queen. It pained Eleanor to see such a strong woman still unable to speak of her daughter's death in concrete terms.

"It's okay, Mom. It's not what you're thinking," Eleanor said.

As always, she felt cornered by her mother's overbearing nature coupled with the fact that she loved her like crazy and despised seeing her vulnerable.

"How do you know what I'm thinking?"

"You're worried about me, obviously. But I'm *fine*," Eleanor said pointedly before she headed out of the kitchen.

"Eleanor, have you even cried? I mean, *really* cried. You didn't at the funeral. Your father and I have never seen it since then. What I'm thinking—and what your father is thinking too—is that you're grieving in a . . . well, an *unnatural* way."

Eleanor spun around in the hallway, infuriated by her mother's intrusiveness. "I'm so sorry I haven't wailed and rended my garments sufficiently to please you. Besides, I'm not grieving at the moment, Mom. I'm trying to *live*."

The worry lines on her mother's face grew deeper as she stepped toward her. God, Eleanor did *not* feel up to dealing with this. Not now.

"I think you're dealing with Caddy being gone by trying to embody her . . . the way you're wearing her clothes and coming off so . . ."

"Bold? Pretty? Confident? Did Caddy hold the patent on those things?"

"No, of course not. But it's not *you*, Eleanor."

"Thanks a lot, Mom."

"Don't go histrionic on me. You know that's not what I meant."

"Do you mean I'm not acting like the boring, wallflower librarian who conveniently blends into the background? Is that what you mean, Mom?"

"At the very least, I'd like you to recognize what you're doing and why you're doing it!"

"Don't preach to me from your psychoanalytic pedestal. I know you're thinking about Caddy and missing her just as much as I am with our first holiday season coming up without her. Don't project all your stuff onto me."

"You couldn't be more mistaken," her mother said imperiously.

Eleanor pointed toward the kitchen. "*Beef pirog?* It was Caddy's favorite. You made it a lot for her, but you made it for Dad and her *every* Thanksgiving. You haven't made it since she passed." She noticed her mother's incredulous expression. "You see? You're not the only one who can psychoanalyze, Mom."

Her mother inhaled, gathering herself. She straightened to her full height of five foot seven. Even though Eleanor had topped her by two inches for a decade now, she still felt about five years old whenever Catherine Briggs took on that regal stance and expression. She made a sound of exasperation.

"Do you *really* want to know why I'm dressing up in Caddy's clothes? It's *not* because I'm trying to embody her, or at least that's not the main reason."

"Then what is it?"

"It's because before she died, she told me to live every day like it was my last. She told me to stop being afraid and to take a bite out of life. *That's* why I'm acting the way I'm acting. It's not because I'm trying to bring Caddy back by being *like* her. It's because I'm trying to take advice she gave me while she was dying. Do you think I should ignore her deathbed advice, Mom?"

Her mother's lower lip quivered. Eleanor immediately regretted her sharp outburst. She'd had the nerve to say those taboo words—*dying* and *death*—in association with Caddy.

"I'm not so sure that taking her advice and embodying her are two separate issues," her mom said after a moment.

"Please, Mom—"

"Did she *really* say that to you?" her mother asked shakily.

Tears stung her eyes, witnessing her mom's vulnerability.

"Would I lie about something like that? Of course she did," she said, her voice breaking.

"Hush, now. I didn't come here to fight with you." She stepped forward and took Eleanor into her arms. Eleanor stood stiff in her embrace for several seconds.

"You always say that, but we usually do," Eleanor mumbled. Despite her annoyance and uncertainty about her mother's argument, after a moment she hugged her back tightly.

She may be infuriating, but she was Eleanor's mom, and Caddy's too. She was a fellow sufferer. How could Eleanor possibly withhold her love, knowing that?

No matter how much he wrestled with his concentration, he couldn't seem to pin it down on his book. How could he care about the social intricacies of a Regency country ball, how much money Mr. Bingley made in a year or *anything* about that stuck-up jerk Mr. Darcy, when *her* seat was empty?

People were creatures of habit. Trey had taken his exact same cushy armchair, and it seemed to him that most of the people in the crowded, hushed coffee shop had done the same with their former seats. It also was apparent that he wasn't the only man in the room who kept glancing over at the empty chair by the window. He certainly noticed that Black Beard kept peering up from his book to beadily scan the room.

There was a clock on the wall next to a newly erected Christmas tree. The second hand ticked off another minute. It was quarter past eight. His temptress—the very same woman he should be avoiding at all costs—was either late, or she wasn't coming.

Hopefully it was the latter.

Unfortunately for him, if it *was* the latter, he knew he wouldn't be able to rest until he'd found out precisely *why* she was avoiding him.

How *dare* she avoid him, anyway?

What kind of a woman put on a show like the one she'd put on in her window last night, a mind-blowing display of sensuality and raw eroticism, and then backed off? She'd walked away . . . fucking *walked away* after turning him into a steaming, frustrated, teeth-gnashing sexual voyeur. He, Trey Riordan, didn't *watch* passively, damn it. At least not for the long term, he didn't. When it came to sex, he participated. He initiated.

He *did*.

For seemingly the thousandth time since last night, he relived that moment when she'd gone belly down on the bed, stuck her gorgeous bare ass in the air and reached between her spread thighs. He'd known the precise moment when she'd climaxed. He'd seen her body stiffen and quake, perfectly sensed her rush of relief and pleasure.

His cock swelled at the mere memory.

Unwanted erections happened with the regularity of his remembering, which wasn't helping his straining attempt at celibacy in the least. Hell, sometimes it seemed like he couldn't see anything else in his sex-warped mind's eye than the vision of her lithe, curving body moving so sexily while she played with her breasts. It'd been damn hard concentrating at work today, and nearly impossible to sleep last night next to the window that she'd single-handedly turned into a giant erotic television screen with no off button.

She'd known where he lived all along. There was no other conclusion to be made. She'd seen him in his home before, and knew precisely what she was doing by inviting him to become a voyeur.

The idea blew him away.

She'd been so beautiful. So uninhibited, so subtle, and yet so blatantly precise in her seduction. She'd been so skilled at jerking his strings, she might as well have been the puppet master born to manipulate not only his cock, but also his brain.

No.

Frowning, he moved restlessly in his chair and stared down at his opened book. Hadn't he grown weary of being manipulated? He did *not* want to know anything more about her. Enough was enough. She'd given him the relief of an explosive orgasm while he watched her do her Salome's dance and bring herself off, but *he* wasn't going to lose *his* head to that little tease.

In reality, any relief he'd experienced had been far too brief anyway. Thirty seconds after she'd walked away and left him standing there like an idiot with his streaming cock in his hand, he'd craved her all over again. He'd been pissed as hell, but still . . . he'd wanted whatever measly glimpse she'd give him.

Pitiful.

His pocket buzzed.

He glanced aside at his fellow readers, feeling vaguely guilty. He'd given his tablet to the woman at the entrance along with one of his cell phones, but he'd kept a spare in his pocket. TalentNet was in the process of hiring a renowned programmer from Singapore for its website for its rapidly expanding Pac Rim market. Trey really needed to talk one-on-one with this guy, but due to the time difference, they kept missing each other. Before he'd left the office this evening, he'd told his admin, Theresa, to give his alternative cell phone number to the programmer and left instructions for him to call no matter what time it was. He'd be forced to duck into the bathroom and secretly take the call. Business was business, as abhorrent as that philosophy was to the aims and goals of the reading event.

As unobtrusively as possible, he slid the cell phone out of his pants pocket, hiding it behind *Pride and Prejudice.* He saw the photo on the screen of a beautiful woman. He grimaced and pushed the ignore button. A text message popped up with amazing rapidity.

> Hey you. Do you know what today would have been? Our six-month anniversary. I'll be in town over the weekend. I miss you, Trey. So much. Meet me Friday at our usual spot for a drink, say at five?
>
> No strings attached.

Shit. Definitely *not* a work call. It was Alessandra, his former girlfriend whom he'd met in London and with whom he'd carried out a hot-and-heavy, volatile and increasingly unpleasant affair. He wouldn't reply. And he *certainly* wouldn't meet her on Friday. Alessandra was British and didn't celebrate Thanksgiving. She hadn't realized it was a holiday weekend when she proposed to meet. Or she *had* realized it, and had just assumed Trey would be spending the holiday conveniently alone. He'd spoken of his family often enough in front of her, but talk of his parents, his brother and his sister's family seemed to skim right past her. He'd never offered to introduce her to them, so for Alessandra, it was easier to act like they didn't exist.

He'd forgotten Alessandra had this number. Although he *shouldn't* have forgotten, because the reason she had it related to their breakup. She'd discovered his alternative cell phone number by digging through his other phone's texts while Trey was in the shower one morning. She'd located the message where he'd supplied Theresa with the alternative number. Then she'd proceeded to accuse him of sleeping with Theresa behind her back. Trey had been so pissed she'd been nosing around in his texts that he hadn't bothered correcting her about Theresa being his administrative assistant, not a bedmate. Let her think whatever she wanted.

Alessandra had eventually found out the truth later, of course, and been contrite. She would have made a great detective. When she set her mind to it, she could choke the truth out of almost any situation. Her manipulations could strangle almost *anything*, including a relationship.

Alessandra was beautiful, yeah, and enthusiastic and skilled in bed. But like too many women he'd dated in the past, it was just way too hard, not to mention depressing as hell, to figure out what was real about her and what was a lie.

He was sliding the phone slyly back into his pocket when he saw rapid movement. He looked up in time to see *her* drop into her seat just feet in front of him, all legs and sexy, tousled hair. She gave him a sideways glance, and he stiffened.

Why did she look so skittish?

Her gaze flickered down his body. He knew she'd noticed the phone when she quickly glanced back up at his face and gave a wry, knowing smile. He found himself smirking conspiratorially back. He pushed the phone all the way into his pocket and straightened in his chair, looking her over more carefully and with mounting interest.

She'd come.

He glanced across the room when he noticed restless movement in his periphery. He wasn't the only one in the room who had perked up at her entrance. Little minx. It annoyed the hell out of him. He didn't want to share her. He wanted her to himself, like he'd had her last night.

No . . . he wanted her in his bed, tied down to it preferably, at his mercy while he proceeded to do whatever he wanted to her, and she screamed in pleasure. This game she was playing was starting to grate on him and yet . . .

He couldn't look away from her.

She looked edible again. Sexy and sophisticated, but also

very . . . *doable*, for lack of a better word. There was a softness to her, an approachability that he liked. Her eyes were amazing: large, especially in comparison to her delicate face. They shone like her brown hair did. Despite her polish and sleek, fashionable clothing, she didn't come off as hard and brittle like so many women he knew. Her combination of boldness and freshness was unexpected, unusual, and too damn appealing.

But there was a new expression on her pretty face he couldn't quite pin down tonight. She was flushed. Was that because she'd been rushing to get here? Or possibly—*hopefully*—from excitement? Arousal?

She regarded him anxiously from beneath long lashes.

No. She was *embarrassed*.

His unlikely realization was only confirmed when she ducked her head, letting her long mane of glossy brown hair partially obscure her profile. She grabbed her book out of her purse so rapidly, it was like she thought it was a sacred relic that was going to save her. He half expected her to hold up the unlikely book as a shield against him.

Then she crossed those long, booted legs that had become indelibly etched into his brain. And with her brow wrinkling in a kind of furious determination that—he couldn't help it—he found adorable, she parted the pages. Without even removing her coat, she began to read her erotic book like she thought it held the truth of the universe in its pages.

Her determination began to disintegrate the closer she got to the museum. If she hadn't caught him breaking the rules of the event by sneaking a glance at his cell phone, she might not have had the nerve to stay. Witnessing Trey's small instance of rule breaking had humanized him a little, though, making it easier for her to continue her daring charade.

It'd been one of the hardest things she'd ever done, to walk into that coffee house tonight and meet his stare . . . to face up to a man she didn't even know, but for whom she'd stripped and masturbated the night before. A mixture of embarrassment and arousal caused heat to rush into her cheeks at the memory. She quickly ducked her head and forced her fragmenting focus onto the page.

He pinned my wrists behind my back and forced me against the front of his body. I struggled, but I was almost choking with excitement at his dominance . . . at the obvious evidence of his arousal.

"Stop fighting," he said, his mouth slanting in impatience and anger.

I immediately went still. I looked up at the harsh lines of his handsome face, panting. The anger left his expression as he studied me. A fire seemed to ignite and flare in his black eyes.

"Have you ever been restrained, Katya? Have you ever been tied up by a man and punished? Have you ever been fucked very hard, and for the man's pleasure alone, and had no choice but to take it?"

"No. And I don't want to be," I replied quickly.

"You're lying," he said without any heat, as if he stated the obvious. His gaze lowered over my neck and chest. I felt his cock jump against me, the sensation making my blood race. "Your pulse is going a mile a minute. Your nipples are hard," he added grimly as he stared down at my breasts. "Would you like me to kiss you?" he asked, a small, deadly smile shaping his beautiful mouth. And I hated him in that

moment, despised him, because I wanted his mouth on me
so much, the desire sliced straight through me.

"No," I seethed.

His eyes narrowed, his stare boring into me.

"I'm going to taste you anyway. Aren't I, Katya?"

Liquid warmth rushed through me. My lungs froze.

I lifted my mouth to him. Slowly, entranced by his mes-
merizing eyes, I opened my lips. A blazing look of triumph
crossed his features before he leaned down, plunging his
tongue into my mouth, shaping my lips roughly to his. He
kissed me hard at first. Ruthlessly. I cried out into his mouth,
but he held me at his mercy, taking from me with savage,
focused greed. He hurt me a little.

But then he softened. He made love to me with his
mouth . . . just his mouth. He sipped and sucked and stroked
me. He made his desire my own, and my pain slowly turned
into a golden, decadently sweet surrender.

Finally, he lifted his mouth. I quaked against him, completely unmasked.

"Alex Jordan is due for a meeting here in a few minutes,"
Xander said.

My heart stopped beating.

"Go to the door and lock it. Alex will have to wait until
you've gotten what you deserve."

My heart leapt. He was going to have me now. He was
going to do what he'd said: Tie me up. Punish me. Fuck me.
The idea of feeling his cock finally driving into my body
stole my breath. I left his arms and crossed his large office,
my breath coming choppily. I flipped the lock.

When I turned, I saw that he stood behind his desk. He
took some keys from his pocket and bent. He was unlocking
it: that very drawer that I'd tried to open so many times

*before while I was alone in his office, my heart beating out
an excited warning in my ears that he may return any
moment and catch me at my little crime.*

I heard the forbidden drawer slide open.

*He reached inside. I watched him place first one set of
leather cuffs, then another on his desk. He leaned down
again and withdrew a two-foot wooden paddle. He straightened and met my stare, grasping the handle with one hand
and caressing the striking portion with the other.*

*"You've tried to get into this drawer before, haven't you,
Katya?" he asked me calmly.*

I started to deny it, but his eyes wouldn't let me.

"Yes."

"You were curious, weren't you?"

"Yes," I whispered.

*He nodded once, unsurprised by my admission, and set
down the paddle next to the cuffs. He bent again, grabbing
one more item before he slammed the drawer shut. I trembled when I saw what he'd withdrawn: a box of condoms.*

*"I'm glad that you were curious. It pleases me," he said
as he began to loosen his tie. "But you'll have to accept the
consequence of your curiosity." She saw his eyes spark with
dark amusement. "That will please me as well," he said.
"Now. Come here, Katya."*

Oh my. Eleanor resisted an urge to fan herself. This book
certainly helped her forget her insecurities and self-consciousness.
Still, just like the other night, it was the man sitting just feet away
from her that was the actual focus of her arousal. Lord, it was
hot in here, wasn't it? It suddenly struck her that she'd been so
flustered when she entered late a few minutes ago, she hadn't
removed her coat.

Would she like to do the things written about in this book? Maybe. But if Trey wasn't there, she wasn't so sure she'd find the book quite so exciting. Xander and Trey might both be sexual dominants, but somehow, Trey was different than the infamous fictional icon. He was infinitely more vibrant and scintillating, at least to *her* he was. She'd spied on him making love maybe six or seven times in the past, enough for her to reach that conclusion. The thing that turned her on the most about Trey was his strength in the bedroom, the way he confidently and precisely positioned a woman in order to give pleasure or to take it wholesale. He didn't seem to get off on seeing his lover in pain. Instead, he seemed determined, forceful even, in his mission to challenge a woman, to amplify pleasure.

Eleanor also didn't think she was the "born submissive" that Katya was supposed to be, but she had to admit . . . the combination of reading the racy book and Trey watching her with that smoldering stare and stern expression was making her *hot*.

Gritting her teeth for courage, she set her book facedown on the table and stood. Very aware of Trey looking up at her movement, she seductively flicked open the belt of her coat, her fingers stroking the fabric. She paused in the action, heat pouring through her. It'd hit her that she'd used the same movement to unfasten the laces on the suede camisole during her striptease last night.

She glanced sideways at Trey. Her lungs stuck on an inhale. One look had told her he was recalling the exact same moment. His stare was glued to her hands at her waist, his expression rigid.

She pulled apart the belt and slowly unfastened the buttons of the coat. She cautiously glanced sideways around the curtain of her hair. When she reached the button above her crotch, she pressed the cloth tighter, giving her pussy a little jolt of pleasure with her twitching fingers. Trey flinched slightly, his gaze jumping to her face. He looked so tense. Wait . . . was he *angry?* She was pushing him too far. He was getting pissed off at her teasing.

Maybe he'd like to spank me.

She mentally rolled her eyes at her stupid cliché thought, but arousal swelled in her nevertheless at the mere idea. She pushed the coat off her shoulders. Her back arched slightly. It was conceited of her to think it, but she knew her breasts looked good beneath the clinging knit: firm and full and nicely shaped. She draped her coat on the back of the chair and sat. With her fingertips, she traced the top hem of the romper and the bare skin of her thigh, seemingly pulling down the fabric, but being pretty ineffective on purpose.

She glanced to the left. His gaze was still glued to her, and it was positively ravenous. Arousal swelled in her. She couldn't help it. She loved getting a reaction out of him. It was addictive.

She picked up her book and uncrossed her legs, feeling the air tickling her warm, tingling sex. With Trey's stare scoring her, she continued reading.

> *He made me strip naked, while he remained dressed in his suit, his loosened tie his only concession to the raw eroticism of what was happening. But I found I loved even that, the reminder of his dominance over me. This was an equal exchange, but ours was a very different sexual currency. My skin seemed unusually sensitive when I finally stood before him naked, my arms hugging my waist in a self-conscious gesture.*
>
> *"Put your hands at your sides. Never hide yourself from me," he said. When I'd done what he asked, his gaze trailed down over me, such a cold stare to make me burn like it did. Finally he looked at my face again. "You're so beautiful," he said. Maybe it was my imagination, but his deep*

voice seemed to crack slightly. He moved, picking up one of the leather restraints from his desk. He knelt in front of me and tapped my left ankle gently. "Spread your legs several inches. Good," he said. He fastened a black leather cuff on each of my ankles. There was a foot-long chain attached to the cuffs. He straightened, his face impassive, and reached for the other restraint.

"Put your hands behind your head," he directed, walking behind me. My breathing hitched at the sensation of him tightening the cuffs around my wrists. "Now cup the back of your head with your palms to give yourself support," he said. "If you should begin to cramp or become uncomfortable, you must say so. A paddling on your ass is your punishment. I won't have you in any discomfort for other reasons. Do you understand?" I nodded, too breathless to speak. "You agree to tell me if your arms become uncomfortable? Say it out loud, Katya."

"Yes."

"Excellent." He stepped behind his desk. My heart jumped when he picked up the wooden paddle. He used it to point at the floor several feet away from him. "Come stand here in front of me."

I felt awkward walking naked, with my cuffed ankles and my hands behind my head, but for some reason, my nipples pinched tight in arousal as I came to a standstill before him. I looked up at him, uncertain, feeling very small in comparison to his tall, strong male body. Very aroused. His nostrils flared slightly.

"You will come to fear the paddle a little," he said. He extended the hand that held my instrument of punishment. My breath caught, but all he did was use the tip of the polished wood to caress the side of my waist. A puff of air left

my lungs. He used the paddle to stroke the side of my now heaving rib cage. Then he lifted one of my breasts with it from below and slid the paddle along the side of the globe. He pressed it tenderly, and then let go. My breast jiggled at the movement. I moaned softly. He watched like a hawk while he moved the paddle over the top of my breast and gently circled the tip over my rock-hard nipple. "But you will come to love it as well, Katya. You'll tremble with excitement every time you see this paddle in my hand."

I already was shaking with excitement. He gave a small smile, and I realized he'd known that. He slid the tip of the paddle down my sternum and over my belly. Lower. My eyes widened and I shifted on my feet.

"Stay still," he said sharply, his eyes flashing up at me. I remained unmoving with effort, my muscles tensed hard, holding my breath. "I'm going to make you burn, Katya. All of you. Now turn around." I did so with his guiding hand on my upper arm. "And bend at the waist. Flex your knees slightly." He used the paddle to gently tap at the back of one knee. "It will help you to take the paddle on your ass. Good," he purred from behind me when I'd taken the position for my punishment. He swept the paddle along the back of my one thigh, then another. He came to the side of me and placed his hand on my shoulder, bracing me for the punishment. The anticipation was killing me.

"Breathe, Katya. Don't forget to breathe." I inhaled deeply. He pressed the paddle into the flesh of my ass and circled it subtly. I couldn't stop myself from moaning, my arousal had grown so sharp.

"Are you ready to begin?" Xander asked me, his deep, mellifluous voice washing over me, soothing the prickling nerves all over my body.

"Yes," I replied.

He lifted the paddle and struck. My body started slightly at the blow, but he steadied me with his hand on my shoulder. The loud crack of contact rang in my ears. The paddling had stung, but that wasn't what made me whimper. It was the feeling of Xander pressing the paddle again to my ass and sliding it erotically against my skin, soothing the firing nerves.

Good God. She could feel Trey's stare boring into her like a hot lance. Eleanor brushed the back of her hand against her upper lip, wiping away the slight perspiration that had gathered there. Her sex had grown wet too. It prickled in arousal. Her breath coming unevenly, she nervously ran her finger along the exposed skin beneath the hem of the romper, wishing she could touch herself. Her aching sex was only inches away from her gliding fingertips. A fever had settled on her. She pressed her fingers to her flushed mouth. She glanced up at Trey, feeling both vaguely guilty at the idea of becoming so aroused in public and unstoppably excited.

She flinched. Xander MacKenna had *nothing* on Trey in the burning-stare department.

His mouth was pressed together in a tight line. He looked *furious.* She glanced down to his lap instinctively. He was covering his crotch with *Pride and Prejudice* again. He made a taut gesture with the hand that wasn't holding the book. Next to his abdomen, he pointed, the action small, stabbing and distinct.

Her stare jumped to his face, her eyes widening at his fierce expression and glittering, stormy blue eyes. She glanced to where he'd pointed. He'd indicated the exit and the lobby.

"Bathroom," he mouthed silently.

Her eyes widened. He was telling her to go to the bathroom in the lobby, and he'd meet her there.

Of course she'd go. She *had* to. This is what she'd been plotting for, wasn't it? Was he going to take her in the bathroom in a hot, sweaty tryst? The very idea made her light-headed.

She stood abruptly, dumping the incendiary book into her bag and grabbing clumsily at her coat. Her mind was awhirl with what was about to happen. Trey Riordan had signaled—no, he'd *ordered*—her to go to the bathroom. He was about to confront her, talk to her . . .

Quite possibly yell at her for getting aroused in public and teasing him so mercilessly for two nights in a row. She couldn't quite be sure from his fierce expression what he planned. This was uncharted territory for her.

Her lungs tight, she plunged down the two steps to the main floor of the coffee house. She instinctively veered away from Trey's chair like she might from the smoke and heat of a raging fire. Regret slinked into her awareness when she noticed that several men were tracking her progress toward the exit, their excitement obvious.

Shit. She'd been doing her little act for Trey, of course. But others had unintentionally been as caught up in her performance as she was.

FIVE

Stacy Moffitt frowned at her disapprovingly when Eleanor breathlessly requested her phone at the counter. She'd be tattling to Jimmy, Eleanor's friend, about Eleanor's odd presentation at the event. Her behavior hadn't been outrageous to anyone but Trey, but still, it'd been notably unusual for those familiar with Eleanor.

She glanced furtively back into the coffee house, positive Trey would be stalking toward her, perhaps intent on retribution for her daring at teasing him. The idea excited her unbearably. Her eyes widened in alarm when instead of Trey, she saw the black-bearded guy rushing her.

"Are you ever going to actually stay for the whole event?" Stacy hissed as she extended the envelope that held Eleanor's phone.

"I'm starting to doubt it," Eleanor mumbled, snatching the envelope from Stacy's hand. The bearded guy was almost to the desk. She hurried out of the exit, intimidated by his glistening, feral-looking black eyes.

She'd been so caught up in being late to the event . . . and then utterly captivated by Trey and her book. She'd forgotten about the guy's rabid stares from last night. She increased her pace, anxious to avoid him. Her heels tapped rapidly on the tile floor of the lobby.

"*Hey*, come back here," he ordered.

She broke into a jog, alarmed by the roughness of his tone.

"Come *back* here, you little cock tease."

Her breath hitched when his footsteps grew faster. He was *chasing* after her. Alarmed by his aggressive snarls, she blindly headed for the doors and the street. Abruptly, the pursuing footfalls halted. There was a skidding sound on the tile floor.

She looked over her shoulder as she plunged out the doors, her heart pounding like crazy in her ears. She saw Trey holding the bearded guy's arm while the man spun around at the unexpected restraint. She halted in the doorway, horrified to see the bearded man lift his fist in preparation to strike. Looking beyond irritated, Trey caught the man's arm, halting the blow with shocking ease. The bearded guy cursed and started to struggle, but Trey was much the superior as far as size and fitness. He held him off with both hands with relative ease. He looked over at Eleanor, his glare singeing her.

"Go. Get out of here. *Now*," he growled between clenched, white teeth.

She inhaled sharply, experiencing his words like a slap. It'd been the first time he'd ever spoken to her.

It'd probably be the last.

Could you have screwed this up any more royally?

She plunged into the November night, racing toward the curb blindly. Only one thought guided her: escape. She wanted to shut her eyes and block out Trey's furious expression.

Frustration swept through her when she saw how snarled traffic was. It was the Tuesday before Thanksgiving. For many people, the holiday had already begun. Spotting a cab with its light on, she jogged into the halted traffic.

"Eleven sixty-one Lake Shore Drive," she gasped, slamming the door shut and locking it. She strained to see into the museum's lobby, but couldn't make anything out from here. What was happening inside? Was Trey fighting that man? What if he got hurt, all because of her selfish lust?

The light turned and the cab inched forward sluggishly. She couldn't stand it. She *had* to get out of here.

"Just turn right up here," she told the cab driver.

"You want to take North Avenue? It's worse than LaSalle."

"Whatever . . . just get me away from here."

She saw the driver glance at her suspiciously in his rearview window, but she didn't care. Her entire awareness was focused on getting out of there. He turned right. The museum disappeared from sight within seconds.

What would have usually been a five-minute cab ride took four times as long because of their meandering route and heavy traffic. She mentally lectured herself on her stupidity the whole way. She wanted to explore her sexuality with Trey, and she wanted to be daring in her attempt.

But maybe she was too inexperienced to recognize the possible consequences?

The cab finally pulled into the turnabout in front of her building. She paid the driver and rushed out of the car, shoving her wallet back into her purse with frustrated forcefulness. She shivered, realizing she'd never donned her coat. The temperature hovered around freezing, and she was only wearing the finely knit romper without a stitch of underwear. Her legs above her stockings were bare to the frigid lake wind.

Against her will, she recalled her mother's concerned voice.

"It's not you, Eleanor."

Awash with mortification, she hurried into her coat as she approached her building. She glanced up distractedly in the process of pulling the coat around her and froze in her tracks.

Trey Riordan stood outside of her building's front doors, his hands deep in the pockets of the black wool peacoat he wore. His eyes glittered at her from beneath his lowered brow.

"Do you want to tell me what the hell this is all about?" he asked her coolly.

She opened her mouth, but nothing came out but a stupid little squeaking sound. Before she could think of anything remotely plausible to say, he took several steps toward her, his gaze narrowing.

"What's your name?" he demanded.

"Ah . . . er . . . Eleanor Briggs," she managed, her voice sounding thick and husky. Her tongue felt like it was about a foot thick. She swallowed with effort. "Are you all right?"

"What?" he asked distractedly. He was studying her like she was some kind of weird-looking, possibly toxic mold he'd never seen before.

"That man. The guy with the beard," she said. His stare flickered to her face. Eleanor's heart jumped. This was the closest she'd ever stood to him. His eyes looked darker beneath the night sky, a midnight blue with shards of light reflecting in them. His mouth was hard, but *so* sexy. Just looking at it caused a surreal feeling to come over her. "He . . . he didn't hurt you, did he?" she asked, her gaze scanning his face worriedly and finding only rugged male perfection.

She was *talking* to Trey Riordan. Well . . . sort of, anyway.

"No," he said pointedly, his brows arching. "He finally saw the wisdom of walking away. It surprised me, to be honest. You really had him worked up this time."

"I'm sorry," she blurted out. "I honestly didn't mean for that to happen."

He took another step closer, until less than a foot separated them. Despite the fact that she wore heels, she had to look up to focus on his face.

"You mean you weren't trying to turn him into a sex-crazed idiot?" he asked, and she saw the hard glitter in his clear eyes. He *had* been angry at her performance. He still was.

"Of course not. I couldn't care less about him," she mumbled, awash in embarrassment. A gust of wind off Lake Michigan lifted several strands of her long hair, spilling it against her burning cheeks. She brushed it aside impatiently.

"I see."

She started. "You do?"

He nodded, his face completely sober. "You weren't trying to make him or any other guy in that coffee shop crazy. You were just trying to torture *me*. Is that right?"

"Yeah," she blurted out, relieved he understood. Then she saw the furious slant of his mouth and realized how callous her admission had sounded. Her eyes went wide.

"Listen, Trey—"

"How do you know my name?"

She flinched. After a pause, she pointed lamely at their two buildings. "We're neighbors," she whispered.

His took another small step toward her, his fierceness palpable. He seemed to tower over her.

"How. Do you know. My name?" he grated out succinctly.

She couldn't swallow. She couldn't breathe. It was like she was a cringing little bug and he was a giant about to stomp on her.

"Eleanor?"

Her breath hitched at the sound of him saying her name. Her guilty confession came spilling out of her.

"Our doormen are friends. Harry knows Ralph, your doorman. I . . . I saw you . . . in your bedroom from my condo a few times," she said, blanching and glancing up at him apologetically.

Maybe he was going to report her to the police for being a Peeping Tom? The fact that she couldn't read his rocklike expression made her desperate. Her lame confession, fueled by guilt, just kept bubbling out of her. "And like I said, I caught a glimpse of you a few times, and I . . . well, I got curious. To be honest, I couldn't stop thinking about you," she mumbled guiltily. "So I asked Harry to ask Ralph who lived in the penthouse next door, and Harry eventually told me it was Trey Riordan, the BandBook and TalentNet founder . . . *you*." She paused to gulp uncomfortably. She noticed his slightly incredulous expression as he stared down at her. "And that's . . . that's how I knew your name," she finished stupidly.

For a few excruciating seconds, he didn't say anything.

"Bastards," he finally said. She blinked in surprise at the irritated slant of his mouth. Surely his curse hadn't signified *her*.

"Who?"

"Our doormen."

"Don't be mad at them. I know they breached your privacy in telling me your name, but—"

"No, it's not that. After that little *performance* you put on last night, I asked Ralph if he could get me the name of the woman in the unit across from mine. I described you to him and Harry."

"You did?" Eleanor asked, stunned.

"Yeah. He and Harry are thick as thieves. They always go to each other's lobbies to gossip while they're on their breaks, and Harry was there this morning. But they got all closemouthed when I brought up you. They blabbed *my* name, but acted like they had no idea who I was describing."

"Harry is kind of the protective type," Eleanor explained apologetically. She still was vibrating over the news that he'd tried to find out who she was after her window dance.

"And so after they told you my name, you recognized me at the reading event?" he prompted.

She just nodded, her mouth hanging open. There was a little more to the story than that, but she'd already overplayed her hand in all this. A gust of wind whipped at her unbound hair again. He stood so close that several long tendrils blew up onto his shoulders and brushed his face. One clung to his whiskered jaw. A quiver of awareness went through her. It was like the strands joined them. Their gazes locked. So did her lungs.

Slowly, he reached up and pinched a tendril between thumb and forefinger. His fingers slid down the length several inches as though testing the texture before he reached, placing it carefully on her chest. Her skin in the proximity of his fingers tingled.

The first time Trey Riordan ever touched her.

It probably would be the last.

"That was quite a show you put on last night. In the window," he said gruffly.

"Oh . . . yeah, that."

She found herself staring at his broad shoulders, the tree in front of her building, Harry's distant figure behind his station in the lobby . . . *anything* but Trey's face in that moment.

"Are you embarrassed?"

She blinked. Once again, he'd sounded confused. Suspicious. He was seeing through her mask. *You're blowing this, Eleanor, blowing it straight to hell.*

"No." She met his stare boldly. "Are you?"

"I'm not sure what to think or feel about you, to be honest."

The image of how intense he'd looked in the coffee shop and peering out his window leapt into her mind's eye. Vividly, she recalled him bracing himself against the window and reaching to cup his erection.

"*Really.* No idea what you're feeling?" she dared him softly.

For a second, he just regarded her narrowly. Then he smiled and gave a rough bark of laughter. He shook his head.

"Are you planning on continuing to torture me?"

"Only if you want me to," she said, gratified at how quickly she'd countered him this time. Being so close to him was unsticking her man-awkward, gummed-up Eleanor brain. Miraculously, he had that effect on her. *Some* of the time, anyway.

His smile vanished. "I'm not the type to appreciate a woman at a distance." His stare dipped over her face. She experienced a swooping sensation in her belly. "Especially one like you."

Her heart flopped like a fish against her sternum.

He jerked his head in the direction of his building. "Do you ever go over to Gold Coast?" he asked her, referring to the upscale bar-restaurant on the ground floor of his building.

Yeah, plenty of times. Usually looking for you.

"Once or twice," she replied, her smile widening at the miracle of the fact that she was talking one-on-one with him and not tripping over her tongue.

"Come have a drink with me?"

"Sure," she replied, shrugging nonchalantly as if it were the most natural thing in the world to agree to a drink with Trey Riordan.

He couldn't figure her out, Trey admitted to himself a half hour later. He watched her while she took a sip of red wine, those beguiling cat's eyes fixed on him over the rim. Sure, she'd been a mystery from the first, but he was a pretty quick study when it came to drilling down into a woman's character once he met her. Eleanor, though . . . she was different. Her beauty and sexy factor were over the top. That was a given. Right now, for instance, her stare was hot. Not like a flirting glance. Hot like she was imagining taking a bite out of him. Those eyes of hers were like a beacon, golden and liquid, warm as heated honey. He found himself melting every time he got stuck in her stare. Somehow, she softened something inside him and yet turned him rock hard all at once. She was the epitome of sexy confidence.

Some of the time, anyway.

Just thirty seconds ago, she'd almost knocked over her wineglass when he'd asked her what she did for a living. She'd righted the goblet and twitched her hands, like she was brushing away his question like a pesky fly.

"My job? It's not that interesting, really. Nothing like yours. Did you say you were a musician, and that's how you first got involved with creating BandBook? What instrument do you play? My mother made my sister and me learn piano when we were little, but it never stuck. Do you still practice? It's really hot in here, isn't it?"

"Which question do you want me to answer first?" he'd asked her dubiously.

For the life of him, he couldn't figure out how she could be as sexy and as comfortable in her own skin as an in-heat minx one second, and clumsy and rambling the next. He got that her inconsistencies signaled a deeper truth about her. Problem was, he couldn't grasp what that truth was.

"Why don't you tell me what your job is, and I'll decide if it's interesting or not," he said presently. Her eyes widened and she set down her wineglass with a clinking sound. She'd thought she'd sidestepped him on the job question, of course, and was inconvenienced he'd brought it up again. He'd noticed over the past several minutes that she had a tell, an anxious habit of playing with her cocktail napkin. He found himself watching her long, pretty fingers fidgeting with the paper edges, oddly aroused even by her show of nerves.

"You won't. Find it interesting, I mean."

"Try me," he challenged.

She inhaled. At the movement, he glanced down at her breasts. *Beautiful* breasts. Mouthwatering. He couldn't decide what he liked better: the memory of her first baring them to him through the window, or right now. Up close. The way the black knit clung to the lush curves, the way the point of that weird, big white collar just covered her nipples; all of it was driving him nuts. She wasn't wearing a bra. Or *maybe* she was, as firm and high as the mounds were. He wanted to just reach across the table, cup her in his hand and find out once and for all. He grit his teeth at the very idea, his cock going heavy at the mere thought.

Bra, no bra, there definitely *had to be a bra—*

"Well . . ." she said, interrupting his imbecilic self-argument. *This* is why he needed a vacation from women. They turned him into an idiot. He focused on her face. An idea seemed to come to her. She brightened. "I work there. At the museum."

"At the Illinois Historical Museum?"

"Yes. I'm an executive there."

"An executive of *what*?" He had the impression her outer self froze while her brain whirred like a spinning top.

"Membership," she said suddenly.

"That doesn't sound boring at all. It sounds interesting. I like that museum. I'm a member there. My company makes a donation to the annual fund, as well."

"I know."

His gaze sharpened on her.

"It's a real adrenaline sales job, wooing the patrons, keeping the machine running by constantly bargaining for the lifeline that keeps us in business. But that's how I love things. I'm not happy unless I'm running on the fast track."

His gaze narrowed on her flushed cheeks. Was she *blushing*? Was she a man-eater, or was she an adorable goofball? He couldn't believe he couldn't figure it out.

"This isn't all about you trying to get a bigger donation from me or my company, is it?" he asked suspiciously.

"No, of course not," she exclaimed, looking insulted. "If I ever suggest you give a dime more than you already do for the museum's sake, you have my permission to turn and walk away."

"I'm sorry. But you're really sending me mixed messages," he stated bluntly, picking up his highball glass.

She went still. "I am?"

He nodded and took a drink. He took his time swallowing, letting the taste of the bourbon soak into his tongue, studying her face the whole time for clues.

"You blew me away last night with that dance," he said quietly after he swallowed, setting down his glass. "You could be a professional dancer."

"The second person on the planet to think so aside from my mother," she said with a patentable, mischievous grin.

"You've blown me away since I first set eyes on you. The sexy book. The sexy clothes. The way you move. Everything."

Her grin faded. Her mouth trembled.

He put his elbows on the table and leaned toward her. "Is that what turns you on, Eleanor? Having a man watch you? Is that what gets you off? Is exhibitionism your kink?"

He saw her elegant throat tighten in the charged silence that followed.

"I like it," she admitted softly. Her cheeks deepened in color, but she didn't look away. "I liked having you watch me."

"I've known a few women who had a proclivity for exhibitionism. I was never into it—or them—personally, but I can't blame a person for having their own thing. It always seemed relatively harmless." The thought of how she'd looked in that window, of how she'd dangled him on her hook, flamed in his brain. So did irritation. "*You*, however, were downright mercenary about it."

"I wanted you to notice me."

He straightened, taken aback by what struck him as a burst of honesty and annoyance on her part.

"How could you think I wouldn't *notice* you?" he asked baldly. "Wouldn't it have been easier to just arrange a meeting with my doorman? Or, you said you knew I was a member at the museum, right? Couldn't you have just introduced yourself sometime, maybe while I was there for an exhibit opening or something? How come you wanted to torture me?" *Jesus, she'd flashed him her pussy the first time he'd ever sat in a public place with her. She couldn't just have said hi instead?* Not that he was complaining about her alternate form of greeting.

Well, maybe a little part of him was. The part not located at his crotch.

She bit at her shapely lower lip. It might have been a nervous gesture on her part. It might have been intentional seduction. In that moment, he didn't care. The result was one and the same.

"I did it because *you* tortured *me*," she said. He made a sound of disbelief at the unexpected flash of fire in her eyes as she said it.

"*I* tortured *you*."

Her indignation vanished as quick as it came. She glanced aside, her fingers moving faster as she flipped at the edge of the cocktail napkin. "That didn't come out right. I know you didn't do it on purpose . . . torture me those times."

"Eleanor?" he prodded. She glanced up skittishly. "*What* times, precisely?"

Her mouth pressed tight. He had a strong urge to pry it open with his tongue. For a few seconds, he thought she'd refuse to answer.

"Those times I saw you naked," she finally said, her voice just above a whisper, her eyes downcast. His body tensed. He couldn't unglue his gaze from her moving mouth. "The times I saw you . . . with other women."

Her hoarsely uttered words seemed to hover in the air between them.

"That's an invasion of my privacy."

"I realize that."

"Maybe it's partially my fault for leaving open the curtains. But you could have looked away. You could have drawn your own curtains. You didn't have to *keep* looking."

"Yes. I *did*."

She inhaled choppily, her eyes going wide, like the words had escaped her throat without her permission and surprised even her.

"So you got off on watching me with other women."

"No," she replied, shaking her head rapidly. She looked a little desperate. "I mean . . . I got off on watching *you*."

The clink of glasses and the low murmur of other patron's conversation blended into a low, pulsing hum in his ears.

"Do you just want to torture me, or have actual sex with me?" he demanded succinctly, sick of thrashing around in confusion and lust.

"*Can* I?"

Air puffed out of his lungs. He glanced around the sparsely populated bar, again half expecting to find someone filming his gobsmacked reaction for an Internet joke. None of the other patrons looked remotely interested in him and Eleanor. This was real. *She* was.

He didn't quite know what to make of her, but at least she was honest about what she wanted. He had to give her that.

"If you want to," he said, unable to hide his puzzlement. "God knows *I* want to."

"Oh, good," she gushed as if relieved. She smiled then, bright and sexy, like the first time she smiled at him in the coffee shop. He reacted just the same as he had then: by sweating and growing stiff as a board. Her effortless effect on him sent up a red flag. He leaned forward intently. Whatever expression he wore caused her smile to fade.

"But let's get this straight," he said. "If you've seen me in the bedroom a few times, then you might already know this: I call the shots. You're not going to yank my chain anymore. Do you understand?"

She nodded, eyes wide.

"Well . . . not unless I ask you to," he added after a moment's consideration. Her mouth curled. He felt that grin all the way to his crotch. He couldn't help but smile back. Sure, her seductions were torture, but it'd be entering new erotic territory, to know he controlled the climax of her brain-twisting little displays.

"When do you want to start?" she asked.

"I've actually sworn off sex for a while."

Her face fell.

"But I was thinking of starting again soon. Like . . . right now?" he added hopefully.

He noticed her pulse was fluttering like mad at her throat. He suddenly didn't think he could stand waiting another minute before he felt it beneath his mouth.

"I was thinking the same thing. But I don't want to encourage any bad habits on your part."

"Yeah, you do," he corrected her grimly. She didn't argue, just wore that cat-that-ate-the-canary smile of hers. "You're being straight with me, so I should be honest with you in return, though. I'm not looking for a relationship at the moment. If we do this, can we just keep it . . . light?"

"*Light?*"

He exhaled in frustration. He'd never actually *said* that to a woman before, and realized how selfish it probably sounded. But he was just trying to be honest about his intentions. "I just lost some people that I cared about, and I've had some pretty bad dating experiences recently. I've been trying to take some time to myself. Get some perspective."

"I'm sorry to hear that," she said, sounding like she meant it.

He nodded. "I was trying to do some self-examination," he admitted. "Hopefully some self-improvement. That's why I'm off women for a while. Or I'm supposed to be, anyway. Women have been kind of . . . unhealthy for me recently," he explained, lifting his glass and taking a swallow.

"Are you worried you're a sex addict?"

He snorted into his drink, startled by her earnest question. "I *wasn't* . . . but *now* I kind of am."

She appeared regretful and amused at once. "I'm sorry, I wasn't trying to suggest you were. *Really*," she insisted when she noticed his dubious expression. "It's just . . . you seem to know a lot of women. And you said they were *unhealthy* for you—"

"They tend to make me stupid, that's all," he mumbled.

"Women make you stupid," she repeated flatly, her brow creasing in that sweet, curious expression he liked.

"Yeah, you're right. I probably sound like an ass saying that. I might be the one who's the problem. Maybe I'm not cut out for the relationship thing, I don't know. Point being, I was trying to figure things out, one way or another. I was doing okay until I looked up and saw you sitting at the coffee shop."

"You're making me feel guilty."

"I'm not trying to. I'm telling you all this because if we do this, it'll just be about sex. I can't commit to anything else at the moment. Or better to say, I *shouldn't*. Is that all right with you?"

"Of course. That's all I want too."

He searched her face, but all he could see was the sexy flush of her cheeks and lips and the excited shine in her eyes. He was finally going to get to touch her, consume her, possess completely what had only been dangled so enticingly in front of him. Yeah, he was falling off the abstinence wagon.

But it was going to be the best fucking fall in the world.

"Then let's go," he said with an air of decided finality. He stood, grabbed his coat and reached for her hand.

SIX

They stepped out of Gold Coast into his building's lobby.

"Is my place okay?" he asked her quietly.

"Yeah, sure."

"Ralph," Trey said as they passed the doorman's station.

"Evening, Mr. Riordan." There was an edge to Trey's tone and an icy gleam in his blue eyes as he passed the desk and Ralph returned the greeting. He wasn't pleased that the doorman had helped her to breach his privacy, and then had refused to supply him with her name. If she had to guess, Ralph would be hearing more about it from Trey when she wasn't there to hear it. Ralph looked at her and blinked in surprised recognition. She ducked her head in fleeting embarrassment.

It only took a second for stunned excitement to take center stage in her awareness again.

I'm going to have Trey Riordan!

The idea was too unbelievable to absorb. He'd been such an untouchable fantasy for so long. And now, she was standing right next to him and he was taking her up to his penthouse. *Incredible.*

The elevator door dinged open. Trey got on and she followed, his gaze landing on her when he turned. He reached, and her heart jumped. But he wasn't reaching for *her*, she realized. He had a card in his hand, which he swiped along the elevator button console before he pushed the eighteenth floor.

A billowing silence descended once the doors slid closed.

"What are you thinking?" he asked her quietly.

"I'm thinking it's weird."

His brows slanted. "Weird?"

"That I'm about to go to bed with you, and we've never even held hands . . . or kissed."

His eyebrows arched. He grabbed her hand. He tugged firmly. The front of her thumped against him. *Oh my*. He was every bit as lean and hard as she'd imagined. More so. She inhaled his subtle scent: spice and fragrant wood and something indefinable . . . the essence of Trey. She stared up at him wide-eyed, her pulse hammering at her throat, her body coiling tighter by the second.

He lowered his head and brushed his mouth against hers, exploring her gently at first. His lips sandwiched hers, first the lower, then the upper, his caresses firm, unhurried. Delicious. Taut anticipation coiled in her belly. She couldn't breathe.

Then, ever so deliberately, he dipped his tongue between her lips, tasting her. A floodgate of sensation opened. She whimpered softly into his mouth. She clung on to his shoulders, feeling the hardness of his muscles through his shirt. She'd long admired all of his tall, beautiful body, but she was particularly drawn to his broad shoulders. To feel the rounded, dense muscles curving into her palm while his deft tongue explored her mouth struck her as surreal.

He laced his hands between her coat and her body and encircled her waist, fingers stroking her back, discovering her. They both turned their heads in unison. The kiss turned deep. Liquid. Electric.

The sound of the elevator opening barely penetrated her awareness. She blinked, bringing him into focus with effort, when they parted several inches.

Talk about a helluva first kiss.

He reached around her, and she realized he was catching the closing doors.

She couldn't unglue her stare from his small, hovering smile.

"Now we've done both," he said, squeezing her hand. She regarded him stupidly. His stare on her was sharp. Hungry. "Held hands and kissed," he prompted her sluggish brain. His gaze narrowed on her. "This is going to be really good, isn't it?"

"Oh yeah," she replied, unable to hide her eagerness from her tone.

His smile widened. Keeping a firm grip on her hand, he led her off the elevator. She gasped in surprise.

"The elevator leads straight into your house?"

"Yeah," he said, reaching for her coat. She relinquished it dazedly.

She was reminded that he was the sole inhabitant of the eighteenth and nineteenth floors. They stood in a high-ceiled, elegant hallway. Through an arch she could see his living room. Trey hung up the coats and took her hand. He led her through the arched entry. She gazed all around at the wide-open space, entranced. She'd never seen any of his penthouse, except through the windows of his bedroom.

The living room was enormous and modernly decorated with streamlined yet comfortable-looking furniture featuring leather and beige, brown and ivory upholstery. The ceilings were at least twelve feet tall. The east wall was completely made of iron beams and glass and faced Lake Shore Drive and the lake. The other walls served as the background for a fantastic art collection. Enraptured, she tugged gently on her hand. He released it and she walked to the center of the masculine, sophisticated room while he remained in place. Slowly, she spun around, absorbing all the amazing details, aware of Trey watching her the whole time.

"It's fabulous. All of it. Is that a Lichtenstein?" she asked breathlessly, pointing at an original painting.

"Yes."

"And a Stella? And a Paschke . . ." she murmured in awe.

"You know your art."

"I have degrees in art history and textile preservation," she said dazedly as she walked the length of the room. The painting over the soaring ivory marble fireplace caught her eye and she wandered over to it in wonderment. "And I love this Hearn of the blues musicians. Is it an original?"

"Yes. Jeanine gave it to me when TalentNet showcased her work several years ago."

She glanced back to where he stood at the far side of the room. He just watched her soberly, his expression giving nothing away. Eleanor had met Jeanine Hearn, the painter, at an exhibit the museum did featuring young and upcoming Illinois artists. Hearn was extremely pretty and disgustingly talented. Not only was she a renowned artist, she was also a violin virtuoso, thus her favorite topic for her paintings: musicians at work. She was *precisely* the kind of woman Eleanor could easily picture with Trey.

She also had a pretty good idea that Hearn had given Trey the painting for reasons beyond jumpstarting her career.

It was intimidating, to think of the brilliant, beautiful women he'd known . . . the ones he'd slept with. How would he think she measured up: boring, bookish Eleanor Briggs?

"Come here, Eleanor."

She turned slowly, fully facing him. He looked beautiful and somber standing there, his face shadowed and grim with determination. Looking into his eyes at that moment, she knew it didn't matter if he potentially gave her a low grade for her lovemaking. At least in the *moment*, it didn't matter. With him, she played the part so well. She became someone other than Eleanor, someone more interesting and exciting. Liberated. The only thing she could think of in those seconds was finally touching him. She dreaded the idea of disappointing him, but she feared the idea of missing her chance to be with him even more.

She started toward him, her lungs tight. He moved in her direction, their paces increasing as they drew nearer.

They crashed together. His arms closed around her, bringing her flush against him. His mouth seized hers in unapologetic possession.

Finally, she knew his strength. Finally, she was drowning in it.

He inundated her, his scent, his taste, his bold, ravenous kiss, the sensation of his spread hands moving up and down along her waist and her sides, his fingers delving into the flesh of her hip and into her back. He intoxicated her. She grew dizzy on him. He plunged his tongue deep, exploring her thoroughly, drinking his fill and sucking on her subtly. She felt that pull all the way to her sex.

His opened hands moved hungrily along the side of her body, cupping her flesh, detailing her shape unerringly. She felt small in his big hands. Feminine. Beautiful. His palms skimmed the sides of her breasts, and she moaned shakily into his kiss. Suddenly he sealed their mouths and muttered a rough curse.

"No bra. I've been wondering all night," he said, plucking at her lips with focused hunger. She smiled when she saw his small, wry grin, but he didn't stop kissing her or pause in his explorations. He cradled her breasts and massaged her gently. She felt his cock jerk against her lower belly. His eyes glittered down at her. "God, you're firm. So nice," he breathed out, his rough, awed voice causing her nipples to shrink tighter and the little hairs on the back of her neck to stand on end.

His hands shifted, and suddenly he was finding the tab of the zipper at her neck. He drew it down to the top of her buttocks in one swift, sure motion. His expression grim, he pushed the romper off her shoulders, peeling it off her arms and down to her hips. He let it drop and the fabric slithered down her ass and thighs and past her knees. He backed up several inches, his stare scorching her.

She was naked now, save for the thigh-highs and boots and the bunched romper at her ankles. She'd never been so aware of every patch of her skin in her life as she was at that moment. Her lungs hitched, making her breasts rise in the air. One of his spread hands glided along the indentation of her waist and hip, and the other cradled a breast, shaping the flesh to his palm. She grew mesmerized by his enthrallment.

"Jesus, Eleanor. You're so beautiful," he said, sounding stunned. Gratified? Then his expression darkened. "You showed up at those reading events, wearing nothing but your gorgeous skin and some skimpy, clinging fabric. You've really got nerve, you know that?"

Her breath froze in her lungs when she saw the glitter in his eyes. He wasn't particularly happy with her about that fact. Horny because of it, yes, but *not* happy. She didn't have the opportunity to try to plead her case, because suddenly, he dropped to his knees in front of her.

She cried out shakily in surprise. He pressed his face to her belly and pulled her tighter against him with his hands at her back. His hot mouth moved, scorching her, sending shivers of pleasure along her skin and down her spine. She trembled, overwhelmed by his erotic adoration. His lips skimmed the sensitive strip of skin just above her sex. He nuzzled the top of her mound, making her cry out helplessly. She delved her fingers into his thick hair. He planted his lips at the crevice of her shaved labia and inhaled, catching her scent.

"*Trey,*" she muttered, awed at his boldness. Increasingly desperate.

"It's okay," he soothed, his warm breath feathering her outer sex. He rose slightly, running his lips along her hipbone, back and forth, back and forth, as though he were memorizing the sensation of her against his mouth. Eleanor knew he probably could feel her quaking. "I've never felt skin this smooth. This soft. *God* you smell good."

He rose in front of her, and she glimpsed his face. His somber expression barely cloaked a primal edge that sent a thrill through her.

Jesus. What kind of storm did I brew up?

He reached for her. He gathered her naked body to him, and her feet left the carpet. The romper slipped past her boots and fell to the floor. He swung her into his arms, muscles flexing hard, and she was reminded of his sexual boldness and displays of raw strength. But now, *she* was the focus of it. The room flew past the periphery of her vision. His face eclipsed her entire awareness.

"You're going to be all mine," he told her.

I already am, she thought wildly. She dug her fingers into his hair and brought him to her mouth for a kiss, forcing him to halt in a long, dim hallway. He made a rough sound in his throat, accepting her invitation. Their tongues tangled. He was delicious. She was reminded she must get her fill now.

This could be her one and only night with him.

The thought amplified her hunger. She deepened the kiss, pulling him tighter to her. He dropped her legs and her boots hit the floor with a clunking sound. She found herself pressed between Trey and the wall. He leaned down over her, a dark, demanding shadow, feeding from her with a single-minded fury that she loved. The noise of her heartbeat pounding in her ears mingled with their moans. His hands moved along her sides, owning her nakedness, stroking the curves of her hips, the indentation of her waist, her ribs and the sensitive sides of her breasts.

Suddenly, it struck her as unbearable that he could touch her nude body at will while he still wore his clothing. She wrenched her hands between their pressing torsos, her fingers frantically searching for the buttons of his shirt. She found one and yanked it through the opening, but suddenly his hands were on her wrists. He spread her arms in a wide V-shape and pressed them against the wall. He wasn't rough with her, but he was firm. She couldn't move.

"Not now. You're about to make me come in my jeans," he muttered tensely against her lips. Her heart soared at his words, and then his mouth was tracing a molten path down her neck, pausing to flick his tongue over her pulse. Eleanor moaned, her desperation mounting. He bent to kiss and lick at the skin of her chest. Pinned against the wall like she was, she stared down at him, helplessly aroused. His lips brushed against the top curve of her breast. Her nipples pulled so tight they hurt.

"Trey," she entreated.

He slicked his warm, wet tongue over a nipple, and her legs almost gave way. Maybe he sensed her trembling, because he let go of her wrists and grasped her rib cage, holding her firmly against the wall for his erotic assault. His mouth closed over a nipple, encasing her in his heat. She gasped. Her head banged softly against the wall. His mouth felt velvety warm. Firm. Insistent.

He sucked on her, then laved her nipple with his tongue. She felt his fire, knew his honest, pure hunger firsthand. She grabbed at his head, her hips shifting restlessly, needy for pressure against her sex. His hands moved to the sides of her breasts. He pushed the mounds together as he released her nipple. He pressed his face between her breasts and made a thrilling, feral growling sound. His hands were so matter-of-fact on her, shaping her flesh masterfully, any way he wanted it. He dipped his head, sucking the other protruding nipple into his hot mouth, drawing on her with a single-minded purpose that knocked the wind out of her lungs.

In that moment, Eleanor knew for *certain* that she'd been foolish in teasing Trey Riordan. But even that misgiving thrilled her to the core.

His hands went to her hips, lifting her effortlessly again. This time, he carried her with her front pressed to his, high up on his body, so that her gaze matched his. She dipped her head, his mouth calling to her.

"Don't, Eleanor. You're making me fucking crazy. At this rate, I'll never make it to the bed," he said sharply, and she stilled herself. Then he was lowering her, and the back of her thighs and ass hit a mattress.

At last, she was in Trey's bed.

"Lie back," he said, his tone grim. She looked up at him, half in trepidation, half in lust.

Now she was going to have to face the consequences of torturing him.

A flash of guilt went through him when he saw her flinch slightly at his harsh demand. He couldn't help it. He'd never been this primed for a woman. There was something about her that went beyond her firm, svelte curves, exotic features and eyes he could drown himself in. She was so fresh. So unexpectedly honest in her passion.

And her *taste*—he'd like to see how long he could survive subsisting solely on her, three meals a day, afternoon and midnight snacks . . . maybe he'd never *stop* eating—

A loud roar started in his ears at his erotic thoughts while staring down at Eleanor lying on his bed, naked, save for those sexy stockings and boots. The curtains were open, allowing in enough light from the city for him to see the paleness of her skin against the dark blue of his bedspread and her high, full breasts rising and falling so enticingly, such delicate, mouthwatering prey. He lunged toward the bedside table and flipped on the lamp to a dim setting. There was no way in hell he was going to miss any detail of this.

Her nipples were dark pink in color. They glistened from his mouth. The areolas puckered incredibly tight. She was extremely responsive. They'd been so hard and distended beneath his tongue. He resisted an urge to fall on her like a wild animal.

"There's no one in your condo who can look over and watch while I have *you*, is there?" he asked her sardonically. He tore his stare off the intensely erotic vision of her naked, flushed labia. She'd strike him dead from an overdose of lust. He forced himself to attend to the mechanics of undressing.

He realized she looked confused by his statement.

"The curtains are open," he clarified. Even the rote task of undressing was nearly impossible with her lying there, her naked skin gleaming, breasts heaving slightly as she panted, her large eyes shining with excitement. She leaned up on her elbows, dragging her gaze off him, and glanced over her shoulder at the window. All was dark in her condo across the way.

"Oh . . . no." She faced him. "I live alone."

"*That's* good to hear," he muttered dryly.

He discarded his shirt, feeling her gaze move down over him. He grit his teeth, annoyed at the response he had to her eyes on his naked skin. One of his shoes skidded several feet under the bed, he'd kicked it off so forcefully. He lifted a foot and ripped off one sock, then the other, tripping slightly on the second one because he couldn't take his stare off her.

His cock plagued him. He couldn't think about anything else but finding blissful relief in that sweet little pussy. He watched her, gritting his teeth as he tore open the button fly of his jeans and jerked them off his body. By the time he drew the waistband of his boxer brief out and over his erection, he was wincing in agony.

His freed cock fell forward, heavy and hurting.

Now naked, he opened the bedside drawer to retrieve a condom. He glanced over his shoulder. She was checking out his ass and cock in profile with what he could only call openmouthed wonder. Her unguarded appreciation made his cock jump up in the air. He fisted himself, wincing at the sharp tug of lust she'd inspired.

"Move back on the bed, honey. Spread those beautiful legs."

She looked a little startled, but her golden green eyes definitely glowed with arousal. He planted his feet, his cock still in his hand, and watched her as she scooted back on his bed and opened her thighs. God, she was gorgeous. That smooth, golden skin, those succulent breasts, those long, long legs . . . and *oh* Jesus. That pussy. He pumped his fist, stroking himself more strenuously. She watched him with wide eyes. He halted, letting his cock go.

"No more coming alone while you torture me, Eleanor."

"Did you . . . come?" Her voice trembled. "Last night?"

"Do you honestly think a straight man could have watched you and not come?" he asked her bluntly.

She didn't reply, and he was too abuzz from lust to decode the expression on her face at that moment. He rolled the condom onto his cock. It felt like he was going to burst through his skin, he was so hard. He scrambled onto the bed between her opened legs.

"I'm afraid this first time is going to have to be hard and fast," he said. He glanced up at her as he took his cock into one hand. "That's a natural consequence of teasing me mercilessly."

Her lips parted and the color in her cheeks mounted. If he'd had his guess, he'd say she'd been turned on by him saying that. Would miracles never cease?

"Open your legs farther," he instructed. "Good. Now reach above your head and grasp your wrists. Don't let go."

"Ever?" she asked incredulously.

"Not until we're done. I'm going to own *you* right now, honey. Not the other way around."

She did what he'd demanded with gratifying eagerness. The position stretched the skin tight across her rib cage and thrust her breasts forward.

"God, you're so pretty. Open wider, Eleanor."

Her long, slightly bent legs slid along his suede bedspread until she was practically doing the splits. He recalled vividly her flexibility from the night of her striptease. Tonight, with her spread out before him like a wanton feast, he could see every jaw-dropping detail of what had previously been denied him.

He made a rough sound in his throat and inched forward on the bed, drawn irrevocably. He reached between her thighs, feeling her wetness. Her softness. Brutal arousal sliced through him. He moved his hand in a taut circular motion, stimulating her outer sex. She cried out in excitement, but his gaze remained fixed on what he was doing. Such a pretty, pink pussy. He used his middle finger to penetrate her while he rubbed her clit with the ridge of his thumb. A groan ripped his throat. It was like pushing his finger into a squeezing channel lined with warm honey.

"Ah Jesus," he muttered, crazed by the sensation. He might want this to be a fast, hard ride for the first time, but she was so small. He'd have to either be patient or cruel. Trey may be many things, but he wasn't the latter.

Time to see if all that control he was supposedly learning in his tai chi lessons actually worked.

Her hips twisted on the mattress. He glanced up at her whimper.

"You okay?" he asked, all the while massaging her outer sex with the lower part of his palm and plunging his finger deep.

"God, yes," she whispered.

"Because you're very small. You haven't done this in a while?" he asked, puzzled. Concerned.

The color in her cheeks deepened. He'd embarrassed her with his bluntness.

"I don't want to hurt you."

"You're not hurting me. It feels so good." He could feel her flesh trembling around him. He pressed his finger deep and circled his palm. She gasped, opening her flushed, pink lips wide. He thought of plunging his tongue between them while he did the same with his cock into the tight, slippery sheath of her pussy.

"Fuck me, Trey."

Her whisper clung in the air between them, locking his lungs. He inched forward, his cock in one hand. It wasn't a request he was capable of resisting. He leaned down over her, supporting himself with one arm. She watched as he moved his swollen cock-head in her smooth, wet sex. He stroked the cleft between her labia, stimulating her clit. She twisted her hips, her moan sounding frantic.

"Hold still."

She stopped thrashing, biting her lower lip while he continued to move his cockhead in her cleft.

"You're nice and wet," he said gruffly, glancing up into her strained face. "Did you get wet for me there at the reading event? Or were you turned on by your book?"

"You," she whispered. "The book. Both at once."

He snarled, shifting his cock and finding her channel.

"And now?" he demanded.

"You. Just you. *Please*," she gasped. Her hands tightened reflexively on her wrists. Her skin would be reddened there when she finally let go, she was exerting so much pressure. Her willingness to follow his instructions to restrain herself, even when she appeared to want to let go, pleased him enormously. He looked up and watched her flushed face, wanting to see every detail of her reaction while he entered her for the first time. He thrust his hips, her gasp echoing in his head.

"God, you're tight," he muttered, incredulous on many levels, but mostly because her narrow channel now clutched his cockhead. He couldn't uncross his eyes for a second, it felt so good. "Tilt your hips back, beautiful," he managed to say through a tight throat. She rolled her hips, her thighs coming off the mattress a few inches, granting him a better angle. He flexed his hips and a groan rattled his throat. He thrust again and grunted in pleasure. She stared up at him with huge eyes, looking stunned.

"Don't look at me like that, Eleanor," he chastised, pushing his cock in her another inch higher. "This is what you wanted, wasn't it?"

She nodded and made a high-pitched, shaky sound.

"Good. Then try to relax. Lift your legs a little higher." He surprised himself by sounding calm enough. The edges of his eyesight were growing blurred. She existed at the center of his vision, a golden, flushed goddess. He was determined to exist at the very center of *her*. He watched, panting, while she lifted her boots higher off the mattress. Her flesh yielded some. A rough groan vibrated his throat as he slid farther into her. He found himself grabbing at one of those sexy boots, urging her more stringently. He sawed his cock several inches in and out of her. *God*, it felt good. She grit her teeth and clamped her eyelids shut. "If you want me inside, *tell* me, Eleanor."

A high-pitched moan escaped her throat.

"Open your eyes," he said sharply. "Look at me."

She opened heavy eyelids and focused on him with apparent effort. Her body and face looked so strained, he was afraid he was hurting her. But he was on the brink.

"Say it," he commanded. His entire world narrowed down to her mouth.

"I'm going to come."

It hadn't been what he'd expected she'd say. Not by a long shot. It sent him straight into the fire.

"Then come, you beautiful girl," he grated out. He thrust, feeling initial resistance. Then her flesh melted around him. He pierced the hot core of her. He grabbed her other boot, holding her steady, while he ground his balls against her outer sex, giving her the pressure she needed to ignite.

She cried out, her eyes going wide. He felt her heat rush around him.

And then . . . well, he wasn't sure what happened there for a moment.

The next thing he knew, he was fucking her in short, hard strokes while she screamed, feeling her spasms of orgasm vibrating into his driving cock. His brain, body and cock crackled with energy. It was like running a race in heaven: a golden, sweet, agonizing bliss as every fiber of his being strained for the finish line.

Open your eyes. Look at me.

She'd been on the brink when he'd said it.

She'd never been so filled. It didn't hurt, having his large, swollen cock in her body. It *was* slightly uncomfortable, though, in addition to being intensely arousing. The indirect pressure on her clit from the thick, piercing shaft was unlike anything she'd ever experienced.

She opened her eyes, her trembling amplifying when she saw him. He was still tanned from some recent travel destination, his skin a beautiful golden brown color. She'd been dazed into near-muteness watching him undress earlier, mesmerized by the ridged tautness of his abdomen, the powerful muscles of his chest and shoulders, the bulging, rock-hard biceps. His cock was straight and thick, the crown flushed and defined. Succulent. He was so erect, she couldn't help but feel proud he found her so arousing . . . even if she was a little intimidated as well.

Presently, he looked rigid and tense as he pierced her. She could see every defined muscle in his beautiful body. It was like he was straining against an invisible cord. His eyes blazed. He looked so powerful staring down at her. He held one of her booted legs in his hand, keeping her open to his possession.

"*Say* it," he insisted, but Eleanor had no idea what he wanted her to say. Her brain was flooded with sensation.

"I'm going to come," she said stupidly, feeling the wave of pleasure about to crash down on her.

"Then come, you beautiful girl," he snarled.

His voice thundering in her head, she shuddered. Wave after wave of pleasure rolled through her. As if through a layer of thick insulation, she heard his ominous growl. And suddenly, she shook from more than climax.

A furor barraged her, rattling her consciousness. She experienced a mixed sense of heady bliss combined with an uncomfortable pressure for a muddled moment. His cock was large, and he rode her like he'd reached his limit. That excited her. A lot. She wouldn't have wanted it any other way. But for a moment, it was too much. She didn't black out, but perception became a swirling, pounding chaos.

She came back to full awareness at the feeling of him thrusting into her with firm, short strokes, his pelvis smacking against her outer sex in an arousing, staccato rhythm. She heaved a ragged breath and focused on his face.

Trey.

He'd rolled back her pelvis and was firmly planted between her thighs, his hips moving in a jaw-dropping liquid glide, his cock moving like a piston in her pussy. He knew how to fuck. He held her booted legs wide, his chest and arm muscles flexed hard. God help her, he looked so powerful in that moment, so hard. So determined.

"You feel like heaven," he rasped from between rigid lips.

"So do you," she managed.

"*Don't* let go of your wrists," he said sharply, never hesitating in his smooth, forceful pump. She blinked dazedly. She'd nearly forgotten he'd told her to hold her arms over her head. Watching him just now in her disoriented, postorgasmic state, all she'd wanted to do was touch him. She'd started to let go. With his insistence that she hold her wrists above her head, all she could do was watch him helplessly as he fucked her . . . as he took his pleasure. Because that's *definitely* what he was doing. She'd fantasized incessantly about what it would be like to be with him.

But she hadn't prepared herself to be owned by him.

She gripped her wrists tighter. Her hips began to move in a counter rhythm to his. It felt sinfully good. A light sheen of perspiration gleamed on his ridged torso. His nostrils flared slightly as he stared down at her. The tempo of their slapping bodies increased in her ears.

"You act like you want it good and hard," he said. "But can you really take it, Eleanor?"

"I can take it," she told him from between clenched teeth.

"Open that beautiful mouth. It's tortured me long enough," he ordered.

She parted her lips, confused by his words, but excited by his intensity.

He fell down over her, his tongue plunging into her mouth.

His taste overwhelmed her. *He* did, because at the same moment he kissed her savagely, he thrust harder inside her . . . *longer*, fucking her from tip to balls. She screamed into his mouth; the pressure was mind-blowing. He rolled her hips back farther with his grip on her calves. Her feet were now parallel to her head. She was at his mercy.

The headboard began to bang against the wall stridently with his thrusts. She struggled for release from his kiss, and yet she'd never craved anything more. Her lungs burned. Her clit sizzled. At this ruthless angle, she could perfectly feel the swollen head of his cock carving into her, the delineated head rubbing previously untouched flesh. There was only one thing she could do.

She shuddered in orgasm again.

He ripped his mouth from hers, grimacing.

"Fuck yeah. I can feel you coming," he grated out.

Eleanor forced her eyelids open a slit, desperate to see him despite her short-circuiting brain and body. "Oh *God*."

His cock jerked inside her. He withdrew and then pounded forcefully into her, his face clenching tight in pleasure. He growled, the sound ominous. Wonderful. His muscles rippled as he finally tore through his restraint.

He roared in release.

Their stares held for a pleasure-infused moment, his blue eyes seeming to shoot fire at her. Then he clamped his eyelids shut, his face pulling tight in pleasure as he continued to thrust.

As the heart-pounding seconds passed, Eleanor opened her eyes wider, staring with stark wonder at the image of Trey Riordan finding bliss in her body.

The moment was the one she'd been dreaming about for over a year now. It'd been everything she'd anticipated and schemed for.

It'd been more. *Much* more.

He was.

She didn't want it to end. One time with him definitely wasn't enough.

He released her legs and fell down over her, bracing his upper body. His rib cage heaved in and out as he panted from his strenuous effort. His head was lowered, his eyes shut tight as he recovered from a blast of pleasure.

Eleanor unclasped her wrists. He'd said she only had to remain that way until they were done, after all. Slowly, she lowered her hands and glided them across his beautiful shoulders, his heaving ribs and down over his narrow hips and the tops of his smooth, hard ass. He was so lean and hard. She felt power emanating from every inch of him. She soothed his agitated state with her fingertips. She absorbed the incredible feeling of him with wonder.

Knowing he was only hers to touch for a short, undefined period of time, her caresses were nothing short of worship.

Each frantic, eager touch may have been her last.

SEVEN

The feeling of Eleanor caressing him slowly penetrated his short-circuited brain. Her hands struck him as sweet and soothing, like they were cooling the fire in his crackling nerves. But there was something else in her touch, an urgency he didn't understand.

He pried open his eyelids and realized his forehead was planted in the pillow next to Eleanor's. His cock was still embedded deep in her. He needed to withdraw. Her flesh quickened around him. She was so warm. So sweet. He groaned as reanimated pleasure rippled through his body. Instead of withdrawing, he flexed and groaned again, planting himself deep inside her once more. Her arms surrounded his head, hugging him against her. Had she too experienced that stab of desire to fuse even more than they already were?

It didn't matter. He had to withdraw or risk spilling in her. He did so, grunting in displeasure at the harsh deprivation of her body.

"Give me a second, okay?" He leaned down and kissed her parted lips. He'd only meant it to be a quick peck before he rose, but her lips were so warm. Delectable. Responsive. It took him a minute to realize he was kissing her wholesale, and was only growing hungrier by the second.

He sealed their kiss, growling in dissatisfaction, although he couldn't exactly say *what* he was displeased about. He rolled off the bed. Instead of walking to the suite's bathroom, he walked out of the room and disposed of the condom in the powder room down the hall. The air felt cool against his perspiration-damp skin when he walked out into the open space of the living room.

He'd worked up quite a thirst. He'd been honing his self-discipline lately, forcing himself to practice his guitar, submitting his body to the most strenuous exercise of his life, beating his brain into submission with his tai chi. But none of that had tested him more than restraining himself with Eleanor just now. And despite expending every ounce of self-discipline he owned, he'd still taken her like a madman. He felt a little guilty about that, but that didn't stop him from wanting to do it again.

And again.

He entered his kitchen, pausing when he glanced out the window. He heard Eleanor's voice in his head.

All those times I saw you naked . . .

It was something he did with relative frequency, to be honest: walk around naked, sleep naked, even check his e-mail naked once in a while. He wasn't a nudist, but he was pretty insouciant about what he wore or did within the confines of his own home. He hadn't thought about the condo next door much, but when he had, he'd always assumed it was empty. It was usually dark, wasn't it?

Yes. He peered into the adjacent high-rise, but only saw darkness.

He didn't like the idea of someone spying on him when he thought he was alone or when he was with a lover. Few *would* like it. But when Eleanor had made her confession about looking inside to his private world, there'd been something else mixed up with his annoyance. Her honesty had turned him on. And he supposed it was excitement at the idea of a beautiful woman watching him and becoming aroused. *That* must be what had tempered his anger.

Although, when he tried to imagine other women he knew confessing the same thing, he didn't experience quite the same reaction.

There was something about *her* looking into his world with those big, expressive eyes that excited him.

She was messing with his ideas of what he found arousing, and he wasn't sure how he felt about that. He wanted control sexually. He wanted his lovers to experience intense excitement and pleasure, but he wanted to be the one to sharpen it to a fine edge and then finally grant that blast of precise pleasure. He wanted to be the one in the driver's seat. Eleanor had yanked that control from him with her exhibitionist displays and admissions of voyeurism. He'd been excited by her confession too. Incredibly so.

But he'd been even *more* excited by the idea of having her under him . . . completely at his mercy.

It'd been incredible.

When he walked into his bedroom a minute later, two glasses of water in his hands, the first thing he saw was Eleanor scurrying out of his bed. She paused in a sitting position at the edge of his bed when she noticed him. Her eyes went wide, like she'd just been caught red-handed at something.

Escape? he wondered darkly.

"Where are you going?" he asked her, his brows slanting as he walked toward her. She looked adorable, her long hair disheveled and falling over heaving breasts. Debauched. Sexy as hell.

"Nowhere," she replied breathlessly.

He thought of asking her if she needed to go home to get some sleep. Maybe she had an early workday in the morning? That would be the logical assumption, wouldn't it? But then her gaze dropped down over his naked body hungrily. His skin prickled beneath her stare. His cock stirred, which both gratified and annoyed him.

And instead of offering her an easy exit, he tilted his head toward the pillows. "It's chilly. Get under the covers."

She complied with an alacrity that soothed his ego a little. When she started to climb beneath the sheet, he set down their waters.

"Eleanor."

She looked up at him, wide-eyed, in the process of pulling the covers over herself. He glanced down pointedly at a protruding boot.

"Oh," she mumbled. She slid her feet and legs over the edge of the bed. Chuckling, he knelt and unzipped the boots one by one, letting them drop to the floor. Relishing the next part, he slipped his fingers beneath the top of her thigh-highs and began to roll them down her long legs, his fingers brushing against her satiny skin with more frequency than was necessary. He hadn't lied while they'd been in the heat of things earlier. Her skin was remarkable.

He straightened, his flash of humor at her getting into bed with her boots on now mingling with renewed sexual interest. She pulled her legs up, lay back and yanked the covers all the way up to her chin, looking a little embarrassed.

"Don't laugh at me," she told him, a smile flickering across her mouth. "You robbed me of all common sense."

He leaned down and grabbed the edge of the bedspread and sheet. He ripped them away from her. She stared up at him, aghast.

"All your boldness too?" he asked, quirking up his brow in a challenging gesture. His smile faded as he checked out her naked body. His stare stuck on her pussy when he noticed the glint of moisture on her smooth labia. Suddenly, she shifted from her huddling position, her thighs parting, her hips shifting in a come-hither movement. Heat flashed through him. His cock perked up to attention. His gaze darted to her face, and there it was. That small, sexy, "I hold all the cards and then some" grin.

"Not *all* my boldness," she assured.

He shook his head and sat at the edge of the bed. "Ingénue or witch, that's what I'd like to know," he mumbled to himself, leaning back next to her on the bed.

"*Witch?*" she asked, sitting up and propping herself on one elbow. He noticed her scowl and hid his smile by reaching for the water glass. "*That's* what you'd call a . . . you know . . . a sexually confident woman?" she accused.

"No," he replied calmly, turning toward her. "It's what I'd call *you*."

She blinked, her scowl fading. "Sit up. Drink some water," he told her matter-of-factly. She followed his instruction, sitting up against the pillows, despite still appearing dazed. Puzzled. Miffed? She drew the sheet up over her breasts. He scowled at her covering herself, but she ignored him and reached for the glass.

"Because in my experience, men are always doing that," she said, taking a big gulp of the water and swallowing. "Making women into either whores or virgins, sluts or saints."

"Men think that, in your experience," he repeated levelly, taking a swallow of his water.

"That's right," she said, eyes flashing.

He leaned back into the pillows. "It's hard to imagine a guy having the ability to think much of anything when you're flashing your pussy at him in a public place one second and running like a scared rabbit the next."

She gave him a disgusted glance at his sarcasm. "You don't understand at all."

"I think I've been pretty up front about *that* from the first." He set down his water glass and turned to her, thinking it might be advisable to change the subject. He'd never experienced anything like it before: the way he disapproved of her exhibitionism and boldness for some stupid reason, and yet was still turned into a rutting pig by it. "So . . . what are you doing for Thanksgiving?" he asked her.

"Spending it with my mom and dad in Evanston."

"Just the three of you?"

She nodded. "What about you?"

"I'm driving to Rockford for the long weekend."

"For . . ."

"My parents are there. That's where I grew up, on a farm a few miles out of town. My sister and her family will be there too. I think my brother is coming from New York as well."

"So you have a brother and a sister? And your parents are still together?"

"Oh yeah. They're still disgustingly in love too even after forty-four years."

"Really?" she asked slowly. "That's nice."

"Yeah."

"It all sounds so . . . normal."

"*Normal?* What's that supposed to mean?" he wondered.

She looked a little guilty. "I don't know . . . you're so . . . *not* normal. I was just expecting you'd spend your Thanksgiving holiday in a more exotic way."

"So you think I'm abnormal?"

"No. I think you're *exceptional.*"

He blinked in surprise at her small outburst. He leaned closer, catching her clean, floral scent mingling with the fragrance of sex.

"I'm just your basic Midwestern boy," he murmured, captured by the shine in her green gold eyes. He noticed her doubtful look. "I'm *serious.* I may have taken some forays into exotic lands as an adult"—he paused when she rolled her eyes at his lame attempt at symbolism—"but I've always remained a simple Midwestern kid at heart. You don't believe me?"

"Let's just say I believe you're anything but simple."

He laughed. He pulled down on the sheet covering her breasts. She tried to pull it back up. For a second, they played tug-of-war. Then he merely looked up at her, slightly exasperated but patiently waiting. Slowly, her fingers relaxed. He lowered the sheet deliberately, teasing his senses. He exposed the pale gold mounds and then the pink tips. Her nipples were in a state between arousal and relaxation. They appeared flushed, fat and luscious. He wanted to make them hard as pebbles all over again.

"You've got the prettiest breasts," he said, admiring her openly. He gently ran his fingertips over a nipple. She inhaled sharply, sending the mounds higher. He glanced up at her. She looked a little flummoxed. "Please don't hide them from me. Ever."

He saw her throat convulse as she swallowed.

"Eleanor?"

"Yes?" she mouthed silently.

"Can you explain what your motives were again for turning me into a drooling animal in a room full of high-minded, serious people?"

Her eyes appeared huge in her finely wrought, small face. She lifted the glass and drank determinedly. When she'd drained the water, she had no other excuse but to answer him.

"I *told* you why I did that," she replied shakily.

"Because you saw me from your condo, and you decided you just had to have me?" he asked, trying to restrain his sarcasm. He saw her expression and knew he hadn't succeeded in disguising anything. She leaned across him aggressively and set her glass down on the table with a clunk. She looked irritated enough that he didn't think she'd dragged her nipples across his ribs on purpose. That didn't lessen his appreciation any.

"What's so hard to believe about that? I mean . . . have you *seen* you?" she asked with incredulous sarcasm, waving down at his body. "So I went after what I wanted. That doesn't mean I'm a slut. *Or* a witch."

"Fine. If you say so."

"I *say* so."

"Okay," he said, putting up his hands in a "don't shoot the messenger" gesture. He stopped himself from laughing—barely—because somehow, he just knew she'd move from spitting to hissing if he did. "So . . . do you like your book?"

The fire drained out of her. She gave him a blank look.

"*Born to Submit*?" he prompted.

"Oh . . . yes," she recovered, her voice sounding a little high-pitched.

"Is that your typical reading choice?"

"Erotica, you mean?" she asked, straightening her spine and meeting his stare determinedly. "Yes, it is. I read it exclusively. Do you like it?"

"Erotica?"

She nodded, her demeanor serious.

"I can't say I've ever read any before. What's it about?" he asked seriously, trying to match her mood.

"Oh . . . you know."

He quirked his brows in a polite query.

"Sex, of course," she said, rolling her eyes.

"That's it?"

"Well, no . . . I mean . . . it's about this couple: Xander and Katya."

"Nice names."

She gave him a sharp glance. "Someone named *Trey* really doesn't have the high ground for making fun of names."

He just smiled and waited expectantly.

"Well, anyway, he's her boss. She's his secretary and . . ." Her cheeks flushed and she gave him a repressive glance. "Don't look so smug. I know it's cliché-sounding, but it's actually pretty good. Better than I thought it'd be. Anyway, they enter into a dominant-submissive relationship."

"Relationship?" he prodded doubtfully.

"Yes, *relationship*. There's some really sweet give and take between Xander and Katya, at times."

"Sexually?"

"Yes, *and* emotionally. Why do you find that so hard to believe?"

"I don't," he defended. "I'm just prodding you, because you're not giving me much to go on. You were turned on. Reading it, I mean."

She blinked at his abrupt turn of topic.

"Well, you were, weren't you? What was happening in the book? When you were getting turned on, there at the coffee shop?"

At first she looked annoyed. Then, ever so slowly, a grin slid across her lips. His cock popped up against the sheet. He couldn't decide what was sexier about her face, her big, expressive eyes or her sometimes sweet, sometimes X-rated mouth.

"Why don't you just read the book and find out? I have a feeling you'd like it."

He straightened against the pillows and leaned toward her. "What's that supposed to mean? Eleanor?" he prodded suspiciously when she didn't reply.

"Just read it and see," she told him, lifting her chin. And despite her play at haughtiness, she gave him a sideways, curious glance. "What about you? Do you like *Pride and Prejudice*?"

He shrugged and turned to retrieve his glass of water, a little disappointed she wouldn't give him some dirty details from *Born to Submit*. "I don't know," he replied, taking a sip of water. "It was kind of hard to concentrate on it, with you there. But I don't think so."

Her mouth dropped open. "You don't like *Pride and Prejudice*?" she asked, clearly scandalized.

There it is. The feminine outrage. He groaned and set down his glass. He turned in the bed and reached for her, hauling her up against him, their naked skin sliding together. It felt good. She gasped and wiggled against him, surprised by his abrupt action. He liked the way that felt too. A lot. He put a hand on her hip, keeping her in place. When she stilled, he slid his opened hand along the warm, silky curve of her hip to her waist. Sure, it was a dirty way to defray a disagreement, but it seemed to work. Her eyes went enormous in her flushed face.

"Don't lecture me about *Pride and Prejudice*. If you want me to tell you that it's deep and romantic, I will."

She blinked, and he had the impression that for a moment, she'd forgotten what they were talking about. Then he felt her touch him on the back of his hip, the tentative caress striking him as shockingly erotic. Pleasure snaked down his spine to his groin. His cock stiffened and brushed against her satiny, taut belly.

"But you don't really think it is? Any good, I mean?" she asked weakly.

"Good? Sure, I mean it's well-written. I don't get why you women think it's so romantic, though. Darcy's a jerk."

"He isn't a jerk," she exclaimed. He gave her a *"seriously?"* glance. "Well, maybe at first he is. You just haven't read far enough. That's the whole premise of the book. They misjudge each other upon their first meetings, and both of them have to work through their pride to admit it. '*I could almost forgive his vanity had he not wounded mine.*'"

He glided his hand to her back and pulled her closer against him, his cock pressed along her stomach, his balls resting at the top of her moist mound. "Are you quoting *Pride and Prejudice*?" he asked, peering down at her, incredulous. *Pleased*, for some reason. She'd sounded sort of prim saying it. It turned him on, the way she came off all girls-gone-wild one second and a proper Sunday-school-teacher type the next.

"What if I am?"

"You just said you read erotica exclusively," he reminded her drolly.

"Well, I might have exaggerated a little," she mumbled, her gaze darting around the room.

"Yeah. You do that sometimes, don't you?" he said without any real heat. She made him want to crack up. She also made him hornier than a stag in heat. "Do it more," he growled, leaning down to kiss her nose and then her lips. They were cool from the water, but he sensed her heat just beneath the surface. "It's better than dirty talk."

"You shouldn't make fun of *Pride and Prejudice*," she scolded him, but her tiny smile as he plucked at her lips only encouraged him.

"It's not *my* bible."

"Why are you reading it, then?" she demanded, backing away slightly.

"Because all you women take it so seriously. I was just trying to figure out the secret to it, that's all," he said, unable to pry his gaze off her lips and highly aware of how soft and curvy and firm she felt against his stroking hand. He lowered to her ass, shaping a buttock to his palm. *Incredible* ass . . . the things he'd like to do to it. He liked her soft gasp of pleasure, and then her obvious attempt to look serious again.

"There's no *secret* to *Pride and Prejudice*. It's funny . . . and it's *fun*. Elizabeth was making fun of herself when she said that line I just quoted. You said you were interested in something *light* right now," she reminded him with a remonstrative glare. "Well *Pride and Prejudice* can be downright froth. You shouldn't be approaching it so seriously."

He considered what she'd said for a minute.

"Maybe you're right," he conceded. "I told you I was having trouble concentrating on the book. You were the one who was responsible for me being distracted. You have no right to be pissed for me not getting the nuances," he said before he nuzzled her ear, inhaling her scent. He cupped a breast and ran his thumb over a beading nipple. She shivered against him. "Quote some more to me, Eleanor," he growled next to her ear before he kissed it.

"I will *not*," she said, but her arms encircled his neck. He pushed and she rolled onto her back. He came down over her. She smiled that witch's smile up at him. "Why should I bother? You're a heathen."

"At least I don't deny it," he said, nibbling at her succulent lower lip.

"At *least*?" she mumbled.

"Yeah. You got all defensive when I called you a witch," he reminded her, lowering his head to her beautiful breasts. He leaned down, anticipation building in him, and glided his lips against the silky skin at the top of one globe. She whimpered and dug her fingers into his hair. Was her hand *shaking*? Could she really be that excited, just from chatting in bed? Maybe it wasn't that much of a shock she was aroused from talking, because God knew *he* was. Her fingernails scraped his scalp. His skin roughened in excitement.

"See, unlike you," he explained gruffly as he brushed his mouth over her breast and kissed the sweet tip, "I'm just heathen enough not to bother denying it when I'm called one," he finished before he firmed his hold on her rib cage and lifted her breasts to his feasting mouth.

EIGHT

Eleanor awoke while it was still dark outside. She was turned on her side facing the floor-to-ceiling windows. Instead of being disoriented upon waking up in a strange place, she immediately knew where she was. It was strange, to be looking at her condominium from a whole new angle.

She'd gone through the looking glass. She was *inside* Trey Riordan's world.

Her sex ached, but pleasantly. She hadn't had sex for over a year before last night, but that didn't fully explain her tender state. Trey was a passionate, skillful, demanding and . . . *potent* lover. They'd had sex three times before they'd finally fallen into an exhausted sleep. Each time had been more exciting than the last.

There was no precedent for her, no prior experience that had remotely prepared her for him. Just thinking about what he'd done to her in this bed—about the things he'd proposed they do in the future—made her shift her hand beneath the sheets. Carefully, so as not to awake him, she cupped her sex and closed her eyes, drowning in the memories for a moment.

Trey embraced her from behind. He was like a subtle furnace. She wanted to curl farther into him like a content cat. The exciting memories, his long, solid male body pressed to her backside, and the pressure of her hand on her sex created a languid state of sensual arousal in her.

After their second round of scorching sex, where he'd again owned her body and soul, he held her against him in the darkness for a while. Neither of them spoke, but she sensed he was awake from his stroking hand on her hip. She found their silence strangely full. Relaxing. Comforting. Before she'd drifted off to a satiated sleep, he'd spoken gruffly next to her ear. She recalled every detail of that exchange now in the early morning darkness, her heart and her senses waking up before her brain fully did.

"Eleanor?"

"Yes?" she whispered.

"Before, when you told me I should read Born to Submit *because you thought I'd like it . . . were you hinting that you've seen something before, when you were looking into my bedroom?"*

Her heavy eyelids sprang wide.

"What do you mean?" He stroked her thigh and then her ass in the tense silence that followed.

"Did you ever see me restrain a woman . . . spank or paddle her?"

Shivers rippled down her spine.

"Yes," she finally admitted, intensely aware of him caressing her bottom. She waited tensely for him to reply, but for a moment, he only stroked her.

"Did you know in advance I'd be at the event, because you work at the museum? Is that why you chose the book you did?"

"I thought it might get your attention," she confessed breathlessly.

Another silence, this one swelling with unsaid things.

"Do you like to do those things? From the book?" he asked her after a pause.

She hesitated. Of course she knew she was supposed to be playing the part of the sexually liberated, bold woman with him. But she increasingly longed to be honest with him, as well.

"You mean do I want to be tied up, spanked . . . things like that?"

"Yes."

"I liked reading about them . . . while you watched. But submission or bondage really hasn't been my area of expertise or interest in the past," she admitted cautiously.

He squeezed her buttock before he gently spanked her in a gentle reprimand. She jumped in surprise and made a little squeaky sound.

"Right. Your area of expertise is voyeurism. Exhibitionism. Driving a man nuts," he stated rather than asked, and she'd sensed his frown from his grim tone. Is that what he thought? That she was an expert on something sexual? There were times that she was sure he remained humorously unconvinced by her act, but on this topic, he seemed strangely certain. Excitement flickered through her at the realization that she'd fooled him so completely on at least one thing. She forced herself to focus and not break her role.

"That's right. I like watching. And I like being watched," she whispered. She left out the fact that she'd never dabbled in either voyeurism or exhibitionism until him. He was her motivation, not some sexual preference somehow worked into her genes. But if he thought she was an expert on a particular area of kink, well . . . it only helped her performance.

More important, it put her on more level footing with him, something she sorely needed when it came to the arena of sex. He was vastly more experienced than her. And she knew she came off like a fumbling fool at times. But her supposed expertise in voyeurism and exhibitionism? Miraculously, Trey never seemed to question it.

He continued to stroke her in the silent seconds that followed. She could almost hear him thinking.

"I'm not sure what I think about voyeurism or exhibitionism. And you say you're a novice to any kind of bondage or submission—although if I had my guess to the way you were reacting to that book and the way you are in bed, I'm hopeful," he'd added dryly under his breath. She wiggled against him, made restless by his words. He stilled her hip with his hand and thrust his cock up the furrow of her ass. She whimpered. He was growing stiff.

Again.

Was that because of this talk they were having?

He spoke directly into her ear, his hoarse, low voice sending shivers down her neck and spine. "But maybe we could share what we know with each other . . . make our light little experiment together more of a challenge?"

"You mean, agree to"—she swallowed thickly—"scenarios that take both our preferences into account?"

"Yeah. It doesn't have to be just about that. As you probably have guessed by now, I don't need kink to turn me on. When it comes to you, I definitely could just focus on the basics, and be happy." He circled his hand on her ass, pushing the cheek against his cock. He grunted softly. "Very happy. But it might be interesting, blending our kinks a little?" He squeezed her ass. "God knows all I can think about when you're teasing me is tying your hands behind your back, bending you over and spanking your ass bright pink before fucking a good, hard lesson into you about the risks of being cruel."

She turned slightly at that. "I'm not trying to be cruel," she protested. "I thought you'd like it."

"I did," he replied, sounding exasperated. "Why else would I have leapt off the abstinence wagon without a backward glance?"

After their tense exchange, he'd made love to her again in the same position in which they'd talked, both of them on their sides, his front to her back. It'd been a heated, passionate exchange, but somehow tender, as well. She'd given of herself without restraint, and felt him straining to give in return.

Following the storm, Eleanor had fallen into a deep, dreamless, satisfying sleep for two solid hours.

But now, it was time to go. She was unsure how to make her exit. It wasn't something she'd ever done before, engage in a purely sexual affair upon a prior mutual agreement. But she had work in a few hours. She dreaded the idea of waking him, of any awkwardness that might ensue. Perhaps he'd feel obligated to ask her for coffee or breakfast, but all the while, he'd be increasingly focused on the details of his day and wishing she'd leave. She didn't want him to be annoyed by her presence. Best to just fade away, leaving him with the memories of their night.

Always leave them wanting more.

Very carefully, she eased out of his embrace. Her heart stalled for a moment when he moved restlessly, his long body curling toward her several inches, as if he missed her heat. But then he stilled and seemed to fall back into a deep sleep.

She inhaled deliberately, absorbing the unique, subtle scent of him . . . of their essences combined. She told herself to hold on to that evocative detail before carefully sliding off the far side of the bed.

Just one night with him, and yet already she despised the feeling of leaving his arms.

The museum was opening a Mary Todd Lincoln exhibit on the Tuesday following the Thanksgiving holiday. As the preservation and conservation librarian, Eleanor was not only in charge of gathering and displaying the Historical Society's own Mary Todd Lincoln letters and personal belongings, but was also responsible for making sure that every last item that was donated to them from individuals' collections and other museums was safely handled and exhibited.

She'd discovered something during the buildup to the exhibit that she was personally excited about, although she knew from experience that it would capture little attention from anyone else. A private donor had provided several books of fiction, religion and philosophy that had been owned by Mary Todd Lincoln. While examining the collection, Eleanor had discovered handwritten notes in the margins. Their handwriting analyst had confirmed it was Mary Todd Lincoln's own hand. Eleanor had done extensive research, making sense of the handwritten notes and setting them in the historical, familial and personal context of Lincoln's life.

No one really cared about her efforts, with the possible exception of her friend Jimmy, who as the director of special events was the prime organizer of the show. They both knew it was the "glamour items," as Eleanor called them, that would make headlines and sell tickets, not Eleanor's hours of research on seemingly mundane scribbles in old books. In her profession, she'd come to accept that sort of thing as a reality. She'd learned long ago to be proud of these little accomplishments, even if few people ever even noticed.

She was also proud to have negotiated a loan of Mary Todd Lincoln's dresses, shoes and pieces of jewelry from the National Museum of American History at the Smithsonian. The dresses and the opulent jewels would be a big hit, even if Eleanor's extensive research would likely go unnoticed.

That day before she left work for the Thanksgiving holiday, the museum staff, board and members of the press were given a private showing. Almost everyone, including Jimmy *and* Jimmy's and her boss, had labeled the exhibit a resounding success. So by the time she left work for the long holiday weekend, Eleanor was in pretty good spirits.

She left directly from work to go to her parents' house in Evanston. With all the bustle of the private showing that day, and then maneuvering through city holiday traffic, she didn't have much of a chance to dwell or worry about what had happened with Trey Riordan.

It wasn't until she drove through the familiar, sedate neighborhood where she'd grown up that evening that the detailed memories of the night before began to wash over her. It seemed right and adult of her to have snuck out before dawn without his knowledge.

It also struck her as cowardly and stupid.

He said he wanted to see me again . . . that we should undertake a sexual discovery that blended their kinks. He doesn't even have my phone number. How's he supposed to contact me, even if he wants to? Why didn't I leave some kind of simple, evocative note behind on the bedside table with my phone number on it?

Because I'm crap at this, that's why.

Her ruminations sent a rush of anxiety through her. Why did she always feel like she was on the very verge of either making something big happen with Trey Riordan or blowing it entirely? In reality, it was probably something in the gray area in between, where one stupid move on her part could leave him puzzled or turned off, all too ready to walk away with a shrug.

The recollections of her night with him struck her as sensually vibrant and intensely real, and at the same time, felt like she was having memories of another person's life. The museum was Eleanor's world, the basement archives, the temperature-regulated storage facilities, the endless rooms filled with precious ephemera. *This* was her world too—or at least it once had been—she thought as she drove down the tree-lined Evanston street with the attractive, older houses.

She pulled into the driveway and put her car in park. For a minute, she just sat there, staring out the windshield at her childhood home. Hers and Caddy's.

After Caddy's death four months ago, Eleanor had been to the house almost every day for weeks on end. Quite a few relatives had stayed there during Caddy's last days, and then through the funeral. Eleanor had been there to help out her parents, provide meals, drive people back and forth to the airport and hospital, pick up the groceries—all the minutia and details that gave structure to a day and helped a person cope when death loomed. After Caddy had passed, and the house had cleared out, she'd also returned frequently. She was uncomfortably conscious of just how empty the house would seem to her parents, all too aware of how that ringing silence could just crash down on you one day.

Over the past two months, however, she'd come here less often. There didn't seem to be as much need. Her parents had returned to their normal routine and functioning. On the surface, anyway.

But here it was: a holiday. And suddenly Eleanor knew with absolute certainty why all the psychological experts said the first holidays and anniversaries without the loved one were the hardest. Last year on the Wednesday before Thanksgiving, she'd pulled up into this very driveway just like she had ever since she'd left for college at eighteen.

None of them had had a clue about how their lives would change forever that following year.

She glanced over at the empty passenger seat. Last year, Caddy had sat there. She recalled her sister had been going through the pros and cons of taking a partner position in a legal practice in Los Angeles.

"Yeah, it's an amazing salary and opportunity . . . but come on," Caddy joked as Eleanor put the car in park.

"What?" Eleanor asked in confusion.

"Me? L.A.? We just don't mix," Caddy said with a sideways grin as she gathered up her purse and discarded coffee cup. She noticed Eleanor's puzzlement. *"Okay, for one thing, people in L.A. drive everywhere. I like to drink, Nora, but I don't drink and drive. Nobody walks there. Nobody takes mass transportation."*

"You're not going to take this fantastic job because of alcohol?" Of course Eleanor knew that wasn't the truth. There were likely tons of good reasons Caddy wasn't going to take the job. But Caddy wasn't one to hash out boring details and get all serious . . . even on a serious topic, like a job change.

Caddy just rolled her eyes humorously and opened the car door. *"I've turned down jobs for much less of a reason. Oh, here comes Catherine the Great,"* Caddy hissed over her shoulder. *"Don't say anything to Mom about L.A. She'll dig her teeth into the topic and gnaw it to pieces by the time we leave on Friday. I'll have no choice but to take the damn job just to contradict all her arguments against it."*

Eleanor gave a sad smile at the memory. Caddy always did have a way of stating the truth with hilarity.

It was a Thanksgiving tradition for Eleanor and Caddy to watch the Dallas-Detroit game with their dad while her mother did the post-meal cleanup. On holidays, Catherine Briggs got out her good dishes, and no one in existence could handle, wash and store them in the way she wanted. Caddy, Eleanor and their dad had learned long ago to leave her to fuss over her china and crystal while they sought safe refuge in front of the TV.

Today, the chair where Caddy usually sat in the family room seemed almost obscenely empty.

"I'll be there in a few minutes," Eleanor heard her mom call loudly over the sound of rattling dishes and the cheer of the crowd on the television. "We're going to watch the video I found in the attic!"

Eleanor gave her dad an "oh no" look. Her father grimaced in shared understanding.

"She found an old video of a ballet recital in the attic, and insisted we watch it while you were here," her dad said under his breath.

"Of both of us?" Eleanor asked quietly, meaning Caddy and her.

"That's what your mom says," he muttered resignedly, turning up the volume on the television.

Last night and today, an alarm had started to wail in Eleanor's head in regard to her dad. David Briggs seemed largely his wry, brilliant, jocular self, but there was an indefinable heaviness to him that was only growing since Caddy's death. His complexion looked a little gray. Of the three of them, Eleanor worried her father had taken the loss of Caddy hardest. Eleanor had always been the quiet, serious, bookish type. Catherine's intensity and passion were unquenchable. It was her father's cheerful character, his light-hearted tendency to find a joke or a bright spot in even in the most serious of situations that was most similar to Caddy. It was the part of his personality that seemed to wither a little after Caddy had passed.

Her dad was a physicist, so a lot of people assumed he'd be an academic bore. He always proved them wrong, however. He was urbane and knowledgeable about everything from art to pop culture to good food and gracious entertaining. As a graduate of the school and a longtime professor, he was a huge Northwestern sports booster. Some of Eleanor's earliest memories were of their fun, well-attended tailgate parties before football games, her dad relishing his role as chief cook, her mom's homemade Russian kolbassa and his burgers sizzling side-by-side on the grill.

Over Thanksgiving, Eleanor noticed that her dad didn't laugh as frequently as he used to. He was just a little more terse and short with his wife.

"We don't have to watch the video," Eleanor said after a moment, picking up a magazine from the table and pretending to be interested in the cover. "I'll tell her it'll upset me."

"Will it?" her dad asked, his green eyes going sharp on her behind his wire-rimmed glasses.

"No. I just meant . . . if you don't want to."

Her dad smirked and looked back at the television screen. "You don't have to make excuses for me, bug." Eleanor flipped randomly through the pages of the magazine, her dad's pet name for her ringing in her ears and making her eyes burn. "But thank you for the thought anyway," her dad added gently after a moment.

She glanced up and they shared a smile.

"Dad, have you been to see Dr. Chevitz recently—"

But her query into her dad's health was cut off by the entrance of her mother.

She came bustling into the living room, a box cradled against her body. She set down the box and pulled an old video tape player from it. While she talked, she quickly hooked it up to the television.

"You're going to love this, Eleanor. You've never seen it before. It's of Caddy's sixth grade recital. Your dad and I didn't record it; Mrs. Kandiver did," she said, referring to Caddy's and her childhood ballet teacher. "She gave it to me years ago because she said she thought I'd like it more than anyone, but I didn't pay much attention. I thought she gave it to me because Caddy was the star of the show, but I knew Dave was filming from a better angle than Mrs. Kandiver. So this tape got stuck in a box in the attic. I just rediscovered it last night, when I was pulling down the Christmas decorations."

Her mother hit a button and an image resolved on the screen of eight tutu-wearing little girls moving in an approximate synchrony to the beginning of Tchaikovsky's *Sleeping Beauty*. Mrs. Kandiver was filming the recital from stage right. Jeez . . . that old, polished oak stage they'd performed on at the dance studio on Dempster Avenue, those dusty red velvet curtains . . . and there was Caddy, front and center, skinny as a rail but uncommonly graceful for an eleven-year-old.

"I thought you said Eleanor was in it too," her dad said.

"Just be patient and watch," her mom said with a smug smile.

It was about then that Eleanor realized that the camera angle allowed them to see all the way across to stage left. There was a little girl with a brown ponytail and bangs sitting on the floor between two curtains, her knees drawn up and a book in her hand.

A smile flickered across her mouth at the unexpected image. It was *her*—Eleanor—six years old and staying after her kiddie lesson to watch her big sister's recital. Mrs. Kandiver had allowed her to observe from behind the stage. Unlike the girls adorned in white on the stage, Eleanor wore a black leotard and tights along with a pair of white Keds and a bright red sweater. As the dance progressed, the little girl huddling in the curtains put down her book.

"Do you remember it, Nora?" her dad asked, and she heard the smile in his voice.

She nodded. "Vaguely. Some of it clearly. I remember the music perfectly and Caddy's dance. She practiced it nonstop for the whole summer. I even remember what book I was reading," she mused wistfully. "*Eloise in Moscow.*"

"Just like you to remember the book. Do you know what happens next?" her mom asked to the left of her.

Eleanor shook her head, bemused.

As the music built, the little girl across the stage stood up.

"Look how *serious* you are," her dad said fondly.

Eleanor grinned. Little Eleanor clearly had no idea she was being filmed. She wore the kind of serious, yet faraway look a child gets when she's dreaming.

And suddenly she recalled what happened next . . . or rather, she recalled what that little girl's dream had been. It'd been to be the star ballerina, like Caddy.

Little Eleanor leapt into life, twirling and going up on her toes in her Keds, all within the confined space between the curtains. Her dad laughed at her impromptu little performance. Her mother crowed.

"Isn't it priceless? I *told* you two you'd love it. Look how talented you are, and only six years old!"

"Seriously, Mom," Eleanor muttered repressively.

"Do you remember learning the dance with Caddy?" her mother asked.

Eleanor shrugged. "I guess. I told you she practiced it every day for a whole summer. I was always with her. It's only natural I soaked up parts of it. I always wanted to do whatever she was doing, always wanted to be as good as her . . ."

She faded off, suddenly feeling self-conscious. One furtive glance told her that her mother was giving her one of those sad, meaningful looks Eleanor dreaded. She recalled her mother's allegation that she'd been dressing like Caddy lately, playing the carefree, sexually confident, bold female because it was her way of mourning Caddy.

"Look at you," her mom prompted. Against her will, Eleanor

glanced back at the screen. "You were every bit as talented as your big sister."

"You were certainly more determined," her dad joked. Little Eleanor started to spin and leap so stridently, she kicked the curtains and made the sconce above the performing ballerinas quiver. Her dad snorted with laughter. Eleanor couldn't help but smile at his honest amusement. "You look like you think your dance is going to alter the course of the entire planet."

"That's *passion*, David," her mother admonished.

Eleanor rolled her eyes, pressed her hands to her burning cheeks, and laughed. "Give me a break, Mom. That's *nerdiness*, pure and simple."

"Nonsense," her mother exclaimed. "I was proud when I first saw this yesterday . . . proud of your talent and your fire."

"*Fire?* I was dancing around in the curtains. Don't make a bigger deal of it than it is."

"You're embarrassing her, Catherine."

"You were *magnificent*," her mother said, golden brown eyes sparkling.

"I have to agree, bug," her dad said with an apologetic smile at Eleanor. "You're adorable. This *was* quite a find, Catherine. Both girls dancing together."

Caddy center stage, Eleanor on the sidelines . . . like always. Only now, center stage had been left empty.

Was all of this her mother's way of reinforcing the idea that Eleanor was just dancing out to center stage in a desperate attempt to disguise the gaping hole of Caddy's absence? "Mom, is this your way of trying to bring home your point from yesterday?" Eleanor asked quietly.

"*What* point from yesterday?" her dad asked.

"Of course not. If anything, the opposite," her mother insisted, looking dramatically wounded by Eleanor's accusation. "I thought if anything, the video was making *your* point. You've always had as much drive and passion as Caddy, maybe more so. After I thought about it a little last night, I started to think maybe your sister was *right* to tell you to dive in . . . take some chances, live your passion—"

"Would someone mind filling me on the first part of this conversation?" her dad asked. Eleanor stifled a groan. Here was proof positive her father had had nothing to do with sending her mom over to Eleanor's to express "their" concerns. Well, it wasn't like she hadn't suspected it from the start. Her mom often mentioned her dad in her campaigns in order to gain credibility. She *should* call her mom out. But the last thing she wanted was a family confrontation at the moment. She felt too raw.

All day long, it'd been like they'd formed a silent pact to act like everything was okay with just the three of them going through the motions of a traditional Thanksgiving, everyone intent on avoiding Caddy's glaring absence. Now, it was as if her mother was defying that pact—ripping away the bandage from the wound.

"It's okay, Dad," Eleanor mumbled to her father. "Mom came over to Caddy's place yesterday—*my* place—and we had a little misunderstanding, that's all."

"One that I hope I've put to rest with this video and what I've just said," her mother said, looking regally put out.

"Why am I always the last to hear about these things?" her dad asked.

"I told you I made Eleanor a beef pirog Monday night and took it there after work yesterday," Catherine scolded her husband.

"That hardly equates to you two fighting."

"It wasn't a fight. Not really. Everything is *fine*," Eleanor smoothed over, desperately pushing the invisible, askew bandage of their pact of silence back into place. "Thanks for showing the video, Mom. I'm sorry I don't like watching how dorky I was as a kid as much as you," she joked in an attempt to deemphasize her discomfort. At that moment, she just wanted out from under the microscope of her mom's attention.

Damn you, Caddy. Why'd you have to go and die and leave me here alone to deal with her on the holidays? We used to have each other's backs. Now I'm taking all the fire straight on.

She stood and grabbed her empty mug.

"Eleanor—"

"Anybody want anything? I'm going to get more hot chocolate," she said briskly, cutting off her mom. She started toward the kitchen.

And it wouldn't hurt to find the bottle of schnapps Mom keeps hidden behind the flour tin in the pantry.

Eleanor hid her smile, feeling comforted for some reason. It had been her thought, of course. But the voice had sure sounded like Caddy's in her head.

NINE

Eleanor was due to go out with her friend Jimmy Garcia on Friday evening upon her return to the city. Jimmy had been away because of a family situation until the day of the press-employee trial run for the Mary Todd Lincoln exhibit. Because they'd been so busy with the exhibit, Jimmy and she hadn't had much time to talk. She had an idea Stacy Moffitt had gossiped to Jimmy about Eleanor's uncharacteristic sexy outfits at the reading event. Jimmy knew about her interest in Trey Riordan and her determination to attend the event because Trey would be there. He probably was straining at the bit to interrogate her about why she'd chosen to go pursue Riordan in such an atypically aggressive fashion.

Jimmy called that Friday afternoon as she was entering her condo, overburdened with her suitcase and two bags filled with leftovers her mom had insisted she take home.

"Do you still want to meet tonight for a drink?" Jimmy asked her as she wrestled open her refrigerator door.

"Yeah, but can we make it an early one? A couple nights in Evanston have got me wrung out."

"Catherine the Great was in fine form, I take it?" Jimmy asked. Jimmy was very familiar with her mother and father. As a nonfamily member, he had the privilege of looking upon her mom's antics with amused fondness.

"We put up the Christmas tree this morning," Eleanor said. Jimmy's heavy sigh told her that statement had said it all. It was yet another Briggs family tradition that she cherished, the four of them putting up the Christmas tree on the Friday after Thanksgiving before Eleanor and Caddy returned to the city. "'The G' just kept prattling on," she said, calling her mom by the familiar derivative of her nickname created by Caddy long ago. "Acting like nothing was wrong and she was having the time of her life, putting up the decorations. I swear, Jimmy, she completely exhausted my dad. He just sat in his chair and stared at the Christmas tree. Not like he was seeing it, but like the Dementors had just sucked the soul out of him or something, and he was an empty shell. And all the while, my mom's going on about whether or not we should do white lights or colored ones, and should we order the fresh garland from Shreff's Florist or online this year?"

She slammed the refrigerator door shut, a shudder going through her.

"I'm sorry, Eleanor. Your poor dad. Poor Catherine too," Jimmy murmured sympathetically. "She's just dealing in the only way she knows how."

"I *know*," Eleanor agreed miserably.

"I know you do. Doesn't make it much easier, though, does it?"

"Not even a little bit," she agreed, rolling her eyes. "It's a good thing I prepared myself for how hard the first holiday could be. Not that it helped, but at least I was a little less despondent than I would have been if I hadn't prepared for complete and utter catastrophe."

"You need a drink. We can talk about it tonight," Jimmy consoled.

"No, we're done talking about that. I've had enough of the gloom and doom," she replied steadfastly. "But I do want to meet. I feel like we haven't talked outside of work in forever. How does meeting at five sound to you?"

"Fine by me. But if we aren't going to talk about Thanksgiving at the Briggs house, you *will* promise to spill all the details about Riordan?"

Eleanor seriously doubted she'd be describing any of the fine points of her outrageous seduction, but she *did* owe Jimmy some dirt.

"There's a bar in the building next door, Gold Coast? Meet me there at five?" she asked. She'd hatched up a plan on the drive from her parents' house to get Trey her phone number. She'd drop a brief, nonchalant message off for Trey with Ralph, his doorman. She'd do it after Jimmy and her had a drink.

"Isn't that Riordan's building? Are you expecting him to be there?"

"No, are you *kidding*? He's out of town for the holiday weekend. I wouldn't go over there if I thought I'd run into him. Not in a million years," she mumbled under her breath.

"Why? What happened, Eleanor?"

"I'll tell you about it tonight."

She said good-bye to Jimmy. She turned in the kitchen, feeling that familiar, forbidden pull from the guest room in the distance. Leaving the lights in the condo off, she walked down the hallway. She entered the still, hushed guest room. Still wearing her coat, she crossed over to the window and peered out at Trey's penthouse. It was dark, of course.

Dark and empty.

But unlike before when she'd looked inside his home, she now knew what it was to be in that room. She'd switched points of view. *She'd* lain in Trey's bed, his arms surrounding her, and looked back *here*—into the known world of her condo, to a place where she'd lusted and longed so intently. Her lungs froze.

It all seemed so strange. So forbidden and exciting . . .

So unlike her.

Something else had altered too, she realized as she stared out the window. Something elemental. Her perception of Trey himself had changed. He was no longer just the untouchable, beautiful, outrageously sexy playboy.

He was becoming three-dimensional.

Breathtakingly so.

Feeling exhausted by her thoughts, by Thanksgiving with her shrunken family—by *everything*—she made her way to the master bedroom. She stripped and climbed into bed.

When she awoke an hour and a half later, she felt rested and more content . . .

Until she noticed the time, that is.

"Shit," she muttered, scrambling out of bed. She only had twenty minutes to shower and get ready to meet Jimmy next door at Gold Coast.

Maybe because she was aware that her hair and makeup would only get minimal attention with the time constraint, she chose to wear Caddy's clothes to make up for the lack. She picked a pair of designer jeans that clung to her legs, hips and ass like a second skin, a white blouse, which she wore untucked, and a seemingly demure white button-down sweater that wasn't at *all* innocent in the way it clung to her waist and breasts. Feeling restored from her nap and shower, she chose a pair of fun red heels with an ankle strap and fluffed her hair. It'd been unusually warm when she'd left her parents' house earlier, and she was just going next door, so she left her coat in the closet. She grabbed her purse and hurried out of the condo.

She saw Jimmy immediately through the windows of Trey's lobby. He was checking his phone—probably looking for a text from her, explaining her lateness. He stood just outside the entrance to Gold Coast.

"Sorry I'm late," she called across the lobby breathlessly after she'd pushed through the revolving doors. Jimmy looked up from his phone.

"Eleanor."

Eleanor halted in her tracks on the granite tile floor, her mouth falling open in confusion. A man had said her name, but Jimmy's lips hadn't moved. She looked in the direction of the voice.

Trey Riordan stood at the doorman's station. He leaned against the counter, his tall body relaxed as though he'd been having a conversation with Ralph before she'd stormed into the lobby.

Shit.

For a stretched second, she just stared at him stupidly. He slowly straightened and faced her.

"I thought you were planning to be in Rockford over the weekend," she said numbly when he began to walk toward her. He glanced down over her. A shiver ran through her when she saw how hard and serious he appeared, how intense his stare on her was. He looked incredible, all tawny and sinuous, his golden brown hair sexily mussed and the shadow of whiskers on his jaw and upper lip. He wore jeans and a long black winter coat. His blue eyes looked especially vivid in his whiskered, tanned face.

"I came back early." He opened his mouth to say something else, but glanced to her right instead, distracted. She realized Jimmy had approached.

"Oh . . . this is Jimmy Garcia. Jimmy, Trey Riordan," she managed. She saw Jimmy flash her a brief, stunned glance before he put out his hand to shake with Trey. Trey remained stony-faced as they shook. Eleanor knew he was physically imposing, of course, but she was quickly learning he could be *intimidating*, as well. As warm and easygoing as she knew he could be at times, he could be just as easily cool and daunting. She supposed it made sense. He hadn't created a multimillion-dollar company from nothing by coming off as a pushover. At the moment, he peered at a clueless, amiable Jimmy with a narrowed stare.

There was an awkward pause when he and Jimmy dropped their hands. Eleanor shifted restlessly in her heels, made prickly by Trey's stare on her.

"Well, I didn't mean to interrupt your date," Trey finally said gruffly. "You two are going to Gold Coast?"

"Oh, it's not a date—"

"Trey? There you are. I thought I heard your voice."

Eleanor blinked in surprise, her denial cut off by another woman's crisp, British-accented voice. She looked between Trey's and Jimmy's tall bodies and saw a beautiful blond woman standing in the doorway of Gold Coast. The contrast of her patrician, cool features and the smoking-hot leather pants she wore created quite an impression. Eleanor's heart shrunk two sizes when she saw the eager way she was staring at Trey. Her gaze bounced up to see Trey's reaction to the unexpected British bombshell. She searched, but couldn't find any clue on his handsome face. If she'd had to guess, she'd have said he'd forced a carefully blank expression.

"Alessandra," he said.

This can't be happening. He'd come back to town early for a date. Here, at Gold Coast. Or maybe he just lied to me about being away with family for the entire weekend. I should have known that his presentation of himself as a family-oriented farm boy was ridiculous.

The blond woman pointed into Gold Coast. "I just got us a table."

"Right," Trey said. Alessandra stepped toward them, looking politely confused when Trey didn't immediately move to follow her. Or possibly, politely put out, Eleanor decided.

"Are these your friends?" Alessandra asked, glancing between Jimmy and Eleanor.

Trey made introductions, and they all shook hands as though everything were perfectly normal. Which maybe it was for everyone else. On Eleanor's part, her heart had bulged from its previous shrunken state upon seeing the gorgeous Alessandra and was now swollen so large it was pressing uncomfortably against her sternum.

"It's very crowded in there," Alessandra told Trey, gesturing toward Gold Coast. "Maybe we could just go up to your place—"

"You said you had a table," Trey cut her off.

Alessandra blinked. "But it's the only one in the entire place. Maybe your friends would like it?"

"We can all sit together," Trey replied, his tone terse and not inviting argument.

"Of course," Alessandra replied, backing up in her heels toward Gold Coast. Eleanor started from her frozen state when Trey touched her back, urging her toward the restaurant. She gave him a startled look. He just peered down at her, his expression inscrutable, his eyes sharp. The only thing Eleanor felt in that moment was his customary focus, and it was drilling straight down into her.

That was how she found herself sitting at a cozy, candlelit table in the bar, for all intents and purposes on a double date with Trey Riordan.

Something this ridiculous could only happen to me.

There was a single saving grace. At least she'd never spied on him making love to Alessandra. If she had, she didn't think she'd be able to sit there without getting physically sick.

Alessandra and Jimmy made up for Trey's surliness and Eleanor's shock by filling up the silence. Alessandra talked about her glamorous job as a BBC television presenter and Jimmy was describing his job at the museum. When the drinks came and Eleanor and Trey had only said twenty words between the two of them the entire time, Jimmy launched into an enthusiastic description of their newest exhibit. Jimmy was a good friend. He knew what a crush Eleanor had had on Trey for over a year now, and sensed how awkward the situation was. He responded by trying to talk Eleanor up, bragging about her coup in negotiating a trade from the Smithsonian for Mary Todd Lincoln's wardrobe and jewels.

"You told me you were in charge of membership and donations at the museum," Trey interrupted bluntly.

"Everything we do at the museum is ultimately geared toward expanding membership. It's the cold, hard reality of life," Eleanor managed with a brittle laugh. Jimmy opened his mouth—undoubtedly to ask her what the hell she was talking about. Eleanor kicked him under the table. It was the best she could do to shut him up. He wouldn't understand why Eleanor hadn't wanted Trey to know she was a basement-dwelling, mousy conservation librarian. *I mean . . . look at the kind of woman he's used to dating,* she thought, staring at Alessandra and repressing a frown.

"How long have you two been dating?" Alessandra asked, taking a sip of her martini and looking annoyingly glamorous.

"We're not dating. Eleanor and I have been good friends for years, ever since we met doing summertime work during college, restoring paintings at the Art Institute. It's not exactly thrilling work, so we had to keep each other entertained," Jimmy said, smiling at Eleanor.

Jimmy had probably heard her try to deny it earlier when Trey assumed they were dating, and was trying to set the record straight. But at that point, Eleanor would rather have just assumed Trey *did* believe she was on a date, since *he* was on one. Jimmy's friendly words seemed to hover in the air over their table. Alessandra frowned and glanced furtively at Trey.

"I'm sorry, I misunderstood. I thought you two were together," Alessandra said. She reached beneath the table, and Eleanor's stomach lurched. Alessandra had just put her hand on Trey's thigh beneath the table. "Trey and I met in London. Six months ago, right, honey?" she asked, staring up at Trey's stoic profile.

Suddenly, Eleanor couldn't take it anymore. She pushed back her chair.

"Excuse me for a minute," she murmured awkwardly.

Trey tracked her progress through the crowded bar, annoyance building in him. *Why is it I'm always watching her while she makes an escape?* The jeans she wore looked like they were painted on. Her long, wavy hair swayed sexily just inches from the top of her ass as she motored across the room. The red heels with the ankle straps that she wore were killing him. Despite the jaw-dropping rear view of her before she disappeared down a hallway, it was the anxiety in her large eyes and the blank immobility of her usually animated face that remained burned in his mind's eye.

He'd been stunned when he'd woken up alone on Wednesday morning, and then increasingly pissed. Maybe that was cocky of him, to be put out because a woman snuck away from his bed. But the truth was, he couldn't remember it ever happening before in his life. What made the experience even more annoying was that he felt particularly robbed, because it'd been *her*.

He'd *wanted* to wake up next to that fresh, unexpected, puzzling, mind-blowingly sexy woman. He'd craved uncovering more of her secrets.

Yes, he'd told her he wanted to keep things light and casual. True, he had no right to be irritated at her escape.

That didn't alter the fact that he *was*.

"Excuse me as well," he said presently. He ignored Alessandra's tightened, clawlike grip on his thigh and her calling his name in a petulant query. He plunged into the crowd around the bar. Damn Alessandra.

Damn this whole asinine situation.

Okay, it was partly his fault. He'd completely forgotten about Alessandra's text, inviting him to meet her for some no-strings-attached sex. They'd had dinner at Gold Coast a few times, and drinks a few more, so apparently, that qualified in her book as making it *their* place, even though he'd never designated it as that in his mind. He'd never responded to her text, and in truth, hadn't even thought about her invitation until he'd seen her standing in that doorway twenty minutes ago, looking for all the world like she'd been expecting him.

In fact, he'd come home early from Rockford because he'd been distracted while there. He wasn't the only one who'd seemed out of sorts at his parents' house. His brother, Kevin, was in a pissy mood and refusing to talk about it with his usual confidantes: their mom and Trey himself. His sister, Kacy, and Kevin had a long-term rivalry. Kevin's bad mood filtered over to Kacy, making her irritable as well. Add in the fact that Jason, Kacy's son, was suffering from a bad cold and being unusually whiny and demanding, and Kacy was worth avoiding over Thanksgiving as well.

Trey himself was uncommonly on edge, put off by the abrupt ending of his tryst with Eleanor. The simple fact was he wanted to see more of her. Had Eleanor left without waking him because she'd lost interest now that she'd achieved her goal of sleeping with the man she'd been spying on?

He'd tried to recall if she'd ever said if she planned to stay at her parents' for the entire weekend, or if she was coming back to the city after the holiday. No, she hadn't mentioned it. He would have remembered if she had specified. Why hadn't he asked, damn it?

Because I thought I'd still have time left with her to find out.

Evanston wasn't far. If he left Rockford early, maybe he could nudge Ralph into convincing Eleanor's doorman to get him her number? Maybe there was a chance of seeing her this weekend.

That's precisely what he'd been in the process of doing when he'd glanced over his shoulder and saw Eleanor herself, dressed to kill and looking gorgeous, rushing into the lobby. It'd taken him a few seconds to come to the ugly realization she was meeting up with the tall, good-looking, dark-haired guy standing at the entrance of Gold Coast.

Trey was leaning against the wall, waiting in the dim hallway when Eleanor came out of the bathroom a minute later. She started when she saw him and came to an abrupt halt.

"How come you left without waking me up the other morning?" he demanded without preamble.

She appeared taken aback for a second before she rallied. Her chin went up.

"I didn't think you'd want me to. You were sleeping. I was trying to be considerate. I was trying to keep it *light*."

He pushed himself off the wall and stepped toward her, until they were only inches apart. She wavered in the sexy red heels she was wearing, like she wanted to back up, but she held her ground. She looked up at him, the mixture of trepidation and defiance on her face making him grit his teeth. Hard. He might have relived moments about their night together a lot more than he cared to admit, but memories didn't match up to the reality of her eyes. She had to have the most amazing, expressive, *sexy* eyes he'd ever seen.

"I thought we decided we still had business together. I *wanted* you to wake me up," he ground out.

Her expression flattened at his bluntness. Then she straightened her spine and took a tiny step closer, so that their faces were only inches apart.

"I'm so sorry I haven't had time to learn your every preference. Maybe I could ask your girlfriend Alessandra to make a list for me, master," she said, her low, vibrating voice oozing with sarcasm.

"She isn't my girlfriend."

She blinked. "She's not?"

"She used to be. We split a couple months ago. She's one of the ugly breakups I told you about that made me want to go cold turkey in regard to women."

"But then . . . what's she doing here? Why were you meeting her?"

"I wasn't. I forgot that she'd texted me and said she wanted to meet tonight. It was just an accident that I was down in the lobby. I never told her I'd meet her here, she just assumed. The only thing I was doing out in the lobby when you showed up was trying to bribe Ralph into getting your doorman to give me your phone number."

He studied the flicker of amazement on her upturned face. Did she believe him?

"Would it have mattered? If she *was* my girlfriend?" he prodded.

She pressed her mouth together in an obstinate line—that delicious mouth he'd been having the most illicit, vivid fantasies about.

"Would it have mattered if I was here on a date with Jimmy?" she countered.

He realized she'd sidestepped his question, but was too hypnotized by her upturned mouth and gleaming eyes to care. He lifted his hands and cupped her curving hips. Excitement flickered at the base of his spine. He pulled her against him, feeling her gasp fly across his nudging lips. He bent his knees and thrust his hips forward slightly, liking the pressure of her supple, soft body against his cock. Digging his fingertips into the firm swell of her ass cheeks, he shook his head, causing their touching lips to brush together.

"It wouldn't have mattered. I would have still wanted you. Nothing's changed. Or maybe it has," he acknowledged, biting her lower lip gently and dragging his teeth across the tender flesh. She quaked against him. "Instead of wanting you less after that night, I want you more. Even if you were just coming on to me to get a bigger donation for the museum."

"I told you I was doing no such thing," she seethed.

He grinned at the return of her outrage and pierced her lips with his tongue. One of his hands delved into her silky long hair. He twisted his fingers and tugged, tilting her head back farther for his kiss. She whimpered into his mouth, kissing him back. She grasped his waist, clutching him, her fingers digging into his back, stroking and rubbing him. Her anxious movements struck him as wild.

Desperate.

Satisfaction and sharp arousal swept through him at her returned display of lust. He bent over her, his kiss growing furious. What right did she have, making him want her this much, causing him to be so distracted and restless on what was supposed to be a relaxing family weekend?

She started against him and moaned, pulling back slightly. He put a hand on her jaw, keeping her in place while he took his fill. But then he felt her jerk back more firmly, and the sounds of approaching footsteps pierced his lust. He realized she'd heard someone approaching before he had.

He sealed the kiss, but didn't release her from his hold. He just stared down at her as she cast a nervous glance around his upper arm. A door opened behind him.

"It was some woman," she whispered. "Not Alessandra."

He still fisted a bunch of thick, silky hair. He tugged gently and she looked up at him.

"It wouldn't have mattered if it *was* Alessandra. I didn't ask her here tonight. What I told you was the absolute truth."

"Well I'm telling the absolute truth when I say I didn't do what I did for a bigger donation!"

"I wasn't serious about that." It was true, for the most part. She clearly was being evasive about her job, for some reason. But he honestly didn't think the reason was because she was going to hit him for a donation at some point.

Her lips trembled, fracturing his curiosity and puzzlement. He wanted to punish that gorgeous mouth of hers again for the crime of tempting him so outrageously.

"Here's what we're going to do," he said quietly, coming to a decision. "We're going to go back out there. You're going to say you don't feel well and that you're going home. You'll go back to your condo. Then I'm going to make an excuse to Alessandra and go up to my place."

"But they'll know we're lying," she said, eyes flashing.

"I don't care if they do. Do you?" he challenged. She closed her mouth slowly. She shook her head.

"Jimmy seems like a good friend, he'll understand. Is he straight?" he asked distractedly.

"What?"

"Jimmy, is he straight?"

"Yes," she replied, looking confused.

"Maybe you should warn him about Alessandra before you leave. She's going to be a royal bitch when I make an excuse and go. Then to bandage her pride, there's a fifty-fifty chance she might come on to Jimmy."

"Jimmy can take care of himself." She frowned. "Unless you're trying to tell me she has some horrible communicable disease or something."

"No, it's not that. She's just a handful, that's all. It doesn't matter. They're both adults. What matters is that in ten minutes flat, at"—he checked his watch—"five forty-five, you're up in that window."

"Huh?"

He nodded his head once, admiring the rush of color in her cheeks and her flabbergasted expression. "Do what you did that first night again."

"You . . . you want me to . . . to dance for you again?"

"Hell, yeah," he muttered, releasing her hair and rubbing her hip and ass. He plucked at her mouth. "Put on a nice show for me, Eleanor."

"*Really?*"

He pushed her into him and ground his cock against her lower belly. "Do I *seem* serious?"

"Yes," she squeaked.

"Then you go out first and make your excuse. Don't wait for me. Just go."

"Okay." He released her and she started to move past him, seeming a little unsteady on her two feet.

"And, Eleanor?"

She looked over her shoulder.

"Two things," he said tensely. "One, sign a consent form for your doorman, allowing me to come up to your place. Leave your unit number and let him know I'll be there soon. Don't lock your front door. Tonight, this isn't going to end with me standing there like an idiot with my cock in my hand, do you understand? I'm going to punish you for teasing me."

Her eyes widened. She looked adorable, but he didn't relent an inch.

"And two"—he pointed down at her feet—"the only things I want you wearing when I get there are *those* shoes."

TEN

Eleanor's heart fluttered erratically in her chest and she was panting by the time she entered her condo and shut the door, remembering not to lock it. She bubbled with nervous excitement. She still couldn't believe Trey was here, or that he was matter-of-factly insisting they put their plan into play for mixing their kinks right that moment. Despite the unexpected turn of events, she knew precisely what she was going to do for her performance for Trey.

Earlier that year, the museum sponsored a special exhibit on the 1933 Chicago World's Fair. Eleanor had organized a subunit on glamorous actress and dancer Sally Rand, who had scandalized Chicago with her provocative fan dance at the fair. Sally would dance with two large feather or fur fans, seducing the audience by twirling and gliding them across her seemingly naked body. Eleanor had been responsible for displaying two pairs of Sally's own beautiful fans along with other artifacts, photos and ephemera, but her exhibit had required some extra decoration. So she'd found a place where she could purchase more fans, and on a whim, had bought two for herself. She'd been seduced by how soft the feathers were, and perhaps by the idea of Sally Rand herself. She admired the woman's boldness. Even before she'd discovered her penchant for exhibitionism, Eleanor had recognized the potent power Ms. Rand held over the audience as she teased them relentlessly with her peekaboo dance. Of course it'd all been an illusion. Sally hadn't really been naked behind the fans.

But Eleanor would be.

Trey would hate it. He'd love it too.

The very idea of having his total attention, of working him into a frenzy again sent her blood to racing. He'd said he'd punish her for teasing him. That made her a little anxious, but not enough to dampen her excitement.

Even though he'd said he wanted her in the window in ten minutes, and she only had five remaining, she still got under a hot shower. Tonight, she'd seduce him from a distance, but he'd be up close, eventually. She wanted to be perfect. After her shower, she took her time applying a bergamot and peach body lotion that contained a subtle glitter that sheened her naked body. She put on a robe and went out to the living room to select some music.

She smiled as the first notes of the sexy, bluesy number— "Going Down Slow"—began to play. As always, the right music was like a shot of potent whiskey. It got her in the mood. It made her bolder than she really was. She put the red heels back on, buckling the straps around her ankles, her heart drumming in her ears when she recalled how on fire and intimidating Trey had looked when he'd given her the instructions to be wearing them, and nothing else, when he arrived.

She glanced at the clock, her eyes going wide when she saw it was going on five fifty. She was late for her performance. But that'd only amp up Trey's anticipation, wouldn't it?

It'll only increase your punishment, a dark voice in her head said.

She tingled with excitement at the thought. She took her time, fluffing out her loose hair and applying blush, eyeliner and lipstick. A minute later, she located the fans in a cupboard in the exercise room. They were made of white feathers and shaped like palm leaves, about two and a half by two and a half feet in size. Standing in front of the floor-to-ceiling mirror, she dropped her robe. Holding the handles, she slid the fans along her body, loving the sensual feel on her naked skin, admiring the way the white feathers looked against her body. She'd never tried a fan dance herself, but she'd studied videos of Sally Rand doing it dozens of times. The trick was to manipulate the fans as she moved, sliding one off a breast or her butt or her sex just as the other fan glided into place.

The whole dance was one gigantic tease.

I can do this.

But can you face the consequences?

Eleanor only knew for certain she was about to find out.

One fan flirtatiously covering her front side while the other shielded her ass, she walked down the hallway to the guest bedroom.

Where the hell was she?

Trey stood next to the floor-to-ceiling window, annoyance and anticipation building in him. The room across the way remained dark. He glanced at his watch. It was a few minutes until six.

Just keep pushing it, Eleanor, he thought grimly. His body flickered with arousal. He couldn't believe he allowed her to push his buttons this way.

But she did it so freaking *well.*

A light blinked on in the room. He tensed, all of his attention zeroing in on the distant figure. She moved gracefully around the foot of the bed toward the window. He stepped closer to the window, completely forgetting his self-command to hold back and to watch her performance with some element of restraint.

She was naked, the pale gold, luminous skin of her shoulders and legs gleaming in the lamplight. But she was holding something white against her breasts, belly and crotch . . . some kind of fan. Just as he recognized the object, she began to dance, moving her hips seductively.

Holy shit. It was made of feathers. He could tell by the movement the fan made as she danced and it slid against her skin. Plus . . . the feathers weren't opaque. As she stepped toward the window, her hips gyrating, he realized he could see the outline of her beautiful body shifting beguilingly to some unheard music. He watched, spellbound.

She spun several times, nearing the window, revealing the sides of her body and willowy bare back, making it clear she *was* completely naked. His cock swelled. He frowned in mixed arousal and disappointment. She held another fan over her ass.

Little tease.

He watched her dance for a moment with her back to him. Keeping the fan in place over her ass, she lowered the other fan and caressed the back of her legs with it, all the while moving to the music. Her long mane of hair swished sexily against her lithe back as she stroked her naked thighs with the fan.

Then she turned and looked coyly over her shoulder. That stare went straight to the core of him.

"Eleanor," he growled softly in warning. He swore he saw her smile. He didn't have time to decide for sure, because suddenly she straightened her long legs and bent at the waist, ass in the air. He placed his hand on the glass of the window, every ounce of his attention straining toward her. She moved both fans at once, her skill at the task surprising him. Just as she slid one down a buttock and caressed her thigh with it, she moved the other up, gliding it over her ass, obstructing his view.

He ground his teeth together, held hostage by her. He couldn't move or breathe. All he could do was salivate and ache, and pray he'd catch even the slightest glimpse of what she so cleverly hid from him.

Then she started to sway her ass as she continued her peekaboo show. As she shifted her hips to the music, he glimpsed a bare suspended breast. He'd seen plenty of breasts in his day, but just that obscured vision from a distance electrified him. He grabbed his cock through his jeans and groaned. She bent her knees and ground her hips in a circular motion, all the while sliding the feathers against her naked skin, provoking him without mercy.

That was it. He was going over to her place right now. He was going to spank that beautiful ass and take her as mercilessly as she teased him.

But then she straightened and spun several feet away from the windows, sliding the fans across her naked body. He froze, utterly enthralled by her. She faced him, her hair tousled around her shoulders. He sensed her excitement, saw the color in her cheeks and her small, daring smile.

He gripped at his cock through his jeans and grimaced. She knew she had him exactly where she wanted him.

It's okay, Eleanor. Have your fun. Because I'm going to have you precisely where I want you in just a few minutes.

With one leg in front of her, knee cocked, she began to manipulate both fans across the front of her body, stroking herself. He suspected she liked the way the soft feathers felt against her flushed, tingling skin. She was such an innate sensualist.

Such a born tease.

She began to shift the fans lower on her body with each hypnotic pass, until he stared fixedly at the tops of her beautiful bare breasts while she feathers slipped and glided across her naked skin, mocking him. He swallowed thickly. Could he see her nipples, or couldn't he?

Damn it all to hell, show them to me now, Eleanor.

She experienced his rising tension as if it were her own, sensed his arousal coiling tight. He was straining at the bit, and she loved it.

She also loved the feeling of the feathers tickling her belly, her hard, sensitive nipples and her tingling labia. In the window's reflection, her flushed face looked extremely well pleased. She was having fun teasing him, but her seduction was far from one-sided. Unable to take it anymore, she slid the fan beneath her breasts, exposing them to him. She began to gyrate to the music, manipulating the fans across her body, still obscuring her sex from him, but letting him catch glimpses of her bare breasts and grinding hips and naked, swiveling belly. She watched him the whole time, enthralled by his rigid features and his hand moving faster and more strenuously at his crotch. His stare on her might as well have been lightning, the way it electrified her flesh.

She closed her eyes, growing increasingly blatant and drunk with her power. The dance took control.

She spun and teased him with her backside again, this time giving him glimpses of her bare ass as she gyrated to the music. Her heart pounded out an excited warning in her ears, and her sex ached unbearably.

She finally bent over and removed the fan entirely from her ass, sliding the feathers up and down the backs of her thighs in a wicked counter rhythm. All the while, she gyrated and popped her butt in a brazen invitation to trouble. She lost herself to a pulsing trance.

Suddenly hands were on her wrists, halting her movements. She gasped in shock, her head jerking back and her hair swinging onto her back.

"Trey," she cried out when she saw him towering over her bent form. How much time had gone by? The reality of him standing there hit her like a slap to the face. His blue eyes gleamed with arousal. His face looked rigid. "I . . . I didn't hear you come in." She tried to stand up, but he pressed her wrists to the small of her back, keeping her in place in her bent-over position.

"That's because you were having too much fun, isn't it?" he asked between tight lips, his even tone of voice not matching the tension in his body and feral stare down at her. "No. You were caught up in your little game. You were *loving* having me at your mercy." Holding her wrists in place with one hand, he took one of the fans from her. Suddenly, she felt the silky feathers gliding between her thighs and brushing her damp sex. Her clit throbbed in arousal. She moaned and trembled as he manipulated the fan over her pussy, his actions much bolder than hers had been during the dance. She bit her lip. "You know, I don't think I've ever seen a person enjoying torturing another human being so much. Now it's payback time, Eleanor."

He withdrew the fan from between her thighs, and then grabbed the other one she held. She heard the fan handles thump on the carpet when he dropped them. He reached into a back pocket. She blew her long hair out of her face, desperate to see what he was doing. Her eyes widened when she saw he'd removed black padded handcuffs from his pocket.

"I'm going to bind your hands behind your back and spank you. You know what's going to happen after that."

Her gaze zoomed to his crotch. From this angle, his arousal was blatant and daunting.

His brows furrowed. He stepped toward her and pushed back her hair from her face. "Don't look like that, Eleanor," he said, and she was surprised to hear how gentle he sounded. She tilted her head, fully meeting his stare. Her breath caught in her throat. The things he was saying and doing made her both thrilled and anxious at once. But when she looked into his blazing eyes, she was reassured. "I'm not going to cause you any serious harm. I'll just make your ass

burn. I'll make all of you burn, just like you've been doing to me,"
he said, his mouth going hard. "Do you not want to do this?"

"I want to," she managed shakily. "It's just . . . I've never done
it before."

He nodded in understanding. "Then I'll tell you what I'm going
to do. I'm going to put the handcuffs on you and then I'm going to
touch you any way that I please. I'm going to spank your ass,
because you've earned it, but I'm going to make you feel good too.
I told you that you'd have to accept the consequences, didn't I?"

She felt heat rush into her cheeks at the memory of her dance, of
how shameless she'd been, how she'd lost herself to the intoxication
of it. Her sex tingled and her nipples pinched in anxious anticipation.

"Eleanor?"

"Yes," she whispered.

He stepped toward her. She stared at the carpet blindly from
her bent-over position as he restrained her wrists at the small of
her back. Once she was bound, she found it difficult to exhale
normally, she was so tight with nervous anticipation. Would it
hurt? She hated even getting a shot at the doctor's office. She
shuddered. Then he stepped closer, pressing his crotch against her
hip. Air ripped out of her lungs at the feeling of his heavy erection.

"Shhh, baby," he soothed, and then his hands were on her,
one sliding up her spine, the other caressing her waist. "You have
quite the imagination, don't you?" Through the buzz in her brain,
she wondered how he'd guessed her anxious thoughts. "It's not
going to be scary," she heard him say, and she took a shaky breath
at the warmth in his deep voice. "Look," he said, and one large
hand cupped one of her ass cheeks. He let go and popped her ass
matter-of-factly with his palm. She started and squeaked.

"That wasn't that bad, was it?"

"Uh . . ." It took her a few seconds to decide *what* it was, her mind
and body were so revved up. Her ass prickled where he'd spanked

her. But now his warm hand was there, circling over the tingling flesh, and that was delicious. "No," she breathed out. "Not bad."

He placed one hand on her far hip and pushed his cock against her, his other hand caressing her bottom the whole time. He groaned. "God, you feel good. Do you have any idea what you were doing to me in that window, Eleanor?"

"I was trying to turn you on," she said, exasperated.

He smacked her ass again, one cheek and then the other in quick succession.

"You succeeded," he said tersely. "In spades. Here." He paused, and she felt his hand move down the crack of her ass. He tapped gently on her inner thigh. "Spread your thighs some. Bend your knees a little. That's right." He placed a hand on her left shoulder. "Stay in this position while I spank you. It'll help steady you. Do you understand?"

"Yes," she said shakily.

"I'm going to give you fifteen strokes," he said, rubbing her ass. "You deserve more."

"I . . . I do?"

He ground his cock against her hip and groaned gutturally. "You deserve to have a sore ass for a week for that dance. It was fucking amazing."

"So you're going to punish me for it?" she asked incredulously.

"Oh, *yeah*."

She didn't have time to respond to his gruff, absolute reply, because he firmed his hold on her shoulder and swatted her ass hard enough to make air pop out of her lungs.

"Ouch," she blurted out. His hand rubbed the burning flesh. She shuddered in excitement at the sensation of him soothing the firing nerves.

"I told you it was a punishment, not playtime. Try to stay still and not jump," he said, and she heard the hint of humor in his tone. He lifted his hand and she tensed. He spanked her on her other buttock, the sound of flesh striking flesh ringing in her ears. She managed not to jump this time, but her body lurched forward slightly. He firmed her with his hand on her shoulder. Again, he paused and rubbed the stinging flesh. "You're going to color up nicely," she heard him say thickly, and she knew he was watching himself as he stroked her. "God, you're gorgeous. This ass is made to be spanked. It's made to be spanked for teasing me so ruthlessly," he finished in a hard tone. He lifted his hand and spanked both cheeks again. She felt his cock jump against her hip and groaned. The burn from her ass seemed to travel all the way to her sex.

"Are you okay?" he asked her, now rubbing her flaming bottom again.

She winced. She needed pressure on her sex. Badly. Her knees bent slightly inward, making her dip in the air.

"What's wrong?" he demanded.

"I have to close my thighs," she managed through gritted teeth.

"Why?"

"Because I *ache*," she bit out in frustration.

He made a sound like an angry hiss. He ground his erection against her firmly and spanked her three more times. "Stand up straight, Eleanor. Just bend your knees a little, like I told you," he rasped. She did what he'd instructed, grimacing. Her sex throbbed so badly. He rubbed her ass more lewdly this time, squeezing the flesh in his palms. "Keep your legs just where they are. You'll get relief when it's due." She moaned miserably. "You like this, don't you?" he asked, and she heard the edge of triumph in his voice.

"About as much as you like watching me dance," she muttered.

He let out a bark of dark laughter at that, and knew he'd understood her agonized pleasure perfectly. Holding her close against his body, he spanked her twice more. "Then you must like it a hell of a lot," she heard him mutter. "Your ass is turning nice and hot," he said, rubbing her lasciviously. "Does it hurt?"

"It burns," she admitted through a tight throat.

He moved away slightly. She tried to look around, missing his heat . . . the mind-blowing feeling of his cock pulsing into her flesh. But he was back as quickly as he'd moved away. This time, when he pressed himself to her, he did so against the side of her ass. He used his hand to bunch her buttocks together, pushing them against the bulge in his jeans.

"Jesus," she heard him say under his breath. Then she felt the feathers gliding across her ass, amplifying the tingle in the nerves.

"Ohhh," she cried out. It felt so good on her prickling skin, so decadently dirty.

"You like that?"

She just nodded strenuously, a squeaky sound leaving her throat. He stroked her ass and inner thighs with the feather, the sensation making her clit simmer. She ground her teeth together and made a sound of distilled frustration.

"Now you know what it's like, Eleanor," she heard him say through the roar in her ears. He brushed the feather between her thighs directly onto her sex. Every nerve in her body seemed to spark, but he withheld ignition. She clamped her eyelids shut and quaked.

"Touch me," she begged. "Oh God, *please.*"

Suddenly, one big, warm hand cupped one of her suspended breasts. His fingers pinched her nipple. She gasped, a shudder rippling through her. It hadn't been the touch she expected. His cock swelled against her ass.

"Your nipple is as hard as a rock," he seethed.

She groaned. "I can't take this anymore."

"You can," she heard him say. There was a thumping noise, and she realized dazedly it was the handle of the fan hitting the floor. He'd tossed it aside. He firmed his hold on her shoulder. "You *will*," he said. He spanked the bottom curve of both her buttocks firmly, popping the flesh. "By my count, you have four more strokes to go." He squeezed one ass cheek, molding it against his palm. His fingers trailed down toward her sex. "You've turned nice and pink, baby. Your ass is hot." She groaned in helpless arousal. His engorged cock pressing against the side of her hip and ass burned her consciousness. "Ask me to give you the last four strokes."

"Huh?" she asked, her brain hazed by thick lust.

He squeezed her ass cheek harder. "Ask for the last four strokes."

"I . . . Give me four more. Spank me."

"Good girl," he murmured, and she heard the smile in his voice despite how roughened it was with lust. "I'm going to move my hand off your shoulder, so bend your knees a little more to steady yourself. *Eleanor*," he said when she just panted. She was so aroused, she was having trouble interpreting speech. He repeated the instruction, and she did what he'd asked. "That's right. Hold steady."

He squeezed one buttock in his hand and spanked it with the other. She gave a surprised cry at the act.

"Too much?" he asked tensely.

"No," she managed, but it was a lie. Her pussy was enflamed and her butt burned and there was nothing to relieve the pressure. She'd combust from the tiniest spark. She was going mad.

"Good. Only three more strokes."

He squeezed her other cheek, molding it to his palm. Her heart lodged at the base of her throat, she waited. He spanked her ass briskly. Air popped out of her lungs. She moaned in misery.

"Just two more," he said, and she knew from the tension in his voice he was just as aroused as her. "You count them off, Eleanor." He squeezed an ass cheek, holding the flesh captive for his spanking hand. He swatted her.

"Fourteen," she gasped.

"Last one."

Sensation burst through her as he smacked her burning ass again. "Fif—"

But before she could ever finish the count, Trey's hand was on her shoulder and he was lifting her from her bent-over position. She suddenly found herself pressed tight against his hard length. His mouth seized hers, and she was drowning. It was like being kissed by a furnace. He overwhelmed her. Then his hand was cupping her sex. Her lungs locked and her eyes sprang wide.

"Jesus, you're soaking wet," he said, sounding agonized. The ridge of his finger slipped between her labia and rubbed her clit. Eleanor tensed and mewled. It was the stimulation she'd needed for so long now, but been denied with her hands bound behind her back and the position he'd had her take with her legs spread. Her breath was siphoned out of her lungs as a huge wave of orgasm loomed. He thrust a finger inside her while he rubbed her outer sex. His other hand grasped a burning ass cheek. He flexed his arm, pushing her against his fingers with insistent force.

She screamed and ignited. Pleasure roared through her.

The next thing she became aware of was the sensation of Trey's whiskers abrading her neck and jaw. His lips plucked at her mouth urgently. His hand still moved at her sex as climax seized her. She opened her eyelids sluggishly, her eyelids widening when she saw the blazing quality of his blue eyes.

"Okay?" he asked.

She nodded, gasping.

"Then come over here," he said, his mouth slanted in a hard line.

He turned her in his arms and guided her a few feet, halting her when they were directly in front of the window. She could see their reflection. Eleanor dazedly realized that while she was naked, he was still completely dressed in jeans and a button-down shirt. She opened her mouth to comment on the disparity, but he pushed gently on her back and shoulders.

"Bend over," he said, and she heard it: the strain and tension in his voice. He was a man about to break. And he was going to break on her . . . in her.

She bent agilely, her body still humming with recent pleasure. She may have just come, but she was eager for this. In the window, she saw him tearing at the button fly of his jeans, his actions terse. He reached in his back pocket and withdrew a condom, then jerked his jeans down over his ass. He stretched the waistband of his boxer briefs out and down. His cock sprung free, the shaft thick and long, the head fat and succulent. It brushed against her tingling ass. She sensed its weight . . . his burning arousal.

"*Trey,*" she said shakily.

She saw his head go up. Their eyes met in the reflection.

"I'm going to fuck you so hard, Eleanor. You're so beautiful. You make me crazy."

She couldn't think of how to respond to his blistering intensity. She just watched him in the window as he rapidly rolled on the condom, her breath starting to come in jagged pants. He put both of his hands on her ass, his thumbs digging gently into the flesh of her buttocks. He moved behind her.

"Your ass is bright pink," he muttered. He lowered his hand to his cock. "Is your pussy as hot as your ass?"

She felt the head of his cock push against her entry and gasped. He penetrated her, his rough moan vibrating in her ears. "Oh yeah. Even hotter," he groaned, answering his own question. His hold on her ass tightened. He thrust his hips firmly. He carved into her, and her flesh melted around his hardness. He thrust to the hilt, fitting his pelvis against her ass. Her cries mingled with his guttural groan.

"Hush," he said, circling his hips and grinding his balls against her outer sex. Eleanor realized she'd been wailing like a banshee and halted herself, gasping for air. She'd never felt so full. So incendiary. His thumbs dug deeper into her spanked ass. "This is for me, Eleanor. This is what's going to happen every time you tease me. You're going to get it. Hard. Now, hold still and take it."

He drew his cock out of her. Eleanor turned her head, watching his reflection as he watched himself screw her. When only the head of his cock was buried in her, he flexed and thrust deep inside her again, making the air gasp out of her lungs.

He was off like a rocket. He fucked her with smooth, relentless precision, never letting up. She watched him in the mirror for a moment, staring in wonder at the vision of his pistoning cock, pumping hips and the tops of his naked, flexing, round buttocks above the waistband of his white boxer briefs. His face looked rigid and fierce as he watched himself fuck her.

Then the friction grew so intense from his ruthless possession, she no longer was able to focus on his image. He rattled her consciousness. She stared down at the carpet blindly, wailing and gasping, overwhelmed by sensation. It stung a little each time he hammered into her, his pelvis smacking against her spanked bottom, his swollen cock filling her . . . overfilling her.

It dawned on her that he wasn't just rocking her world in the figurative sense, but in the literal one. He fucked her so hard, his rough grunts and growls raining down on her, that her entire body shook and shot forward with each thrust. His hold on her hips and ass kept her mostly a stationary target, however. He finally paused, his breathing remarkably even, given his strident, rapid movements. *She* was panting like she'd just run a race. He released her ass and she felt his hands moving on the padded handcuffs at her back. Her arms fell forward, liberated, the cuffs still attached to her right wrist.

"Put your hands on your knees, Eleanor. Support yourself," he said, his voice sounding harsh in her ringing ears.

When she'd done what he'd demanded, he resumed his assault on her senses, this time with perhaps greater rigor. She was reminded firsthand of his supreme physical condition and raw strength. The sound of him smacking into her body grew so rapid it was like gunfire going off. Was it possible for a man to fuck that fast, that hard . . . that *well*?

Apparently so.

A scream tore out of her throat as she started to come.

"Jesus, Eleanor. You little—"

She was so lost in a cyclone of pounding sensation, she hardly knew what was happening to her. Suddenly his forearms hooked beneath her elbows and he was lifting her upper body, never stopping in his rapid, fluid thrusts. He pulled her back, leaning down until his front pressed against her shoulders and arching back. He bent his knees beneath her, causing her ass to slap forcefully onto his pelvis and hard thighs as he fucked her. All the while, his cock kept up its relentless thrusting into her captive body.

She felt him swell inside her, and then his deep, rough voice vibrating ominously near her ear.

"I'm going to come in your teasing little pussy now, Eleanor."

He cupped one of her breasts in his hand and pounded into her with short strokes that jolted her entire body. His growl sounded savage. Thrilling. Days later, she'd recall that tense, electrical moment and become uncontrollably aroused. He roared as he came, holding her immobile for the first blast, and then using his hold on her breast and shoulder to ride her on his cock while he finished. She bounced to and fro, gasping for air, completely and deliciously frayed.

Slowly, his forceful manipulation of her body eased. He finally stopped pumping, some of the palpable tension leaving his corded muscles. She couldn't get over his strength and stamina. He wrapped his arms around her waist with his cock thrust high. He bent his head, his face against her shoulder. She absorbed the sensation of his warm breath brushing her skin as he panted for air.

ELEVEN

"I think you turned me inside out," he muttered thickly after a moment next to her shoulder blade.

"You're telling me. You're *looking* at my insides," she mumbled through numb lips.

He tensed at that, straightening and bringing her with him. His cock slid out of her body.

"*No,*" she said with exhausted irritability.

"Come here," he soothed quietly, holding her upper arm and guiding her over to the bed. They fell down heavily onto the mattresses, making the springs squeak in protest. His arm went under her head to her shoulders, and she rolled against him. For a few seconds, they just panted as their bodies recovered and steadied.

Her face pressed against a solid pectoral muscle. As the minutes passed, she became attuned to the rise and fall of his chest and the feeling of his cotton shirt pressed against her nose and lips. Sluggishly, she raised her hand and began to unbutton his shirt. He touched the back of her hand with his fingertips, and for a moment, she thought he was going to try to stop her. He didn't, though. He just caressed the back of her hand as it moved down his chest and abdomen. She drew open the shirt and ran her hand over the glorious stretch of his nude torso, sliding against his hard abdomen, heaving rib cage and powerful chest. A thin layer of perspiration covered his thick skin. Arousal flickered through her, surprising her a little. All the while, he kept his hand in contact with hers, and she had the weird, random thought that he was experiencing what it was like for her to touch his naked body at that moment. She felt exquisitely attuned to him. She found a small nipple and circled the tip of her forefinger over it, air soughing into her lungs when she felt it pebble.

He gripped her hand tighter in his.

"You're turning me on again," he stated, his tone both blunt and vaguely incredulous.

She pulled her hand free of his and came up on her elbow, staring down at him. He looked magnificent lying there, his burnished brown hair mussed, his bronzed, muscular torso exposed, his blue eyes lambent and fierce-seeming in his otherwise utterly relaxed state. She could smell him too, the lingering scent of his aftershave mingling with the musk of his arousal and climax. Wanting to experience his fragrance more, she pressed her nose next to his rib cage and inhaled. He muttered something—she wasn't sure what—and laced his fingers into her hair.

She ran her fingertip from his collarbone downward, trailing it through the brown hair on his chest and down over his smooth sternum. His heaving rib cage stilled, and she knew he'd held his breath. She liked the way his ridged, flat abdomen jumped beneath her touch. His cock lay at a diagonal along his pelvis and belly, his boxer briefs and jeans still shoved heedlessly at his thighs and beneath his testicles. The condom looked very slick with her juices. Heat swept through her.

He was magnificent.

She could just lie there for hours and touch him, and her fascination would never wane. Mounting arousal might fracture her attention, but boredom?

Never.

She shifted her head, pressing her mouth to the side of his waist. She sunk her teeth gently into smooth skin and dense flesh. He jumped and tightened his fingers in her hair. His skin roughened beneath her lips.

"Take it easy, gorgeous. If you're that hungry, we'll order in."

She grinned, her lips sliding against his skin. She kissed him playfully and rose up over him.

"I *am* kind of hungry, come to think of it."

She liked the way his gaze trailed over her face and his small, knowing smile. "Then let's get something to eat," he said.

"I've got enough to feed an army in the fridge," she said. "That is if you like either goose or Russian food."

His brow quirked. "Russian food?"

"Yeah, some pelmeni, bliny, pirog?"

She smiled when he gave her a blank look.

"Dumplings, crepes or a meat pie?" she interpreted. "Along with loads of sour cream, it's your basic diet for guaranteed clogged arteries."

"My favorite kind," he said, turning on his side and propping his head up on his elbow. The action brought him into easier striking distance. She leaned forward and ran her lips along his ribs. He grunted and plunged his fingers back in her hair, scooping it onto her back. "Your hair is ticklish," he murmured, his fingers continuing to run the length of it. "And very soft." She made a satisfied sound in her throat and buried her face in a rock-hard pectoral muscle.

"You're lying. You must eat kale and cabbage, raw fish and steamed chicken to have a body like this," she said, nuzzling his chest and squeezing a bulging bicep through his shirtsleeve. "You've lost weight, haven't you? Not that I'm complaining. You look extremely healthy." *Phenomenal, in fact.* "But is the weight loss on purpose?"

"It's just from working out like a madman. Especially lately." He ran his hand down her naked spine and she sighed next to this skin.

"So you've been spending more time at the gym?"

"I have to."

She lifted her head and gave him a dubious glance.

"Because of my new self-improvement routine. Well . . . my former one, since I'm apparently off it now." His gaze lowered to her breasts in amused lechery.

"So that's *it*? You're *completely* off self-improvement, just because you slept with me?"

"You disapprove?" he asked, his voice gruff and low and delicious. He cupped the back of her head warmly. He brought her to him and kissed her mouth. He held her against him, their foreheads pressed together. "In my opinion, you were more than worth it."

"I shouldn't be blamed for ruining your self-improvement campaign. There's no reason why you can't better yourself and have sex with someone at once," she insisted against his mouth.

"Maybe for most people. I seem to be the exception," he said, loosening his hold on her.

"Why?"

He shrugged casually, but his expression was serious. She regretted ruining his mellow, playful mood with her questions, but she was so curious about him.

"I guess because my career has been my absolute focus for the past twelve years. When I did get involved in relationships, they tended to be a sideline to that."

"A sideline?"

He grimaced. "That sounded bad, didn't it? I just mean that BandBook, and then TalentNet, took up my whole focus. They became my entire life. Sometimes out of preference, but more

often than not, out of necessity. Relationships with women tended
to be more about . . ."

"Sex," she filled in for him.

"Yeah," he admitted. "Sometimes I wanted it to be more than
just about that. It just never worked out that way. I'm starting to
wonder if it ever will." She became aware that he was studying
her reaction very closely, and made an attempt to wipe the anxiety
off her expression. She'd assured him she was fine engaging with
him on a purely sexual basis, after all. His gaze narrowed on her.
"Are you wondering if I'm a sex addict again?" he demanded.

"No. I never really thought that," she insisted, laughing.
"*Really*. I wouldn't be with you if I believed that."

He looked vaguely pacified. "My relationships *do* tend to be
of the intense, short-lived variety."

"Wild and out of control, and then they burn themselves out
as quickly as they blazed to life?" she asked with false lightness.
Kind of like what's happening with us, for instance? What will
happen eventually?

A feeling of dread began to settle on her.

"Pretty much, yeah," he mused, his fingertips stroking her
scalp. "I have to say, though . . . this thing with you is unusual."

She did a double take. "Really?"

"Yeah," he said, his brow furrowed thoughtfully. "If my former relationships could be described as fiery at first, you're more
like an explosion of epic proportions. I can't believe that fan dance
you did," he mused. He focused on her face. "It was incredible."

She flushed. "Thanks."

"You're so in the moment at times. So present. Really honest."

She started, guilt sweeping through her. "I am?"

"Yeah. You're upfront about what you want"—his mouth
twisted—"even while you're manipulating the hell out of me to
get it. You're a little tease, and you totally lose yourself while

you're pushing all my buttons . . . but at least you put it all out there."

She ducked her head, suddenly afraid he'd see straight through the façade she donned for him with those laser beam eyes of his. He tugged gently on a tendril of her hair, and she was forced to meet his stare.

"Do you date a lot?"

"Are you asking me if I do stripteases a lot?" she asked him, holding his stare, determined not to flinch.

His gaze narrowed. "I've told you about my bad luck with women. I was just wondering about your history with men. Is that too intrusive for me to ask?"

"There've been some men in my life." She swallowed thickly. "Not a lot."

He touched her cheek. She went very still, her skin prickling with awareness beneath his fingertips. "You looked like sex personified doing that dance. You must have . . ." A frown creased his brow. "Practiced it a lot," he said after a pause, his mouth going hard.

Her breath caught. She didn't know what to say. He alluded to the fact that she must have done that dance to seduce other men on many prior occasions. If she was the sexual libertine she was pretending to be, and the exhibitionist to boot, she should lay claim to a great *deal* of practice. Instead, she found herself wanting to tell him it'd been her first time, and he'd been her entire inspiration.

But suddenly he gave a crooked smile. "Never mind. You're right. I don't want to know how many times you've done that dance. It's nicer to pretend it was just for me. Besides, I have no right to grill you about your past. Not when I've admitted to being ashamed of my track record."

"Trey—"

He shook his head abruptly, as if to both silence her and clear his thoughts. He shut his eyes. She studied his sober expression. She really liked talking to him. He was interesting, genuine . . . complex. She wanted to know more about him.

The only problem was, it felt like she was navigating a minefield, given the narrow parameters they'd put on their dalliance.

Given her dishonesty in portraying who she really was.

"This issue you're struggling with when it comes to women is really bothering you, isn't it?" she asked him cautiously. He didn't reply for a few a seconds. Finally he opened his eyes.

"It just seems like one minute, I'm having fun with a woman, enjoying her company whenever we're able to get together, and then . . ."

"She suddenly wants more, and you don't?"

"More than that. As time goes on, I feel like the mask runs thin, and I don't like what I see underneath. It gets to the point where a lot of what she says, no matter how nice or seemingly complimentary to me, starts to feel like I'm being tactically maneuvered."

"And you got sick of that," she said, full understanding settling. "That's why you were going cold turkey on sex and relationships."

"It's my fault," he said gruffly after a pause. "Or at least partially. That's what I'm starting to think. It's only natural that a woman starts to expect more over time. And more often than not, I just don't want to give it."

"*Is* it? Natural, I mean? For a woman to want more?"

"*Isn't* it?"

"You make it sound like it's some kind of behavior gene linked to the X chromosome," she said, lying on her back and staring blankly up at the ceiling. "I don't think that's true, necessarily."

"It's not true for you, that you'll inevitably want more from a guy the longer the relationship continues?"

"No. It's not *inevitable*, anyway," she insisted. It wasn't a lie.

She'd dated guys whom she'd wanted more with as time went on, but the opposite had occurred as well. With *Trey*, wanting more might be an inevitability, but that's not what he'd asked her.

Technically.

Lie or not, their conversation was making her feel a little bereft. Not to mention like more of a fake than ever, given her scheme to don a sexy playgirl persona and fulfill her selfish fantasies.

He exhaled and also flipped over onto his back. "All I know is that I have a tendency to get mixed up with the kind of woman who isn't really honest about what she wants in the beginning. When I don't give her what she needs, she starts to turn manipulative. Underhanded. Dishonest. But maybe you're right. They probably sense my lack of commitment, my lack of focus on them. That's why they start acting that way."

She gave a dry bark of laughter. "*I* never said that their being manipulative was your fault. *I* wasn't trying to make some big point. And you can't know if I'm right or full of crap. You don't really know *what* to think of women, do you?"

"I haven't got a clue," he said. He glanced sideways at her. "I'm starting to think I don't have what it takes, Eleanor."

A feeling of tenderness for him went through her, such a different, unexpected experience in comparison to the usual sexual hunger and single-minded determination he typically inspired in her.

She reached up and caressed his whiskered jaw.

She turned her head farther on the mattress. "I think you're being too hard on yourself," she said softly.

"Maybe. Or maybe I'm not being hard enough."

"Do you *really* think you'll find answers in the pages of *Pride and Prejudice*?" she asked, a smile tickling at her mouth. She couldn't help it. He was *Trey Riordan*, after all, full of confidence, considered a unique path blazer in the fields of business, technology, art and popular culture. He'd just expanded her vision of how she saw herself sexually a thousandfold, not to mention turned her into a mass of quivering sex goo. Yet he seemed genuinely baffled about how to interface with a woman on anything else but a playing field for sex and good times.

"I never said I thought it held some kind of golden key to truth, but I didn't think it'd hurt to look."

She chuckled. He gave her a dark glance.

"I'm sorry," she said sincerely, reaching to brush back his thick hair. "Your search for something real seems genuine. What's more, so does your campaign for self-reflection and improvement so that you can be more worthy of finding it. It's very admirable, actually." Her smile faded and her stroking fingers paused. Their stares caught and held. "I hope you find what you're searching for, Trey."

"Thanks," he said.

He was regarding her so solemnly. Something about the way he was looking at her made her heart jump erratically.

"Why the Russian food? Briggs isn't a Russian name, is it?" he asked gruffly after a moment.

She laughed, mostly at herself, for thinking he was about to say something else . . . something meaningful. Of course he'd try to keep things casual. He'd made it clear what he wanted from their fling. She had to admit, however, that if this was *light* with him, she couldn't even imagine what the depths would be like.

She really was playing way out of her league.

"No, Briggs is English. My dad's ancestors were mostly from England and Scotland. But my mom is one hundred percent Russian: brilliant, imperious, always right and a fabulous cook. We call her Catherine the Great, or just 'The G' for short. Instead of being insulted, she loves it. She probably wishes we weren't kidding, and that was her official title," Eleanor told him, grinning. She loved his easy smile and the sound of his gruff laughter. "Do you want to try some of it? Her cooking, I mean? She loaded me down after Thanksgiving."

"Yeah," he said, sitting up on the mattress. "I do. But how about we have it for breakfast?"

"What?" she asked, confused. "You aren't hungry now?"

"Let's go out for a walk," he said, standing. Her eyes widened at the too-brief view of the top half of his bare ass before the tail of his shirt fell down over it. "It's still early," he said, shifting his underwear and jeans. "I'll take you out to dinner somewhere."

"*Really?*" she asked, sitting partially up on the bed.

He glanced back at her over his shoulder. His brow creased.

"I know I've been honest with you about my lousy relationships with women, but you don't have to look so shocked, Eleanor. I'm not that much of a louse. I like you. I want to spend more time with you, have dinner. Breakfast too, if I'm invited."

"But I thought you said—and I agreed—that this was just going to be about . . ." She waved lamely at the discarded feather fans on the floor and the place where he'd just spanked her and then screwed her brains out.

"I thought we'd already established I don't know what I'm talking about half the time," he muttered under his breath. "If you don't want to go out, that's fine. Is that the bathroom?" he nodded toward a door on the right.

"Yes," she said, her heart plummeting down to her navel. *You're blowing it again, Eleanor.* But how was she supposed to know how not to lose when she didn't understand the rules of the game . . . a game of her own making?

He made a movement with his hand at his crotch and she realized he was removing the condom. He started to walk toward the bathroom.

"Trey," she called, made anxious at the vision of his retreating back.

He paused and glanced over his shoulder, frowning slightly.

"I don't know what I'm talking about half the time either. And I *do* want to go for a walk with you," she blurted out before she could stop herself.

His forbidding expression melted slowly. She saw his small smile before he turned. She was still experiencing a rush of euphoria from his sexy grin when she heard a buzzing noise. It was his phone in his pocket, she realized. His focus on her fractured. He started toward the bathroom.

"I'll be back in a second," he said.

For a few seconds, she just lay there, basking in the unexpected turn of events, disbelieving at her luck in being able to spend more time with him. *Nonsexual* time, even. That had been far more than she'd allowed herself to hope for, let alone expect.

Suddenly energized, she jumped up and grabbed an afghan at the foot of the bed, wrapping it around her naked body. She heard the sound of running water in the bathroom. She waited, thinking she'd tell Trey she planned to jump in the shower for a minute before their walk and dinner.

He walked out of the bathroom a few seconds later, his pants fastened and his phone in his hand. He looked up at her. Her ebullient bubble popped, just like that. There was something in his expression—

"I'm really sorry, but can I take a rain check on dinner?" he asked.

"Of course. Is everything all right?"

He glanced down at his phone, appearing both distracted and vaguely stunned. "I'm fine. It's my brother," he said.

"What about him?" Eleanor asked, holding the afghan around her breasts and walking toward him.

"That's just it, I don't know. I knew something was bugging him at Mom and Dad's over Thanksgiving, but he wouldn't open up about it. But he texted that he's just a few miles outside of Chicago and needs to talk to me. He asked if we could meet over at my place."

"Do you think it's something serious?" Eleanor asked quietly.

Trey shook his head and slid his phone into his back pocket. He began buttoning up his shirt. She watched his fleet fingers covering up his cut, powerful torso with a sinking feeling. That simple action on his part, more than his words, brought it home to her that he was really leaving.

"I'm guessing it *is* serious," he stated dryly.

"Why do you say it like that?"

"Because even though my brother and I are close, he's never actually been to my place. I'm talking never *once*, not since I've been an adult. He's ten years older than me. I came a lot later than him and my sister, Kacy. Kevin's a pilot. When he has a layover in Chicago, or when I'm in New York, we meet up at a restaurant or bar if we're both free. But he's been flying to Europe for the past few years, so I've seen him less and less. Usually, we just see each other on holidays at Mom and Dad's. He's a pretty independent guy. Some people would call him a loner." Trey paused, frowning. "He's certainly never driven to Chicago just to *talk* to me."

His flashing glance landed on her standing there clutching the heavy afghan above her breasts. Something darkened his features. He took two long strides over to her and delved his fingers into her hair. His head dipped. He cut off her soft gasp with his mouth.

His kiss told her he regretted having to leave. Or at least that was her impression when he stood close and his taste and scent filled her.

When Trey was next to you, and his mouth was moving on yours, there wasn't much room for doubt.

Once he was gone . . .

Well, that was a different story altogether.

TWELVE

Kevin Riordan carried his forty-three years extremely well. Most people guessed he and Trey were five years apart instead of almost eleven. Both of the Riordan boys had gotten their father's height and their mother's blue eyes, but Kevin was darker than Trey.

He'd always looked up to Kevin. As a kid, he'd worshipped him like a hero. As he'd gotten older, he'd grown to genuinely respect his brother's skill and courage as a Navy pilot, his easy confidence with other men—who also seemed to immediately admire him—and his even easier confidence with women, who typically adored him.

As Trey entered his living room that night, however, and saw the back of Kevin's shadowed form staring broodingly down onto Lake Shore Drive, the unusual thought struck him for the first time in his life that Kevin Riordan wasn't just a loner. He was lonely.

He cleared this throat and his brother turned. Trey held out the glass of bourbon Kevin had requested.

"Thanks," Kevin rasped, immediately taking a sip. He closed his eyes and sighed. "God, that's good. Heaven compared to that crap Mom keeps at the farm."

Trey chuckled and sat down on the couch, placing his glass of ice water on the coffee table.

"If you think that, you should bring her the good stuff," Trey said.

Kevin dropped into a chair. "Yeah, you're right. I'm a shit guest. Dad and Kacy were certainly making that clear by the time I left Rockford a few hours ago."

"Everyone knew something was bugging you," Trey said honestly.

"You weren't in the best of moods either."

Trey shrugged his acknowledgment. Thinking about why he'd been so restless over Thanksgiving brought up the image of Eleanor standing there a half hour ago, that afghan wrapped around her breasts, her hair wild and sexy, her golden green eyes glistening. Why had she looked so somber as she regarded him?

Damn, I wish I could figure her out.

Kevin grimaced and rubbed his eyes. There were lines of tension around his brother's mouth and eyes that Trey had never seen before this Thanksgiving.

"I know I was an ass. I apologized to Mom and Dad before I left. Kacy, Mike and Jason had already left, so I didn't get a chance to apologize to them yet." He winced. "Christ, my eyes burn. I haven't been able to sleep lately."

"You're starting to freak me out. Are you sick or something?"

Kevin gave him an incredulous glance. "Do I *look* sick?"

"Uh . . . *yeah*, a little. Mom was all worried because you hardly ate any of her stuffing or pumpkin pie."

Kevin suddenly broke out into harsh laughter and leaned back in the chair. "No, I'm not sick. Not in the way you're thinking, at least. Damn," he muttered, shaking his head as if he were going over some morbidly funny joke in his head. He took another drink of his bourbon, still grinning like a madman.

"*What?*" Trey demanded. "What the hell is going on with you?"

Kevin looked around his penthouse, his grin fading. "Jesus, will you *look* at this fucking place? My little brother, the billionaire."

"I'm not a billionaire," Trey said, frowning because his brother had changed the subject.

Kevin gave another bark of incredulous laughter. "You're a hell of a lot closer to it than I'll ever be. It's funny. Kacy and I always had the big sibling rivalry, but it's *you* we should have been jealous of all along."

"What purpose would that serve?" Trey asked wryly.

"It would have given me a break from Kacy, and Kacy a break from me."

Trey laughed. His brother joined him. Again, Kevin's narrowed gaze traveled around the penthouse. "It's huge, isn't it? It's not much of a place for a family, though, is it?"

"Since when would something like that have bothered you?"

"Maybe for about a month now."

Trey paused in the action of reaching for his water, stunned. Kevin was quite the playboy. He couldn't believe what he'd just heard.

"Are you serious?" he asked quietly.

Kevin just nodded, his dazed expression making it clear he couldn't quite believe it either.

"You've fallen for someone?" Trey clarified. "That's what your pissy mood and the lack of sleep and—"

"The fact that I look so sick are all about?" Kevin finished darkly. "Yeah. That's what they're all about." He took a drink and swallowed. "I'm worried I'm terminal too."

Trey snorted. Kevin gave him a sharp, annoyed glance. "What are you griping about?" Trey wondered. "It's a good thing, isn't it? You're in love with someone."

He shook his head in amazement when Kevin didn't argue.

"What's she like?" Trey asked.

"It's no good," Kevin said bitterly, tossing his glass down on a table.

"*What's* no good? *She's* no good?"

"*She's* fantastic," Kevin corrected, blue eyes blazing.

Trey threw up his hands in a surrender gesture. "Okay, okay. So . . . spell it for the feebleminded. *Why* are you so upset?"

"You don't know what it's like," Kevin said, sitting forward restlessly in his chair. Trey saw a wildness in his eyes he'd never seen before. "I can't stop thinking about her. I've traveled all over the world for most of my adult life, and never thought twice about the distance. Now all of a sudden, I hate every single fucking mile, because it's taking me farther away from her. And the thing of it is, she's all wrong for me."

"In what way?"

"She's too young, for one thing. Twenty-seven."

"A mature twenty-seven?"

Kevin scoffed. "Elizabeth was *born* more mature than me."

Trey smiled. It was weird seeing his brother like this, so discombobulated over a woman. "Good. You need someone to keep you under control . . . balance you out."

Kevin gave him a dirty look. "Like you should talk, Mr. Viral Sex Video."

"Elizabeth," Trey mused, pointedly ignoring Kevin's barb about that infuriating video with the stupid Scarpetti sisters. No, *he'd* been the stupid one on that occasion. What the hell had he been thinking? He *hadn't* been, that was the whole problem. He still cringed inwardly in regret and embarrassment every time he thought of his mother hearing about it. Plus, his dad had bought her a computer recently. He'd told his mom point-blank about the rumors regarding the video a couple years back, wanting to prevent her hearing about it from one of her girlfriends or a cousin or something. But what if she'd actually *watched* it?

"I like that name," Trey decided. "It's got substance. Like Elizabeth Bennet from *Pride and Prejudice*."

Eleanor was a name of substance too.

Kevin gave him a look like he was losing his mind, scattering Trey's weird, out-of-nowhere thought. "That's Elizabeth, all right," Kevin said, obviously too distracted to notice Trey's momentary oddness for long. "She's got so much substance, sometimes I feel like I'll learn something new about her every day."

"So she'll keep you on your toes for the rest of your worthless life, then. What are you so worried about?"

Kevin hesitated. It was beyond strange, seeing his cocky brother so unsure.

"But . . . what if one day, I learn something about her I *don't* like?"

"Like, if you discover she's not perfect?" Trey asked, frowning.

Kevin gave him a startled glance. "No, it's not that. I don't think she's *perfect*."

"Sounds to me like you do."

"Like you don't demand perfection of the women you date," Kevin muttered, rolling his eyes.

"I *don't*," Trey defended. "I demand honesty."

"Yeah, honesty about all their faults. How many people do you know who want to spill all their ugly secrets on the first date?"

"Did you come here to talk about my love life, or yours?" Trey countered.

Kevin seemed to deflate. He struck Trey as seeming hopeless in that moment, more vulnerable than he'd ever seen him. It worried Trey. Is *that* what love did to you?

"*Do* you actually love her?" Trey asked, thinking it'd be best to start at the basics.

Kevin looked him straight in the eye. "Like crazy."

"Well there you go. Look, you *know* I'm no expert at this. Recently, I've kind of been struggling with what it all means too."

"Of course I know you're no expert. Maybe that's why you're the only person I felt comfortable talking to about it," Kevin said glumly. "Everyone else would have just patronized me."

Trey exhaled heavily and sunk back in his chair. He was glad his brother felt okay talking to him about this, but at the same time, he couldn't help but feel it was a bit of a backhanded compliment. They just sat there gloomily in silence. It was like they'd just attended a funeral and were wrestling with the heaviness of their thoughts. Death made you feel all alone with your insecurities and doubts. Maybe that's what love did too. The Riordan brothers' reaction to their first encounter with true love would have struck Trey as both pitiful and funny if it didn't feel so damn serious.

"That's what you're worried about the most?" he asked Kevin eventually. "That you'll find out something about her you don't like?"

"I guess. Or maybe worse, she'll find out something about me she doesn't like and can't live with."

"Yeah, I hear you," Trey agreed, understanding that angle completely. For a few seconds, they didn't speak, each of them lost in their thoughts. Something occurred to him.

"You know how Dad makes that disgusting, weird noise in his throat all the time while he's watching TV at night? Because his sinuses start to drain once he's settled down from all the activity of the day?"

Kevin blinked. "Yeah."

"I heard Mom say once that you know it's real when you encounter another person's phlegm on a regular basis, and you're still in love with them."

A grin slowly broke over Kevin's face. "That sounds like Mom."

Trey chuckled in agreement.

"So you're telling me that I have to expect phlegm along with all the brilliant, sweet, *incredibly* sexy things about Elizabeth?"

"I'm saying you shouldn't be *afraid* of the phlegm." Kevin's eyebrows went up. "Because it's *Elizabeth's* phlegm. As for your phlegm, well . . . let's just hope Elizabeth is a hell of lot more generous than you."

Kevin just stared at him with a blank, stunned look.

Trey gave a helpless shrug. "Hey man, *you* came to me. What the hell do I know?"

Kevin laughed gruffly, some of the tension leaving his body. He reached for his glass.

"Maybe you know more than either one of us thought you did," he said before he stood and walked over to the windows again, this time wearing a small smile.

On Saturday morning, Eleanor got up early and showered. She was determined to get out of the condo and do something purposeful. It'd been a long, restless night. She didn't want to prolong the unpleasantness into the daytime by bingeing on Netflix and Russian dumplings all day, thinking about Trey's abrupt departure, or wondering when she might see him again. One thing was certain: her mental conversations would drive her stark raving mad if she let them.

What if that text he got wasn't really from his brother at all? What if he just needed an excuse to leave? What if he'd really just wanted to get away to reconnect with the gorgeous Alessandra?

Okay, now you're just being completely paranoid.

Really? How many men do you know who would turn down a woman like Alessandra for you?

One. Trey. He did it last night.

Yeah, but the night was still young when he left . . .

God, she hated that snide little bitch in her head.

Besides, she didn't even have a *right* to be concerned about him sleeping with someone else. She'd agreed with Trey that all she wanted was an unconditional agreement for mutual pleasure.

Yeah, but when you made that agreement, you were in the midst of a performance, weren't you? The adventurous little slut you were playing might not mind. But you're sure as hell starting to.

Those were the type of self-dialogues she longed to escape by the time she left her building at eleven that morning.

She'd called Jimmy and they agreed to meet for an early lunch in Logan Square at a favorite cafe. She owed him another apology for her abrupt departure last night. Plus, she was dying to hear how Alessandra had reacted to her and Trey leaving within minutes of each another.

It ashamed her a little, that she was so gratified when Jimmy told her the cool English beauty had abruptly altered into a snarling bitch when Trey had calmly stood, tossed a hundred-dollar bill on the table, shook Jimmy's hand and told Alessandra he hoped she had a safe flight back to London.

"She calmed down after a bit, though," Jimmy said after they'd been served their lunch.

"Trey said there was a fifty-fifty chance she'd come on to you after she was rejected by him. Did she?"

"No. But we did stay and have a couple drinks together. She's not bad."

"I have a feeling there's more to *that* story," Eleanor said, studying the way Jimmy suddenly seemed completely focused on arranging his cheeseburger garnishes.

"I can take care of myself."

"That's what I told Trey. But still . . . watch out, Jimmy. I'm serious. Trey says Alessandra is a handful."

"Just because she's not right for Riordan doesn't mean she's not interesting."

"Not to mention disgustingly gorgeous," Eleanor said sarcastically under her breath. Jimmy gave her a wry glance.

"Enough about Alessandra. You're the one with the big story. Give me dirt. What's been happening with Riordan? Start from the beginning," Jimmy insisted.

She owed him some kind of story. As her closest friend, Jimmy had been in on her obsession with Trey ever since she'd discovered his name from her doorman. He'd been the one to tell her about Trey signing up for the reading event.

She outlined some of the basics of what'd been happening with Trey and her, leaving out most of the details about her uncharacteristically bold exhibitionistic displays. Jimmy probably wouldn't believe her if she told him the full story, anyway.

"So after you guys left, you guys just went up to your place and had fantastic sex?" Jimmy asked for the third time after the plates had been cleared and they sipped their coffee.

Eleanor rolled her eyes. "How many times do I have to say it? Why does everyone have to act so surprised when I do something sexy?" she complained. "Am I really that boring?"

"No, it's just . . . *Trey Riordan*. He's quite a catch," Jimmy said, raising his eyebrows in a lecherous gesture.

"And to think," she said drolly, "that I told Trey you were straight." Jimmy laughed. "But seriously, you think it's weird too, don't you?"

"What?"

"That Trey thinks I'm attractive. Sexy," she added hesitantly.

"Why would I think that?" Jimmy asked, frowning.

"*You* don't think of me that way. Almost no one does. I just don't . . . *wear* sexy well, do I?"

Jimmy set down his coffee cup with a clanging sound. "Are you serious? You're beautiful, Eleanor. You've never been very obvious about it, but that's just part of your charm. What is this? Are you fishing for compliments?"

He looked so bemused, so incredulous—possibly even more so than when he'd asked her repeatedly about her and Trey having sex last night. Eleanor thought maybe she should just change the subject. Jimmy couldn't understand.

Especially when she wasn't certain she understood it herself.

Sure, she knew she cleaned up well, and could be attractive when she made the effort. It just wasn't in her nature to *choose* to put a lot of energy and time on her looks.

Although recently, she had to admit, she was starting to get why some women indulged in clothes and hair products and shoes. Maybe the beauty industry wasn't *exclusively*, as she'd always thought in the past, a multibillion-dollar bandage to female low self-esteem. It was just like Caddy had said several times in the past. You should look good because it pleased *you*.

"Eleanor?" Jimmy asked, interrupting her thoughts. "Is all this about Caddy?"

"Huh?" she asked, stunned. How had he known she'd just been thinking about Caddy? *Oh no. First Mom, now Jimmy.* This topic made her practically writhe in her own skin with acute discomfort. Her heartbeat started to thrum uncomfortably loud in her ears.

Jimmy must have noticed her panicked expression. "It's just . . . ever since Caddy died, you've started doing your hair different once in a while, wearing makeup, dressing more . . . you know."

"Sexy?" she asked through a tight throat.

"Yeah. And it looks great on you, it really does," Jimmy said.

"You don't actually believe that. You don't think it looks good on me, do you?" she asked hollowly, thinking about her mom saying, *It's not you, Eleanor.* "You think I'm just pretending to be like Caddy?"

"*No*, it's not that. I don't think you're pretending to be like Caddy."

"Really?" Eleanor asked, taken aback by his confident denial.

"Yeah. I'm not lying. Your new style does look great on you. I'm sure most people would agree. Didn't you notice the way all the men at Gold Coast were drooling over you last night? You probably didn't, since Riordan was one of them, and you weren't looking anywhere but at him."

She flushed, taken off guard at the very idea of Trey drooling over her.

"Then . . . what's the problem?"

Jimmy shrugged and picked up his coffee cup. "The problem is *you* don't seem to believe in your new look. Not completely."

"Okay. So I'm working on my self-confidence. So what? What's that got to do with Caddy?"

"This new look only appeared once Caddy passed."

She grimaced. "I told you why that was. She told me to live my life, step out of the shadows . . . stop being so afraid," Eleanor added in a small voice.

Jimmy nodded. "I know. And I'm glad Caddy did that. She was an amazing sister. She was amazing, period."

Eleanor just nodded, her throat feeling tight.

"But the thing of it is, Eleanor, Caddy wasn't telling you to be someone *different*."

"Oh *no*," Eleanor exclaimed, a tear shooting out of her eyes unexpectedly. Jimmy started at her atypical reaction.

"*Jesus*, Eleanor. I'm sorry, I didn't know it'd—"

"Have you been talking to my mother?" She wiped at her cheek irritably. "She thinks I'm grieving *unnaturally*, as well."

Jimmy reached across the table and grabbed one of her hands.

"*Eleanor.*" She blinked away more tears at his abrupt gesture and met his stare reluctantly. "Of course I haven't been talking to Catherine about you. Do you think I'd do that behind your back?"

She shook her head.

"I don't think there's anything unnatural about you or your grief or your new look. I think Caddy would have *loved* the fact that you're giving her clothes a spin. I just think she'd want you to feel comfortable with what you're doing. She'd want you to *own* it all."

"Versus playacting at it?" Eleanor sniffed. "Well, Rome wasn't built in a day. Neither will Eleanor be."

Jimmy looked like he was about to say something else, but then he seemed to think better of it. He released her hand and sat back.

"Maybe you're right about that. Everything works itself out, in time," he conceded. "So . . . when do you think you'll see Riordan again?"

Eleanor paused to compose herself. What was wrong with her, getting so emotional all of a sudden? It was this thing with Trey that was making her feel so frayed. Or maybe it was her worry that her mom was right, and this was all about Caddy. About grief.

She didn't understand her own motivations anymore.

"I don't know. Trey's going to find out that I'm not being honest with him eventually," she confessed miserably.

"What are you talking about?" Jimmy asked. "What aren't you being honest about?"

Everything.

She gave a bark of laughter. "I've led him to believe I'm as coldhearted as someone like Alessandra, for one. I've told him I'm fine with a no-strings-attached sexual relationship."

Jimmy gave her a sharp glance over his cup of coffee. "That *is* what you went into this wanting. Isn't it? You wanted to climb Mount Riordan and plant your flag."

Mortification swept through her. "Don't remind me. It sounds *horrible* hearing it. I was no better than a guy intent on one thing: sexual conquest."

"Hey, I resent that."

"Yeah, but you know it's true. *You're* the one who's always warning me that I'm kidding myself if I don't think men have sex as a primary motivation even for the simplest *hello*," Eleanor countered. Jimmy shrugged sheepishly. She laughed. "And I was just as mercenary when it came to Trey," she added, her amusement fading. "But all that was before."

"Before what?"

"I actually knew him."

"You think he's that special?" Jimmy asked her quietly.

It suddenly hit her then, how far out of her depths she'd swam. She couldn't even see the shore anymore.

"I *know* he is," she admitted with a hopeless sigh.

"Don't overthink it," Jimmy murmured after a pause.

She sat up straighter. "Is that what I'm doing?"

Of course it's what you're doing. It's what you always *do.*

"I think that you're very attracted to Riordan and he's extremely attracted to you. You guys couldn't take your eyes off each other last night. I think you should just take it one step at a time. And, Eleanor? Try not to get in the way of yourself having a good time."

She and Jimmy went to a movie that afternoon and had coffee afterward. By the time she got back home it was dark. The condo seemed even larger and more shadowed than usual. As she got dressed in some workout clothes, she mentally acknowledged a fact she'd been trying like hell to avoid. This was the weekend she and Caddy would have usually put up their Christmas decorations in both of their apartments.

A sharp pang of loss went through her. She sat down heavily on the bed in her room. It took her several minutes to catch her breath and gather herself.

This year, she couldn't bear to do it alone. She suddenly doubted she'd ever be able to put up a Christmas tree for herself again.

She forced herself to rise out of her bout of grief and stand. It was a good thing she didn't believe in ghosts, because otherwise, the empty condo and the ringing silence would have struck her as more than just oppressive.

She returned a phone call to her mother. Afterward, loud music and exercise seemed like a great way to eclipse her worrisome thoughts about her parents, about the absent Christmas tree, about what Jimmy had mentioned about Caddy . . .

About what she'd realized at lunch about Trey being so special.

Would she see him again before the reading event Monday night? About thirty seconds after she'd come out of the spell from his good-bye kiss yesterday, and the door had closed behind him, she realized they still hadn't exchanged phone numbers.

She'd just turned down the music from her aerobics and exercise routine when she heard the house phone ringing. She raced to pick it up.

"Hello?" she said breathlessly into the receiver.

"Eleanor, there you are."

"Hi, Harry," Eleanor said, recognizing her doorman's voice.

"You've got a Trey Riordan here to see you. I saw that you'd filled out a permission form for him to enter for the next month, but you filled it out with Alan last night. I don't trust that guy,"

Harry stated bluntly, referring to his relatively new night replacement at the security desk.

Excitement shot through her veins, but embarrassment chased quickly behind it. Trey was undoubtedly standing right there at the doorman's station, listening to Harry on the phone. And Harry had just blabbed that Eleanor had checked the category "one month" on the permission to enter form, not "one time only." For a second, mortification choked her. What was Trey *thinking* of her naïve, wishful impulsivity?

"Eleanor? Is it okay if he comes up?" Harry prodded.

She should make an excuse. She didn't want Trey to see her all sweaty like this.

"Uh . . . yeah, of course."

Great. Apparently, it wasn't in her makeup to deny him.

She hung up and stared around her kitchen wildly. Although she was typically a neat freak, the kitchen was a bit of a mess. Plus, she wore shorts and a perspiration-damp Northwestern T-shirt.

And Trey was going to be there any second.

Desperate, she lunged over to the sink and hastily washed her hands before splashing water on her face to cool herself. When his knock came on her door, she was tossing a few random items in a drawer to straighten the countertops and wiping her damp face off with a paper towel at the same time.

Trey knocked again.

"Damn," she muttered heatedly and threw away the paper towel.

THIRTEEN

She flung the door open. For a few seconds, he just stood there, a little stunned by her abruptness. She wore a pair of gray shorts and a Northwestern T-shirt that was slightly damp around the collar and in the valley between her breasts. He jerked his gaze off the vision of her full breasts snugly encased in cotton. She wasn't wearing a bra, and this time, it was gloriously obvious. She panted slightly, and her smooth, golden skin was dewy with perspiration. Her long brown hair was pulled into two pigtails.

She looked adorable, not to mention sexy as hell.

She also appeared worried.

"What's wrong?" he asked tensely.

Her green gold eyes widened. "Nothing."

"I'm sorry for not calling first. I still don't have your—"

"Phone number. I know. It's okay."

"I'm catching you at a bad time, aren't I?' he asked, regret and disappointment swooping through him. He pointed toward the elevator and started to edge toward it. "I should go."

"No."

He blinked and halted at her terse command. She flinched in embarrassment. "Why are you leaving? You just got here."

"I caught you in the middle of something."

She shook her head. "No you didn't. I just finished exercising."

He waited two expectant beats, but she just stared at him with those big, expressive eyes.

"And there's also the fact that you haven't asked me in yet," he added pointedly.

Her eyes widened and she started back. "I'm sorry, I was just a little surprised. Come in."

"Are you sure?"

"Yes, absolutely," she insisted.

As often was the case with her, he was getting the strangest mixed signals. How was it that she could be such a skillful seductress at times, and others, come off like she did right this second: like an awkward, adorably sexy Mouseketeer? She looked so innocent and undone. He felt a little guilty for leching after her at that moment just as much as he did when she seduced him so ruthlessly.

He followed her down a short hallway to the kitchen. "Can I get you anything to drink? I was just going to have some water," she said.

"I'll have the same, thanks."

He watched her while she moved around the kitchen, admiring her from the back. She kept pouring the water from the pitcher into the second glass when it reached the top. It overflowed and splashed onto the counter, making her jump back in surprise. He snapped a towel off the stove and went over to dry her off.

"Here," he said. She turned toward him. He grabbed her hand and wiped off her wrist. He slowed when he noticed her looking up at him anxiously. "Why are you so jumpy, Eleanor? You want me to go, don't you?"

"No," she insisted, shaking her head forcefully and making her pigtails rustle against her shoulders.

"Why are you acting so nervous, then?" he asked her quietly, enfolding her captive hand in both of his.

"That's what you do to me sometimes."

She bit her lip, like she'd regretted saying it.

His nerves prickled in heightened awareness. Her admission interested him. It gratified. He couldn't help but smile in relief. He'd been worried she didn't want him there. "Not *all* the time though," he murmured, stepping closer to her. He'd caught her scent: sweet sweat and fragrant Eleanor. He was drawn like a bee to honey. Something caught and flamed in her pretty eyes.

"No," she replied huskily. His head dipped toward her upturned face. "Not all the time."

"There's no reason for you to act skittish around me."

"How do you know?" His smile twitched at the appearance of her frown.

"Because I've seen you naked and done outrageous things to you. You've been pretty outrageous in return," he reminded her before he brushed his mouth against her soft, slightly pursed mouth. He tensed in excitement when she opened her lips.

"Trey? What did you come here for?"

He blinked, his trance broken slightly. Was she asking because she thought he'd come over here just to fall on her like a rutting animal? If she did, it was because she had precedent for thinking it.

"I came to ask if we could take that walk we missed out on last night," he replied. He was being honest. That *had* been his only intention upon coming there. It had been until he'd seen her big eyes, and pigtails, and a T-shirt that hugged her beautiful bare breasts like a second skin, anyway. "I was hoping to take you to dinner."

"Really?"

"Yeah," he replied earnestly, thinking it was wise to release her hand and take a step back before he revealed his other, less admirable, motivations.

"But I need to shower," she said, waving down at herself self-consciously.

"That's okay, I'll wait," he said, picking up one of the glasses. He took a swallow of water to cool off. He needed it. "If you don't mind, that is."

She shook her head. This time, he was glad to read nothing but excitement brimming in her eyes.

"If you want anything to eat or drink, just—"

"I'll be fine."

"I'll just be a minute," she promised, walking out of the kitchen.

"Take your time."

"All set," he heard her say ten or fifteen minutes later. He'd just wandered into her living room a minute ago. He turned from examining the contents of a bookshelf.

"You only read erotica, huh?" he asked her dryly, pointing at her large, diverse collection of books.

She grinned. "I told you I might have been exaggerating about that."

His smile slowly faded as he took her in.

"What?" she asked, frowning.

She wore jeans, a dark green sweater, a scarf, a black overcoat and a pair of supple walking boots. Her long hair was pulled back into a high ponytail. She'd scrubbed her face of perspiration, but as far as he could tell, she wore little or no makeup. Nor did she wear any jewelry. She looked so fresh.

So lovely.

"I never know what to expect from you," he said, walking to her. He stepped close. She looked up at him with those enormous, soulful eyes that had started to haunt both his sleep and waking moments. He smoothed back a stray curl at her temple. His fingers lingered, brushing the delicate, soft shell of her ear. He liked feeling her slight shiver at his touch.

"Is it . . . okay? How I'm dressed?" He blinked at the hesitance in her tone and focused on her face. He kissed her to erase the anxiety he read there, losing himself for a moment in her soft, responsive lips.

"Of course it's okay," he assured. "You look adorable."

"But you said dinner. Maybe the place you want to go to is dressy?" She glanced down at him. "You look really nice."

"I'm wearing jeans and boots and a coat, just like you," he murmured humorously, nipping at her lower lip.

"You manage to make it look a lot more sophisticated than I do." She shifted on her feet. "I think I'll change."

He grabbed her shoulders, making her an immobile target. He seized her mouth in a hard, swift kiss. By the time he lifted his head, she wore that dazed, flushed look that always gratified him to the core.

"Plans should change, not you. You're perfect," he said with a pointed glance. He pulled her toward the front door.

Once they were outside walking south on the inner drive, he didn't even bother to button the coat he wore. "It must be in the forties. It's even warmer than it was yesterday," he said to Eleanor.

"I didn't get a chance to ask you: how is your brother?"

"He's okay. He left for New York this morning. It wasn't anything life-threatening that was bugging him. Life-altering, maybe," he added under his breath.

He saw her questioning glance and explained about his playboy big brother falling hard for a woman, and being pretty torn up by it.

"He's forty-three years old and never been in love before?" Eleanor asked after he'd finished.

"I know. Hard to believe, but true."

"That's a really long time to go without ever being in love," she mused. He studied her profile as they crossed Division Street. What was she thinking? He opened his mouth, intending to ask her how old she was, and if she'd ever "fallen" yet. But she cut him off.

"Oh look. They have the lights up," she said, referring to the Christmas lights on all the trees lining the shopping district on Michigan Avenue.

"They've had them up for at least a week," he said, both relieved and irritated by her changing the subject. Why did he feel compelled to ask her such an intimate question? It was the kind of topic he usually avoided with women. Her wistful smile snagged his full attention.

"I love Christmas in the city. I usually walk over for the lighting parade," she said, referring to the annual event that inaugurated the beginning of the holiday season.

"How come you didn't this year?"

A shadow fell over her face. "Too busy, I guess. And my work is in the opposite direction, so I just hadn't noticed they'd decorated already. I missed it."

"I would have thought a fashionista like you treaded a beaten a path to Michigan Avenue."

"Fashionista? Oh, well I guess I do like clothes."

"For their performance value?" he asked quietly, casting a sideways glance her way.

She gave a small grin. "I know that's what *you* like my clothes for. Are your offices in the Loop?" she asked him.

"Yeah, on South Wacker Drive," he replied, highly aware she'd changed the subject yet again. He reached for her hand. It seemed like a natural thing to do on his part, but she gave him a startled glance at the familiar gesture.

"What? I can't hold your hand? After everything we've been through?" he teased her.

"No. I mean . . . of course you can," she muttered, flustered. It was dark out, but the streetlights gave off enough luminescence for him to see that she blushed. She'd given him mind-blowing displays of exhibitionism. They'd had scorching sex, not once, but several times, and by all available evidence, she'd loved every bit of it.

But she'd started and blushed when he held her hand.

They paused with half a dozen other pedestrians at the light on Oak Street. He leaned down and spoke quietly near her ear. "I'm going to figure you out, Eleanor."

Her big eyes looked anxious when she looked up at him. *Alarmed?*

"What do you mean? What's to figure out?"

He frowned down at her. "*Some* kind of mystery," he muttered darkly before the light changed, and he pulled her out into the street.

Eleanor's heart had started charging when Trey had said matter-of-factly near her ear that he planned to figure out the mystery of her. Why had she broken the role? She should have dressed more seductively and put on some makeup before they went out. She'd had the chance.

The truth was, she'd grown hopeful there in the condo. He'd seemed attracted to her, even when she'd been sweaty and disheveled. She'd given in to a romantic notion that maybe, just *maybe*, he'd like her without all the theatrics.

And that's a pretty dangerous hope to be having, isn't it?

That's not what this thing with Trey was supposed to be about, what is? No, it was supposed to be about taking that greedy bite out of life she'd promised herself she'd take following Caddy's death. Still, it was only a matter of time before he figured out she was nowhere near as daring and bold as she'd pretended to be to get his attention. Sometimes, she thought he *already* knew. Part of her expected him to call her out at any second and walk away for good.

She glanced over at him furtively as they walked, and he caught her looking. His grin melted her insides. It was the kind of smile that just made you want to let go and relish the moment. Jimmy had been right. She needed to stop overthinking this.

They made their way down a crowded Michigan Avenue, Eleanor absorbing the pretty holiday scene. When she'd realized earlier that the lights and Christmas decorations were up already, a feeling of sadness had swept through her for a moment. She, Caddy and Caddy's best friend, Sandra Banks, who lived nearby on Oak Street, had a tradition of attending the Christmas lighting parade every year. Afterward, they'd drop in on a few stores and then cap off their festive evening with a drink at the Four Seasons bar. It'd been weird, seeing the street all cheerily lit up. It'd been a harsh reminder that life went on, with or without Caddy.

With or without *her*—Eleanor.

The bustling, festive mood on the street quickly dissolved her melancholy. That, and the man at her side. Tourists and locals flocked the sidewalks and poured in and out of the stores, taking advantage of early Christmas sales and the extended holiday weekend. It seemed strange for her, to be out in public, walking hand in hand with such a handsome, exciting man.

Strange and wonderful.

She'd been startled when he'd grabbed her hand earlier. Holding hands in public seemed so sweet. Romantic. Innocent. She'd have thought he wasn't interested in such a vanilla display, but she'd been thrilled he was. She recalled what he'd said about being a basic Midwestern boy at heart. Could it be true?

Then she remembered that the very hand that grasped hers so innocently that very moment had previously spanked her ass until it burned hot last night and worked explosive magic between her legs. Arousal flashed through her at the mere memory.

No, Trey was anything but a simple farm boy.

A horde of rowdy teenage girls swarmed against them, causing them to break hands and go around them. Trey was so tall, it was easy to see his head above the crowd. She returned his grin when they joined up again, captivated by his gleaming blue eyes. Her hand went out, and his was there, ready to grasp it. She ducked her chin, embarrassed at the flood of pleasure that went through her from the simple act of holding his hand in public. If she didn't watch it, he was going to recognize that she was as giggly and goofy as those teenage girls they'd just passed, and then where would she be?

As they neared the Chicago River, a harsh wind whisked down Michigan Avenue. She shivered, and Trey noticed. He herded her inside to the atrium of a vertical mall.

"It's getting colder. Button up your coat. Do you like hot chocolate?"

She nodded eagerly. In truth, it was a favorite of both hers and Caddy's since they were kids.

"Whipped cream?"

"Oh yeah."

His grin told her he'd anticipated her answer. She usually compensated for her guilty pleasure by getting the sugar-free, low-fat hot cocoa, but it seemed like a very good night to splurge.

"Wait here, I'll be back in two seconds," he said before he sprung up a flight of stairs, his black coat billowing out behind his long body. When he returned, he held two hot chocolates in his hands. She couldn't repress her grin. They stood face-to-face, sipping the hot, creamy ambrosia for a few moments while shoppers streamed around them, each of them as lost in her or his own world as Eleanor was in Trey's eyes.

"I know of a nice, casual little Italian place close to where I work. It won't be so crowded down in the Loop," Trey said loudly over a bell-ringing Santa Claus once they'd returned to the sidewalk. "But you said you were hungry earlier, and it's still quite a way if we walk. Do you want to grab a cab?"

"I'll be fine. Let's walk there," she insisted. Was he kidding? *How could I not be fine, walking down the street with you, hand in hand?* She could walk all the way to central Illinois in the mood she was in, if he was by her side.

They approached the Michigan Avenue Bridge and she glanced down over the balustrade to the river. She saw a sign posted on the stairs leading down to the quay. "Oh look. This is the last weekend for the Water Taxi before it closes for the winter. I always wanted to take it, but never have."

"It has a drop-off close to the restaurant we're going to. I should warn you, though, it'll probably take longer than walking. It's slower than dirt, and they make every stop, even though no one is interested in being on the river in late November."

"But us?" she asked hopefully. She loved the sound of his low, rough laughter.

"But us," he agreed, pulling on her hand and leading her down the stairs.

They were indeed the only passengers on the large water taxi. Trey had been right. It was chillier on the water than up on the street, and people didn't even consider a boat for transportation this time of year.

They found refuge from the wind in the indoor portion on the upper deck as the water taxi pulled away from the quay. "Over here," Eleanor called out to him. "There's a heater on the floorboard. It's nice and warm."

They sat side by side on a polished wooden bench, Eleanor clutching her still-hot cup of chocolate to warm her hands. Windows surrounded them on all sides, making her feel like they glided in their own private atrium with a panoramic view of the glittering city all around them. She twisted her head and looked out the window over Trey's shoulder.

"Look at all the Christmas lights decorating the riverside. You never see them from the sidewalk or street," she said in a hushed tone as she untied her scarf.

"Yeah. It's a whole new world down here."

She looked into his face, thinking he'd put it exactly right. Funny, how being with him made the whole world seem like it was unfolding second by second, just for them.

Really, Eleanor? Stop being such a romantic idiot.

She really needed to watch it. It was dangerous, feeling so fanciful. So *happy*. But she couldn't help herself. The moment *was* magical.

Maybe he was.

"Do you like Christmas?" he asked her.

She nodded. She didn't want to ruin the moment by telling him that for the first time in her life, she was dreading Christmas this year. "Do you?"

"It's always been a pretty big deal at the Riordan farm," he said. "Mom goes nuts with the indoor decorations, and Dad goes crazy with the outdoor lights. I think their electric bill for December must be about equivalent to all of the other eleven months of the year."

They shared a smile.

"Thanks for coming on the water taxi with me. I don't know why I never took it before," she confessed, staring wistfully out the window. "I've lived in the city for ten years now, and never taken it."

"That's how it is sometimes, living in the city. You walk by so many things, and you hear of so many amazing events, but you don't get to most of them. Life gets in the way, and you never seem to take advantage like you should."

"Exactly." She sounded a little breathless, and realized it was because of the way he was watching her mouth narrowly. "But you sound like you've taken the water taxi before."

"I have." He set down his hot chocolate cup on the seat next to him. He reached for her cup and took it from her. "But I've never taken it with you."

Her breath caught at that. He calmly turned toward her and grasped her upper arms. "Come here," he urged.

She gasped in surprise, but soon divined what he wanted. She came down over his lap, her knees on the bench, facing him. Before she could question what he intended, he grabbed the ends of her scarf and pulled her to him. His mouth seized hers.

There was something about Trey's kiss. It was all or nothing. He ravished her with his mouth. There was no way for her to respond but wholesale.

She moaned shakily, melting against him. His lips were cold and firm, but his mouth was hot and tasted of sweet chocolate. His hands slid along the sides of her legs and up under her coat. He cupped her hips and then her ass. She felt her body quicken and heat. He urged her and she slid closer on his hard thighs, her arms encircling his neck, their kiss deepening. She flexed her hips, pressing her sex against his, eager for the sensation of him. He groaned roughly and squeezed her ass, bringing her closer yet.

His hands shifted between them and she realized he was unbuttoning her coat. She broke their kiss, her forehead pressed against his.

"What are you doing?" she whispered near his mouth.

"Being original."

"What?" she asked when his nudging hands pushed her back slightly. He grabbed for the hem of her sweater and lifted it over her breasts.

"I've never fooled around on a water taxi. You've never *been* on the water taxi." He brushed his fingertips over the top swells of her breasts. His expression turned serious. City lights reflected in his eyes as he watched himself touch her. His fingers slipped beneath the edge of her bra and pushed it down beneath her nipples. "By all logic, then, this is an original moment for both of us," he said before he leaned forward and sucked a nipple into his mouth.

Eleanor gasped at the shock of pleasure. She stared blankly out the window behind him as the nighttime landscape of the city rolled slowly by her vision. He tugged on her gently with a firm suction. She felt that pulling sensation all the way to her sex via some invisible cord. She wriggled in his lap, needy for pressure. Her fingers dug into his thick hair. She held him to her as he lashed at her nipple with a warm, deft tongue.

"Trey," she called plaintively, pressing her sex against the lengthening column of his cock.

He loosened his taut suction on the tip of her breast.

"I like the way you say my name," he said hoarsely, his breath rushing across her damp nipple.

"How do I say it?" she whispered.

"Kind of shaky. A little surprised . . . like you really mean it. That's what I like to think, anyway."

Her breath stuck in her lungs. Did he worry she wasn't sincere about her desire? He lifted his head and she saw the pinpricks of light in his night-darkened eyes.

"You *do* surprise me," she said with quite force.

"That's good. Because just about everything you do surprises me in the best kind of way."

For a few seconds, they just regarded each other in their private little world as the city slid by them. And then, still holding her breath in her lungs, Eleanor pushed herself back off his lap and slid down his shins until her knees hit the floor.

"What the hell are you doing?"

She reached under his coat and planted her hand between his thighs. "Surprising you," she whispered fervently. His face was shadowed, but she saw his smile slowly fade from his face as she moved her hand along the shaft of his cock where it pressed against his jeans. She wanted to crow when she felt him swell against her palm.

Greedier now, she rapidly unbuttoned the lower buttons on his wool coat and then started to attack the fly of his jeans. He suddenly caught one frantic hand and curled his fingers around the base of her skull, halting her. She looked up at him wide-eyed.

"Not now, Eleanor."

"Why not?" she wondered, because the idea of bringing him to climax with her mouth in this romantic setting had enflamed her. She wanted to hold him captive again, have him at her mercy. She saw his jaw clench tight.

"Because I don't want to feel pressured. I want to take my time and savor it the first time I watch my cock slide between those beautiful lips of yours."

"You don't want to do it in a public place, do you?" she asked breathlessly after she'd recovered from his illicit description.

"It's not that. We're all alone up here. I just don't want you to do *me* the first time in a rush or in bad lighting," he said matter-of-factly, reaching for her. He urged her to come back up on the bench. She sat next to him, their sides pressed tight. "I mean, I *do* want to. Trust me, I do," he amended gruffly. "It's just not the moment." She glanced at him hopefully, his addition going a long way to soothing the sting of hurt at being rejected for her impulsivity.

He shook his head. "You're something else, do you know that?"

He slipped his hand beneath her coat and cupped her rib cage. Her sweater was still bunched up above her breasts. His warm hand felt divine rubbing against prickly skin. Her nipples pulled tight. He dipped his head and spoke next to her lips.

"You love to be the one in control, don't you?"

"No, it's *not* that," she whispered. "You must know how much I liked it when you . . . did what you did last night."

His curving mouth caused something to tighten at her core. "I was hoping you liked it as much as you seemed like you did."

"Oh, I liked it, all right," she admitted dryly. "I'm not interested in being in control of this. I just . . . like to make you happy."

"And that means torturing me?" his hand slid over a breast. Her nipples were still exposed over the top of her bra. He squeezed the flesh, his fingertips rubbing the aching crests.

"No. It means exciting you," she whimpered.

"You *do* excite me. *You* like seeing the evidence of that. Don't lie, I know that turns you on, Eleanor."

She pressed her lips together in a stubborn gesture, but mostly she was focused on his hand massaging her breast. His mouth went hard when she refused to reply.

"If you really want to send me over the edge, then do what I say," he said. "*I want to tell you to suck me. I want to watch* while I spread those lips I've been fantasizing about nonstop. I want to control the pace. I want to come when I'm ready, not in a rush because we're pulling up to the dock. Okay?"

A quiver of anxious arousal went through her. "Okay."

She saw the flash of his white teeth. He circled his palm over her breast, applying a delicious, firm friction against her turgid nipple. "I can't believe you don't have any experience with sexually dominant men or being a submissive."

"Why?"

"Because," he murmured, plucking at her parted lips. "You're a natural submissive . . . unique, because you like to work me into a frenzy . . . but still a sexual submissive. In the end, you are."

"I don't know," she whispered doubtfully, distracted by his firm, warm lips.

"I do. Hold up both your breasts for me. Push them together."

She did it without pause. She cupped them, plumping them together. Her forefinger hooked the edge of her bra and pulled it down an inch, fully exposing her thrusting, sensitive nipples.

"*Very* nice," Trey murmured appreciatively. He pushed his hand between her clamped thighs and dipped his head.

FOURTEEN

His warm, suctioning mouth, lashing tongue and rubbing hand made every nerve in her body go on high alert. Her fingers delved into his hair.

He lifted his head, the hand between her legs pausing on her aching flesh.

"I said to hold up your breasts for me."

She made a frustrated sound, but cupped her breasts for him again in an offering. He resumed his feasting, his hand moving again between her thighs. He stroked her extra firm there, as if he knew he needed to amplify his usual force due to the extra covering of her jeans and panties. His occasional rough groan and her soft gasps of pleasure twined with the lulling sound of the boat's chugging engine. He clearly was as expert stimulating a woman above the pants as he was under them. It was hard to argue with the results. She stared out the far windows at the sparkling black river and the cars zipping down Lower Wacker in the distance, feeling her body rising to a low boil.

He lifted his head, his mouth making an erotic, wet suctioning sound as her nipple popped out of his mouth. "Push them closer together," he demanded starkly, just inches from her aching breasts.

Eleanor complied. Then his mouth was everywhere, licking and sucking at both nipples at once. She cried out shakily, her hands automatically doing what her body craved, pushing the crests even tighter together in order to feel as much of his ravenous, pleasure-giving mouth as possible. He rubbed her pussy harder and she found herself slipping beneath the surface of everyday, mundane reality.

She writhed in a hot, boiling sea of abandonment.

Trey lifted his head again. It took her sex-muddled brain a moment to recognize the unpleasant lack of his mouth. He was making her nipples a little sore with his greediness, but that slight ache mixed with her intense pleasure, spicing it.

Amplifying it.

She opened her eyes dazedly. She realized the boat was approaching the Washington Street Bridge.

"Unbutton your jeans and peel them down your ass a couple inches," he said.

"Huh?" she asked stupidly, her acute arousal making her as thick as an old tree stump.

"Unbutton your jeans and slip them down your hips a bit," he grated out. His lust-bitten tone cleared her brain a little. She hastened to follow his instructions, ripping open her button fly and wiggling her hips to lower her jeans some.

"That's fine," he said tensely. "Hold up your breasts again."

She presented her breasts to him, her breath sticking in her lungs at the sensation of his long fingers burrowing beneath the waistband of her panties. At the same moment that he slid the ridge of his finger against her slippery clit, he fastened on a nipple.

Her eyes sprung wide.

"Oh no. Oh *God*." Her entire body coiled tight and quaked. She slipped down in the seat, instinctively raising her pelvis to the heaven of his stroking fingers. His hand moved firmly between her legs. Insistently. She pushed her breasts tight together and felt his hot mouth drawing on both her nipples at once, then the cool air, and then his whipping tongue.

Oh, it hurt.

It felt divine.

She bucked her hips against his hand. She stared past his lowered head. Later, she recalled seeing the lit-up opera house as if in a fever dream. Then his shadow rose to block it out. With his free hand, he cupped her hip and firmed her against the seat.

"Stop squirming around, baby."

She moaned in anguish, her mouth hanging open. His entire arm powered his movements, rubbing subtly but forcefully between her legs. He kept her immobile while he stirred her into a frenzy. She made a choked, helpless sound.

"Are you going to come?"

She just bobbed her head once, unable to speak as she came face-to-face with a towering wave of orgasm.

"Let me feel it, then."

She heard him through a dull roar. He shifted his hand, plunging a finger into her slit, replacing his forefinger on her clit with his thumb. Just as orgasm blasted through her, he covered her mouth with his, eating her desperate cries as pleasure pulsed through her body.

She came back to herself at the sensation of him kissing her mouth hungrily. She inhaled shakily, trying to gain her bearings, but finding it extremely difficult with her nerves still zinging in the aftermath. Around Trey's head, she made out the lights from the skyscrapers on the far bank of the river.

The water taxi was at a standstill.

"All off at Monroe. This is the last stop!"

She started in shock at the sound of the man's voice bellowing from below. It'd been the boat captain.

She instinctively jerked the lapels of her coat over her tingling breasts.

"Slow down," Trey said, his finger still inserted in her.

She blinked at the sound of his voice. He sounded quiet, but she heard the edge of his arousal.

"He's not coming up two flights to get rid of us. Not in a hurry, he's not. Did you get a good look at him when we boarded?"

Eleanor briefly recalled the older, stout man who had taken their fare. "But we should—"

"Shhh," he hissed, and she saw a gleam of determination in his eyes. He withdrew from her. The next thing she knew, he was pressing his fingertips against her lips. She instinctively parted for him. He slid across her tongue, holding her stare. She whimpered and closed around him.

His fingers were thickly lubricated with her juices.

"Suck, Eleanor."

She did what he demanded without thought, tasting her essence for the first time. He made a low, rough sound of aroused satisfaction in his throat. Before she could divine his intent, he withdrew his fingers. She watched in wonder while he dipped the same two fingers into his mouth. Then he kissed her, hard and thorough, sharing the residue of her pleasure.

The pilot shouted again, this time sounding closer. And more annoyed.

He stood abruptly, startling her from her sex-drugged state. He grabbed her hands and helped her stand, immediately jerking up her jeans. In the distance, she heard a slow, heavy tread on the stairs. She hurried to assist him. He just continued to help her adjust her clothing, his actions methodical, but not frantic like hers were. The hard slant to his mouth gave her the impression that any harsh words the boat pilot might hurl at them for their truancy would bounce straight off him. He'd gotten what he wanted.

And he was far from sorry.

She seemed distracted during dinner. If he'd ever thought that about other women he'd been out with before, that would have been a negative. What guy wanted to be out with a preoccupied woman? But somehow, Eleanor even made distraction fascinating.

Perhaps *distracted* wasn't the right word. She seemed dazed, but happy. He liked to think that small smile she wore and the shine in her limpid eyes had something to do with him. He was sure the rosy color of her cheeks and lips related to him, or at least what he'd done to her on the water taxi. Heat expanded in him at the memory. He watched through a narrow-eyed stare as she lifted a glass of wine to pink, slightly puffy lips and tipped the red liquid between them, her stare trained on him over the glass. He'd kissed the hell out of those lips on the taxi.

Before the night was over, he planned to ravage them even more. Maybe *that* prospect was what was distracting him the most.

It took him a moment to realize that he'd been thinking of them being on a date, even though he'd established from the first he wasn't interested in getting involved in a relationship. When had that shift occurred?

And what would Eleanor think of it? He found himself wanting both to know the answer to that, and dreading it at once.

"What are you frowning about?" she asked him amusedly.

He blinked. "Nothing. You're not eating very much," he said, never breaking their stare across the candlelit table. She'd ordered a salad and a side dish of fettuccine. She'd plucked at the salad ineffectively while her gaze skittered around the restaurant, and then frequently landed on him and stuck. The fettuccine hadn't been touched. If he'd had to guess, he'd say she felt nervous about them staring at each other like moony human versions of Lady and the Tramp, and forced herself to look away from him. He, also, typically disliked displays of lovesick infatuation.

So he couldn't figure out why he kept getting annoyed every time she ripped her stare off him, like she did now.

"You haven't eaten much either," she observed, nodding at his half-eaten plate of chicken Parmesan. He liked the sound of her voice: low and a little husky. Sexy as hell. "I guess we weren't as hungry as we thought we were."

"Not for food, maybe."

She rolled her eyes at his lame joke, but it was her curving, lush mouth he focused on. He pushed his plate back and put his elbows at the edge of the table, leaning forward slightly.

"Why are *you* so preoccupied?" he asked.

She set down her fork and took a drink of water. "I guess I was thinking about . . ."

She trailed off, biting her lower lip.

"The water taxi?"

She laughed and the color in her cheeks deepened. "Well yeah, obviously." They shared a laugh. He had a strong urge to go over to her side of the table, push her down on the booth cushions and ravage her like an animal. Her bee-stung lips alone were turning him into a wolf, but add in the sparkle of her big eyes, and her delicate, pretty face, and the fullness of her breasts behind her sweater and the memory of how sweet her mouth was, or the incredible responsiveness of her nipples beneath his tongue and . . .

Well, it was a wonder he could even go through the motions of being a civilized man in a restaurant.

"Go on. You were thinking about something else, right?" he prompted her.

"I was thinking about your bad luck with women and how you were taking a break from them." Her gaze jumped up to his and then returned to her picked-over salad. "I mean . . . before all this."

"Before you walked into that coffee shop, you mean?"

"I guess. It's just—"

She cut herself off and swallowed thickly.

"What, Eleanor?" he persisted, her obvious trepidation on the topic making him even more curious.

"Well . . . it's . . . the windows. I mean, I've only seen you through them seven, maybe eight, times over the past year or so. It's not like I was spying on you every night or something. Recently, you've been alone, of course. And usually, your curtains were closed . . ."

"Yeah, okay," he prompted when she faded off yet again. He wasn't exactly comfortable with the topic of her having watched him having sex with other women, but it *was* part of Eleanor's story. He accepted that she had a proclivity for voyeurism, even if he was far fonder of her bent for exhibitionism. When she exhibited for *him*, at least.

"Well, it's just . . . the most I saw you take a woman to bed was twice."

"And you're wondering if I'm even capable of monogamy, is that it?" he asked her dryly, sitting back in the booth.

"No. I'm wondering, given your track record, if a long-term exclusive relationship is even something you're *really* interested in, or you just *think* you are because you keep running into women who try to manipulate you. And when they show their true colors, you have a ready excuse to . . ."

"Dump them?" he asked when she faded off.

She nodded.

"So you *do* think all my problems with women are down to me."

"No, I wasn't trying to make it black-and-white. Things like this are usually a lot more complicated than that."

He shrugged and tossed his napkin on the table. "Maybe you're right. That's one of the things I'm trying to figure out. But the fact of the matter is, honesty *is* important to me. Do you know why I broke up with my last girlfriend?"

"Alessandra, you mean?"

"No. There was someone after Alessandra. Jamie. *She* was the last straw."

"Oh," she mouthed before she cleared her throat. "I'm a little scared to ask. What did Jamie do?"

"I caught her poking holes in my condom supply with a pin."

She blanched and leaned back in her seat. She looked genuinely appalled . . . maybe even a little sick, and Trey didn't think it was an act.

"That's *despicable*."

He shrugged his agreement and took a sip of his water.

"I'm not surprised you swore off women," she said. He glanced up and met her stare. "I'm shocked you're willing to be with me, to be honest."

"So am I, a little. But the whole thing with you, the entire setup . . . it felt different than any time before," he admitted slowly.

"Because I was so bald-faced about it all?"

"Maybe."

He saw her throat convulse as she swallowed.

"Usually, when I find out that a woman is a liar, it turns me off. I can't see her in the same light. But maybe that *is* an excuse for me to bail."

"I hardly think you needed an excuse to cut all ties, in Jamie's case."

"Yeah, but Jamie was the exception. Most women aren't that blatant. Like I said before, maybe I'm the one who is encouraging them to be underhanded, because I'm too distracted by other things. Eleanor? What's wrong?" he demanded when she made a face he couldn't quite interpret.

"So you want a woman to be completely honest about her motivations. If she told you up front that she wanted a serious, long-term, monogamous relationship with you, you'd be happy about it?"

"You and my brother should get together. He told me something similar yesterday. No, like I've said. I'm willing to take some of the blame. Maybe I should just accept that all I'm interested in is sex when it comes to women." He paused. "But the thing is," he added slowly, "I'd be lying."

"You would be?" she asked in a hushed tone.

He grimaced. "A few months ago, my human resources manager had one of those inspirational speakers come in for a day seminar for the staff. I popped in for a few hours of her talk in the afternoon. For a motivational exercise, she was having people write out two versions of their obituaries."

"Obituaries?"

"Yeah. One version was supposed to be what it might read like if you died today. The other version is what you hoped it would be ideally."

"That sounds like it could be pretty interesting."

"It was pretty enlightening, that's for sure. For one thing, it annoyed the crap out of me."

Her eyebrows arched in a question.

"I couldn't sleep because I kept thinking about it. The thing was, in the professional arena, I was right where I wanted to be. No regrets."

"You're light-years beyond most people your age in that arena," she said.

"Thanks. But my point is, in the personal and family categories,

I was pretty damn skimpy. It just brought it all home. I *do* want what my parents have, and what my sister and my brother-in-law have. Someday. Actually, I was relieved as hell when I heard Kevin had fallen hard for someone last night. I was beginning to wonder if the male Riordans in this generation were born with a faulty gene or something."

She'd set down her fork. She was listening to him with focused intent, her eyes shimmering in the soft lighting. "And that's definitely what you want too?"

"I've started to think so, anyway," he admitted honestly. "I just don't know how to go about achieving it. I'm not so sure I get what women want. Or worse, if I'm remotely able to give it. That's what I was trying to figure out when I went off dating. And yet here we sit."

She started slightly.

"What's that supposed to mean?"

He shrugged. "I was just thinking before, this feels an awful lot like a date. Dinner. Wine. Conversation. Candlelight. Is that okay with you?" he asked her, studying her reaction closely.

"Of course."

"Because . . . that's not what we specified from the first, is it?"

"No, it's not," she agreed, sounding breathless. He'd pushed her too far. She was going along with the conversation, but he was *definitely* making her nervous.

"Jesus, we're a pair," he muttered under his breath.

"What do you mean?"

"I'm not sure if I've got what it takes for the long haul and you prefer things at a safe distance. Like—from a building away?"

She dropped her hand on the table with a thump. "Is that what you think? That I enjoy"—she hesitated—"*exhibitionism* because I'm afraid of being close to someone?"

"The thought has occurred," he replied bluntly. He felt a little guilty at her stunned—or was it hurt?—expression. "Don't look like that, Eleanor. So what if we have intimacy issues? They say most of the population does."

Her lips parted in amazement. "*Intimacy* issues? Me? I don't have intimacy issues."

"*Really?*" he asked, unable to disguise his disbelief and—face it—a little anger. She turned him into an animal with her sexy dances, but it also drove him crazy that she liked seducing him from a distance. For a few seconds, he thought he'd gone too far with his sarcasm. She looked like someone had just taken a swipe at her.

But then she recovered. She shook her head and laughed raggedly.

"*What?*" he asked.

"It's just so *weird* . . . having this conversation with you, hearing you say that you fantasize about settling down. That you grapple with intimacy issues—"

"Why is it weird? Do you think I'm too stupid to have an existential crisis?"

"No." She threw him an Eleanor glare. "You're obviously brilliant. It's just . . . you're so different than what I thought you'd be."

"Am I disappointing you, Eleanor? Because the thing is, it's pretty hard to actually know someone when your entire idea of them comes from either the Internet or spying on them from the building next door."

For a few seconds, the silence between them seemed to ring in his ears. Then her eyes flashed fire. She leaned forward.

"Do you think I'm being prejudiced about you? Is that it? Well fine. Because you've been doing your fair share of being prejudiced

when it comes to *me* too. I'm not some cold, controlling bitch. I
don't always like things at a distance. I *like* that you're struggling
with these issues. I mean, I don't *like* to see you're suffering," she
muttered, rolling her eyes in frustration at expressing herself, "but
I like you better as a person. You seem more . . . more *human*."

"I'm all too human when it comes to you."

She started, looking as surprised by his comment as he was by
saying it. God, she made him nuts sometimes. He reached across
the table and snatched her hand. She looked startled at his action.
For some reason, all the irritation drained out of him. He shook
his head and smiled in disbelief.

"Jesus. When are you going to get used to me holding your
hand?"

"I don't know." Her annoyance seemed to evaporate as quickly
as his had. A smile flickered across her beautiful mouth. "It's hard
to get used to something so . . . so . . . *nice*."

He squeezed her hand at that little, potent compliment. She
confused the hell out of him. She could be so skittish at times, so
bold at others, so edgy, and sometimes . . . so sweet. So giving. "I
don't have all the answers," he said quietly. "I don't pretend to.
That's why I was taking this time off and trying to figure things
out."

"That's why I brought it all up again just now," she admitted,
leaning forward, her expression earnest. "I'm just not saying
things right. I *want* to . . ." She swallowed thickly. "Spend time
with you. Very much. But I don't want to distract you from your
mission. I'm starting to feel really selfish, knowing that I am."

"You're not. Don't worry about it. I can take care of myself."

"Okay," she said breathlessly.

Their stares held until the waiter arrived, asking if they wanted
coffee or dessert. Eleanor shook her head once, never taking her
gaze off him. His nerves prickled with awareness of her. Acute

anticipation coiled inside him. He handed his credit card to the
waiter, eager to be finished with dinner.

Very eager.

"They say fantasy and reality rarely intermingle," he said
gruffly once the waiter was gone.

"What makes you say that?" she asked softly.

"It's just that in your case, they do. Mingle, I mean." He saw
her pulse leap at her throat and knew she was caught in the same
spell as he was. "You've basically been a fantasy come to life for
me ever since I saw you walk into that coffee house," he told her
bluntly.

"You mean a sexual fantasy?"

He nodded. "When I saw you in that window . . . you made
fantasy reality. It was like magic."

She didn't reply, just stared at him with huge, glistening eyes.

"Is it okay if I'm honest right now?"

She nodded.

"It's driving me crazy, sitting across this table from you and
not being able to touch you more."

She blinked. "You really *do* like honesty."

"Is that okay?"

She nodded. He liked the way she looked a little flummoxed,
but pleased. She peered up at him from beneath long lashes. *There
it was. In that single look was the entire paradox of Eleanor: sweet*
and curious; delectably, outrageously erotic all at once. He leaned
forward and spoke to her quietly.

"I want to get you back home the quickest way possible. I've
got some plans for you, Eleanor."

"Like what?" she whispered.

"You've shown me how incredible you are in putting on a show
for me when I'm in the building next door. How do you think
you'd do if I was in the same room with you? How do you think

you'll like it knowing full well what you're going to get when the performance is finished?"

She didn't really get a chance to respond to his loaded questions. The waiter came, and Trey took care of the bill. Then he stood and extended his hand to her. All the while, his questions kept replaying in her head, mounting her anxiety and excitement.

Because the thing was: she *was* intimidated by his proposed plan. Very. Despite her earlier denial, she now realized there was something about him being at a distance that gave her courage during her dances. She'd been able to plan everything in the past. Did that mean what he'd said tonight was true? She needed to be in the driver's seat?

That she had *intimacy* issues?

She didn't think she could lose herself to the extent that she did when he was in the building next door, and she could imagine him a hapless near stranger. But that wasn't fair to Trey anymore, was it? For her to continue envisioning him as a distant, unobtainable object to be manipulated for her sexual fantasies?

Fair or not, her mind went blank with anxiety when she tried to imagine what it'd be like to perform with him right there in front of her.

They got a cab on Monroe Street. Trey held the door open for her and then climbed in after her. Eleanor opened her mouth to tell the cab driver her address, but then Trey gave his address in a brisk tone, overriding her. A hand seemed to seize at her heart. He wanted her to exhibit herself directly in front of him, to titillate him sexually, all within the relatively unfamiliar territory of *his* home, not hers?

Once he'd settled beside her, he grabbed her hand and placed it on top of his coat-draped thigh, the gesture amplifying her already acute awareness of him and her mounting anxiety. What if she froze with the startling spotlight of his stare directly upon her? She was going to get stage fright, balk and make a fool of herself.

At one point, she noticed he leaned toward her and opened his mouth as if to say something to her, but then glanced uneasily toward the front seat and the cabdriver. There was no separator between the back and front of the cab. He shut his mouth and stared straight ahead.

He didn't really speak again until they were on the elevator in his building. By that time, she was spinning in a cyclone of anxiety.

"What's wrong?" he asked.

She started. "Nothing."

"You've looked skittish ever since I said I had plans for you. Do you not want to fool around?" he asked very quietly.

"It's not that."

"Then what *is* it? Eleanor?" he added when she glanced everywhere in the elevator car but at his face. The door opened into his penthouse. She got off before him. He caught her arm in the entryway, urging her to turn and face him.

"What is it? Tell me," he demanded.

Mortification struck her, but she couldn't think of anything else to say but the truth. "It's not as easy for me as you're making it out to be."

His brow creased in puzzlement. "What do you mean?"

"I don't know! Maybe you're right. Maybe I *do* like to be in control of it . . . *I* choose the music, *I* pick what I wear, *I* decide when I begin—"

"Okay, fine. I had no idea it was such a big deal for you. We don't have to, it was just an idea I had," he insisted. "I didn't mean to take away your control."

"You don't understand. It's not that I don't want to have sex,

I *do*. But I don't have any clothes here. I don't have any . . . you know . . ." She was very aware that her cheeks were burning, but there was no help for it. "Props," she finished.

"Props?" His face went carefully blank. "You mean like the fans?"

She nodded.

"I suppose you have whole closets full of props for your dances?"

"*No,*" she scolded, hearing the hint of sarcasm in his tone. He was imagining her performing sexually for a long line of men. "I'm not a professional stripper. I'm not a whore either," she defended heatedly.

He blanched. "Jesus, Eleanor, I know that."

"*Do* you?" She'd never wanted to set the record straight more than at that moment. It seemed that every minute she spent with him, she dug herself a deeper hole.

"Yes," he grated out.

He looked angry. She swallowed thickly, straining to get ahold of herself. "The thing of it is, I have more options than I do over here," she said in shaky frustration. She glanced down at her jeans and walking boots. "Look what I'm wearing. It's not *sexy*." She stalked through his entryway into his large living room, having difficulty meeting his slightly incredulous expression at the moment.

"You're wrong. You look fantastic. Look how crazy you've been making me all evening," he said from behind her. She spun around, exasperated.

"You're missing the point. This isn't a *striptease* outfit!"

"Okay," he said, holding up his hands in a surrender gesture. "We'll skip it, then. Do you want to watch a movie or something?"

"*No,*" she growled, frustrated. "I want to . . . you know. Make you feel good like you did me . . . on the water taxi."

"Okay," he said slowly, clearly wary about what to say next, worried he'd step on another mine. "Maybe we should go over to your place, where you feel more in control."

"It's not just that. I've never really *done* it while someone was in the same room as me," she said, frustrated by her inability to put concisely into words her dilemma. It wasn't a topic she was used to discussing. She was a little alarmed at how difficult she was finding it to communicate her discomfort. She did a double take when she saw his speculative, pleased expression and reflected back on what she'd just said. "You *like* that, don't you? That I've never done a striptease in close proximity to someone?" she asked him in amazement.

He shrugged. "I do like the path not taken. At least with you I do. Or so it would seem," he added wryly.

She stared for a moment, her attention entirely caught by his small, sexy grin.

"Look, I'm sorry I don't understand all the details and nuances about your preferences yet. It's not that I don't want to learn," he said quietly, taking a step toward her.

"Thanks for that," she whispered. She replayed their conversation in her head and winced in regret. "That means a lot to me. Really. I'm sorry for seeming so . . . hysterical about it. I'm not sure how to put how I feel about it into words."

"You don't seem hysterical," he muttered, smoothing back a strand of hair at her temple. Her skin tingled beneath his touch. "I'm not getting you, and it's making you nervous. Right?"

She nodded. "I told you on the boat: it's not that I'm a control freak when it comes to sex," she hastened to say. "I want to turn you on. The control I want is in service. To you."

His fingers paused just above her ear. *There.* She'd said it right. Hadn't she?

His expression went rigid. He suddenly seemed much closer

than he had before, his hovering face just inches away from her upturned one. She saw the gleam in his blue eyes.

"That's one hell of a sweet thing to say."

She smiled tremulously, warmth rushing through her. He'd understood her. He opened his hand along the side of her head and brushed his lips against hers. She sighed and stepped closer, placing her palms facedown on his chest.

"I tell you what. We could either go over to your place. Or . . ."

"Or?" she wondered breathlessly.

"I could give you complete control over my bedroom. It'll be your stage to set as you like," he said quietly, nipping at her lower lip. "I'll even open up my closets and cupboards for you for props. Anything in them is yours to use."

"Really? You'd allow that?"

He grabbed her hand and led her in the direction of the hall-way. "Sure, I'm willing to sacrifice for the benefit of the arts."

She laughed. He turned and smiled over his shoulder. Her heart gave a little jump. God, he was sexy.

"I'll show you around a little, and then leave you to it. How would that be? If you don't find what you need to inspire you, we could go to your place." They crossed the threshold into his bed-room suite and he turned on a light. He halted next to the bed and turned toward her. She glanced around the luxurious, mas-culine bedroom and seating area.

"I'm not sure I'll find much of use in a man's room."

"Maybe not as far as clothes, but you're welcome to whatever is here." He led her over to a door. They entered an enormous walk-in closet, including shelving and rows upon rows of hung clothing.

"Jeez, and you called me a fashionista," she murmured amusedly, running a hand admiringly over the shoulders of a row of neatly hung suits.

"Use what you like. And as far as props, well, I might have some inspiration over here. If you're feeling particularly bold, that is." There was something she heard in his voice that made her arch her brows. He walked out of the closet and over to a large armoire in the seating area. He opened the cupboard. "I've got a Techilicious in here—"

"Techilicious," she exclaimed in excitement, poking her head around his back to peer into the cupboard. "*Oh*, it's a stereo system." He grinned at her obvious disappointment.

"What'd you *think* it was going to be?"

"I don't know," she mumbled, blushing. She frowned at his widening grin, and then couldn't stop smiling back when she noticed the humor dancing in his blue eyes. "It sounded kind of racy: *Techilicious*. I thought maybe you kept something . . . naughty in here."

"*Oh,*" he said as if in sudden understanding. "Well I'd hate to disappoint you."

He slid open a deep drawer. Her eyes sprang wide. He didn't say anything while she looked into it and the nerve endings on her skin tingled and her breath stuck in her lungs. She saw several boxes of sex toys, more padded handcuffs and restraints, a black leather paddle and a crop with a slapper on one end and a leather flogger on the other. Heat rushed through her. Her heart started to drum in her ears.

"You really *are* kinky," she said, still staring into the drawer.

"Am I?" he asked, reaching up and cupping her jaw. He brushed his finger against her cheek, and she knew he felt her heat. "Don't be scared, Eleanor."

"I think maybe you *want* me to be."

He gently lifted her face until she met his stare. All traces of amusement had left his handsome face. "No. Never afraid, that's not what I want for you. But I'm going to be honest. I like when you're a *little* nervous, like right now. Your eyes look so beautiful. So sexy. God, I can't wait to look down at them when I put my—" He broke off when a thrill went through her, and she shuddered. "Shhh," he soothed. He brushed his thumb against her parted lips. Her lungs hitched and she inhaled his scent. "Mostly, *that's* what I want, Eleanor. I want you to be excited. I want to watch while whatever anxiety is there gets burned away by pleasure and lust."

He placed his opened hand on her throat. She swallowed thickly, knowing he felt her leaping pulse against his palm.

"Anything in a box is new, never been touched," he told her quietly after a pause. He nodded toward the drawer. "Whatever is in that purple bag has never been opened either. I'm not even sure what's all in there. I got it as a favor at a fancy unisex bachelorette party I was invited to at a club in London for Abigail Chasen."

"The hotel heiress?" Eleanor asked him breathlessly, peering at the foil magenta bag curiously. "Rumor has it she's pretty wild."

"Rumor is dead-on, in Abigail's case. Maybe you *should* check out what's in there," he said dryly.

"You and she didn't—"

"No, are you kidding? She married Gerald Sturgis, the lead singer from Easy Blood? Gerald and I were friends."

A chill passed through her. "But didn't Gerald Sturgis pass away recently?" she asked, studying his face in mounting concern. She wasn't super familiar with the punk rock band, but it seemed she'd seen something in the papers about the colorful, irreverent British rocker dying.

He nodded. She didn't see his sadness at that moment as much as sense it. "Yeah. Last spring of a drug overdose. Gerald was truly one of a kind. Easy Blood exploded on BandBook, and that's how I first met him. We weren't best friends or anything, but he was the kind of person who makes an impact on you. He didn't know shit about taking care of himself or thinking about much beyond the next second and a good time, but he was extremely talented. Always smiling. It still seems weird. He was so full of life."

"And then one day . . . gone," she whispered. "I'm really sorry, Trey." She realized Sturgis's abrupt death was probably one of the reasons he'd been plunged into an existential crisis, left wondering what his life meant. Sturgis and Trey were far from being the same, of course, but both of them had led a privileged and unrestrained existence. In many ways, she could imagine Trey viewing Sturgis as a kind of amplified, bigger version of what he—Trey— had been like in his youth.

"I don't want to give you the wrong impression," he said. "Gerald and I weren't super close. I only saw him maybe once or twice a year. In my business, I meet a *lot* of people, loads of big personalities, tons of talent. It comes with the territory. But Gerald wasn't just a work acquaintance. He was a friend. It hits deeper than you'd think, when it happens so unexpectedly like that."

"You're not giving me the wrong impression," she said softly. "He meant something to you. His death is part of why you're reexamining your life, isn't it?"

He nodded once.

He didn't say anything for a moment. She listened to her heartbeat thrum in her ears. Then she felt his fingertips caress her cheek.

"Talk about a mood spoiler. I'm sorry," he said.

"*Don't* be," she assured. She smiled up at him. He smiled back. The moment stretched. She swallowed back the ache in her throat.

"Would you . . . you rather not?" She waved anxiously at the opened drawer.

He blinked. "Oh, I'd *rather*, all right." Her smile widened at his adamancy. "Unless you would rather do something else?"

"No," she laughed. "I haven't changed my mind."

He looked a little relieved. "Good. Anyway, like I said, use anything in the room that you'd like. But you don't have to use any of the stuff in the drawer, Eleanor. It's your call. Speaking of calls, do you have your phone on you?"

She nodded, reaching for her back pocket. She handed her phone to him. He put in his number before handing it back to her.

"I'm going to go upstairs to the loft," he said quietly. "You get things the way you want them down here. Text me when you're ready, and I'll come down. And we'll begin. Does that sound good to you?"

She just nodded, too overwhelmed by his low, sexy voice, his smoky stare, his nearness and his scent to speak.

Trey played his guitar while he waited in the loft. But he was too preoccupied to get serious about any songwriting, too distracted with the idea of Eleanor down in his bedroom, touching his clothing, setting the scene . . . maybe (hopefully) selecting something from the cabinet. He kept replaying in his head how big her eyes had gotten when he'd shown her the contents of the drawer, how her flushed lips had parted. It was almost ludicrous, how much he was anticipating having his cock in her mouth while she looked up at him with those big, golden green eyes. Ever since he'd stopped her from going down on him earlier on the water taxi, he'd become obsessed with the idea. He wanted her at his mercy, as helpless to resist him as he was her.

He lifted his hand off the guitar strings and reached between his thighs, tugging at his erection and wincing. He glanced at his watch. She'd been down there alone for over half an hour now. What the hell was she doing, transforming his bedroom into the Chicago Theatre?

His phone buzzed on the table next to him. He jerked to attention, picking it up to read the new message.

Please don't be mad at me. I'm doing the best I can. Honest.
For now, if you want your show, you're going to have to look
out your bedroom window to get it.

He started. *What?* Had she *left* the penthouse while he was
sitting up here, smugly imagining he had everything under control?

He clamped his teeth together, realizing there was a photo
attached to her message. Knowing he'd probably regret it, but
unable to resist her, he opened it.

It took him a few seconds to realize that he probably looked
as wide-eyed and stunned as she had when he'd opened that
drawer downstairs.

Damn, she had a way of turning the tables.

He'd thought he'd talked her into performing for him, up close
and personal. He was willing to admit, he'd even selfishly enjoyed
that she appeared to be a little anxious at the prospect, because
she'd never done it before for another man.

But in typical Eleanor fashion, she'd snatched the reins from
him yet again.

It was an up-close photo of her face. In it, her eyes shone with
heat and just a tad bit of mischief. Her lips were pouty and parted.
She pressed the flaring crown of a dildo against her mouth, just
the tip touching her pink, wet tongue. His cock jumped at the
outrageous precision of the teasing photo. He'd never seen the
dildo before, so he suspected she'd raided Abigail's racy gift bag.

I should go straight over to her place and damn her little show.

He'd gratifyingly learned that evening he had access to her
place for a month, after all. Yeah. *That's* what he'd do.

But of course when he got to the bottom of the steps, his feet
didn't take him to the elevator. He found himself entering his
bedroom, his body already coiling tight in mixed irritation and
arousal in response to the torment he was about to receive.

Frowning furiously when he saw the empty room—part of him had been holding out hope she hadn't really left—he flipped out the lights and stalked over to the window. Almost immediately a lamp illuminated in Eleanor's condo in the distance.

He came to a halt when he saw her standing at the far side of the room. He was familiar with the room now. She waited near the bathroom door.

Despite the fact that she'd snuck out of his condo, she'd still borrowed from his wardrobe from her performance. She wore one of his button-down striped shirts, the white of the fabric shining brightly against her pale gold skin. In addition, she wore one of his black ties loosely around her neck and a leather belt cinched around her waist. His shirt fell to mid-thigh on her. Her long, sexy legs were bare.

She suddenly burst into motion, her long hair rippling back from her shoulders. He only caught a glimpse of her feet briefly before she neared the windows, but whether he'd seen them or not, he would have already known she wore heels just by the way she strutted so boldly. It was like her feet and legs became entranced every time she put on a pair of sexy boots or heels. He couldn't hear the music, of course, but just looking at her, he felt it. The music seemed to transform her into another person . . .

. . . Or fully into herself.

She planted her feet, long legs parted, and began her dance, swiveling her hips, outlining the supple curves of her body with her cupping hands. He sensed the driving beat with the precise pulse of her pelvis and limbs.

And the torment officially began.

She placed both hands on her belly and undulated her torso in the most erotic fashion, all the time taking several steps toward the window. Her hands moved up her rib cage, cupping her breasts, her fingers straining toward the V of the fabric between them and the buttons.

"Come on, Eleanor," he growled.

Her fingers flicked at the button, parting his shirt and revealing the inner swells of her breasts. No sooner had she done it than, with a little smile, she turned and started teasing him from that direction. He'd never seen a woman move her ass like Eleanor did. It was excruciating, the gyrating hips, the tight little pops of her butt, the movements designed to remind him of how well she moved when his cock was deep inside her.

She used her hands to mold the cloth of his shirt against her buttocks, but it wasn't enough. Gritting his teeth, he stepped closer to the window, straining to see beneath the cotton shirt. He'd never be able to wear that damn shirt again without a perennial erection.

Suddenly, his cinched black leather belt loosened and slipped down over her buttocks. Standing with her legs parted, she pulled the belt tight against her ass and shimmied shamelessly. His cock pulsed in aroused annoyance, as if it had a mind of its own, and was protesting about being kept from what it wanted. He instinctively clutched at his aching testicles, his fingers squeezing the shaft.

She shifted the black belt, using it to shift his shirt higher, wiggling her ass the entire time. She played him like that for a minute, dancing and maneuvering the belt until he would have sworn she'd done the dance a hundred times before, she was so fucking skilled at it.

Had she?

The two-word question cut through his enthrallment. He thought of how discombobulated she'd been in the hallway tonight, trying to explain to him her anxieties.

No. Somehow, he didn't think she *was* as practiced at all this as she came off as being at times.

He didn't have time to question the logic or likelihood of his fevered realization, or the flash of savage satisfaction that accompanied it. Eleanor *finally* revealed the bottom curves of her plump ass beneath the edge of his white shirt.

"God bless it, you have about one more minute, girl," he rasped, and his hand moved more strenuously between his thighs. She bent and slid the belt beneath her bare ass and started to jerk upward on the firm globes.

He hissed. That was the final straw. He started to back out of the room, unable to look away from the ridiculously erotic image she made, manipulating her gorgeous ass with the black belt. She stretched it tight now beneath her ass, making her flesh jump up and down as she gyrated to the music. Where the hell did she learn this stuff? It was outrageous. Abruptly, she released one side of the belt and it snapped below her buttocks. He saw her jump slightly, and knew the leather had stung her.

He froze.

Again, he was held hostage to her. He was strung tight as piano wire. He couldn't wait to see what else she was going to do with that belt.

A thought fractured his enthrallment.

Jesus . . . Had she taken that dildo from the photo with her to use in her dance, as well? If so, what torture did she have planned for him with *it*?

The thought gave him the motivation he needed. He turned grimly and headed over to the cabinet. He pulled out the magenta bag, in search of some of his own ammunition.

She jerked on the belt, gasping at the sting of leather flicking against her upper thighs. It stung, but her clit flared with pleasure. The burn quickly segued to a tingle and she found herself emboldened. Straightening, she lifted the tail of Trey's shirt seductively to her waist and doubled the belt in her hand. Swinging her hips to the beat of the loud music, she reached around her waist with the belt and swatted her gyrating ass.

Ooh, it felt good.

She lost herself to the mounting, increasingly familiar heat. Her swats on her naked ass and thighs weren't harsh, but they enlivened her nerves, making them prickle and burn. She ached, thinking of Trey watching her, imagining him boiling with want. It was unbearable. She couldn't take it anymore.

Still standing with her back to the window, she let the shirt fall partially down over her burning bottom. She slipped the belt between her thighs, pulling up on it from the front and back, using the leather strap to stimulate her wet sex. She moaned loudly, the pounding music and her racing blood spurring her onward. Her hips pushed her pussy against the tightly drawn leather. Her eyes fluttered closed as she tensed in excitement. She felt herself rising to orgasm. It felt divine, but she hadn't planned for this to be the climax of her dance.

A sound like a bullet going off fractured her bliss. She opened her eyelids, air hissing past her lips. The bedroom door had bounced against the wall as it opened forcefully. That had been the noise she'd heard. Trey strode around the foot of the bed, looking tense, irritated, magnificent . . .

Aroused as hell.

Before she knew what'd hit her, he reached around her with one hand, grasping her wrists. He urged her to straighten.

"Let go," he ordered tensely. Her fingers loosened, and he took the doubled-up belt from her. He slid the leather strap between her legs. She looked up at him, her breath coming erratically. His eyes appeared alight in his rigid face. The music continued to pulse around them, but it was as if they stood inside a vacuum. A roar started in her ears.

He reached up and ripped open the shirt she wore in one swift movement. She gasped, feeling falling buttons tap her legs and feet.

"Do you have any idea what the hell you're doing, Eleanor?" he seethed.

"That was *your* shirt," she exclaimed. "*I* didn't just ruin it."

"Screw the damn shirt," he muttered through a snarl. His gaze moved hungrily down the front of her naked body. He cupped a breast possessively, running his thumb over the nipple. Eleanor trembled, the gentleness of his caress following his terse shirt-ripping undoing her. He noticed her quivering at his touch. His stare jumped to her face.

"You can't stop yourself, can you?"

"Can't stop myself from what?" she whispered, unable to look away from his blazing eyes and moving lips. She experienced an overwhelming urge to press against his male body, to press him *into* her.

"Torturing me."

She felt something smooth and hard glide across her nipple. Her breath hitched when she realized it was the belt. She started to move into him.

"Stay still," he bit out.

She froze, recognizing not only the authority in his tone, but his edginess. A thrill coursed through her. She'd gotten to him.

Again.

"Get that witch's grin off your face, Eleanor."

Despite the fact that she saw his lips tilt ever so slightly in amusement, she responded to the flash of fire in his eyes. She wiped any traces of satisfaction from her expression. She'd forgotten her smugness in two seconds flat anyway. He looked down at her, holding her eyes in a trap, and began to slide the belt against the sides of her ribs, and then down over her belly. She was so pitched with excitement, it was like she was a sponge, absorbing every detail of him, soaking him up thirstily along with all the pleasure he gave her.

God, he was amazing.

She held her breath when the leather strap dipped lower. Her hips swayed slightly. "I told you to hold still," he said.

Her tensed facial muscles convulsed. Their gazes held for an excruciatingly exciting moment as he rubbed the leather loop against her labia. He looked between her legs, watching the belt slide against and between the slippery folds of her outer sex. She whimpered, her thigh muscles going tight. He lifted the belt and tapped the loop against her pussy several times.

She jumped and made a choking sound as arousal tore through her. His gaze flashed up to her face.

"Turn around," he said grimly.

"But—"

"Just do it, Eleanor."

She spun slowly, her heart in her throat. He lifted the tail of his shirt over her ass. She heard him groan behind her. He grasped a buttock.

"You made yourself pink. You're so bad. Aren't you?" he asked thickly as he massaged her ass lewdly. Suddenly, he flicked the loop of the belt against her bottom. She jumped and made a squeaking noise. The belt landed again, making her skin burn. She instinctively started to walk away, but he caught her upper arms, holding her in place. His hands slid down to her wrists. He grasped them together in one large hand at the small of her back, restraining her.

"You can dish it out, but you can't take it?" he asked her, and despite the roughness of his voice, she heard his amusement.

She flashed him a defiant glance over her shoulder. "I can take it," she assured.

"Good. Because you've been very, very bad, Eleanor. You're teasing is getting out of hand." Her heart jumped at that. "Lean forward, but only slightly. Pop your butt back. I *know* you know how to do that," he said sarcastically, referring to her favored dance movement. He grazed the looped belt against her buttocks gently, and she pushed back her tailbone several inches, presenting her bottom. He groaned roughly. He snapped the belt against her skin.

She whimpered and quivered. It stung, but in truth, he didn't strike her much harder than she'd been whipping herself during her striptease. She rested her chin on her shoulder, watching him fixedly and biting her lower lip. He lifted his hand and struck her ass with the belt several more times. He flipped his wrist as he did it, whisking the leather back and forth, from one side of the loop to the other, snapping the leather surely until her bottom seemed to radiate prickly heat and her legs grew shaky.

Once again, she was the focused target of his easy mastery in the bedroom, the way he positioned her with so much confidence and strength, the way he punished and pleasured her flesh with outrageous certainty. Watching his rigid face as he watched himself flick the leather strap against her ass aroused her unbearably. She was disappointed—actually *disappointed*—when he told her to turn around and face him. She followed his instructions, feeling the burn of her ass . . . the sizzle of her clit.

He arched his eyebrows. "Where did you put that dildo?" he asked her. Her gaze betrayed her, flickering to the table and chair at the left. He lifted his hand. The loop of the leather caressed the sensitive strip of skin just above her mons. Her quivering amplified. He gently tapped her labia with the belt, just over her clit. Air shot out of her lungs. She trembled uncontrollably.

He was killing her.

He hitched his chin toward the chair where she'd placed the dildo.

"Go and get it," he said.

She went to the chair and picked up the rubber cock. She repressed a frown as she walked back to him. A smile flickered across his mouth.

"You're disappointed, aren't you? You were planning to use it in your dance to torture me. You just hadn't gotten around to it yet, had you?"

She came to a halt several feet away from him and feigned a bright smile. "You wouldn't have liked that?" she asked, letting her fingers glide across the shaft of the dildo. She tugged firmly at the defined rim of the cockhead. Triumph raced through her when she saw how he watched with narrowed eyelids as she fondled the fake cock.

"I'm going to like *this* more. Come over here. Stand in front of me."

Her feet moved automatically at his tone, despite her show of defiance. He reached into his front jeans' pocket and removed what appeared to be a small jar. He opened it and dipped his finger into it.

"Oh," Eleanor gasped when he matter-of-factly reached between her legs and started rubbing a dollop of cream directly onto her clit. She shuddered at the unexpected jolt of pleasure. "What are you *doing*?"

"Stay still," he murmured. "It's a clit sensitizer."

She grasped mindlessly at his forearms, because even as he'd said it, she'd felt her nerves begin to sizzle and burn beneath his rubbing finger.

"God, you're nice and wet. You do love to tease, don't you? Or was it the belt on your ass that got you this hot?" he growled softly near her ear. She was too preoccupied with his rubbing finger to reply. If he kept it up, she'd be coming soon. "Eleanor?" he prodded more sharply when she didn't answer.

"Both," she managed.

"I thought so. Does it feel good?" he asked, referring to his rubbing finger.

She just stared at his chest blindly and nodded. He made a rough sound of satisfaction and dropped his hand.

"Hey—"

"Put these on," he cut off her protest, reaching into his back pocket. Much to her dazed amazement, he handed her what appeared to be a black pair of silk panties. She hesitated. "Don't worry. They're brand new, courtesy of Abigail Chasen. Take them, Eleanor."

She reached. Almost immediately, she felt the weight among the froth of the silk. She glanced at him, confused. He sunk his hand into his pocket yet again and held up a small, black mechanical device.

"They're vibrating panties. Time for you to take what you dish out, Eleanor."

FIFTEEN

Yes, she was an adorable, teasing little witch, but he'd had enough of her wrestling the control from him. He was so aroused, he had little sympathy for her when he made his proclamation and her eyes went wide in uncertainty and arousal. He watched her slide the panties over the black pumps she wore and up her long, toned legs. She still held the dildo, which made the sight even more distracting. He waited until she'd slid the underwear into place, and then stepped forward and reached between her thighs, making sure the inserted vibrator was in place for optimal stimulation. Her breathy whimper at his touch swelled his already ponderous erection.

He stepped back and met her stare. "Go down on your knees."

He saw her swallow thickly in the tense seconds that followed. For a few seconds, he wondered if she'd do it. She had to be the most uniquely sensual women he'd ever met, but she wasn't a typical submissive. She did surrender in the end, but she loved to get him as worked up as she could beforehand.

"Don't worry, baby," he said quietly. "It's going to be the best kind of torture for me, as well."

That helped, as he suspected it would. She'd meant what she'd said earlier. Her ultimate goal was to excite him, just as his was to ultimately excite her.

She slowly dropped to her knees in front of him. He ripped his gaze off the mouthwatering vision of her bare breasts heaving between the plackets of his shirt and located the buttons on the miniature remote he held. He hit a medium setting and looked up to gauge her reaction. She started slightly in her kneeling position, and then her lips parted. More color stained her cheeks. A dazed expression dawned on her pretty face. Her hips pulsed slightly forward in rhythm to the music.

"Is it . . ." She faded off in wonder, biting her lower lip and moaning.

Raw satisfaction swept through him at her fresh, unscripted reaction. It couldn't be clearer she'd never had the experience before. *Now* he had her where he wanted her. "Yes. It's sensitive to sound. It vibrates to the beat of the music. Gives whole new meaning to one of your dances, doesn't it? Now show me what you planned to do with the dildo," he ordered gruffly.

"What?"

"Show me what you were going to do with the dildo in your dance." He saw her wariness. He also saw the speculative gleam dawn in her gorgeous eyes as she looked up at him.

"Do it, Eleanor."

Her gaze dipped down to where his cock pressed against his jeans. He resisted a strong urge to stroke himself in front of her and instead turned up the power on the vibrator one notch. She whimpered, her entire body quaking subtly, her bare breasts trembling. Her nipples looked hard and incredibly edible.

She lifted the dildo to her mouth. Her hips jerked slightly, and then she swiveled them to both the beat of the vibrator and the music. He groaned.

She was killing him.

He watched her like a hawk as she began to lick the flaring head of the dildo. She lifted it slightly and trailed her tongue all the way down to the testicles. Her tongue was pink and wet and sinuous.

Raw arousal shot through him. He cupped his aching balls at the flagrantly erotic sight. "God, Eleanor."

He saw the spark in her eyes, and knew his response had emboldened her. She clamped her lips shut and pushed the dildo between them, spreading them wide. *Ah Christ.* He ripped open his button fly. His was about to burst. He watched, utterly enraptured as she slid the rubber cock into her mouth several inches and then pulled it back. She sucked hard. He could tell by the way her cheeks hollowed out. The dildo was shorter than his cock, but the diameter was similar. It was a concise, agonizing tease of what was to come.

He thrust his hand into his boxer briefs and fisted the shaft of his cock. He removed it from the fabric of his underwear, never taking his gaze from the vision of Eleanor sinking the dildo between her tightly pursed lips again.

"Faster," he insisted.

She began to plunge the rubber cock back and forth, her taut rhythm matching that of the driving dance music. He noticed she pulsed her hips against the panty vibrator in the same rhythm. He groaned and began to jack his cock to the same tempo.

After a moment, he released his heavy erection and stepped toward her. She made a shaky sound as he withdrew the dildo from her squeezing lips. Her wide-eyed stare up at him made his cock jump in the air. *This* was what he'd been anticipating so acutely. He palmed her jaw and traced the flagrant color in her cheeks with his thumb.

"Little witch," he said. He pushed the rubber cock between her flushed lips, back and forth, absorbing the erotic sight, enjoying the buildup so much the ache of arousal began to cut at him.

"I should blindfold you next time," he told her as he withdrew the dildo from her sucking mouth with an erotic popping sound. "Your eyes are going to make me come sooner than I want."

He dropped the dildo to the floor and stepped into her. Her eyes seemed to swallow up her face. He grasped his cock from below and trailed the head against her cheek.

"So hot," he murmured, utterly enthralled. "Part your lips, Eleanor."

She opened her mouth. He hit a button, turning the vibrator in the panties up to the highest level before he dropped the controller to the floor. He heard her disbelieving moan of pleasure before he pushed his cock between her lips and slid onto her tongue. She vibrated into his flesh. Pure pleasure snaked through him. He groaned roughly.

She sucked him deeper. He cupped her head gently and pulsed his hips, and for a moment, knew nothing but bliss. They worked together to get his cock a little deeper with each pass. He was glad when her eyelids drifted closed.

Her eyes alone were nearly as erotic as her soft, warm, squeezing mouth.

He cupped his balls while she sucked him, frustrated to encounter his underwear still partially covering them. Grimacing, he flexed back, sliding his cock from the heaven of her mouth. She opened her eyes, looking dazed and debauched and so damn beautiful. He kicked off his shoes and attacked his jeans, never taking his gaze off her the whole time. He realized as he stepped toward her, now completely nude, that she breathed in shallow gasps and her entire body shook very subtly. Realization struck.

"Are you about to come?" She looked just as incredulous as he sounded. He'd never used vibrating panties before. Apparently, he'd been missing out. Still, he was glad he'd discovered their potential with Eleanor. The eroticism of the moment was razor sharp.

"I don't know," she gasped dazedly. "It feels *good*."

He cursed and stepped into her. He slid his cock into her mouth. She moaned, and then closed around him like a vise. Her mouth was so pink and soft-looking, but damn, she was strong. He thrust, snarling. She was there to meet him, ducking her head, bobbing back and forth at a brisk pace. She took him eagerly, never balking. He could feel her heat. Her arousal. It fueled his hunger, until he couldn't tell where his need ended and hers began. He became aware of the near-constant trembling of her body. It didn't break, as it would if she were climaxing. It was a continuous quaking. She'd been pitched into an uncommon state of excitement.

So had he.

He cupped the back of her dipping head and thrust between her lips more forcefully. "Use your hand, Eleanor," he guided her.

Her squeezing hand joined in the urgent pace they set, jacking the base of his cock while he plunged into her mouth. He grimaced. God, it was *good*. He was going to come. She started to scream onto his cock, breaking their fluid, rapid pace.

"Eleanor?" he called tensely. A violent shudder went through her. He grabbed the base of his cock and withdrew, thinking he'd been too forceful. She pulled at him so hard with her mouth, his eyes crossed. He stared down at her, panting, the slick, ruddy head of his cock pressed against her parted lips. Her breath struck him in erratic bursts. She looked up at him, her eyes dazed and shining, her body shuddering as she climaxed.

It was the most erotic sight, bar none, he'd ever seen.

A shout burst out of his throat. He plunged into the heaven of her mouth again, desperate to be buried in her heat. He thrust rapidly and broke in orgasm. Because she was still climaxing, she hadn't really been ready for him. He started to come with her mouth only loosely clamped around him. He shuddered, groaning gutturally as pleasure racked him. His ejaculate spilled around her puffy lips.

It was a wild, delicious mess. He palmed the back of her head, groaning, undone by her yet again. Suddenly, her mouth tightened around him. He slumped slightly, gasping for air.

Their stares held as she cleaned him thoroughly.

Afterward, they collapsed together on the bed, too exhausted to get beneath the covers. Her face was pressed into his chest; his arms encircled her. It felt like heaven and hell at once. She couldn't stop panting, even after Trey's breathing slowed. She wiggled against him, needing stimulation against her fevered body. After a minute, he propped himself up on one elbow and lifted her chin from his chest. He peered at her closely. Concern tightened his features. Confusion penetrated her dazed state.

He moved quickly, sitting up and jerking the panties down her hips. Eleanor gasped loudly at the deprivation of the vibrator. She'd been so out of it following her explosive orgasm, she hadn't realized it had continued to stimulate her overwrought body. She gasped shakily in relief, but an achy pressure continued to plague.

"I'm so sorry, baby. I've never used the panties before. I didn't mean to leave you hurting," he murmured after he'd shoved off her pumps and then jerked the panties off her feet. His hands went to her back. He reclined on his side and slid her body higher on his with a flex of his powerful arms. Now their faces were only inches apart. He studied her closely. Suddenly, his fingers were at her sex.

"Let's just bring you off one more time," he murmured.

His hand moved at her sex, amplifying the friction the panties had created. She moaned in fevered pleasure. He looped his arm around her head. His fingertips caressed her fevered cheek while he watched her rise to climax. Somehow, Eleanor knew that the memory of him looking down at her with such tender possession while she burned in his arms would stay with her until she was an old woman.

A moment later, she shuddered in orgasm against him. He dropped a kiss on her temple while she shook and spoke gruffly near her ear.

"You're the most beautiful thing I've ever seen."

She gasped, overwhelmed with feeling. "That was—"

"Incredible," he finished for her. He kissed her lips softly. Did he realize they were a little sore? He hadn't been harsh with her, but he *was* very demanding. She'd loved it. His kiss was so sweet in the aftermath of it all. She found herself straining for more of his taste. It was like drinking deeply after finishing the race of a lifetime. A moment later, he cupped the side of her head and backed up slightly, examining her face narrowly.

"You okay?" he asked, his deep, rough voice a delight to her prickling nerves.

"Better than okay."

His gaze roved over her face. "I don't know how you do it."

"I could say the same of you," she whispered.

A tiny smile twitched at his mouth. Her slowing heart hitched a beat. "Well, that's something, at least."

"What do you mean?" she murmured when he reached down and loosened his tie that she'd looped around her neck. He pulled the tie over her head and down her long hair before tossing it aside. Then he pulled the shirt down over her shoulders, and she helped him get it off her arms.

"It's nice to know it's not totally one-sided, that's all," he said, reclining fully on the pillows and closing his arms around her.

"It?" she asked breathlessly.

"The obsession," he replied, stroking the side of her body. Her gaze darted up to his face to gauge his expression. She couldn't locate a trace of humor.

"Is that what you'd call what's happening between us?" she asked him softly.

He didn't reply immediately, but his hand continued to caress her sensitive skin. Finally, he rose up partially over her and pressed her back onto the mattress. He looked so beautiful to her in that moment, his hair mussed and falling onto his forehead, his clear, cobalt blue eyes holding a banked flame. She stared up at him, her breath sticking in her lungs.

"I don't know what else to call it. Do you?" he asked solemnly.

She shook her head, unable to speak because of the invisible balloon that had expanded inside her chest.

"It's not like anything I've ever felt before, Eleanor."

He leaned down and kissed her softly, and her breath broke on a desperate whimper.

SIXTEEN

They lay there, kissing and touching and talking quietly, until their bodies cooled. When his caress on the side of her ribs made her shiver, he roused her enough to get both of them under the covers.

"I heard you playing your guitar in the loft when I left your place earlier," she said dreamily a while later as she stroked his chest. She loved the feeling of his thick, soft skin gloving dense muscle. "You're incredible at it," she said, remembering his rapid, complicated finger work. He really had gifted hands and fingers. How *well* she knew it. "What was that you were playing? I didn't recognize it."

"Just something I've been working on."

She lifted her head. "I didn't know you wrote your own music."

He nodded distractedly as he cupped the side of her head, using his fingers to brush back her long hair from her face. "I haven't been doing it as much as I used to, either composing or playing. That's one of many things that got shoved to the wayside when I started BandBook and TalentNet. I've been trying to get back to it more regularly."

"What you were playing . . . it sounded like both classical and rock guitar at once. It was melancholy one minute, exciting and wild the next. It was *really* good, Trey."

His stroking fingers paused. "Thanks," he said, looking a little taken aback and pleased by her praise. His brow creased suddenly. "How long were you listening?"

She lowered her head. "Five or ten minutes or so."

He laughed gruffly and resumed stroking her. "And I was up there tearing at the bit to be with you the whole time."

She started to speak, but halted herself.

"What?" he prodded her.

"Well, I don't know if you'll like this or not. But what you were playing was very . . ." She ducked her head to hide her embarrassment. "Romantic."

"*Romantic?* Really?"

"Why do you sound surprised?" she asked, peering up at him.

He grinned wryly. "It's just not a descriptor I've heard applied to me or anything I do much."

"It's the right word," she said simply. "Do you have any recordings of you playing?"

"As a matter of fact I do. We have a couple recording studios at TalentNet."

"Do you think I could have one?"

"Sure . . . if you really want it," he said doubtfully.

"I do. I'm not flattering you. I really loved it. It was sort of . . . sweeping, what you were playing, like the score for an epic movie or something. Just listening to it made me—"

She swallowed thickly, overwhelmed for a moment. She'd stood at the bottom of the stairs and listened in awe for breathless minutes, the notes flowing down the stairs carrying her spirit like a rapid stream. A sharp longing had expanded in her chest cavity, hearing him play. She felt it again, lying there while Trey held her.

She felt his fingers beneath her chin and she looked up to meet his stare reluctantly.

"It made you what?" he asked.

"Feel," she whispered hesitantly, her gaze flickering up furtively to his face.

For a moment, he just studied her soberly. Then he leaned forward and kissed her mouth so tenderly that, to Eleanor, it felt like a silent blessing.

After that, they lay quietly for a while, both of them awake, both of them thoughtful. Eleanor grew warm and extremely content in the circle of his arms, inhaling his singular scent, feeling his strong, slow heartbeat against her cheek.

Her stomach growled loudly. Trey laughed and reached down to stroke her belly.

"I knew you didn't eat enough at dinner," he said gruffly.

She lifted her head from his chest. "Let's go raid the fridge," she proposed excitedly.

"Of Catherine the Great's feast?"

"We *should* eat some of it. I haven't touched any since she gave it to me. She makes enough food for an army." She threw back the covers. "My mother drives me crazy sometimes, but her cooking makes up for it. And that's saying something."

He dragged on his jeans. She threw on the shirt she'd worn for the striptease.

While she heated up the food, Trey wandered out of the kitchen. After a moment, a feeling of trepidation snuck into her awareness. She tried to pin down why she suddenly felt so anxious, and it came to her.

Her living room was dimly lit, but there were some family

photos over in the far bookcase by the window. If Trey saw them, he'd probably ask her questions.

She hadn't ever mentioned Caddy to him. Was that because of everything her mother and Jimmy had insinuated about her recent liberated, bold behavior relating to Caddy's abrupt death? What if all of it—including this thing she had going on with Trey—*was* due to her mourning Caddy?

What if she really was, as her mother insinuated, grieving unnaturally? What if she was exhibiting some kind of *intimacy issue*? She wished Trey had never said that dreaded phrase. It sounded like some kind of incurable, chronic illness.

She wouldn't let it get to her. She wasn't ready to broach the topic of Caddy yet with Trey. Not when things between them were getting so amazing. She hastened out of the kitchen, hoping to distract him from the photos by telling him the food was ready. She came to a halt when she reached the living room. Her secret was safe. He hadn't gotten to the far side of the room, where the photos were. Instead, he was somberly examining the contents of a near bookcase. The dim light from the hallway gilded his lean, cut torso and rounded, dense shoulder and arm muscles. For a few seconds, she just soaked in the miracle of him being just feet away, peering at her book collection.

He glanced aside, noticing her as he pulled a book from the shelf.

"*Pride and Prejudice*," he said, walking toward her. "A *very* well-read copy of *Pride and Prejudice*."

"It's one of my favorites," she admitted. "I was shocked to see you reading it at the event."

"Were you?" he asked gruffly, leaning down to brush his lips against her temple. She shivered in pleasure and looked up at him.

"I was then. Less so every moment I spend with you," she whispered before she went on her tiptoes and pressed her lips to his.

"You don't still think I'm a heathen, then?" he asked quietly against her mouth a moment later.

"Maybe. But a heathen with potential," she conceded.

His mouth twitched in humor. He held up the book. "I've kind of been remiss in my commitment to it lately. Maybe you can read it to me . . . teach me how to appreciate it."

"I don't know if I have the power to do *that*."

His grin widened before he swept down, his firm, hot kiss stealing her breath for a moment.

"I'm starting to think that if anyone does, it's you, Eleanor."

They decided to eat their feast in bed. Eleanor made a tray for each of them and they started toward the bedroom.

"Hey," she called when he turned right in the hallway. He looked over his shoulder. "Where are you going?"

He glanced down the hall dubiously. "To bed?"

"*Oh.*" It struck her that he'd never been in the master suite before. "That's not my bedroom. That's the guest room," she said. She tilted her head to the left. "I'm in here."

He followed her into the master suite. "This is nice," he said, looking around when she turned on the light. He went around the far side of her bed and set down his tray. When they both sat on the bed, she noticed his brow was creased. "So we just used that room all the time because—"

"Because it was the room with a view," Eleanor said, keeping her gaze downcast to hide her embarrassment.

They started to eat, Trey growing more and more enthusiastic by the minute. He raved about the food. She couldn't help feeling a little proud of her mother's cooking when she saw how eager he was.

"So how is it that you ever saw me?" he asked once he finally took a pause from wolfing down his meal to swallow down half a glass of ice water.

She paused with a pelmini halfway to her mouth. "What?"

"How is it that you saw me through the windows, when you stay in here?" he asked.

Her heart seized a little. "Oh, it was just by chance, really. The first time, it was. After that . . . well, I knew to look." He gave her a questioning look while he chewed. She flailed for a likely answer. "My parents stayed here one weekend last year. I gave them my room, because it has the larger bed. I stayed in the guest room. That's when it happened," she said, pretending to focus on eating again. For a few tense seconds, she thought he was going to ask her more questions. But then he reached and plucked the last bliny from her plate. She nodded down at her tray, wryly encouraging him. He grinned and dipped the pancake into her dish of sour cream. He bit into it and groaned.

"God, this stuff is good."

She laughed.

After they'd finished and removed the dishes, Trey insisted she read to him from *Pride and Prejudice*.

"Are you *serious*?" she asked him incredulously when they returned to bed and he handed her the book.

"Yeah, completely," he said, deadpan. He flipped open the book to the last page he'd read and handed it to her before he collapsed back on the pillows. Eleanor opened her mouth to protest, but then soaked in the image of him reclining there, his beautiful, cut torso bare, his arms bent and above his head. He looked completely relaxed and unguarded. She quickly changed her position about reading to him.

If he grew interested enough in *P and P*, he might just let her touch him to her heart's content while she read. It sounded like a plan, anyway.

After only ten minutes of reading, however, he caught her hand abruptly as she caressed his abdomen just above his jeans, her fingers straying beneath the waistband. She'd sensed the tension coiling in him, so she wasn't exactly surprised. She stopped reading and glanced at his face.

He lifted his head off the pillow. His blue eyes were alight with arousal.

"Don't give me that innocent look, Eleanor."

She hid her grin. She really had been petting him shamelessly while she read. He grabbed the book from her hand and tossed it on the nightstand.

"I'll never get through that damn *romantic* book," he said, reaching for her. His fingers twitched at her ribs, tickling her. She giggled and squirmed against him. "And it's your own damn fault. You're supposed to be teaching me to appreciate it. You should be ashamed of yourself."

He dug his fingers deeper and she snorted with laughter. He grinned wider at the sound. She poked between his ribs in payback, and for a moment, they engaged in a tense, exciting tussle.

After a moment, she gave up and encircled his neck with her arms, bringing his mouth an inch within her own.

"Give up?" he asked her with a cocky, sultry stare.

She pressed tight against him. He was so hard. It felt wonderful.

"Not really," she sighed in pleasure when his opened hand went beneath the shirt she wore to stroke her naked hip and ass, all signs of teasing vanished. She arched against him, so hungry for his heat. "It's just that I agree. Who needs fiction when the real thing is so close at hand?" she asked softly just before his mouth captured hers.

SEVENTEEN

She made omelets for them for breakfast. Trey did his part by making toast and coffee. After eating, they spent a lazy morning lounging in bed, watching television and making love. Every new thing she learned about him she cherished, no matter how small and seemingly inconsequential. He loved Thai, Italian, German and Japanese food. Despite the fact that he added Russian food to his list of favorites after their meal last night, Eleanor was tickled to discover that just the mention of caviar made him look like he was going to throw up.

When he was in college, he played in a cover rock band with drummer Adam Keyes, who later became a member of the bestselling band Commuter Toss. Adam Keyes was also a computer science major who shared Trey's fascination with online culture. He'd been a big influence in helping him develop BandBook, and BandBook, in turn, had been instrumental in sending Adam and his group to the top of the charts.

Even as a kid, his interests had been diversified. He was a devotee of both American and British football. He could ride a horse by the time he was seven and had started driving a combine when he was only thirteen. He was the only kid in high school who was on the football and soccer teams, a member of

Future Farmers of America, the technology club and a newly created jazz band. After growing so frazzled his senior year with all his schoolwork, his social life and helping his dad on the farm, his advisor suggested quitting one or two extracurricular activities.

"Did you end up quitting something?" Eleanor asked him as they lay entwined together in bed. She loved listening to the sound of his deep voice rumbling up to her ear while she pressed it against his chest.

"Yeah, dating." She lifted her head and gave him a stunned look. "Only for a few months, just before and during final exams. I had a scholarship I didn't want to lose." She arched her brows. He eyed her suspiciously. "Oh, I get it. I know what you're thinking. That the precedent goes way back, is that it?"

"Relationships with women were the first to go, even back then. We were the first to be lopped off the list of importance," she murmured.

She'd been teasing him a little, so she was a little shocked when he grew so sober. "You're right," he said. "I never really thought about that before."

"Why do you think females were the most expendable thing?"

He thought about it for a few seconds. "I don't think it's fair to say it globally about all females."

"Really?"

"Really. Janice Hoffman, the girl I was dating my senior year, made the bottom of the list. That's not the same as saying every woman does. *Is* it?"

"Nooo," she agreed slowly.

"There's definitely a *but* in that *no*, Eleanor."

She smiled. "It just strikes me that you often describe the women you date as high maintenance. Maybe you consider relationships work instead of fun, just another project on your to-do list. Isn't it possible that if you see relationships that way, you might attract the type of woman who fits that pattern?"

"What are you? An amateur psychologist?" he asked her, raking his fingers through her hair and scratching her scalp. Her eyes fluttered closed and she moaned in pleasure.

"That's a pretty good description of a psychologist's daughter. I just think relationships and sex and romance should be a lot more lighthearted than you envision them, that's all."

"More fun?" he growled softly, planting a kiss at the corner of her mouth. He rolled her onto her back and came on top of her.

"Certainly less like an obligatory task," she teased.

He laughed and flexed his hips, rubbing his growing erection against her belly. She reached for him, scraping her nails against his neck and shoulders. God, she loved the way he felt. Everywhere. She saw that familiar spark in his blue eyes, and knew he enjoyed her touch, as well. He cupped her breast and feathered the nipple with his thumb. Her smile faded.

"There's no issue with putting you right at the top of my to-do list, Eleanor," he said gruffly. "Trust me on that."

He dipped his head to kiss her. Maybe it was wishful thinking on her part. But even though it was seemingly a teasing, sexy type of thing to say while they were in bed, she couldn't find a trace of amusement on his face when he'd said it.

Trey wanted to go to the gym that afternoon, and then stop by his office, where he said he had something in the works that needed his attention. Eleanor said she needed to run some errands herself.

"Plus, I told Mom I'd take some of her containers back to her," she reflected as they stood together near the front door. She was feeling a little nervous at their parting. Their time together this time had been intensely erotic, intimate and . . . special. It was one of those kinds of nights and days she wished she could do all over again. She was a little heartsore it was finished.

"Yeah, I kind of cleaned you out of your mom's cooking, didn't I?"

She patted his hard belly and smirked. "Who knew Mom's food could feed either a platoon or Trey Riordan?"

He took her into his arms and dipped his knees to bring his head down to hers. His low laugh struck her as delicious as his lips moved on her neck and then plucked at her lips. She'd given him a new toothbrush to use earlier following his shower. He smelled like mint and clean male skin. "Thank your mom for me. Tell her the food was fantastic. I think I'm addicted," he said, eyelids heavy as he peered down at her.

Her pulse started hammering at that, but she played it cool.

"Trust me, she already knows it was fantastic, but I'll tell her anyway."

Their mouths brushed together and clung. "Have a good rest of the day, then," he murmured, showing no signs of leaving.

"You too," she said, hoping he couldn't see her pulse thrumming at her throat. Her heart hitched when he gave her one last kiss and finally parted from her.

He halted a second later with the front door open.

"Can I take you to dinner tonight?" he asked her over his shoulder.

Relief broke over her, feeling like a physical sensation, it was so intense. "I'd love that."

"Good. Because the thing of it is . . ."

"Yes?" she asked him breathlessly when he faded off.

"I really don't want to leave."

She blinked at his admission. He'd sounded a little surprised saying it, like he'd just fully experienced the realization at that moment.

"I don't want you to go either."

He gave a half grin and leaned back toward her. He planted another kiss on her mouth. "That makes going a little easier. Not much, but a little. I'll call later and we'll decide what time for tonight?"

She nodded. He studied her for a second before he turned and left.

He was right. Watching him walk away this time was better after they'd made their confessions.

Not much, but a little.

She couldn't get over how different Trey was in reality versus magazine articles' slants on him, or given her own expectations of him from spying into his private world. He was surprisingly forthright and easy to be with. It had started to become clearer and clearer to her since spending time with him that she'd been seeing him in the one-dimensional light of her sexual attraction.

Her hunger.

His honesty made him exponentially more attractive, but it also added to her guilt.

Although she wasn't precisely sure she *should* feel guilty. He'd proposed a sexual, no-strings-attached affair initially, and she'd accepted. Since then, they'd started to tread in deeper waters, but it was still the beginning of a relationship that they'd both agreed was primarily based on an uncommonly strong physical attraction.

So what if she'd made herself more exciting in his eyes than she really was? Her playacting at being a sexually confident woman only added spice and excitement to their affair.

Maybe it was because he'd intimated at dinner last night that he was aware that things were going deeper between them. And the deeper she went, the more honesty became crucial.

Stop overthinking things, she admonished herself at least a couple dozen times that afternoon as she picked up her dry cleaning and drove up to her parents' place in Evanston. *Everything is going great with him. You're finally tasting that big, juicy, delicious bite of life Caddy encouraged you to take.*

And it's not like your dishonesty equates to sticking a pin into his condom supply. Everybody pretends a little at the beginning of relationships.

Just enjoy it while you can.

Her self-lecture must have worked a little, because by the time it came for her to get ready for her date with Trey—yes, for all intents and purposes, it definitely was a date—she was feeling more optimistic. More than optimistic . . .

. . . Excited.

Trey called at around three thirty and said they had reservations at the Park Grill for seven, but that he'd be by to pick her up at five if she thought she could be ready by then.

"Five? Why five?"

"Something's been cooking over the long weekend, and we got things all finalized today while I was in the office. It should be pretty amazing," he said on the phone.

"*What?*" she asked, her curiosity piqued.

"It's a surprise. We were talking about how we don't take advantage of things in the city. This is a chance to improve our record. Do you think you can be ready by five?"

She assured him she could.

"Wear shoes you can stand in for a little bit without getting sore feet, and a warm coat," he told her before he signed off.

There'd been something in his tone that made her think he was really looking forward to this mysterious event as well. That only spiked her excitement even more.

In deference to the fact that it sounded like they'd be outside for a while, she chose to wear a pair of jeans, supple brown over-the-knee boots, a thick ivory sweater and a darling ivory faux fur coat that had belonged to Caddy, which was not only extremely fashionable, but warm. She wore her hair up because of the thick turtleneck on the sweater and took some time with her makeup. By the time she'd finished getting ready, the mirror told her she looked chic and confident.

On the inside, however, it was like a swarm of bees was trapped inside her stomach.

Once Harry had called to announce Trey's arrival, she spritzed on her favorite perfume and went to grab her purse. She answered his knock a moment later, brimming with excitement. She could tell by his warm, admiring gaze that her nervousness was her secret.

"Wow. You look fantastic."

"So do you," she told him. It was a bald understatement. He looked monumentally handsome, wearing a pair of black jeans, a stark white cotton mock turtleneck shirt, a rust-colored scarf and his black peacoat. There was a slight scruff on his jaw and his golden brown hair was sexily mussed. She wanted to eat him up.

He smiled and stepped into her, dropping a kiss on her mouth. He inhaled and nuzzled her ear. "You smell even better," he said gruffly, causing her skin to prickle in pleasure. He pressed his lips to her throat, and she sighed.

She felt him press something in her hand. "What's this?" she asked, glancing down to see he'd put a thumb drive in her hand.

He shrugged sheepishly. "An audio recording of some of my music. I picked it up while I was at the office. Be kind while you listen to it. There's a reason I'm the CEO of a company that represents some of the most talented artists on the planet, but I'm not one of them."

"I don't believe that for a second," she insisted earnestly. "I've heard you play, and I know your focus. If you decided that you wanted to play as a full-time job, you'd be as successful at that as you are at running TalentNet."

He smirked and kissed her briskly on the mouth. "Nice to know that if I did ever decide to go in that direction, I'd have one other person beside my mom buying my records." She gave him a rueful glance and he grinned. "Come on. We don't want to be late for this. There's already a lot of traffic. I have a car waiting."

She set the thumb drive on a foyer table and followed him out the door. "A lot of traffic for what?"

"You'll see," he said mysteriously.

She laughed and scurried to keep up with his long-legged stride down the hallway.

It was crisp, windless December night, the temperature right around the freezing point. A black sedan was waiting for them in her building's turnabout.

"Eleanor, this is Billy," Trey introduced once they'd climbed into the back of the car. "Billy drives for me a lot."

Eleanor and the middle-aged man in the driver's seat exchanged hellos. "They've made the announcement to the media," Billy said to Trey as he turned down the radio and he pulled onto the inner drive. "Lake Shore Drive is already bumper to bumper."

"Just get us as close to Millennium Park as you can using the local streets, and we'll walk the rest of the way," Trey said as he checked his watch.

"Bumper-to-bumper traffic for what?" Eleanor asked him. He just gave her a small smile, his eyes gleaming in the shadows, and grabbed her hand.

Billy turned off a jam-packed Michigan Avenue early on, but

it was enough for Eleanor to notice that most of the people on the crowded sidewalks were moving south. Even though the local residential streets weren't as busy, she still saw a lot of people leaving their residences and walking rapidly in the direction of Millennium Park. By the time they reached Randolph Street, the crowd was thick.

"They've closed off Randolph," she said, seeing the police cars stationed to the right to block off the street. "What's going *on*?" she asked Trey in bewildered curiosity as they exited the sedan and joined what looked like hundreds of people crossing the street. She could see the huge city Christmas tree alight in the park. There was the distant sound of music echoing in the air. A feeling of excitement and good cheer seemed to emanate from the moving crowd.

"It's a surprise concert," Trey said, pulling her along. "They just sent out an announcement on social media a few hours ago, and now the radio and television has picked it up. Looks like people are flooding into the park from the shopping districts now that the stores are closed."

"A surprise concert?" Eleanor asked breathlessly. "Who's performing?"

But the crowd had grown thick and the music was getting louder. Trey was prevented from answering. He had to go ahead of her to cut a path. He kept a tight hold on her hand, weaving his way through the mass of chattering people. After a minute of this, the crowd broke as they descended down a slight hill to the seats and grassy area in front of the Pritzker Pavilion.

"Oh my God, look at all the people," she murmured in wide-eyed amazement. The seats were already filled and the grassy area was packed to the brim with standing and dancing people. The music was upbeat and loud, being performed by fifteen or so dancing and singing women on the stage. Trey led her in the direction of the large pavilion.

The performers were belting out a jazzy version of "Santa Baby" and the crowd was loving it. A huge wide-screen television on either side of the stage made the performance visible even to people at the farthest reaches of the park. Eleanor watched the flashy performance as Trey pulled her along. Her feet started to drag when he urged her so close to the edge of the pavilion she started to lose sight of the performers.

"Come on." He urged her around the side of the pavilion. "I think they're about to go on."

"Who's about to go on? Where are we *going*?" She laughed incredulously when he pulled her to the side of the pavilion.

"Backstage," she heard him say before he led her to a door with several men standing in front of it. His hand dipped into his breast pocket. A man studied the piece of paper Trey showed him with a stern expression. The security guard glanced up, a smile breaking over his face.

"Enjoy the show, Mr. Riordan. And thanks for setting it up. Looks like quite a crowd."

"Thanks," Trey said when the man opened the door for them.

Then he was pulling her up some stairs, and her heart was beating in wild excitement. In the distance, she heard a man on a loudspeaker, his voice a little muffled by the sound of their feet pounding on the metal stairs and the loud cheers from the crowd. Her heart jumped, and there was a huge explosion of applause.

Had she heard the announcer correctly?

Trey led her through a shadowed area. Over his shoulder, she saw a slice of the brilliant lights of the stage between two rows of curtains. The opening notes to "Sock It to Me Santa" rang in the air around them and vibrated the floor beneath them. Before

Trey could draw her close to the stage, she pulled on his hand, halting him. He turned.

"Did he say *Bruno Mars* and *Sam Smith*?" she shouted incredulously over the music. The men started singing, and Trey didn't need to answer. She grinned hugely, and he smiled back. He leaned forward and spoke near her ear. "A holiday performance. It was an impromptu thing. TalentNet and the Magnificent Mile Shopping Association planned it with the artists. Come on," he said.

She followed him to the wings eagerly. Awe overcame her as she stared out onto the brightly lit stage onto hordes of glittering, shimmying backup singers and the two incredibly energetic, talented performers. She was almost within touching distance of some of the dancers, and she could feel the heat of the stage lights.

She looked up at Trey. He noticed and squeezed her hand warmly. She laughed as a wave of pure happiness went through her. Sure, it was partially excitement from the novelty of standing on the stage, so close to an amazing performance.

But mostly, she experienced sheer joy from standing next to him at that moment. He was what made everything so colorful and vibrant.

He was what made her feel like the world was a fresh, new, amazing place to be.

Her ebullient mood continued when they'd been seated later that evening at the Park Grill. Her brain and body were still abuzz with excitement from the treat of the surprise concert.

"I don't need this," she told Trey when they lifted their champagne-filled glasses for a toast. She beamed at him over the top of the flutes. "Who needs champagne after a night like that? I'm still bubbling inside. *Thank you*. It was so amazing."

His smile faded. He dipped his head toward hers. "Do you

know you're glowing right now? Actually *glowing*?" he repeated, his gaze moving over her face.

"I'm flushed from the dancing. It was hot under the lights," she told him. She still couldn't believe it, but during the finale of the concert, they'd been pulled onto the stage along with several other people who had been watching in the wings. She'd remember that forever, dancing under the bright lights with Trey to an unforgettable "Santa Claus Is Coming to Town" as the crowd sang along and went wild.

That's when she'd first realized it. She'd never been in love before.

Until now.

And she was still flying high in the clouds from that realization. Fear might hover at the periphery of her consciousness, a black anxiety that she'd made the cardinal error of engaging in an affair: she'd fallen in love. But the heat and the glow were what dominated tonight. She couldn't feel anything but euphoric as she stared into Trey's eyes at that moment.

He leaned in and brushed his lips against hers. "You glow because you're beautiful," he said. "Inside and out." Her heart squeezed in her chest at what she thought she read in his eyes at that moment.

After a delicious dinner, Trey took her to his penthouse. They'd barely gotten off the elevator before they were yanking each other's clothes off. It seemed they couldn't get enough of each other, and they couldn't get it fast enough.

After they'd made love, they held each other and Eleanor stared out the opened windows at her building next door. Her eyelids were growing heavier by the second.

"Trey?" she asked him quietly, breaking the silence.

"Hmmm?" he replied as he stroked her shoulder.

"Why didn't you tell me you were such a good dancer?" she mumbled.

He snorted. "I can stumble around in close approximation to the beat, so I'm a good dancer?"

"You did a lot better than that," she insisted, pressing her lips to his chest. "Thank you again."

He laughed gruffly. "You've thanked me dozens of times already. You're welcome. But it wasn't a big deal. I get to go to concerts a lot. It's a job perk. You made it a hell of a lot more enjoyable for me, so I should be thanking you. I'll take you to as many concerts as you like," he finished, pressing a kiss to the top of her head.

Her heart jumped at that, as it did anytime he referenced them being together in the future. Her emotions felt especially sensitive to the topic after tonight, after her realization she'd fallen for him.

Still, he hadn't understood what she meant.

"No, that's not what I meant. Not entirely, anyway," she said, snuggling closer to his warm, hard body and sighing in contentment. All the adrenaline from the night ran thin in her blood, and exhaustion was finally taking over.

"What did you mean, then?"

"I'm not thanking you just for taking me backstage to an amazing, once-in-a-lifetime concert. I've never danced on a big stage like that, right out there in the middle of the spotlight with such a huge audience," she said groggily. "It was a little scary. But I was with you," she whispered. She placed her hand facedown on his chest, feeling his heartbeat. "So everything was okay," she mumbled before she sunk into a deep, content sleep.

EIGHTEEN

She was late getting to work the next morning because she was hesitant to leave Trey's arms. Her one consolation was that he seemed just as reluctant to let her go. One thing was certain: the over-the-top attraction to each other they'd shared from the beginning was only growing stronger.

Nevertheless, she had no choice but to leave him. Not only was her work schedule packed following the holiday, she had the reading event tonight. She and Trey had agreed to get together for a late supper afterward. With the public opening of the exhibit tomorrow, she had her work cut out for her today.

Adding to all that, she hoped to get out of the museum before six to go home and get her sexy on before the reading event. She'd been cooking up a little idea to drive Trey a little wild during it, and yet still put him in the driver's seat. It was risky on her part, but so potentially exciting. She couldn't wait.

She barely got out her condo door that morning in a presentable state, her hair piled on top of her head and wearing a practical, comfortable dress and a pair of ugly flats that would keep her feet from aching as she accumulated her typical miles walking around the museum every day.

Even though she felt a little flustered about being late, she couldn't wipe the grin from her face that morning as she helped Jimmy with some improvements they wanted to make on the exhibit. Every time she thought about the night before with Trey— every time she thought of him, *period*—her happiness swelled.

"Somebody sure is smitten," Jimmy teased her at lunch in the cafeteria that day. She'd told him all about the surprise concert and Trey's backstage pass and dancing on the stage with him and the artists for the raucous, unforgettable finale.

She tried to erase her stupid grin, but couldn't entirely. "What makes you say that?" she asked, pretending nonchalance, and not caring that she was unsuccessful.

"Oh, I don't know. Maybe because you decided that bodice on that Lincoln dress needed an emergency remount to keep the fabric safe, and you normally would have been snarling and barking orders at everyone, half in a panic with the exhibition opening in less than twenty-four hours. Instead, you were all sweetness and smiles, and got it all done in record time. If that's what love does to you, sign me up."

Jimmy arched his brows. He'd been baiting her about the love thing, trying to draw her out. But her realizations about her feelings for Trey were too new. Too raw and powerful.

Too intimidating.

If she started to talk about it out loud to Jimmy, maybe it'd become more real. She'd potentially have to acknowledge that given their mutual agreement at the beginning of their relationship, it was impossible to know *exactly* how intense or permanent things stood between Trey and her. She might have to admit to herself that she wasn't *precisely* sure what the future held for them . . . or have to concede everything could disintegrate to dust at a random flick of fate or a turn of mood.

Picking it all apart in a conversation with Jimmy might dim the magic, and that was something she just wasn't willing to do yet.

"Speaking of which, since we did get everything done for the Mary Todd Lincoln exhibit, is it okay with you if I retreat down below for the rest of the afternoon?" she asked Jimmy, circumventing his fishing-for-gossip expedition. "We just received that private collection that includes the Margaret Harrison inaugural ball gown, and I only have Betsey until four o'clock today to help me start to unpack it all."

Jimmy agreed.

Betsey and she began the unpacking, cataloging and storage process of costumes, photos and ephemera. The collection was all from the last twenty years of the nineteenth century and was associated with the Chicago political and social scene, a favorite topic of Eleanor's. It was a ripe opportunity in which to completely lose track of time.

The next thing she knew, Betsey was long gone, and she heard Jimmy's muffled voice calling out to her in the far distance. She blinked and rubbed her eyes beneath her glasses, coming back to the present moment dazedly.

"I'm back in Room D, Jimmy," she yelled out the door. Her basement workplace took up nearly an entire city block beneath the museum, and included dozens of temperature- and light-regulated storage facilities, workrooms and art studios. She checked her watch and cursed disbelievingly under her breath. She'd done it again, lost herself in history. She began to carefully repack the fascinating photos she'd been studying, all of which related to popular Chicago mayor Carter Henry Harrison's assassination.

It was now six twenty, and she'd wanted to be out the door by six. Thank goodness Jimmy had interrupted her. She straightened her glasses, which had fallen down on her nose. Room D was a storage room for original photographs, so it was kept cool and dim. The chill had penetrated her clothing, although she hadn't been aware of it while she'd been so preoccupied in her study. It hit her now. Shivering, she wrapped the old nappy wool sweater she always kept in her office around her more tightly and hurried over to the closed door.

"Jimmy," she yelled, swinging the door open. "I'm down he—"

She halted abruptly. Jimmy walked down the hallway toward her. Trey was right beside him. *What the hell is he doing here?* It jarred her, seeing him, of all people, in her subterranean domain. The lights in the hall were brighter than the storage room's had been. She saw his blue eyes fix on her. In a split second, it flashed into her brain how he must be seeing her at that moment. Her hair was falling down from the haphazard bun on her head. She wore a shapeless, gray dress and clutched an old-lady sweater around her.

Great. She was basically at her basement-dwelling, distracted, mousy-librarian Eleanor best.

It felt like she had a sudden allergic reaction. Her throat and tongue seemed to swell up. She'd never corrected her spontaneous lie to Trey about being some kind of high-powered sales executive for the museum.

He was going to realize she'd lied to him.

And you know how much he hates dishonesty.

It felt like the floor had dropped from under her. It was going to end with him, and she wasn't ready.

"Look who I found asking for you at the information desk," Jimmy said, grinning. She flashed Jimmy a helpless "I'm going to skin you alive later" glance. The two men came to a halt in front of her. She glanced at Trey furtively. He looked incredible. He must have had some kind of meeting today, because he was wearing a gray suit beneath his long wool coat. Or maybe he dressed that way for work all the time? What the hell she did she know about the most basic routines of his life, after all?

Not only that . . . he'd gotten his *hair* cut. She'd have thought she'd hate seeing his hallmark wavy, sexy hair shorn, but in fact, the alteration made him look even more arresting and attractive. Older, somehow. Distinguished. Almost like someone she didn't even know . . .

Or was her impression coming more from her near-panicked state? His brow furrowed as he studied her narrowly.

"I hope you don't mind," Trey said. "I thought maybe we could get something to eat before the reading event instead of after." He glanced down to where she clutched at her sweater. "But I've obviously caught you in the middle of something."

She looked down stupidly at where he looked. "Oh," she mumbled through a thick throat. She hastily took off the cotton gloves she'd been wearing to handle the photographs. "No, I was just finishing up," she managed through numb lips.

There was an awkward pause. Jimmy cleared his throat.

"So I'll just be going, then," Jimmy said, gesturing down the hall.

"Thanks for bringing me down," Trey said.

"Sure, no problem." Jimmy's smile froze when he glanced at her. She must have been shooting desperate darts at him with her eyes, because he looked a little contrite.

"I'll see you guys later at the reading event?"

"You'll be there?" Trey asked him.

"Yeah, I was just out of town last week," Jimmy said, giving them a quick wave. He suddenly seemed very eager to be gone. They both watched him walking away down the hall, the pressure at Eleanor's throat and chest mounting by the second. Trey finally turned to her and met her stare.

"*This* is where you work?" he asked her quietly.

She swallowed back the lump in her throat. "Yes."

He glanced around at all the doors coming off the vast main hallway.

"It's massive down here. I had no idea," he said. "Do a lot of people have offices down here?"

She cleared her throat. "Not a lot, no." Taking advantage of the fact that he wasn't looking directly at her, she tried to straighten her hair while still holding the cotton gloves. He caught her at it, peering at her closely.

"I didn't know you wore glasses."

She froze at his observation. "Uh . . . these are just magnifiers, for when I'm studying something up close." She pulled them off her head and slid them into her sweater pocket self-consciously. She sort of felt like *she* was under a magnifying lens at that moment beneath his stare.

"What's wrong, Eleanor?" he asked sharply.

"Nothing."

"Am I in the way?" he asked, taking a step toward her. She glanced up to his face incredulously.

"Of course not. I'm just . . . I wasn't expecting you."

He nodded. His new haircut made his face looked more angular and hard and his eyes even more striking.

He suddenly shook his head slightly, his eyelids narrowing. "How is that I can feel like we've known each other forever one second, and the next second, be questioning whether or not you even *recognize* me . . . or worse, wondering whether or not you're wishing that I was long gone?"

His deep voice echoed in her head for several seconds after his lips had closed into a hard line.

"Is *that* what you think? That I wish you were long gone?" Her high-pitched squeak made him blink his eyes in surprise. His subdued reaction amplified her desperation. "I don't wish you were *gone*. I'm just embarrassed to have you see me like this." She glanced down and waved at her frumpy form in a "hello" gesture. "Plus, I told you I was an executive in the membership department," she mumbled, her voice shaking slightly. "And I'm obviously not, working down here in the collection archives."

He rolled his eyes slightly. "Yeah, but you also told me you read erotica exclusively. I've kind of learned to take some of what you say with a grain of salt."

She vibrated like a gong that had just been rung. Was he *serious*?

"I figured you'd been dodging the truth about what you did here at the museum the other night when Jimmy told us how you negotiated for the Mary Todd Lincoln wardrobe from the Smithsonian. That doesn't really sound like something a sales executive would do. Besides, *maybe* a sales executive in a museum would have a degree in art history, but also one in textile preservation? It seemed a little unlikely."

"Why didn't you say anything?" she asked, her voice ringing with shock.

He shrugged those wide shoulders she loved.

"I figured that, for some reason, you didn't want me to know the specifics of what you really did here. I've been known to tell people, for different reasons, that I'm anything from a programmer to a manager to a gofer at TalentNet. In a way, all of them are true," he added with a small smile. "What you said made sense to me, while we were at Gold Coast. *Every* job in this museum is associated with interacting with the public. Educating them. Entertaining them." He leaned forward. "Getting their money to keep this place solvent and the doors open. I don't have a problem with you not giving me your specific job description." He seemed to register her amazement. "I'm interested in *you*. Not your job title, Eleanor."

"Oh," she said, her voice hollow with shock. She'd imagined he'd be furious when he found out she'd misled him. The amazing realization that he wasn't going to dump her any second because of her white lie made her feel light-headed with relief. Would he ever cease to surprise her?

He glanced at all the closed doors surrounding them. "Okay,

I'm lying. I'm actually *really* curious. This place looks amazing. So what do you do down here, anyway?" he asked, stepping closer to her, blue eyes zeroing in on her like a target. "And why *did* you want to keep it from me?"

He saw her elegant throat convulse as she swallowed. If he had to guess, he'd say that she was stunned. She set him off balance so frequently. Maybe it was selfish, but it gratified him to know that he had the ability to do the same to her.

Glossy tendrils of her brown hair were falling around her cheeks and down her shoulders, the mass of it heavier on the right side than the left. When she'd walked out of the room a moment ago, she wore that sweet, curious, intent expression that reminded him, strangely enough, of the first time he'd ever seen her at the reading event when she'd pulled out *Born to Submit* to read. He recalled how he'd had the seemingly random thought that she wore that expression a lot. And here was proof. He'd caught her unawares while she'd been totally absorbed in her work.

He couldn't understand why she was embarrassed about that.

"Eleanor?" he prodded when she pursed and opened her pretty mouth, but no words came out. "Jimmy told me on the way down here that you were the conservation and preservation librarian. Why wouldn't you want me to know that?"

"I . . . uh . . . I didn't think you'd find it very interesting. It's kind of a hard job to explain to people," she finally said.

"So you thought I was too stupid to understand? Or was it too shallow?"

"No, of course not," she said, her eyes lighting up with indignation for a second before she ducked her head. "I just thought you wouldn't find it very exciting."

"Well, you were wrong," he stated matter-of-factly. He glanced down the long hallway. "I think your job sounds a hell of a lot more interesting than pushing memberships and schmoozing companies for donations. Will you show me around a little?"

Her mouth fell open. "You want me to show you around?" she repeated.

"Is it okay? All these closed doors are making me curious. It's like some kind of treasure hallway. I'm thinking anything could be behind them."

He blinked at the sound of her nervous laughter. Her curving lips warmed him.

"That's pretty much true. Well . . . what would you like to see?"

"Anything."

"Hmmm," she considered, her brow wrinkling as she thought. All the while, her gaze traveled over his face.

"I like your hair," she said, surprising him.

"Thanks."

"Why'd you get it cut?"

"I just thought it was time."

"*Time?* What does that mean? Your hair was your bad-boy hallmark," she said, arching her brows in amusement.

He gave her a droll glance. "If that was true, then I'm doubly glad it's gone."

"You wear the new look extremely well."

He stilled, seeing the flash of heat in her eyes. He started to step into her—he'd been straining at the bit not to touch her since first seeing her. She'd looked so disheveled and distracted and *sexy* when she'd walked out of that door earlier. When she'd seen him, she'd frozen up, though. That'd restrained him from reaching out for her.

He paused in stepping forward to take her in his arms when she suddenly snapped her fingers. "Ah, I know what you might like. We just got these in a few weeks ago. Follow me."

She led him to a closed door. She went in and flipped on a very dim light. He entered and saw a room filled with metal shelving racks with long, flat boxes stacked on them. They walked down an aisle between the shelves and he saw that the white boxes were all labeled.

"Here," she said, pausing. "Help me with these three, on top." He grabbed one end of the boxes and she the other. She nodded in the direction she wanted him to go. In an open area, they set down the three boxes on a long table. She started to lift off the lid, and he assisted her on his end. He paused in mid-movement when he saw what lay inside the long box.

"Holy shit," he muttered, setting down the lid. "Is *that*—"

"Jim McMahon's Bears uniform. It's the one he wore in the—"

"Nineteen eighty-five Super Bowl," Trey finished. "I was only two when they won it, but my brother, Kevin, was twelve. He and my dad were such a huge fans, I swear I must have absorbed their enthusiasm in the womb and been born a Bears fan. My mom insists I was too young to remember the '85 Super Bowl, but whether it's from me seeing old clips or Kevin talking about it nonstop or what, I swear I have a memory of sitting in our living room, watching it. Kevin won't believe it when I tell him I saw this."

"Tell him to come by anytime, and I'll show him as well, if he's interested. We'll have it down here for quite a while. We're doing a big sports exhibit next fall," Eleanor explained.

He glanced up and was snagged by her smile. *"Really?"*

Her laugh sounded pleased and a little surprised. "Really."

He glanced down at the boxes. A thrill raced through him when he saw the tag on the bottom box.

"No way. Is that . . . *Walter Peyton's* uniform?"

"Yeah. Do you want to see it?"

"Of *course* I want to see it." She chuckled and helped him move aside the other two boxes. A moment later, he stared down at his hero's uniform laid out in the box.

"You have got the coolest job *ever*." He looked up in time to see her stunned expression. "I don't suppose there's any chance I could—"

"Do you want to touch it?"

"Uh, *yeah*, I do. But I was just going to say take a picture."

"Tell you what," she said, moving over to a cabinet and pulling out a drawer. "Hold it up and I'll take a picture of you. Then you can send it to Kevin and your dad, if you want?"

She handed him a pair of cotton gloves like the ones she'd been wearing earlier. She had him turn off the flash on his phone camera. A few seconds later, he sent off a photo of him holding up Sweetness's jersey, a huge grin plastered on his face.

"They're going to be so jealous," Trey told Eleanor several minutes later as they left the cool, dim storage room. She turned to him once they were in the hallway again.

"Where next?" she asked him. She'd tried to straighten her hair at some point while he was drooling over several other of the museum's collection of many sports legends' uniforms. Now her thick, long hair was piled on her head again in a very messy bun. He experienced a strong urge to rip apart her efforts and see it spilling all around her pretty face and down her back.

He cleared his throat and strained to focus down the hallway of treasures. "I don't know. You tell me."

"Just pick one."

Distracted by her pink, curving lips, he stuck his hand out and pointed randomly.

"Oh, not that one," she said. "That's not really a collection preservation unit. It's more of a work room and storage area for leftover junk from exhibitions and—"

"I don't care," he said, moving past her toward the door. He was fascinated by her work life. "Let's have a look." She trailed behind him. He opened the door. The room was pitch black.

"You can turn on the light. It's to the right," she said from behind him.

He flipped on a switch and started slightly in surprise. Eleanor snorted with laugher behind him at his reaction. He gave her a condemning glance over his shoulder.

"You were the one who barged in. You didn't give me a chance to warn you," she told him pointedly.

The vast room was almost entirely filled with hundreds of mannequins in various positions, some of them missing arms and heads, some just torsos lying on the floor. Seeing an army of mannequins suddenly pop out of the darkness had startled him.

"What are they for?" he asked, stepping into the large room.

"Costume displays," she said. He heard the door shut behind them. "Some of these mannequins are more than a hundred years old and originate from the museum's inception. I'm always telling Jimmy we could do an exhibit on the mannequins alone. Some of the faces on the old ones are exquisitely painted, and just the body size difference over the century is an interesting lesson on its own. Look at this one," she said, walking over to a corner. He followed her and examined the vintage, but still intact figure she indicated. Unlike modern, featureless mannequins, this one had a beautifully rendered, painted female face that wore a vacuous, insipid expression.

"Wow. As a piece of art, it says a lot about the commercialization of women, not to mention what people of the time period thought of them, doesn't it?" Trey murmured. He'd stopped close behind her. He dipped his head, catching the scent of her hair—fresh and citrusy—and swayed closer for another inhale. "So what does it say that all your modern ones have no face at all?" he asked distractedly.

"For my part, it says that I don't want the face to interfere with the study of the costume." She turned and started slightly, her big eyes jumping to his face. She hadn't realized he'd stood so close. Her lips parted. He zeroed in on them like a target. "I . . . I want the mannequin to represent anyone and no one."

"You're very smart," he said, dipping his head, drawn by her scent.

"Thank you," she said softly. "So are you."

"Even though you thought I was too shallow to appreciate what you do for a living?"

Her mouth trembled. "Trey, I don't think you're shallow. That's ridiculous."

"Then explain to me again why you didn't tell me what your real job is?"

"Because it's boring," she said in a burst of frustration. "And you're the opposite of that. You're dynamic, and worldly, and sophisticated. You regularly hang out with celebrities and talented artists. And I'm happy being down here in the dark, hunchbacked and squinting at some dusty, century-old photographs, or deciphering the scribbles in a book, or conserving some ancient pantaloons, for God's sake. I'm—"

"Adorable," he said, stepping forward and taking her into his arms. She halted, looking startled. "You're adorable," he repeated, his hard glance daring her to deny it. "And sexy as hell." Unable to stand it any longer, he dipped his knees and dropped a kiss on her succulent, parted lips. He tilted his head and pierced her mouth with his tongue. She moaned softly, her tongue tangling with his. He opened his hands on her, feeling her slender waist and curving hips. A groan vibrated his throat. *God*, she felt good.

And her taste . . . every time, he was freshly amazed at it. It was like his brain wasn't capable of storing completely how delicious she was. Memory paled in comparison to the real thing.

She pressed closer to him, her hands moving anxiously at his waist and back. Their kiss grew wild and deep. He could feel her breasts crushing against his ribs. He slipped his hands beneath the big, drab sweater she was wearing. If it were possible, her librarian look turned him on more than her chic, sophisticated outfits and stripper costumes did. All he could think about was what was underneath the dull, shapeless fabric, the warm, soft flesh and smooth naked skin. Her dress was relatively thin. He traced her svelte curves, feeling her heat. Blood rushed to his groin. He felt himself go heavy and hard in seconds. She must have felt it too, because she whimpered and circled her hips, stroking him with her body. He inhaled sharply and broke their kiss with effort.

"Jesus. You get me there so fast," he breathed out against her parted lips.

"I could say the same of you," she whispered, panting. She glided her hand down his chest and belly. His breathing halted when she cupped his cock and began moving her hand up and down the swollen shaft. He hissed and grabbed her wrist. He started to tell her to get ahold of herself, but then he saw the heat in her big, glistening eyes.

Little witch.

"Does that door have an inside lock?" he asked her tensely.

"It's the only one that does."

His eyebrows went up. "I really *did* pick the treasure room," he muttered before he went to fasten the lock.

By the time he returned to her, her breathing had turned choppy with excitement. Some little voice inside her told her that she was crazy for fooling around at her job, but it felt mandatory. And in truth, almost the entire staff was gone for the day. The risk was minimal. No one really came down here on a regular basis except her small staff, and they all worked during regular museum hours.

But those were just surface rationalizations.

The only real logic for behaving so impulsively stalked toward her right now, his gaze trained on her. His new haircut made him look sleeker. Harder.

Hungrier.

"Where?" he asked her gruffly.

She swallowed back her mounting excitement and glanced around the room. She pointed toward the only likely candidate, a huge cataloguing table with dozens of small drawers beneath it and clutter from various old exhibitions collected on top of it. He glanced to where she indicated and took her hand wordlessly. When they got to the wood table, he pushed aside several informational signs, some cans of spray paint, some paint swatches and who knew what else. He shrugged out of his long dress coat and laid it on the table, then turned toward her. Before Eleanor realized what he intended, he hoisted her up onto the table and set her down on his spread coat. He hastily took off his suit jacket and tossed it next to her the on the table.

With no further ado, he spread her knees and slid her dress up her thighs until it bunched at her hips. He stepped between her legs and began unfastening the buttons of her dress.

"I've been wanting to do this ever since I saw you standing there in the hallway earlier. You look so sexy."

"Are you crazy?"

His glanced bounced up to her face. "It's better than any of your stripper costumes," he told her bluntly.

"*This?*" she asked incredulously, staring down at herself as his hands moved between her breasts.

"Oh *yeah*. I didn't realize I had a librarian fetish, but I guess I do. In a big way. Jesus, what *is* this?" he asked, pausing at her waist. He opened his hand along her satin-covered ribs. His eyes widened.

Embarrassment swept through her. She started to pull the opened edges of her dress closed. He grabbed one wrist, stopping her halfhearted attempts, and continued to unfasten the buttons of her dress.

"Are you wearing a *slip*?" he asked, sounding stunned. He finally seemed to have enough of her struggling and grabbed her wrists, spreading her arms wide. Eleanor shifted her hips in embarrassment on top of the table. "Do women still wear slips?" he asked.

"It gets chilly in the preservation rooms. They're temperature controlled. I wear slips with my dresses to help keep me warm. So what?" she defended.

He glanced up at her face. "So *what*? I'll tell you so what. It's sexy as hell." He reached behind her with one arm and lifted her off the table with ease. Eleanor squeaked in surprise. With his other hand, he whisked her dress down over her hips and butt and down her thighs. He plopped her ass back on the table and drew her dress down over her feet. He stared at her as he tossed aside the dress heedlessly, his mouth shaping into a snarl. Eleanor held her breath. He almost looked angry.

He put his hands on her thighs and slid the satin slip upward, exposing her underwear. Eleanor knew a moment of panic and sharp embarrassment. She had *not* dressed for a seduction. Just the opposite, in fact. She was wearing thick ivory thigh-high tights and a pair of utilitarian cotton panties. They weren't granny underwear, but they definitely were the opposite of sexy. Trey's warm hand slid across the bare skin at the top of her thigh-high. He stared at her crotch fixedly. Mixed mortification and sharp arousal tore through her.

He reached for her. Impulsively, she tried to stop him. Undeterred, he pushed past her resistance and shoved his hand between her clamped thighs. A surprised, shaky whimper puffed past her lips as he rubbed her pussy lasciviously.

"Jesus, Eleanor. You're gonna get fucked so hard."

She saw his swooping, slanting mouth. He kissed her hard,

almost immediately penetrating her parted lips with his tongue. His exciting declaration echoed in her head. His attack on her senses wasn't violent, but it was close to it. He placed one hand at her back, supporting her, and he leaned farther into her, feeding from her mouth furiously while rubbing her pussy through the cotton panties. She drowned for a moment in the dark decadence of his kiss, clutching at his head and running her fingers greedily through his thick, newly shorn hair. The sensation excited her unbearably. He kept pushing back on her as he came over her, until her knees rose and her feet dangled in the air.

There was nothing, nothing so intoxicating in the world, as being ravished by Trey.

He ripped his mouth from hers, making her blink open her eyelids dazedly. His hand eased off her back, and she compensated for his support by planting her hands on the table behind her. He began to lower the straps of her slip, his expression rigid. His fingers scooped the fabric down over her bra to waist. Then his hands were at her back, and he was peeling her bra off her breasts. He tossed the bra aside, his gaze never leaving her.

"Look at you." He reached to the top of her head, and she felt the pins holding up her hair slide next to her scalp. Her hair tumbled down her back. He sunk his fingers into it and spread it around her shoulders.

She didn't have the wherewithal to puzzle out how or why he could be so excited. All she knew was that he *was*, because his arousal was palpable. His gaze moved slowly down over her. She felt like a feast that was about to be ravenously consumed. She couldn't exhale. He lifted his hands. She whimpered in cutting anticipation.

He cradled and stroked her bare breasts, sliding his palms and fingers across her skin so tenderly. She moaned at the exquisite sensation . . .

And at the unchecked longing she read on his face.

NINETEEN

"**Y**ou're like warm silk here. You're the *softest* woman," he breathed out, his stare on her rapt. He whisked his thumbs over her nipples. Arousal stabbed at her core. Her nipples pulled tight. "And you get so hard here," he added, tweaking and rubbing the crests. She clenched her teeth and moved her hips restlessly on the table, pushing her pelvis forward so that she could feel his cock.

He moved his hands just below her armpits and grasped her rib cage, holding her immobile. His head sunk. He sucked her breast into his mouth. His heat enveloped her, his lashing, rubbing tongue making her cry out. He cupped both of her breasts in his hands and massaged them firmly. Eleanor just stared down at him, panting, burning . . .

. . . Wanting.

His skin was dark compared to the paleness of her breasts. He closed his eyes while he fondled and sucked, his cheeks hollowing out slightly.

"Trey," she moaned. He drew his mouth off one crest with a popping sound and moved over the other. All she could do was continue to prop herself up on the table and take everything he gave her. At one point, he slid his firm lips off a swollen nipple and straightened. He put his hands on her hips and slid her body toward him. "Lean back," he directed. There wasn't enough room on the table to recline completely. Besides, who wouldn't want to watch him at that moment? So she went back onto her elbows, never taking her gaze off him. He was staring at her crotch again. Her thighs tensed when he matter-of-factly reached between her legs and began rubbing her pussy again. She gasped. His mouth slanted.

"You're so warm, Eleanor," he growled, glancing up at her face, triumph flashing in his eyes. "And you're getting your panties nice and wet, aren't you? Does that feel good?"

"Yes," she moaned as she stared at him, spellbound while she twisted her hips slightly against the divine pressure of his rubbing fingers. He moved suddenly, wrapping his arms around her thighs and scooting a good portion of her ass off the table. She cried out in surprise, her back flattening against the table and her head bumping on the surface. He continued to support her lower body with one arm around her thigh.

"Let's just get these off you," he murmured, pulling down on her underwear with his free hand. He maneuvered them between their bodies and off her feet. Before she knew what to expect from him, he plunged a finger into her sheath. She cried out.

She saw his teeth flash. "Soaking. Wet," he grated out as he moved his arm back and forth, penetrating her briskly. "Who would guess that you're as hot as a volcano under all these baggy clothes?" She moaned, bucking her hips against the pressure of his hand. "*Who*, Eleanor?"

"You," she gasped.

"Damn straight," he muttered, and then he was bending her knees and pushing her thighs back, giving the table most of her weight again. "Spread them wide," he ordered, and she opened her legs farther. He kept his hands at the back of her thighs and sunk his head. He swiped the tip of his tongue between her labia, and she made a wild, strangled sound. He rubbed her clit hard with the tip of his tongue. She shuddered.

His mouth conferred pure, distilled pleasure.

"Oh God," she moaned. Her hands clutched helplessly at the lining of his coat. She lifted her head, desperate to see him. He ate her with a furious focus now. His firm lips pressed on her outer sex while his stiffened tongue lashed and polished her clit. He sucked gently and twisted his face back and forth, and she bit off a scream. His intensity, his raw hunger, overwhelmed her. She clutched at his head mindlessly, only vaguely aware that she was moaning nonstop. The soles of her feet burned. Her clit simmered beneath his abrading tongue.

He plunged a finger into her pussy while he rubbed her clit even harder. She went wild, clawing at his head, twisting her hips on the table. He growled into her flesh, holding her hip firmly with one spread hand, forcing her to take her pleasure head-on.

A moment later, she gasped and shuddered in orgasm. He didn't stop. If anything, he was even more ruthless in his actions while she climaxed, plunging his finger deep and using his entire hand to vibrate her outer sex, his fingers delving into her buttocks. The whole time, he tongued her clit forcefully while wave after wave of orgasm coursed through her. He demanded she experience every ounce of pleasure she could, and she obeyed without thought. She'd never had an orgasm last so long.

He squeezed every last bit of pleasure out of her.

Finally, she sagged onto the table, dazed, limp and panting. Distantly, she was aware of him straightening and moving tensely where he stood between her splayed thighs. Then his hands were on her hips again, and he was adjusting her in that matter-of-fact way he had.

"You okay, Eleanor?" she heard him ask.

She lifted her head and blinked sluggishly, focusing on him. His face appeared strained and his blue eyes fierce as he looked down at her. She bit her lip to stifle a groan of reanimated arousal. His firm lips, his chin and his nose glistened from her juices.

"Yeah," she managed hoarsely.

"Good, because now it's my turn."

She knew what that meant. He looked like a wolf that was about to feed. She felt his cock nudging at her entry. His hands pushed on her thighs, rolling her hips back on the table, sending her feet higher into the air. He guided his cock with his hand. He pierced her slowly, but firmly. She moaned shakily at the sensation of him stretching her. Filling her.

He pressed his balls against her wet outer sex and circled his hips slightly. A cry rippled past her lips. *Oh God, it feels so good.* She tightened around him reflexively. He growled.

"You have no idea how sexy you look right now." His eyes flashed. "I'm going to fuck you until your ears ring." He cupped her hips and waist with his large hands, withdrew slightly and sunk back into her firmly. "Is there any reason we should be cautious as far as making noise?"

"Huh?" she gasped, too overwhelmed by the feeling of his big, long cock pulsing in her flesh to decode language.

"Can anyone hear us down in this vault?" he bit out.

She shook her head, rolling her skull against the table. "Everyone who works down here is gone."

"*Good.*"

He laced his arms beneath her knees, forcing her legs open in the air, his shoulders pressing against the back of her thighs, her feet falling behind him. He withdrew until only the head of his cock was still submerged, and then jetted back into her, their pelvises smacking together.

"Jesus, you feel fucking fantastic," he grated out.

And he was off.

He took her with that fluid, strong thrust of his hips, thighs and ass with which she was becoming achingly familiar. Eleanor shook on the table, rattled to the core. She couldn't get in a full breath of air. He was ruthless, his facial muscles growing rigid, his body coiling tight, his cock pounding into her at a hard pace. She found herself grasping at his shirtsleeve-covered forearms, desperate for some kind of hold in the midst of the storm. He caught her wrists and held them immobile next to her thighs, never pausing once in his merciless possession.

His restraint of her arms steadied her, both inside and out. Had he known it would? All the while, he stared down at her, his gleaming eyes piercing her spirit just as surely as his cock did her flesh.

He became so forceful, the antique cataloging table began to heave against the wall. A can of some kind fell, rattling on the tile floor. He never paused. Not until the top of her head began to bump against something behind her. She hardly cared, she was so overwhelmed by the hard, constant pressure of his driving cock.

But apparently he minded.

He abruptly withdrew, making her cry out in surprised protest. Then he was lifting her down from the table and urging her to turn.

"Bend over," he said behind her. She was highly disoriented. The deprivation of his cock had been cruel. All she could think about was getting him back inside her. When she was too slow to respond, he pushed gently but firmly on her shoulders. "Bend over and brace yourself," he said. "Eleanor?"

Crack.

She jumped slightly at the sharp sound and the sting on her bottom. He'd spanked her. He drew her slip up deliberately to her waist, fully exposing her ass. He squeezed both her buttocks at once. He spanked her twice more.

"Ooh," she whimpered, her brain clearing, her hands finding his coat draped over the edge of the table. She bent for him then, presenting herself for his hand. His cock. Anything he wanted to give her. She heard his grunt of satisfaction.

He peeled back one of her ass cheeks and entered her again. Her mouth fell and a harsh moan tore at her throat. He felt huge at this angle. He began thrusting again with deep, firm strokes, their skin slapping together, the sound ringing in her ears in a regular, taut rhythm. She became vaguely aware that she was groaning and whimpering nonstop. As always, he barraged her with sensation.

He paused with his cock embedded in her and his balls pressing hard against her outer sex. He spanked her ass cheek tautly before he reached around her, finding her clit unerringly. She clamped her eyelids shut, her entire body tensing at his touch, her throat vibrating with a groan.

"This is what you get for being so beautiful, Eleanor, so damn sexy . . ." he bit out before he fucked her with short, hard jabs. She had the bizarre, disoriented impression he was trying to push his words into her being . . . to make her believe them.

She exploded like a rocket. Pleasure seized her entire being.

Trey's harsh voice penetrated her brain.

"Hold steady. Eleanor? Brace yourself," he demanded, squeezing her elbow with his hand to indicate what he wanted. Orgasm still rippling through her, she managed to stiffen her arms.

He began to move, his thrusts into her even faster and more forceful than before, if that were possible. She gritted her jaw and tightened her muscles, striving to move her hips in a counter-rhythm to his. With only the head of his cock submerged, he paused, her ass molded into his tightly cupped hand.

"Stay still, honey. I'm about to come," he rasped.

His cock plunged into her, making her gasp. A taut, knocking sound entered her buzzing brain. It was the cabinet striking the wall faster now. She blinked open her eyes, her body rocking to and fro rapidly while his grunts of pleasure rained down on her. He was jerking her hips and ass, serving her pussy to his driving cock. Her mouth opened in a silent scream. His pelvis smacked against her ass. He held her against him, and she felt him swell in her.

A giant shudder went through him and a roar rattled his throat. Her hair stood on end at the thrilling sound.

Then he was thrusting into her again, her body jerked to and fro, and the cabinet rapidly bumped against the wall. Sensation struck her consciousness like bullet fire. And then something really *was* falling on her, hitting the back of her head, her shoulders and back—

"Shit, oh Jesus— *Eleanor?*"

Something large had broken loose that was stacked at the back of the table. But the only thing she experienced for a confused second was dread at the sensation of Trey's cock sliding out of her body.

"No, Trey," she groaned miserably, blinking open her eyelids. "Just leave it."

But it was no good. He was next to her now, lifting the wooden frame that had fallen on her while they rocked the cabinet so forcefully. She pushed herself up and stood, feeling her satin slip falling past her hips.

"Are you okay?" he demanded.

"Yeah, I'm fine," she assured, touching her back dazedly. The plywood frame hadn't been all that heavy.

"Let me look."

She turned slightly. She felt his fingers move along her shoulders and back as he inspected her. "It didn't break the skin," he finally said. "I thought it was attached to the wall. It didn't even rattle like the other stuff piled in front of it did . . . until the end, anyway. It's a mounted photo or something. Damn," Trey muttered thickly. "It's torn. I'm sorry."

"So am I," she agreed, still irritated by his abrupt departure from her body and her sudden emptiness. "I hate that stupid thing."

He glanced at her tensely. "You're not worried about it? It's not a rare photo or something?" He heaved the three-foot by three-foot mounted, wood-framed photograph back into its original position against the wall.

She stood and leaned across the cabinet. "Hardly. Don't worry about it. I told you this wasn't a collection preservation room. There's no art or artifacts in here. It was a photo I had done for a display item for the 1960s Sexual Revolution exhibit we had a couple years ago." She lifted the torn portion of the black-and-white vinyl, making the subject of the photo clear to him. She gave him a wry glance of amusement.

His slow smile made something curl tight in her belly.

God, I'm crazy about him.

He snorted with laughter as they both stared at the image of playboy Hugh Hefner surrounded by a bevy of buxom bunnies.

"Some irony, that ol' Hugh would be the one to interrupt a moment like that. Traitor," she said with amused irritability.

"At least he had the decency to wait until the finale."

"Barely."

"I know. Trust me, I *know*."

"I always hated the stupid thing. Now I have even more reason to dislike it," she muttered, beleaguered.

His low, rough laughter made her sensitive skin prickle with awareness. He turned, taking her into his arms, his blue eyes lambent with amusement and the heat of his previous blazing arousal. She hugged his waist. He bent his knees and dropped a kiss on her mouth. Their lips clung together, hunger still lingering even after their explosive lovemaking. "You know, I think I hate Hugh too," he mused, his warm, fragrant breath brushing against her upturned mouth. "I'm learning that I don't like *anything* that keeps me from you, Eleanor."

A ripple of emotion went through her. She wished she could believe what she saw in his eyes at that moment, but it seemed too incredible, like signing on for a fantasy when she knew better.

She felt him lift his arm and realized he was checking his watch. "It's going on seven fifteen. Do you still want to make the reading event?" he asked her quietly.

"No way. I still need to shower and change. There's isn't time."

"Okay. Then how about if I make you dinner? We should talk."

She froze. *What the hell does he mean by that?*

"We should?" she asked hollowly, her heartbeat starting to drum in her ears.

He nodded. He leaned down and rubbed his lips against her flushed cheek.

"Okay," she whispered.

And then he was kissing her again, deep and wet and wholesale, and her curiosity and anxiety faded. It'd never been clearer to her that she was in *way* over her head.

But before Trey, she'd had no idea that drowning could be so sweet.

TWENTY

They agreed in the cab that Eleanor would go to her condo to shower and change and then go over to Trey's penthouse.

"Can you really cook?" she asked him as the cab flew down the inner Lake Shore Drive.

"Are you surprised?"

She shook her head, smiling. Their scorching, unexpected interlude in the basement had left her feeling euphoric again . . . almost intoxicated. She still couldn't get over the fact that he'd not only not been angry at her misleading him about her job, he'd also—impossibly—found her work persona *attractive*.

"Not really," she replied. "I'm starting to think you're capable of anything."

He arched his brows in a questioning gesture.

"I thought you'd be angry, when you saw me down there in the basement of the library today," she told him impulsively. "*That's* what surprised me most of all."

His smile faded. She saw the city lights gleam in his eyes. "Because you were dishonest with me about what your job was like, you mean?"

Her throat tightened. She glanced ahead, assuring herself that the cab's partition was shut so that the driver couldn't overhear.

"I thought maybe you wouldn't think I was exciting as I was making myself out to be, at the reading event," she admitted quietly, glad for the cover of night to hide her blush. "That's why I misled you about my job."

"I know I've told you how much I value honesty," he said after a pause wherein her stomach had started to grow fluttery with anxiety about what he'd say next. "And that hasn't changed. The thing of it is . . ."

"What?" she asked breathlessly when he faded off, as if he was trying to find the right words.

"Telling me that you're some kind of sales executive instead of a preservation librarian at the museum . . . well, that's not really the kind of lie that I'm concerned about." His face looked serious, but she thought she saw a sparkle of amusement in his eyes. He glanced up at the cabdriver, but the partition was muffling the radio he had playing. There was little chance he could hear their conversation. "We agreed from the beginning this was only going to be a physical relationship, so I can't really blame you for trying to put on a sexy show for me, can I?" Her heart palpitated in her chest at the word *show*. Did he realize she was playacting at being sexy? "You didn't know me well enough at first to guess that I think your real job is a hell of a lot more interesting—and sexy, for that matter—than your made-up job description."

Her breath stuck in her lungs when he started to lean toward her, a lean, hungry look on his shadowed face. She jumped when her cell phone buzzed loudly in her coat pocket at the same time the cab pulled into her building's turnabout. She gave Trey an amused, apologetic glance and dug in her coat pocket for her cell phone, while he paid the driver.

He'd gotten out and was holding open the door for her while she read the text she'd just received. It was from her mom.

Come to the Evanston Hospital ER as soon as you can. Your
father has had a heart attack.

Shivers poured through her body.

"Eleanor?" she heard Trey say, but it was like he spoke through
insulation. She blinked in disorientation, looking up at him. The
stark vision of him made reality jerk into place with the seeming
force of a snapped whip.

"It's my dad. He's had a heart attack," she said numbly.

He pulled her out of the cab and slammed the door. He took
her phone from her. She stared at his rigid features while he
read the text. He handed her back the phone and took her free
hand in his. "Come on. You call your mom and find out what's
going on."

She started to dial, but as she did so, a call from her mother
came through.

"Mom? What's happening?" Eleanor asked as Trey pulled her
along the sidewalk.

She listened as her mom shakily described her dad falling in
the hallway on the way to the bathroom. An ambulance had come,
and her dad had been conscious, but very groggy when they took
him. Her mom had followed the ambulance in her car.

"The EMT said it was a heart attack. Now I'm just waiting to
hear about the lab results," her mother said anxiously. "Why is
this happening? It's too *much*—"

"It's not the same thing, Mom. Dad's going to be okay," Eleanor soothed, knowing her mom was flashing back to Caddy's sudden illness and hospitalizations. Eleanor wouldn't allow her brain
to go there. "I'll get in my car right now and be at the hospital
within the hour. Just text me where to go once I get there. And
Mom, call Dr. Chevitz to let him know what happened," she said,

referring to their longtime family doctor. "He might even be on call and can meet us at the ER. Okay? I'll call—" She caught herself, startled. She'd been about to say she'd call Caddy. That hole opened up alarmingly wide, gaping in her chest when she realized the utter impossibility of reaching her sister at that moment.

"I'll call Aunt Joan and let her know what's happened," she covered her near mistake, referring to her dad's sister who lived near Milwaukee. "I'll see you soon. Everything's going to be okay," she repeated firmly.

She hung up the phone. She blinked in disorientation when she looked around, not recognizing where Trey had led her. They were in a parking garage, but it wasn't hers. Everything looked hazy and weird, until Trey turned and looked over his shoulder. His sharp blue eyes pierced her fog.

"Where are we?" she asked. "I've got to get to the—"

"We're going to my car. I'll take you to the hospital," he said.

"I can drive. You don't have to go," she called out to him, but he kept walking rapidly ahead of her, his hand still grasping hers. Eleanor was too worried to try and stop him. "My mom is freaking out," she said as he led her to a dark blue, sleek sedan. He opened the door for her.

"Has your dad had problems with his heart before?"

She sat. He extended the seatbelt and waited until she took it from him. She stared at the metal clasp as if she were seeing the device for the first time in her life. "No, he's always been pretty healthy. I *thought* he didn't look well over Thanksgiving, though. I should have pushed him to see his doctor then." Fear rippled through her, cutting through her dazed shock. The thought of her father lying crumpled and helpless in the hallway overwhelmed her. What was going to happen?

"Oh *God*," she gasped, panic rising up in her like a wave that was about to smother her last breath.

She blinked when Trey's hand grasped her shoulder. She stared up at him, her mouth hanging open.

"One step at a time," he said firmly. "Put your seatbelt on, Eleanor."

Her head cleared. She inhaled shakily and nodded, thankful for his touch. His presence. It anchored her.

The trip to the hospital passed in an anxious haze. Her brain seemed sluggish. Numb. It was as if some kind of automatic shut-off had occurred inside her. She didn't want to think of what it would be like if they lost her dad. So her mind just went blank.

A half hour later, Trey pulled his car directly up to the ER entrance. "You go on in while I look for parking," he directed.

"You don't have to come in. I can take the L home."

"Do you not want me there? Will I be in the way?" he asked her matter-of-factly.

"No, it's not that, I just don't want to bother you any more than I already have—"

"It's not a bother." He reached around her and opened the passenger-side door. "Go on. Your mom will be anxious to see you. I'll be there in a minute. But if I don't see you in the waiting area, I'll just wait. Don't worry about me."

She caught his eye. "Thank you so much," she told him before she got out of the car.

She immediately saw her mother standing near the check-in station. Her usually immaculate hair looked disheveled and her face appeared wan from worry. She immediately launched herself toward Eleanor when she saw her, her arms outstretched.

"I know you'll think it's all my fault. All that rich food I give him," her mother fretted as they hugged tightly.

"It doesn't matter what I think, Mom. It's what the tests and the doctors say that counts. If diet is the culprit, then you guys will just have to change it and exercise more. People have to do it every day; it's not the end of the world," Eleanor assured through a tight throat. She pushed her mother back and peered at her face closely. "What *are* the doctors saying? What's happening?"

"He's stable."

"Thank God."

"I saw him just a minute ago after they finished the EKG. He was groggy, so he might be asleep by now. They're giving him oxygen therapy and nitroglycerin now. He'll have to start taking some of that clot-busting medicine."

"So it *was* definitely a heart attack?"

Her mom nodded. Eleanor's own heart swelled uncomfortably at the affirmation. Her mom grasped her arms. "But a minor one, honey. The doctor called it a warning sign."

"Some warning sign. Can I see him?"

"I think so. They were going to move him to a regular room soon. Come with me," she said, taking Eleanor's hand and leading her through a pair of swinging doors.

Forty-five minutes later, she and her mother walked back out into the ER waiting room. It'd been sobering, but also a huge relief to see her father, and even speak with him a little. Yes, he'd looked unusually small in the hospital bed for a man she'd always considered to be as big and strong as a giant, and his complexion had been distressingly gray. But he'd also smiled upon seeing her and said, "Don't worry, bug. It's not that bad. It felt like a really bad case of indigestion."

"Yeah, your heart is telling you loud and clear it doesn't like your diet," Eleanor had teased him back before she'd kissed his temple. His laugh had been weak and gruff, but Eleanor had never been so glad to hear it.

A man had arrived with a gurney to take her father to his hospital room. Eleanor had a chance to speak briefly to the attending physician, and then more extensively with their family doctor, Dr. Chevitz, who had been kind enough to come down to the ER after her mother's phone call. Chevitz helped them by decoding some of the lab results and explaining her dad's condition and prognosis in concrete terms. His presence went a long way to soothing her mother. By the time the two of them walked out of the ER, her mother had gone to the bathroom, combed her hair, put on some lipstick and seemingly located most of her typical imperious composure.

Eleanor saw Trey immediately when they entered the waiting room. He sat on a couch, long legs bent in front of him, a magazine in his lap. He looked a little surreal sitting there in his expensive suit, her longtime unobtainable fantasy smack dab in the middle of the harsh reality of a family emergency. Without saying anything to her mother, Eleanor walked over to him. She felt awkward about him being there, but she also was profoundly grateful and touched by his presence.

He glanced up, saw her and stood.

"How is he?" he asked her.

"He's going to be okay. They're only going to keep him overnight. They're moving him to a hospital room now. They told us to wait a little bit before going up, while they get him admitted and situated. There was no major damage done to the heart. He's going to have to get more exercise, take medication, make some major changes to his diet, but he should be good as new before long."

"I suppose the last was aimed at me."

Eleanor blinked at the sound of her mother speaking behind her. She hadn't realized she'd followed her.

"I wasn't aiming anything at you," Eleanor said wearily, turning. "I was just repeating what the doctors told us and what you already knew. Trey, this is my mother, Catherine Briggs. Mom, meet Trey Riordan."

Trey tossed down the magazine and extended his hand toward her mother. Instead of shaking it, her mom accepted his hand and just held it. Eleanor mentally rolled her eyes at the typical Catherine the Great regal gesture.

"I'm sorry to have to meet you under these circumstances," Trey said. "But I'm glad to hear your husband is going to be okay."

Catherine smiled, her gaze running down the considerable length of Trey's person in a sharp assessment.

"Trey was nice enough to drive me here," Eleanor said, sensing the questions brewing behind her mother's polite but inquiring expression. There hadn't been any opportunity to tell her mom about Trey. "We were out together when you texted me earlier."

"How wonderful. I hadn't realized you were seeing someone special, Eleanor."

Eleanor felt heat flood her cheeks.

"My father had something similar happen to him two years ago," Trey said to her mom. "I know what a shock it was for me when I heard. I didn't think Eleanor should be driving unless it was completely necessary."

"How kind of you," her mom said approvingly, finally releasing Trey's hand.

"He did? Your father, I mean?" Eleanor asked Trey, concerned. "How is he doing now?"

"He's doing fine. He complains nonstop about his low-fat, low-cholesterol diet, but he hasn't been as fit as he is today since I was a kid."

"Everyone focuses on diet and exercises in these cases almost exclusively," her mom told Trey, her manner confidential, as if Eleanor weren't even standing there. "What they don't dwell on in the ER is the psychological aspect of things. Eleanor's father has always been healthy as an ox. We lost Eleanor's sister this year. I'm sure Eleanor has mentioned it. David has taken it very hard. We all have, of course. But *grief*," her mother said with a shrewd glance at Trey, "is likely the main culprit here, not my beef pirog. Mark my words. David's heart was broken when we lost Eleanor's sister, Caddy."

"*Mom,*" Eleanor muttered, mortified. A roar had started up in her ears. She noticed Trey's sideways glance at her. What was he thinking? Suddenly, it all seemed unbearable, having Trey exposed to her mother's irrepressible smugness . . . her family's vulnerability.

Hers.

"I saw a sign for a cafeteria. Could anyone use a cup of coffee?" Trey asked, putting his hand on Eleanor's back. She glanced up at him, startled by his calm suggestion. At his supportive touch. As her mother replied enthusiastically to the affirmative, Eleanor searched his expression.

She didn't know what she'd done to deserve it, but something in Trey's warm, steady gaze said it was true.

On this difficult, anxiety-ridden night, he was going to stand by her.

It was past one in the morning when Trey pulled his car into a spot in his parking garage and turned off the ignition. Eleanor just sat there in the passenger seat, feeling wrung out by the events of the night, yet strangely alert too. Despite her exhaustion, she'd been hyperaware of her close proximity to Trey on the drive back into the city. Tonight had begun to teach her a lesson.

Trey Riordan was indeed her fantasy man. He just wasn't the fantasy she'd pegged him as being. Or at least he wasn't *solely* that. He was so much more.

She'd been humbled by his attentiveness and kindness, not only to herself, but to her mother. They'd made sure that her father was settled in his new hospital room. Just before midnight, her aunt Joan had arrived. Joan said she'd be staying at the house in Evanston with her mother, a detail that had relieved Eleanor hugely.

When it became clear that her dad would sleep through the night, Eleanor agreed to leave. She promised her mom to return to the hospital early in the morning. Only then had Trey driven her home, despite the fact that Eleanor had assured him he could go at least a dozen times during the interminable night.

Presently, he put his hands on the wheel and looked over at her, his expression solemn.

"You look exhausted," he said.

"I am. Also wired, strangely enough."

"It's the adrenaline. It does weird things to you."

A wave of emotion went through her, somehow brought on by his low, intimate tone in the close confines of the car. She swallowed it back thickly.

"I like your mom. She's a riot. I see why you guys call her Catherine the Great."

"I love her like crazy, but there's no denying she's a handful," Eleanor laughed wearily.

"The very definition of family. They know our buttons, and are experts at pushing them."

"She liked you too. Adored you, in fact. I'm sorry if she embarrassed you, with some of the assumptions she was making about us," she said, wincing slightly in memory at some of those assumptions, like how she'd proudly introduced Trey to her aunt Joan as

Eleanor's boyfriend. At the time, Eleanor had suppressed a wicked urge to blurt out that she and Trey were just screwing each other.

"I wasn't embarrassed once."

She blinked at his firm tone. Slowly, she unfastened her seatbelt, finding it difficult to meet his stare in that moment. An uncomfortable pressure had started to expand in her chest. "It helped a lot, having you there. You were very sweet, to act as a buffer. We usually cover for each other in handling my mom, but with Dad out of commission, and—" She stopped herself abruptly and stared at her entwined fingers resting on her thighs.

"Why didn't you tell me about your sister?"

His quiet question seemed to hang in the air between them, replaying again and again in her head. It'd seemed to hover between them at the hospital too. He hadn't had a chance to ask her about it all night, with either her mom or Joan being near them.

Not until now, anyway.

She swallowed thickly and inhaled for courage. She turned to him and met his stare.

"I haven't told you a lot of things about me. It didn't seem to be a requirement before, given what we'd decided our relationship would be."

For a moment, he didn't speak. He didn't move. What was he *thinking*? She experienced a wild urge to take what she'd said back, but then he was twisting the keys out of the ignition, unbuckling his belt and pushing open his door. She rushed to get out of the car and follow him.

"Trey, I didn't mean—"

"It's okay," he said shortly, reaching behind him as he walked in order to activate the automatic lock on his car. "You're not saying anything shocking. We agreed from the beginning this wasn't going to be serious."

"But—" She frowned, realizing she was trying to hold a

conversation with his back. She rushed to keep up with his long-legged stride. He opened a door and she caught it. She hurried after him down a flight of stairs. By the time they entered the luxurious lobby of his building, she was out of breath. He punched the button for the elevator and she circled around him in mounting frustration. She stepped into him, demanding he look at her. "Then why are you acting mad at me?" she asked in a subdued tone.

"I'm not mad at you."

She raised her eyebrows incredulously.

"I'm mad at myself. And maybe you too, a little," he admitted under his breath, glancing aside at the doorman's station and frowning fiercely. Ralph sat there, pretending he wasn't listening in on their exchange. "But I shouldn't be."

"You shouldn't?" she whispered, bewildered.

His mouth grew hard. "I'm the one who suggested we should keep this light. I've got no right to get pissed at you for reminding me of that. You were never obligated to spill your life story to me."

She took a step back from him, stung.

"I see," she managed, struggling to steady herself. "Well, thank you again for everything tonight. It was above and beyond what the role required. Obviously," she added bitterly. She started toward the lobby front doors, but he halted her firmly with a hand on her upper arm. He looked fierce.

"Come upstairs with me."

Her mouth parted in disbelieving confusion. She couldn't understand his mood.

"Just to rest. That's all," he added tersely. "You look exhausted."

"But that's—"

"Not part of the agreement. I *get* it, Eleanor," he bit out, his jaw tense. "Come anyway."

She stared at him in openmouthed shock. The elevator door dinged open. For a moment, she just stood there, dazed, well aware she stood on the threshold of some indefinable zone between safety and danger when it came to her heart. But then he held out his hand, and she reached for it without thought, drawn by his eyes. His determination. His heat.

The undeniable fact that she'd fallen in love with him.

Still, she was wary.

"I don't want to talk about anything serious tonight, Trey," she said shakily. She couldn't stand the thought of having to explain why she'd purposefully never opened up much in front of him . . . why she'd never told him about Caddy. She felt too raw on that topic. Too exposed.

"I realize you don't need anything heavy laid on you right now. What you need is some rest. It's only a few hours until you have to get up and go to the hospital again. But I want you with me, Eleanor. I want to make sure you're okay. And I don't give a damn if it breaks any of the rules of our agreement," he stated fiercely. "Okay?"

"Yes," she whispered. His hand closed tighter around hers and she followed him onto the elevator.

When they got up to his place, he asked her if she'd like anything from the kitchen. She told him ice water. While he was preparing their drinks, she wandered into his large living room. There were several boxes stacked near the windows that she hadn't seen on her last visit there.

Leaving the lights off, she stood and looked out at the cars zooming down Lake Shore Drive and the black expanse of the great lake on the horizon. She tried to make her mind go as blank as the lake appeared in the darkness, but it didn't work. As exhausted as she was, she was still very aware of Trey's movements in the kitchen behind her. Something had changed tonight.

Something huge.

She was no cynical player. She never had been. But the fact of the matter was, she'd been okay with their agreement to make their relationship about mutually gratifying sex. The arrangement had felt both incredibly exciting, yet somehow predictable too. She'd felt in control, at least some of the time. But now she'd fallen for him.

And suddenly, instead of being in control, she felt like she was free-falling, already cringing in anticipated pain from the harsh ending.

The back of her neck prickled when she heard him approaching. She watched his reflection in the floor-to-ceiling window, absorbing the outline of his hard male beauty. He'd removed his tie and suit coat and rolled back the sleeves of his dress shirt. She wondered yet again if she could ever get tired of looking at him.

He came to a stop beside her and she glanced sideways. She smiled.

"What's this?"

"An ice water for you and a hot chocolate for me."

"It smells good," she murmured, turning to him, referring to the steaming beverage he held in his left hand.

"Then take it. I actually made it for you. I'll take the ice water."

She glanced at him in surprise. "Are you sure?"

"I know how much you like hot chocolate. I thought it would help you relax a little. Come and sit down," he said, nodding toward a couch.

She took a sip of the sweet chocolate a moment later and sighed wearily. Their arms, hips and thighs pressed close where they sat side by side on the couch. The feeling of his solid body against hers felt indescribably good in her dazed, numb state. They remained silent for a moment, Eleanor sipping the cocoa and glancing around the beautiful room. She spied some framed photos in the distance on the bookcase. She'd never studied them up close before.

"Are those family pictures?" she asked quietly.

"Yeah," he said, following her gaze.

"You told me your brother was a pilot. What does your sister do?" she wondered, taking comfort from the sound of his voice.

"Kacy is the vice president of human resources for a watch factory. She's your basic dynamo—she works full-time, has my nephew, Jason, to take care of, plus she volunteers for a ton of projects. My brother and I have always been lazy in comparison to her."

"Right. You and your brother sound like real slackers," she murmured sarcastically.

"You know how it is with siblings."

"Sibling rivalries, you mean?"

He shrugged. "I'm third born and the youngest. Sometimes I think I had it easy compared to Kacy and Kevin. They were always competing for the spotlight."

She chuckled softly as she took another sip of cocoa.

"What?" he asked.

"Trey. I just got it." She rested her head on the back of the couch and turned her chin to look at him. "Your name. You're third born."

His low laugh struck her exhausted consciousness as wonderful. For some reason, it made her feel like she was sinking into the couch. Into him. Her eyelids felt very heavy.

"My mom has a sense of humor," he said.

"And your dad?"

"My dad likes to play cards. Three is his lucky number."

She snorted with tired laughter. The moment struck her as very sweet and fragile for some reason.

"What are all the boxes for?" she asked a moment later, nodding at the boxes stacked by the window.

"Christmas tree and decorations. My maid got them out this morning. She's going to start putting them up tomorrow."

She blinked to ease the sudden sting in her eyes. "You don't do it yourself?"

"It's not all that much fun alone," he said gruffly, taking a sip of his water.

"Yeah," she agreed, her throat tightening. "Do you usually put it there? In the window facing Lake Shore Drive?"

"Yeah."

She wiggled on the couch, starting to draw up her feet before she realized she still wore her shoes. She slouched back into the couch, too tired to remove them. Trey noticed. He set down his water on the coffee table and matter-of-factly bent to flip off one shoe.

"I'm not going to put up my tree this year," she said through rubbery lips.

"How come?"

"My sister and I used to get together to decorate our condos. It was a tradition."

Trey went still in the process of pulling off her second shoe. Through her haze of fatigue, she recognized she'd startled him. She'd surprised *herself*, by bringing up Caddy when she'd thought she wanted to avoid the topic at all costs. The mention of his Christmas tree had ripped the bandage off the wound.

"We'd do it on the first weekend after Thanksgiving. Drink hot chocolate. Listen to Christmas music. Put up our trees," she continued hoarsely. "I just don't think I can do it alone." She blinked heavy eyelids and focused on his face. "*There,*" she said, her voice just above a whisper. "I've talked about Caddy in front of you."

"You loved her so much."

Unwanted tears swelled in her eyes at his simple declaration. He'd read the truth on her face. She hated it, but her defenses felt threadbare at that moment. Suddenly, his arms surrounded her and his mouth was pressed against her temple. A shudder of emotion went through her.

"Shhh," he said, his lips brushing her ear. "I've got you."

If he'd uttered some platitude, like, "Everything is going to be okay," she probably would have been able to keep herself together. It was his holding her so securely and saying those three words that made her lose it.

She shook. She wept without constraint, in a way she hadn't since Caddy had passed. He didn't speak, but his actions said so much. He just held her while she cried out her sadness and her fear, her grief and her loss. At some point, he broke their hold only to take her hot chocolate from her and place it on the table next to his water. She'd forgotten she'd been holding it. Wordlessly, he snagged a box of tissues from the table at the end of the couch, plucked out several, and handed them to her. Mortifyingly, the tears kept coming. He didn't seem to mind. He just took her back into his arms and held her fast.

In the following fifteen minutes, she managed to use up most of the Kleenex box.

Finally, she just sagged against him, utterly spent. She blew her nose loudly. He plucked up all the discarded tissues in her lap and held out his hand expectantly when she'd finished blowing her nose. She grimaced, staring down at the damp, crumpled Kleenex in her hand.

"No, it's too gross," she muttered hoarsely.

"No. It's not."

She felt his lean body start against her. Startled, she glanced at his face. Strangely, he was *smiling*. She realized he'd been shaking in subdued laughter. He noticed her confused expression and wiped the grin off his face.

"Sorry. Just thought of something. Give it, Eleanor," he insisted wryly, nodding at the crumpled tissue.

Reluctantly, she tried to set the well-used, balled-up tissue on top of the others, but he just grabbed it matter-of-factly. He rose from the couch, holding the used tissues in both hands. He was back within a minute.

"Lean back," he urged, his deep, gruff voice penetrating her groggy, post-crying state. She followed his directions without hesitation or thought, sinking into the couch on her side. He came down next to her, so that they were belly to belly facing each other, their heads resting on the same cushion. He whisked a throw over them, tucking it carefully around her back. She blinked open her eyelids when he cupped her jaw in one big hand. An anxious thought entered her sluggish brain and she opened her mouth to voice it.

His finger slid across her numb lips as if to silence her.

"I have the alarm set on my phone. I'll make sure you're up in time so that you can get back to the hospital early," he said quietly.

She exhaled in relief, moved by the fact that he'd anticipated her concern, and that he took care of her so well. So effortlessly.

The last thing she was aware of before she succumbed to sleep was his kiss on her mouth, soft and sweet, asking nothing from her.

Only giving.

TWENTY-ONE

S he awoke to the same sensation: Trey's mouth moving on hers. She awoke to need.

It was dark, and she felt warm. Secure. So good. She pressed closer to his long, solid body, craving his heat. His strength. Her body quickened in arousal. He groaned roughly when she deepened their kiss, his big hand running along the side of her body, detailing her shape.

Her desperate longing mounted.

She began to claw at his shirt buttons. Frustrated by her fumbling fingers, she shifted her attention to getting him out of his pants. He was busy shoving her dress up to her waist. All that mattered at that moment was the essentials.

All that mattered was that they were joined.

A frantic few seconds later, he lay on top of her on the couch, his cock sinking into her. She stared up at his large, shadowed form, her fingers digging into the rounded muscles of his shoulders. He filled her up so greatly. So perfectly. Not just his cock. She overflowed with feeling. It was all she could do to keep herself from screaming when he pressed his balls against her outer sex.

He went still between her thighs. He leaned down and kissed her mouth, his manner striking her as reverent somehow.

And then he was moving, building that friction in her that only he could, calling her name . . . forcing her to feel more, and then more, until she was bursting with it. He pounded into her body as she climaxed and spoke harshly next to her ear.

"Take it, Eleanor. Take it all. Because I've got so much more to give you."

She thought about it frequently the rest of the day, him saying those words so feelingly next to her ear as pleasure lit up her body. She relived and questioned that moment again and again in her head.

Their lovemaking in the predawn hour had felt so passionate. So soulful. So much more profound than anything that had passed between them before . . . more intense than anything she'd experienced in her life.

Maybe it'd been wishful thinking on her part. But there, in that poignant moment with him, it had felt like he'd been telling her something precious with those fiercely uttered words.

She was surprised and pleased to see how much better her father looked when she returned to the hospital that morning. He was sitting up in bed, eating his breakfast and talking with her mom and Joan, who had arrived just before Eleanor.

"How are you feeling?" she asked her father after she'd kissed him in greeting and taken his hand in hers.

"Other than feeling a little stupid, I'm just fine," her dad told her.

"You've got nothing to feel stupid about," Eleanor insisted.

"Maybe you're right. *This* time," her dad conceded. "Now that I know how things stand with my heart, though, I'm responsible on a go-forward basis. It's nothing that can't be made right, bug," her dad said, patting her hand and giving her a pointed look.

"I know," Eleanor assured. "I'm not worried about that. We'll whip you into shape."

"Where's Trey?" her mom asked.

Heat rushed into Eleanor's cheeks. Last night, her mother's assumptions that she and Trey were an established couple had embarrassed her. Today, everything felt different, although she had no solid evidence to prove *why* it felt different. No spoken words. No promises.

Still, last night felt very amazing to her: beautiful, but delicate. Fragile.

"He's on his way to work, I assume," Eleanor replied lightly to her mother's question. "He dropped me off this morning." After they'd made love, Trey had insisted that he'd take her to the hospital, and he'd pick her up that evening at her parents' house.

"I like him a lot," Joan said, her eyes sparkling with warmth. "It's not often that you run into men who are as nice as they are good-looking. And Catherine filled me in on how successful he is." Eleanor glanced at her mother and rolled her eyes. Her mom had wriggled most of the crucial details about Trey's professional life from him by the time they'd reached the cashier at the cafeteria last night. "He runs his own company, Dave. Big, lucrative tech business," Joan told her brother. "I think you'll approve."

"It doesn't bode well that the first time I met your special man, I was unconscious," her dad grumbled.

"You guys are making more of a big deal about Trey and me than is warranted," Eleanor felt obligated to say. Her dad squeezed her hand and gave her a look. She couldn't help but smile when she saw the glint of understanding in his green eyes. She and her

father had always been unusually close. He clearly had sensed her
bubbling happiness and accompanying uncertainty when it came
to the topic of Trey.

The day passed quickly as they conferred with the cardiologist,
and a nurse educated them on future diet, medication and care.
Her dad seemed so much his normal self that it had Eleanor second-
guessing whether or not it wasn't just wishful thinking on her
part. The nurse assured her privately, however, that in instances
of a heart attack as minor as her father's had been, recovery could
be rapid. Her dad left the hospital on his own two feet that afternoon. If it weren't for the pallor of his skin, Eleanor would never
have guessed what had just happened to him.

After they'd gotten her father home and comfortable, she and
Joan went out to get her father's prescriptions filled and to go
grocery shopping for heart-healthy food. By the time they returned
home and put everything in the refrigerator, it was dark out.
Eleanor prepared dinner with her mom, making sure she stuck to
the low-fat cooking regimen.

Her dad was tired after dinner, and her mom went up with
him to bed. She and Joan were cleaning up in the kitchen when
the doorbell rang. An anxious tremor of anticipation went through
her at the unexpected sound.

"I'll get it," Eleanor said, wiping her hands off with a dish
towel and leaving her aunt in the kitchen.

A tight feeling expanded in her chest as she walked toward the
front door. She knew it was Trey even before she opened it. Her
breath caught at the vision of him standing on the front porch,
his blue eyes sharp on her, his shoulders looking so broad in his
black dress coat, his hands deep in the pockets.

She'd never seen a more welcome sight than that of him there at the front door of her childhood home.

"I hope you don't mind," he said when she opened the storm door for him. "Your parents' address was listed, and I saw the car in the driveway."

"I don't mind at all. We just finished dinner. I was about to call. Thanks for coming. I'm *so* glad to see you," she told him with breathless sincerity. She opened the door wider and beckoned him inside. Her gaze traveled over his handsome face in fresh wonder. It was as if she were seeing him for the first time. She knew her heart was in her eyes, but she couldn't seem to control her zeal for seeing him.

"I should have called sooner, but it's been one thing after another all day," she said. "Here, let me take your coat."

"How's your father?" Trey asked her as she led him into the living room a few seconds later.

"He's fantastic." The Christmas tree was lit. She turned on an extra lamp. "If I didn't know for certain he'd had a heart attack last night, I would have never believed it, seeing him today."

"I'm glad," he said, his gaze running over her face. "You look better too. Relieved."

"Thanks. It *has* been a relief, seeing him so much better today," she said, flushing in pleasure at the gleam in his eyes as he studied her closely. She thought of how he'd been there for her last night, how he'd held her while a storm of grief had shook her. A moment of awkwardness suddenly came over her. He somehow shrunk the dimensions of the familiar living room. He seemed so big standing there, so vibrant. So wonderful.

"Trey? I thought I heard your voice."

Eleanor blinked and looked up at the sound of Joan's voice. Her aunt stood at the entryway, smiling. Trey greeted her.

"We just finished dinner. Chicken, a baked potato, broccoli. It was a little bland, but healthy as can be. Should I warm up something for you?" Joan asked him.

"No, I've already eaten. But thanks."

Eleanor smiled when he glanced back at her. "Just his luck," she told Joan. "He'd just sampled Mom's leftovers from Thanksgiving and fallen hard for Russian cooking. Now there's been a halt to Russian feasts."

"I'm sure he'll have plenty of opportunity to sample Catherine's famous cooking, at least on the holidays, if not every day. All things in moderation. I'm going to get back to the dishes," Joan said with a wave of the dish towel she carried.

"So," Trey said gruffly when they were alone again. He glanced around the cozily lit living room. "This is where you grew up. It's nice."

"Yep. This was home. For eighteen years of my life, anyway."

"Somehow, your childhood home is always home," he said. His gaze skated over her, and suddenly he cursed softly under his breath. He stepped toward her and took her into his arms. He bent his knees and kissed her firmly on the mouth. Eleanor looped her arms around his neck, responding wholesale to his kiss.

"When's it going to stop?" he asked her a moment later, his lips brushing against hers. She plucked at his mouth hungrily before responding.

"When is what going to stop?" she wondered, distracted by his scent, and the feeling of his body pressed against hers, by his kiss.

"That awkwardness. When we first see each other," he murmured, shaping her lower lip between his. "I vote for right now."

"Okay," she agreed. "I'll try. No more awkwardness."

He leaned back, peering down at her closely. "Promise?"

"Yes," she whispered fervently.

A smile curled his mouth. He glanced downward at a table.

"Is that you?" he asked.

"Huh?"

He released her and stepped toward an end table. He picked up a framed family photo and examined it.

"Yeah. I was twelve there," she said, looking around him at the photograph he held. A feeling of mixed amusement and embarrassment shot through her at the idea of Trey seeing her at that age. She resisted a stupid urge to snatch the frame from his hands.

And he thought she could be awkward *now*, at twenty-eight. At twelve, she was taller than all the other kids in her seventh-grade class. She looked like a malnourished foal wearing braces. Caddy, on the other hand, was in the first, lush bloom of an uncommonly beautiful seventeen-year-old girl.

"You're so cute," he murmured. She rolled her eyes. He lifted the photograph closer to his face.

"Some things don't deserve closer examination," she told him drolly. But then she noticed his intent expression and furrowed brow.

He glanced up and looked at the bookcase at the far side of the room. He set down the frame on the table.

"Trey?" she asked him.

A strange feeling went through her as she watched him walk over to the bookcase. He picked up a photo. He studied it as closely as he had the other one. She approached him from the back, a feeling of trepidation rising in her that she couldn't explain. "Trey?" she repeated hollowly when she came alongside him. She looked at the photo he held. It was a photo of Caddy and her when Caddy had graduated from law school.

"Your sister was a lawyer?" he asked, staring at the photo narrowly.

"Yes," she said slowly, perplexed. She examined the photo for evidence that Caddy was graduating from law school, but couldn't find it. She was wearing her cap and gown, but it might have been any graduation. "How did you know that she was a lawyer?" she asked him. She knew she hadn't mentioned it last night. Maybe her mother had told him at the hospital, while Eleanor was in the bathroom or something?

He turned his chin, his blue eyes scoring her.

"Your sister was Arcadia Green?"

The hair on her neck and forearms stood on end. "Yes. We've always called her Caddy for short, and Green was her married name. How did you—"

She broke off when he set the photo back on the shelf abruptly. He turned to her.

"I knew her. I knew your sister," Trey said.

She had a sudden, shockingly vivid image pop into her head of Trey and Caddy together. They'd be such a striking pair, both of them tawny and beautiful, both blessed with that warmth and elemental charm that would open a lifetime of doors for them . . .

. . . Both of them the type to light up a room.

It was too much to take in, too unexpected. An invisible band seemed to tighten around her chest.

Oh God. I can't breathe.

Eleanor just stared at him for several seconds, her mouth hanging open, her large eyes glistening. He felt like he'd just slapped her. Her shock was palpable. He heard a sound like wind rushing past his ears.

Maybe he was in a bit of shock himself, come to think of it. When he'd looked at the first photo, it'd just been a suspicion. He'd known Arcadia for the past several years. There was a big difference between the polished, sophisticated woman he'd known and the beautiful young girl in the first picture. The second photo had slammed the truth home, though.

"Come here," he said, reaching for Eleanor's hand. He didn't care for the fixed, stunned expression on her face. "Let's sit down."

He started to walk over to the couch, but she remained unmoving, pulling back on her hand, resisting him.

"What do you mean you knew Caddy?" she demanded.

"I knew her from work. Dobsen, Mayer and Peterson consults for us at TalentNet," he explained, referring to the consulting legal firm for which Arcadia had worked. "Your sister is our primary contact there. Was, I mean," he corrected, grimacing. He bit back a curse. Eleanor looked even more slain than she had last night, upon finding out about her father's heart attack. "Let's sit down, okay?"

"How well did you know her?"

"Fairly well," he replied honestly. "We worked closely together on building the legal infrastructure of TalentNet as a separate legal entity from BandBook. I've known your sister since TalentNet's inception."

"I don't believe you."

He blinked, startled by the baldness of her statement. "I'm sorry. It's a shock for me too to realize it. I didn't have a clue until I saw those pictures just now."

"She never mentioned you to me. Caddy *would* have mentioned you to me. If not you, then at least TalentNet."

"She told you the names of all of her clients?"

For a few seconds, she didn't respond. He sensed her going through the new information in her head, sifting it, trying to make sense of it all.

"No," she admitted after a moment. "But some of them, she did. I'm sure she would have mentioned you." She stepped toward him, her focus on him absolute. "Is that all it was between you and Caddy? Professional?" she asked him shakily.

He hesitated. It was hard to define *what* his relationship with Arcadia Green had been. It'd been special, that much was certain. He'd never had a relationship with a woman as unique as the one he'd had with Arcadia.

"No. It wasn't just professional. I considered her a friend." He threw up his hands in a helpless gesture. "Jesus, this is bizarre," he said, looking around the cozy, attractive home, seeing it through different eyes than he had just moments ago. *This* was where Arcadia had grown up? Right here, in this very house . . . with *Eleanor*? It was too incredible to absorb.

He recalled his shock when he'd heard about Arcadia passing away months ago. *Impossible* to imagine: that vibrant, funny, smart woman gone forever.

Whatever pain he'd experienced, Eleanor had felt a thousand-fold, he realized, staring at her rigid, pale face. "I'm *so* sorry I couldn't attend her funeral," he told her quietly. "I was on a trip to China at the time. By the time I got home, she was gone. Her funeral was over. I hadn't even realized she was sick—"

"You mentioned when we first met that you were examining your life because you'd lost some important people in your life unexpectedly. Was Caddy one of them?"

He didn't reply for a moment, just staring into Eleanor's golden green eyes. A weird, swooping sensation went through him. Just this morning, he'd felt so close to her. He'd hoped they'd only grow closer, still. Last night, he'd finally put a name to this new, incredible thing that was happening between them. Inside him.

He'd fallen for her. Hard.

But suddenly, it was like she was flying away from him, even though she stood right there in front of him. It couldn't be clearer that he'd just unknowingly backed into a giant hornet's nest. He couldn't fathom in those seconds how to put things right.

"Eleanor, let's sit down," he insisted, nodding toward the couch.

"Just answer me, Trey.

He saw no escape. "Yes," he said. "Your sister's death hit me hard. She was . . . very special."

"Were you two lovers?"

He halted in the process of reaching for her when he absorbed her question. Her whisper clung in the air between them.

"Never mind. You don't have to answer," she said stiffly. She walked past him.

"Eleanor, wait," he called. It was all a mistake. She'd misunderstood. He'd be able to make this right. "Eleanor, the answer is *no*. I wasn't involved that way with Arcadia . . . Caddy."

She turned abruptly. His stomach dropped. Tears swam in her eyes. She looked devastated.

"We were attracted to each other in the beginning." Panic swelled in him when her eyes widened and a tear skipped down her cheek. "It was just an initial attraction, Eleanor, when we first met," he hurried to explain. "That's all. I swear, it never went anywhere. We got to know each other through working together. We respected each other too much to go down that path. She had as much luck with men as I did women. You must realize that about her? We didn't want to screw things up between us. We made a pact to just be friends and to only see each other at work."

"You and Caddy were friends. And you were attracted to each other."

"It sounds bad when you say it like that. I'm just trying to be honest. I mean . . ." He waved at the photo on the table helplessly. "Your *sister*. I had no idea."

"I think you'd better go," she said.

It felt like he'd been shoved. "*No*. I'm not leaving. This is just a misunderstanding."

She shook her head so adamantly that several tears skipped down her cheeks. "It's not a misunderstanding. This whole thing . . . Us." She waved between them, looking dazed. "It isn't right. I should have known there was something strange about you wanting me."

"There's *nothing* strange about me wanting you," he growled fiercely. He stalked toward her, determined to set things straight right that second. She staggered back, flinching. He halted, stunned to the core by the expression on her face. She looked *betrayed*.

"What are you *talking* about? How can the fact that you're Arcadia Green's sister have anything to do with us?"

"You're attracted to *me* because you thought I was like Caddy. But I'm not. Not really. Don't you get it? I'm not an established exhibitionist or a voyeur. I've never done a striptease for anyone in my life until that night I did it for you in the window. I've been acting all bold and sexy and confident, wearing Caddy's clothes, living in her condo . . . trying to be someone you would be attracted to. And you believed in the performance. But it's all been based on a lie."

"What?" *Eleanor's condo had been Arcadia's?* "I never knew Arcadia lived in the building next to me," he stated firmly. "You see, Eleanor? *That* should go to show you that our relationship was completely confined to work. I had *no* idea."

"Go, Trey," she said miserably. "Just go. Please."

"Jesus," he hissed. He was floored. "Eleanor, what the hell is happening?"

"I don't know," she whispered, sounding so incredulous, he couldn't help but believe she was just as bewildered as he was at that moment. "I don't know anymore. Maybe my mother has been right all along. Maybe I have been grieving *unnaturally*." She sniffed and raked the back of her hand across her cheek. "Look, I'm sorry. I know you came all the way out here to get me. But I think I should stay here with my parents tonight. Is it all right if you just let yourself out?"

"*Eleanor,*" he called, but he was talking to her back. He strode after her down the hallway, halting only when he saw the rear of her disappearing up a flight of stairs. A moment later, he heard the sound of a door shutting briskly.

He just stood there for a minute, as dazed as he would have been if someone had just clobbered him on the head for no reason.

TWENTY-TWO

S he arrived back in the city the next day as dusk began to settle. The temperature had plummeted that morning. A frigid wind blew off a lead-colored Lake Michigan. Entering the condo felt like walking into a cold tomb.

She turned up the heat on the thermostat. She walked through the chilled condo, pausing to look out the window onto the traffic flying down Lake Shore Drive. It struck her then, how she had previously imagined asking Caddy for her advice about how to progress with her seduction of Trey.

It'd never once crossed her mind that Caddy had been much more familiar with Trey than Eleanor had ever been. It was so bizarre to consider it, that there was such a crucial thread of Caddy's life that she'd never even imagined. Logically, it made sense, of course. Everyone associated with dozens, even hundreds, of people through their jobs on a daily basis who their family members and intimates never knew about.

But the unexpected connection—a special connection, according to Trey—between Caddy and the man she'd fallen in love with had left her reeling.

Bleeding.

Was it jealousy? Is that what she was experiencing?

Maybe, in part, it was. It was a hard pill to swallow, to realize that her sister and Trey had shared a special relationship way before she'd ever shown up on the scene. But that's not what was mainly paining her.

It was that she'd fallen in love with a man under false pretenses. She'd been pretending to be something she wasn't. Trey's admission that he'd been attracted to Caddy, that he'd found her special, was like a knife in her side, but it also made perfect sense. Caddy was passionate and exciting, beautiful and brilliant. It wasn't difficult to imagine the two of them together at all.

In fact, it was sickeningly easy.

She kept picturing Trey's bewildered expression last night. She'd been shocked to the core by his revelation that he'd known and cared for Caddy, but he'd been sideswiped as well. Confronting Caddy's death in such an unexpected way had obviously pained him. She remembered the look on his face when he brought up losing his friend, that bad-boy rocker Gerald Sturgis, who had died from an overdose.

He'd seemed even more torn up by Caddy's death.

Trey had tried to call her several times since last night. She hadn't answered his calls. With a heavy heart, she'd revoked the permission-to-enter form she'd left at the front desk for him. The idea of him knocking on her front door, confronting him . . . well, it broke her heart to consider it. She couldn't bring herself to talk to him. It was hard to put exactly *why* into words.

It was a little like that first time she'd ever done a striptease for him. She'd gotten so hot during her performance, so lost in her role. After she'd brought herself off, it'd suddenly hit her in a rush. She'd just masturbated in front of a stranger. She'd just been *intimate* with a stranger.

Shame swamped her every time she thought of how baldly, how selfishly, she'd seduced him.

Her need mortified her. Was she really so desperate as to enter into a frenzied, hot, mind-numbing relationship with Trey because she needed to forget her grief?

She suspected now it was true. Her mother had been right.

She'd been acting out, behaving like a bold, passionate playgirl—acting like *Caddy*—because she needed to fill that gaping hole in her chest.

Caddy had advised her to take a bite out of life, to stop being afraid. But Caddy and Trey and her mom—and Eleanor herself—hadn't understood just how ill-equipped she was to take on that role.

The realization that Trey and Caddy had known each other for years, that they'd been attracted to each other, had shattered the illusion somehow, vanished the glamour of what was happening between Trey and her. Last night, when Trey had said he knew Caddy, it'd been like the magic spell had suddenly evaporated. She'd been left standing in front of him naked, all of her inadequacies, her lies, the *thinness* of her character, all exposed to his eyes.

The atmosphere of the silent, oppressive condo swallowed up the sound of her choked sob.

The following week, she looked up when she heard a knock on her opened office door.

"You've been avoiding me ever since you got back," Jimmy said, stepping past the threshold.

"I haven't been." She waved at the mess on her desk. "I've just been buried with work ever since I got behind last week."

More accurately, she'd buried *herself* in the work, eager to focus on something other than the fact that the days and nights not seeing Trey were starting to accumulate. His calls were coming less frequently. She told herself it was what she wanted, but her thoughts didn't ring true.

Every day that passed not seeing him, every night spent without him, seemed to be making the aching hole in her chest gape just a little wider. So she worked. And she tried to forget.

It wasn't working in the slightest, she acknowledged grimly as she watched Jimmy plop down in the chair in front of her desk.

"How's your dad doing?" he asked.

"It seems like he's doing better every day. He got the okay for regular exercise from his doctor, and he and Mom joined a health club. We found one that has a cardiac rehab specialist on staff. Last night when I visited them, my dad was showing off his hip new workout clothes and talking about things like free weights, reps and optimizing his cardio routine," she told him drolly.

Jimmy laughed. "That's great. I should go with you out to Evanston sometime soon. I'd like to see them."

"That'd be great," she said, setting down her pen and stretching.

"And how are things going with Riordan?"

She froze, then sighed and lowered her arms.

"They aren't, to be honest," she admitted after a pause. She *had* been avoiding Jimmy a little, mostly because she didn't want to have this conversation. She'd been evasive about the topic of Trey with her parents too.

But maybe it was time to start coping with the truth.

"Trey and I aren't going to see each other anymore," she said as evenly as possible. "It's over."

"Why?" Jimmy asked, sitting forward in his chair.

She shrugged, feigning nonchalance. "You didn't really think what was happening between him and me was going to last forever, did you?"

He blinked and started back slightly. "I don't know, exactly.

But the way you two were looking at each other that night at Gold Coast, I thought there was enough steam to keep it going for a hell of a long time. *That's* for sure. What happened?"

"It's a long, boring story," she said dismissively, avoiding his stare and shuffling the papers on her desk.

"Eleanor?" She looked up and saw his arched eyebrows. "I've got time."

She exhaled resignedly. The truth came out awkwardly at first. By the time she got to the revelation that Trey and Caddy had known each other for years, and formed a pact not to get involved romantically despite their attraction for each other, the words were spilling out of her throat in an anxious rush.

"So that's it," she said breathlessly after several minutes. "Just my luck, isn't it? That they'd known each other? Liked each other? Back when we first met, Trey told me that he was taking a break from relationships . . . trying to figure his life out. He called it an existential crisis, brought on by some ugly breakups and losing two close friends." She met Jimmy's dark eyes. "One of those friends was Caddy."

Jimmy shook his head. "That's incredible. I guess it's not too surprising, though. They did live right next to each other."

"That's the weird thing. *One* of the weird things," she amended, grimacing. "They didn't know they lived next to each other, according to Trey. Their relationship was strictly professional. They saw each other only through work."

"And Trey told you that they'd decided early on not to date or see each other romantically?"

She nodded, her eyes downcast. "He said they made a pact about it. He said they respected each other too much, and were open about their bad luck with relationships. So they mutually decided to just be friends."

"Wow," Jimmy said, leaning back as he took it all in. "Did you believe Trey when he said it?"

"What do you mean?" she asked, the hairs on the back of her neck standing on end.

"Did you believe him when he said that he and Caddy hadn't slept together?"

"Yes," she said hollowly. "Don't you think I should have believed him?"

Jimmy shrugged dubiously. "You know him better than me. Would he have lied about something like that?"

Her mouth hung open as his question repeated in her head. "No," she stated absolutely after a pause. "Trey's not like that. He doesn't lie. Not about anything elemental. Honesty means too much to him."

Jimmy nodded. "*But . . .*" He made a "next step" gesture with his hands. "It bothered Trey, knowing you were Caddy's sister?"

"No," she exclaimed. "He was blown away when he realized Caddy and I were sisters, but I wouldn't say it *bothered* him, precisely."

"So . . . *why* aren't you guys seeing each other, then?"

"Because it bothers *me*," she stated baldly.

"It bugs you that Caddy and Trey were friends?"

"Yes. No. I mean . . . You don't understand," she blurted out in frustration. She glanced up uneasily from twiddling her pen. Sure enough, Jimmy appeared bewildered. "Don't you get it? Mom's been worried that I've been hashing out my grief over Caddy by wearing her clothes, acting all bold. She never said it, but I assume she'd include doing something as daring as seducing Trey Riordan in that category, if she knew about it. It seems like you think something similar. You said it the other day at brunch," she reminded him. "Now, come to find out, Trey probably *was* attracted to me because I was acting and dressing like someone whom he respected and was attracted to for years. In other words, he was probably attracted to me because there were similarities between Caddy and me, and he recognized that unconsciously. He probably even recognized some of her clothes on me," she mumbled, sinking in her chair, mortified at the idea.

"Whoa, wait a second," Jimmy said, holding up his hands. "*I* never said you were acting like Caddy."

"Yes, you did. Well, you sort of implied it."

"I said the opposite, point-blank," he defended. "I said you *weren't* pretending to be Caddy. That's not what I think your new look is about."

"You told me you thought me wearing her clothes, and this thing I started with Trey . . . *all* of it, was only happening because Caddy had passed."

"Yeah, I did," he said. "I also said that you wore the new look really well, but that I thought you weren't owning it."

"You said that I was playacting!"

"No," he said, his dark eyes flashing. "*I* said that when Caddy suggested you take a bite out of life and live passionately, she meant that you should live your passion. *Not* hers."

She flinched back.

"Right," Eleanor said after a moment, her throat tight. "And you and Mom both think I'm just trying to step into Caddy's shoes—literally—in order to do it. *That's* why Trey fell for me."

"*No,*" Jimmy bellowed. He threw up his hands, clearly fed up with her. Feeling deflated and overwhelmed, she sagged back into her chair.

"Look, I don't know the exact reasons Riordan is attracted to you," Jimmy continued in a calmer tone. She rarely saw him so serious. Despite her agitation, she found herself hanging on his every word. "I think that Caddy knew you had your own passion, and that for whatever reason, you were keeping it buried. Under wraps. I think she was telling you to liberate it. Live it, because life is too short. And maybe you found your passion and set it free by wearing her clothes once in a while, and by taking risks you normally wouldn't have when you moved into her place. But that doesn't make what you were doing, or how you felt, *playacting.* I think . . ."

"What?" Eleanor whispered, utterly focused on him now.

"I think it was *your* passion all along, Eleanor. I think that's what Riordan was seeing. I think that's what he's fallen for. Maybe Caddy gave you the opportunity to borrow her luxurious lifestyle, and her wardrobe and her confidence, a rare chance to find your own passion." Jimmy shrugged. "But don't you think the time has come for you to take full ownership of it now?"

TWENTY-THREE

That night when she got home from work, there was a huge, sophisticated flower arrangement consisting of white lilies, freshly cut ranunculus and larkspur sitting on the doorman's station.

"Someone is trying to tell someone that he likes her," Harry told her when Eleanor commented on how striking the arrangement was.

"I'll say," she agreed, pulling her gaze off the flowers. "Any packages, Harry?"

"Just those," Harry said, nodding at the flowers.

She blinked in disbelief. "These are for *me*?"

"Yeah. Along with this."

Harry stood and opened a closet door behind his doorman's station. She gaped at him in amazement when he walked toward her carrying an equally lovely, colorful, fresh-cut bouquet of wildflowers. Her heart squeezed tight in her chest. Flustered, she accepted it. Her fingers fumbled with the attached envelope. She withdrew a card. It read:

The florist asked which type of arrangement suited you best. I said I wanted to send both of these. She asked if I was

*unsure about which one was right, and I said no. They both
reminded me of you.*

*I'm not giving up, Eleanor. Just give me a chance to talk
to you.*

*If you won't call me, then at least look out your window
tonight at ten. I want to give you something.*

Trey

"He stopped by too. Just fifteen minutes ago. He was hoping you'd
be home," Harry said from behind the desk. She glanced up dazedly
and saw Harry's brown eyes on her, his gaze kind. Concerned.

"He did?" she asked hoarsely. *If you won't call me, then at
least look out your window tonight at ten.*

Her heart started to thrum loudly in her ears. Her doorman
nodded somberly. "He seemed pretty disappointed when I told
him you hadn't come home from work yet."

"Thanks, Harry," she replied thickly. "I'm kind of loaded up
at the moment," she said, looking down at her heavy briefcase.
"Can I come back down to get the big arrangement?"

"I'll have Alex bring them up in a few minutes," Harry assured,
referring to their maintenance man.

The written message kept repeating in her head. *I'm not giving
up, Eleanor.*

*If you won't call me, then at least look out your window
tonight at ten.*

She recalled how she'd written a similar message, inviting him
to watch her striptease on that first night in the coffee shop. It
seemed like ages ago. The memory made a spike of mixed longing
and shame go through her.

Her motivations had been so mercenary toward him in the beginning. But her longing had only grown exponentially since that time. Her sexual attraction had bloomed into a full-fledged, hopeless love.

Her reasons for inviting him to look inside her world that first night were single-mindedly sexual and selfish.

What could Trey's reasons be for asking her to look into his home?

Alex delivered the huge, gorgeous arrangement just as she'd finished putting the wildflowers in water. A moment later, she stood back and admired the pair of bouquets on her kitchen counter, a knot forming in her throat. Trey had been right, of course. It was hard to say which arrangement she loved more: the wild and unassuming, or the sophisticated and sensual.

The beautiful flowers seemed to mock and tempt her nearly as much as the closed guest bedroom door down the hall. Feeling confused and restless, she changed into a pair of yoga pants, a sweatshirt and tennis shoes. A brisk walk would clear her head. Maybe she'd divine the "right" answer as to what precisely she'd be doing at ten o'clock tonight.

Much to her surprise, she found herself determinedly turning down Oak Street a few minutes later. She entered the lobby of an apartment building and approached the doorman.

"I'm here to see Sandra Banks?" Eleanor told the doorman. "I'm Eleanor Briggs. She's not expecting me. I'm not sure if she'll be home—"

But the doorman was already dialing Caddy's best friend's number. It still stunned her a little, that she was standing here in Sandra's lobby. She'd been avoiding Sandra's requests to get together since Caddy died, a fact that pained and embarrassed her as she waited there now.

The idea had occurred to her out of nowhere as she walked

down the inner drive. As her sister, Eleanor had thought she'd known Caddy better than anyone on earth. But Caddy had always taken a big-sister protective attitude toward Eleanor.

There could be no doubt that a sisterly relationship and a best-friend relationship were two *very* different things.

The doorman spoke into the phone. He hung up a moment later.

"She's not here at the moment, but she said she's only a few blocks away, if you'd like to wait?"

Eleanor nodded thankfully and took a seat in the lobby. Within minutes, Sandra was entering the front doors, laden down with several shopping bags and her briefcase. A grin broke over her face when she saw Eleanor standing up to greet her.

"*Eleanor*, how wonderful to see you. What a surprise." She dumped her bags heedlessly on the carpet and rushed her. They hugged tightly, Eleanor laughing, warmed to the core by the other woman's exuberance. "We haven't seen each other since—"

"The funeral," Eleanor said, smiling as she stepped back. Sandra looked healthy and prosperous, her cheeks and nose pink from the cold wind off the lake. "How have you been?"

"Busy. Work, the holiday season. You know how it is," Sandra said, nodding at the shopping bags on the floor that were filled with gift-wrapped packages. "How are your parents?"

"Fine." She made a face. "Actually, there is some news on that front. Maybe I can fill you in over a drink?"

"That'd be great, I'd love that. Have you moved into Caddy's place?" Sandra asked.

"Yes."

"I thought we'd see each other more. I only live a few blocks away. I used to see you more when you lived in Logan Square than I do now, and we're practically neighbors."

"Yeah, well . . ." Eleanor shrugged and they exchanged a quick,

meaningful glance. They both knew the only reason they used to
see each other with regular frequency was their mutual relationship with Caddy.

"I miss her," Sandra said quietly after a pause.

"Yeah. Me too."

"Of course you do. You two were so close. I ran into Schraed-
er's the other night with a bunch of work associates from out of
town. I told them all they had to get a Caddy Green," she laughed,
referring to the specialty martini the bartender at the local hot
spot used to make for Caddy. "Did you know they made it official,
and added it to the menu?"

"No," Eleanor said, shaking her head and smiling. "But it
doesn't—"

"Surprise you?" Sandra finished, and they both laughed.
"You're right. It's just the kind of thing that would happen to
Caddy." She started to pick up her shopping bags.

"Do you have time to grab that drink now?" Eleanor wondered. "There's something I wanted to ask you about."

"Of course," Sandra said, her quick reply and game smile
amplifying Eleanor's guilt over making excuses whenever Sandra
called. She realized now that she'd been afraid seeing Sandra
would just emphasize Caddy's absence.

"Let's go over to the Four Seasons," Sandra suggested. "We
missed the parade this year, but we can still do part of the tradition: the holiday drink. Caddy would like that, don't you think?"

"Yeah," Eleanor agreed. "I think she would."

Twenty minutes later, they sat in the handsome, posh bar at the
Four Seasons Hotel, their drinks in front of them.

"So, you said you had something you wanted to ask me?" she
asked Eleanor once they'd caught up on what'd been happening

in their lives for the past few months and Eleanor had told her about her father's heart attack and recovery.

"Um . . . yeah," Eleanor replied, awkwardness swamping her. She'd told herself in the last several minutes that she'd come up with a good way to broach the topic of Caddy and Trey, but had come up empty-handed now that the moment had arrived. "It's about . . . it's about Trey Riordan."

Sandra paused in the action of lifting her martini, her gaze shooting over to Eleanor.

"So Caddy told you about him?" she asked in an amazed, hushed tone.

"Uh—"

"I'm surprised, to be honest," Sandra said, setting down her drink and looking reflective. "Caddy could be such a paradox. Bold as brass one second, vulnerable the next."

A strange feeling quivered in Eleanor's belly. "Caddy? *Vulnerable?*" she asked in amazement.

TWENTY-FOUR

S andra smiled at her stunned reaction.

"Sure, Caddy could be vulnerable. About some things. *Very* few, the truth be told. Not much got Caddy down. Her confidence was no act." She gave Eleanor an assessing glance. "It doesn't surprise me that you never saw her as vulnerable. She didn't want her little sister to see her as anything but in control. Happy. Carefree. She was very protective of you, you know," Sandra said, fiddling with the toothpick in her drink. "That's why I'm a little surprised she told you about Trey Riordan. *He* was one of her few vulnerabilities." Sandra seemed to rise out of her memories and focused on her. "Why did you want to ask me about Riordan?"

"I met him," Eleanor said impulsively.

"You did?" Sandra asked, her gaze sparking with interest. "I've never had the honor. I've seen a few photos of him in the newspaper and magazines. And of course, I saw that infamous photo of him with the Scarpetti twins. Who didn't, right?" Sandra rolled her eyes and laughed. "And I heard about him from Caddy, naturally. From her description, he's one hell of an exciting man."

Eleanor shook her head, trying to break the surreal feeling that had come over her. "I can't believe Caddy talked about him to you," she admitted. "She never said one *word* about knowing him before she got sick."

Sandra shrugged and took a drink. "Like I said, she tended to avoid topics with you that made her feel vulnerable, or susceptible, or *anything* but the successful, woman-about-town, confident persona she put out there for the world to see."

Eleanor froze. "Are you saying she wasn't those things? That she was a fake?"

Sandra gave her a concerned look. "Of course Caddy was all those things. She was one of the most successful, warm, dynamic, confident women I've ever met . . . I likely *ever* will meet. She was the *best* of friends," Sandra assured feelingly. Emotion seemed to overcome her for a moment. She sniffed and shut her eyes briefly. "Who of us *does* want to wear our vulnerabilities on our sleeve for everyone to see? That's all I meant, Eleanor. You must know how much I adored Caddy."

Eleanor nodded, swallowing back her anxiety. "And Trey . . . Trey was one of her vulnerabilities, in your opinion?"

"I'd say so, yeah," Sandra said. Her brow furrowed as she peered closely at her. "Caddy *did* tell you about Trey, didn't she? I didn't misunderstand that part, did I?"

"Caddy told me a lot of things, when she was dying. Things she'd never mentioned to me before," Eleanor sidestepped, worried Sandra would suddenly clam up. She couldn't have Caddy's friend suddenly stop imparting valuable information before Eleanor could glean anything crucial. That would be unbearable.

"I understand," Eleanor began cautiously, highly aware that she might make a misstep in the conversation at any moment, "that Caddy and Trey formed a pact not to see each other romantically."

"Caddy agreed to it, but she's not the one who came up with the idea. Riordan did that."

"Really?"

"Yeah, she didn't mention it when she told you about him?" Sandra asked, wide-eyed. "That's what made her feel so vulnerable. Because she *did* like Riordan. She liked him a lot."

"But he suggested—"

"That they keep things on a strictly professional basis, yeah. It killed Caddy a little. I remember the night when she brought up the topic of him perfectly. I'd never seen her so torn up about a guy. It surprised me a little, at the time. Of course, I couldn't help but feel for her. Caddy had never once shown regret for playing the field ever since her divorce from Clark. Not that *I'd* ever seen, anyway. She embraced the idea that she wasn't the type to settle down. Her independence was her hallmark.

"But that night, after Riordan told her he wanted to keep things professional between them, she was regretful, all right. Her reputation as a player had clearly preceded her in regard to Riordan. She thought it'd made him wary. It was the only time I'd ever heard her say she wished she'd done things differently when it came to relationships.

"After that night, she kept her feelings locked up tight. If Riordan's name ever came up again between us, she was breezy and matter-of-fact. Anyone else who didn't know better would have assumed that she and Riordan were just work acquaintances who respected each other. If I hadn't seen how upset she was that one night, I wouldn't have ever questioned that Riordan was anything but a casual work friend to her."

Eleanor took a long draw on her wine, staring blankly at the colored bottles behind the bar. It felt so strange, thinking about Caddy being vulnerable. Of course she had been. It was a little embarrassing, to realize that she—Eleanor—hadn't allowed for her sister to be flawed.

Human.

Then again, maybe it was inevitable. The cancer had robbed both of them of the opportunity to discover those sister secrets about each other that full lives would have eventually afforded.

"So Riordan actually *hurt* her," Eleanor said numbly. That idea confused her almost as much as the idea of him sharing some kind of unique bond with Caddy.

"Of course he did," Sandra said. Eleanor glanced over at her blunt tone. "But not deliberately or cruelly. Not in a way that was any different than what we all have to do when we recognize that we just aren't meant to be with that person in a romantic or sexual way. From what I understood from Caddy's occasional references, he was always warm and respectful toward her. It sounded like they ended up having a great working relationship."

"Yeah. That's my understanding too. But . . . when she was passing, Caddy said something to me. She said that she didn't have any regrets as to how she'd lived her life." She met Sandra's stare squarely, determined to understand the truth. "Do you think she regretted her feelings for Trey? Do you think she was just being strong, because she knew the end was coming, and she didn't want me to think of her going with regrets?"

"No," Sandra said with quiet certainty. "I think she meant everything she told you. Maybe I'm giving you the wrong impression. Your sister wasn't the type to crumple if a guy didn't like her. She was strong. Clearly, by the time she got sick, things were on even footing with her and Riordan. She was in several relationships with other men following her crush on him. Caddy was *not* the type to pine, as you know," Sandra said, pulling a face.

Eleanor couldn't help but smile in return. Relief swept through her. No, she couldn't imagine Caddy locked in her condo, wasting away and wetting a photo of Trey with her tears. Maybe she hadn't been getting the full picture of her big sister's personality, but *that* rendering of Caddy was just ridiculous.

"So that's what you'd call her feelings for Trey? A crush?" Eleanor asked.

Sandra reflected for a moment. "I guess. But she was so passionate, even a crush *meant* something, when it came to Caddy. Do you know what I mean?"

Eleanor nodded in complete understanding.

"She was such a vibrant, complicated person." Sandra sighed. "She used to say you were all that way. Caddy would say it was the Russian in you."

"*Who* was all that way?" Eleanor asked, startled.

"Your family," Sandra said with a wistful smile. "Well, at least your mom, her and you. She said your dad was the straight and strong mast that kept you all going in the right direction."

For a few seconds, Eleanor just stared at Caddy's friend. Then a laugh burst out of her throat.

"Did Caddy *really* say that?"

"Oh yeah, several times," Sandra said, grinning at her burst of laughter.

Eleanor shook her head, both disbelieving and inordinately pleased. Her faced flushed with warmth.

"Why are you so surprised?" Sandra asked.

"Because . . . I would have thought she'd file me on the straight-as-an-arrow, boring side of the family, not the passionate side . . . Thank you for this," she said in a burst of honesty. "Thanks for meeting with me and for sharing your perspective on Caddy."

Sandra waved away her gratitude. "It's not a big deal. It's my pleasure."

"But it *is* a big deal," Eleanor insisted. "I'm sorry about . . . about not getting together with you before this." She caught Sandra's stare. "Let's do it more, okay? Caddy would have wanted us to stay connected. *I* want it, as well."

"Me too."

"Stay and talk for a while more, then?" Eleanor asked her hopefully.

"Absolutely," Sandra agreed, reaching for her hand and squeezing it warmly.

A quiet, thick snow started to fall as she walked home that night.

She paused on the sidewalk in front of Trey's building, her gaze drawn to the top floors of the high-rise and Trey's windows. Distant lights were on in his living room and loft, but she couldn't see his Christmas tree on display in the window. That was strange. She would have thought his maid had put it up by now. Maybe plans had changed for him somehow, and he wasn't going to be here during the holidays.

The idea made her feel hollow.

Part of her—a big part—wanted to just walk inside, ask his doorman to call him and request if she could go up to his penthouse.

But her stark longing for him was tainted by a lingering uncertainty. It'd been a relief to learn tonight that Trey had been the one to set the limit on her sister's and his relationship.

He definitely hadn't been holding some kind of secret torch for Caddy.

Thank God. That would have just been too weird, on so many levels.

Plus, from everything she'd heard and observed, she believed that Caddy was over her crush on Trey by the time she passed. Caddy and Trey's relationship truly had been special, but it'd never progressed to any territory that Eleanor would consider dangerous.

She continued down the sidewalk toward her building, her feet making fresh prints in the newly fallen snow. The fact of the matter remained, she'd been far from confident about this thing she'd started with Trey even *before* she'd discovered that he and her sister'd had a friendship. The realization that Trey and Caddy shared a connection had just been the dose of reality that'd made everything go suddenly clear in her head.

Her conflict suddenly crystallized in her awareness.

They'd begun this whole thing with the most basic of motivations: sexual gratification. If she looked out that window tonight, as Trey had requested in his note—which she longed like crazy to do—what if he'd planned something that took them back to that basic place? Something wonderful and primal, but still essentially sexual in nature?

The idea frightened her a little. It also pulled at her. Part of her was willing to go back to that selfish agreement they'd made, because at least she'd get to be with him. Love him . . . even if silently.

And that realization about herself frightened her. She was willing to expose herself to so much hurt, so much heartache, just to see his face again, just to touch him once more.

No one had told her that falling in love could be so *painful*. So risky. Or if they had, she'd never fully understood until that moment.

She entered her apartment, her heartbeat starting to thrum very loud in her ears. Of course, she'd been aware of the time all night.

It was currently a few minutes until ten.

She paused in the hallway for a full minute, listening to her mind screaming caution at her, feeling her heart throbbing another answer altogether.

Her heart won out, apparently. All she knew was that she found herself headed down the hallway like a sleepwalker to the dark guest bedroom. Her fingers paused next to the switch on

the lamp. She listened for a breathless moment to the blood surg-
ing in her veins.

The light switch clicked. The empty room was illuminated.
Her heart seemingly lodged at the base of her throat, she walked
over to the window. Dozens of scenarios flashed through her pan-
icking brain regarding what she might view in Trey's bedroom.

Not one of them included a dark room with absolutely nothing
to see.

She inhaled choppily, disappointment slicing through her.

Then it happened: lights went on in the midst of the dark room.
She stared at a huge, illuminated Christmas tree in the dark
window.

She couldn't believe her eyes.

Blinking back tears, she stepped closer to the window and
placed her hand on the cold pane. She soaked in the vision, incredulous. He'd put up his Christmas tree in his bedroom.

For her. It *had* to have been for her.

She made out a slight movement just to the right of the large
tree. In the soft glow of the lights, she made out his tall figure.
Her heart did a double beat at seeing him step out of the shadows.
He placed his hand on the window, his position mirroring hers.

Trey.

The connection she felt with him in that moment seemed to
cut down to her very bones. It was a feeling that surpassed the
empty space between them, a sensation that canceled out all their
previous selfish, clueless motivations. At that moment, she saw
him clearly. And she saw herself, as he saw her, in all her flawed,
layered, bewildering complexity.

And the truth was, she liked what she imagined she saw
through his eyes.

She inhaled shakily as relief swept through her, cold and
refreshing as a sluicing stream.

He wasn't seeing something false when he looked at her. Even when she'd convinced herself she'd been playing a part, he'd seen her truly. What he'd done for her, putting up that Christmas tree for her to see because she'd told him she'd been too grief-stricken to do it for herself: those weren't the actions of a man who was interested in her just for sex, or for her similarity to her sister, or for *any* other reason but one.

He cared about *her*—Eleanor.

She lifted her hand and gave a gesture of hopeful beckoning. The tension level of his body seemed to break slightly, and she saw him nod once before he turned to leave the room.

TWENTY-FIVE

She'd never been as anxious as she was when she heard his knock on her front door. She felt chilled and prickly with nerves. Hope and uncertainty mingled in her awareness. She kept thinking about the Christmas tree he'd put up for her to view. It'd been the sweetest gift. It took her breath away.

Her hand shook as she turned the knob.

She paused holding open the door, soaking in the image of him as if she were starved and his image could feed her. He wore a pair of faded jeans that fit his narrow hips and long legs with casual, sexy perfection and a striped button-down. His black pea-coat was unbuttoned, as if he hadn't bothered fastening it when she'd signaled for him to come over to her condo.

His blue eyes seemed alight as they moved over her and finally latched on her face. Her mouth opened. She felt so much, but she didn't know what to say. He frowned and stepped across the threshold. He pushed her into the hallway and let the door slam shut behind them. His big hands cradled her jaw, and then he was kissing her with that honest, blatant hunger that she loved, and that heated her to the very core of her being.

"I thought you agreed the awkwardness had to stop between

us," he growled softly next to her lips a moment later. His mouth moved, capturing a teardrop that had fallen down her cheek.

"Thank you for putting the Christmas tree there," she murmured shakily.

"I put it up for you. Me. Not my maid."

"It's so pretty. That was so sweet of you."

His eyes flashed. "I'd give you much more," he said gruffly. "If you'd let me, Eleanor."

She nodded toward the living room. "Come and sit down?" she asked. "I have something I want to tell you."

His face went carefully blank at that, but he followed her into the living room. They sat down together on the couch, a few inches separating them. She tried to gather her words as the silence pressed down on her eardrums.

"I owe you an apology," she finally said, staring at her hands resting on her thighs.

"Why?"

"For not talking to you for more than a week." She swallowed thickly. "But for more than that." She forced herself to meet his stare. "I've been so afraid since we started sleeping together that you'd find out the truth about me."

"What truth is that?" he asked, his eyebrows slanting.

"That I'm not really daring or super confident or exciting," she said in a small voice. "That I was putting on an act in order to get your attention." She cleared her throat uncomfortably. "And like you've said before, I was pretty mercenary about doing it. It was incredibly selfish." Shame slinked into her awareness. She couldn't bring herself to meet his blazing stare. "My mother said she thought I was acting out my grief about Caddy. That I was trying to be like her, to fill the void of Caddy being gone."

"Is that true?" he asked. "You seduced me out of grief?"

"No," she whispered, meeting his stare even though tears had gathered in her eyes. "I don't think it is. Not primarily anyway. When Caddy was dying—" She gasped softly and paused for a few seconds, gathering herself. "She told me she didn't have any regrets. That she'd lived each day to its fullest. She asked me to try to do that with my life, to live my passion." She sniffed and wiped an errant tear off her cheek. "And I did," she said, meeting Trey's stare. "Ever since I first saw you over a year ago, you became the target of my passion. I couldn't stop thinking about you. I would have done anything"—her voice broke, and she inhaled— "to be with you. So I hatched up this plan to seduce you. I wouldn't let myself think about what would happen after I did it. It was single-minded of me, and selfish, and for that, I'm sorry. I refused to examine my motivations, so I didn't understand them."

"Do you now?"

She strained to read his expression, but she couldn't. She had no clue in that moment how he'd react to her confession, but nothing less than honesty was available to her at that moment. Nothing else would do anymore. She'd reached the end of the script as far as her role.

"I think I might have fallen in love with you a little, as unlikely as that seems, just by looking inside your world, just by watching you breathe, sleep, move and exist," she said softly. "It's the only thing that really makes sense, in the end. I know you thought I was some kind of practiced exhibitionist and voyeur, but I'd never done anything like that before. I'm not the kind of woman you were used to." She gave a ragged laugh at the understatement. "I'm not bold or experienced or sexy—"

"Wrong."

She blinked and glanced at him, startled at his harsh utterance.

"You're unbelievably sexy. And you may not want to admit it, Eleanor, but you *are* an exhibitionist. An incredible one. I can't take my eyes off you when you start to dance."

Her lower lip trembled. "I've never really thought of myself that way before. I was the boring one in the family. The book-worm. In seducing you, I felt like I completely stepped out of myself. I became something different." She met his stare entreat-ingly. "But you have to believe me when I say that I wasn't chan-neling Caddy to get through my grief. That *wasn't* it."

"Then why did you get so upset when you suspected Caddy and I had been involved?"

"I wasn't sure *what* I thought then," she said starkly. "It all just struck me as so bizarre."

"Yeah," he said grimly. "Me too."

"But it was more than just strange. I felt like Cinderella for a minute there, like the prince was staring at me in rags. That moment, when I realized you and Caddy had a connection, it just seemed like the magic fell away."

"Magic?"

"Yeah, the illusion I'd created for you disappeared." She sniffed and swiped at an escaped tear.

"Why *then*?" Trey demanded. She heard the puzzlement in his tone, and the lump in her throat swelled bigger. "Why did it dis-appear when you heard I knew Caddy?"

"Because Caddy was the real thing, and I was just a stand-in. That's what it felt like to me for most of my life, even if I don't feel that way anymore," burst out of her throat. She inhaled rag-gedly when she saw his stunned expression. "Not when it comes to us, anyway."

Trey seemed to consider what she'd said for a moment.

"Your sister was a special woman. I liked her a lot. Did you know she and I were the same age, and that we had the same graduation years?"

"I hadn't thought about that," Eleanor said, made wistful for some reason by his question.

"Well, we did. And did you know that my assistant used to bring her hot cocoa when we were working together on something in the office?" he asked with a small smile. Her throat too tight to respond, Eleanor just shook her head. "A little thing you two had in common. The Briggs sisters and their hot chocolate. And I knew about it, first-hand." He reached and grabbed her hand. He squeezed it warmly. "I thought about it a lot in the past couple weeks. It's horrible that Arcadia passed so young. But I'm glad I knew her in the time she was here. I'm glad I knew her for *you*. She was special to you. And I know why, at least partially. That means something, Eleanor."

He was right. It came to her in a rush of amazement, what a blessing it was that the man she'd fallen in love with had known the light that was Caddy before she'd left this world. He let go of her hand and curved his fingers around her jaw. Her pulse began to throb at her throat when he turned her face to fully meet his stare.

"I admired your sister a lot. But I wasn't in love with her, Eleanor. Far from it."

"I know that now," she assured. "I talked to Sandra Banks, her best friend, about you and Caddy earlier tonight. I guess I just needed an outside source for some perspective. She told me that you were the one to suggest you and Caddy keep things on a professional basis. You didn't want to cloud things with her and ruin your working relationship."

"Are you okay with it all, then?"

She met his gaze squarely and nodded.

His finger moved on her cheek. "I don't know what to say about all this stuff about you acting and not being honest with me. Are you telling me you were faking your attraction to me? Or your response in bed? Your feelings for me in general?"

Heat rushed through her. "God, no. Nobody could be *that* good of an actor," she exclaimed.

He exhaled roughly and shook his head. His hand moved,

smoothing back the hair at her temple. Her skin tingled beneath his touch. "Then you *weren't* acting."

"As it turns out," she said incredulously, "I *wasn't*. That's what I've been trying to say that I've come to realize. I thought that I wanted you so much that I was willing to put on the performance of a lifetime. But apparently—"

"You really are bold and daring and hotter than a firecracker?" he asked, the hint of a smile on his lips.

"With you," she whispered. "For you."

This time when he went to kiss her, she was ready for him. His hand rose to the back of her head. He twisted his fingers in her hair. She felt his sexual hunger in that kiss, but she felt more. She felt his focused need.

Or at least she hoped she did.

"Do you have any idea what a turn-on that is? What a sweet gift?" he rasped against her lips a moment later.

"What?" she asked, taken aback by his intensity.

"You're telling me that I had something to do with you finding your passion. That's *incredible*. Because I've seen your passion. I've felt it. And if I had even a *little* bit to do with liberating it, then I must be the luckiest guy on earth."

"Really?"

He rolled his eyes and raked his fingers through his hair. "Yeah. *Really*. Do you want to know what I've figured out in the past week?"

"What?" she mouthed.

"I'm not emotionally challenged or a commitment-phobe or permanently disabled somehow in the intimacy department."

"You're not?"

He shook his head. "No. That wasn't my problem with women, Eleanor."

Her voice box didn't work for a second. "What was?" she finally whispered numbly.

"It was simple. I just hadn't found the right one."

His words echoed and swirled around her head. A strange, wonderful tingling sensation started up on every square inch of her skin as she looked into his blazing stare.

"I have now," he said roughly, leaning into her. He nipped at her lips. "She's really sweet, and she's a little goofy."

"Hey," she protested, but he just plucked at her lips again and continued.

"She's super smart and looks just as amazing in a miniskirt as she does in her librarian clothes. She's fresh and beautiful and so sexy, sometimes I worry I can't keep up with her in bed."

"Trey," she admonished thickly, nipping back at his lips with increasing fervor.

"You're adorable," he stated, leaning back and scoring her with his stare. "I've fallen in love with you. And do you want to know the weird thing about it?"

She froze, her mouth falling open. She couldn't believe she was hearing this. And yet . . . at the same time, it seemed like the most natural thing in the world, like she'd been waiting for this moment her whole life.

"It wasn't hard at all, Eleanor." He breathed out, his gaze traveling over her face. "It seemed like the most natural thing in the world, once it hit me the other night, after we came back from the hospital. I think one of the reasons I didn't recognize it more quickly was that we sort of started in the middle, you know? The chemistry between us was blistering, it wasn't hard to imagine it was just about sex . . . to convince myself that was *all* it was, at first. But once my eyes were opened, it was so easy. So nice. At least, it was nice until you ran away from me at your parents' house," he added, his eyebrows slanting. "Then it kind of became a nightmare I couldn't wake up from."

"I'm sorry. I really am. When that happened, part of me worried my mother was right: that I was acting out some weird combination of a sibling rivalry and filling the void of Caddy's loss at once. It was just so bizarre, thinking about you and Caddy, given everything else I was struggling with. It magnified my fears. My insecurities. I just needed to set things straight in my head before I was ready to tell you the truth."

"What truth is that?" he asked her somberly.

"That I've fallen in love with you," she whispered.

He smiled and kissed her lips softly. Eleanor felt like her heart swelled so big, it might squeeze past her rib cage.

"Are we on the same page now?" he asked her, his warm breath brushing against her mouth.

"I love you, and—"

"I love you back," he growled.

He cupped her head with one large hand and brought her close, pressing his forehead against hers.

"Please hear me when I say this, Eleanor. Really *listen*. There's no one else like you. No one else has ever made me feel like this. Thank God I found you, or else we might have kept going on in life, both of us having the most ridiculous misperceptions about who we really were," he muttered fiercely before his mouth covered hers in a possessive, no-holds-barred kiss.

They stayed on that couch for hours, talking and touching, affirming their bond. Finally, Eleanor took his hand and led him to the guest bedroom. She left the light off, and they sat on the edge of the bed in the darkness. Trey wrapped her in his arms and they stared across to his building and the brilliantly lit Christmas tree he'd put up for her to see.

"The second time I ever saw you in this window, it was Christmas time," she said softly after a comfortable silence.

"I'm not sure I want to ask what I was doing, precisely," he said dryly.

"You were so beautiful to me, from the beginning," she murmured, lost in her thoughts. "You were amazing to look at, but I think it was the way you moved that had me spellbound. You were so confident in your own skin, so vibrant . . . so sexy."

He nuzzled her temple. She turned her chin up to look at him. His face looked sculpted and hard in the shadows, but the city lights gleamed warmly in his eyes. "That's a good description of how I felt when I first saw you in the coffee house," he said gruffly.

"Really?" she whispered.

"Yeah. When you get yourself into a zone, it's like you start to move to the beat of the universe or something. When you dance, it's like you're giving yourself up to it. It's incredible to see. I still can't get over the fact that you didn't do it regularly. I mean . . . I'm glad no one else has seen you like that." He brushed his fingertip across her temple and she saw his small smile. "I'm ecstatic about it, actually. I want you all to myself. But that doesn't negate the fact that you look like you were born to dance. Made to drive me nuts," he added under his breath.

Her lips parted in wonder.

"I'm sorry we missed the reading events last week," she whispered.

"Me too." His finger traced the line of her jaw. "But maybe this way, I can talk you into reading the rest of *Pride and Prejudice* to me."

She smiled. "Only if you read *Born to Submit* to me."

His eyebrows arched. "It's a deal."

She chuckled, but a flash of heat went through her at the idea of hearing Xander and Katya's sexy trysts told in Trey's deep, compelling voice. "I had something planned, for that night you came to the museum . . . the night when we ended up at the hospital."

"What?" he asked, still stroking her jaw with his fingertip.

She hesitated only for a second before she stood. "I'll show you. You stay here. Lean back on the pillows and get comfortable."

A few minutes later, she hit a button on the stereo and the sounds of Trey's fluid, melodic finger work on the guitar filled the entire condo. She loved this particular piece. It'd made her ache again and again during the time period when she didn't see him. Nevertheless, it hadn't stopped her from listening to it more times than she could count.

Her heart raced madly by the time she walked down the hallway. She'd changed into a clinging, revealing negligee and matching robe. She wore her favorite shoes for dancing.

And the panties.

You're really going to do this. Finally. You're going to expose yourself to him, and he's going to be right there.

She was going to strip, just feet away from him. She was going to seduce him . . . and she was going to give him the control. It was a challenge for her, an ultimate act of intimacy. But it was Trey, and it was a challenge she was ready to meet.

When she entered the guest bedroom a moment later, she saw that he reclined at the head of the bed, his shoes off, propped up against the pillows. She didn't turn on the light. There was enough illumination from the city lights to make each other out in the darkness.

She walked around the bed and stretched out her hand to him, the sounds of his strong, fluid fingers on the guitar strings rippling and pulsing in the air around them, seducing her.

"Here," she whispered. "Do what you want with it. Do what you want to me . . . whenever you want it. I trust you."

She handed him the small remote control for the panties she wore. She'd barely registered his look of surprise at her words when she spun around, and begun to dance to his music.

EPILOGUE

Four months later

Eleanor arrived at Trey's office a few minutes past five. She barely had had time to exchange a few words with Theresa, his admin, before he came out of his office, his manner striking her as strangely tense.

"We've got to go," he told Eleanor, taking her hand and pulling her away from Theresa's desk. "See you later, Theresa."

Eleanor rolled her eyes at Theresa. "Apparently, we're late for this mystery event," she said, rushing to keep up with Trey's long-legged stride. Theresa just grinned broadly, waving at Eleanor.

"You told Theresa, didn't you?" Eleanor said as they waited for the elevator, hand in hand. There'd been something knowing about Theresa's smile just now.

"Told her what?" Trey asked, deadpan.

"Whatever the mystery is," Eleanor said, reaching to straighten his tie. It was a likely excuse to touch him. He looked fantastic, wearing a dark blue suit, a blue and silver striped tie and a white shirt that set off the golden brown tan he'd acquired in a recent trip they'd taken to Fiji. The primal urge she'd had since the first day she saw him up close in the coffee shop to bite him all over had only gotten stronger in the past several months. Sometimes, Eleanor wondered humorously if there was such a thing as sexual cannibalism. She restrained herself from nibbling on him now with effort.

"I think my mother knows the mystery too. You must be blabbing about it to all the women in your life, aside from me."

The elevator door opened and Trey hurried her inside the car.

"What *is* it?" she couldn't help but prod him, her curiosity mounting by the second due to his tense, preoccupied mood. "Are you going to whisk me off to London for another surprise concert? Or is it dinner with another celebrity? I hope they like Italian food. I'm starving," she said, rubbing her hollow stomach. "I worked straight through lunch on the Authors of Illinois exhibit."

"It's not anything half so fancy as that. But there'll be food."

"Well, that's fine with me. I'm not in the mood for celebrity schmoozing anyway. I don't want anything fancy tonight. Trey, why are you frowning?" she asked suddenly when a shadow crossed his face.

"Nothing. I just hope this—"

He cut himself off suddenly, and Eleanor was only cast further at sea. What had him in such a wired, weird mood?

They left his office building and walked out onto a glorious early spring evening. The weather matched her mood. She knew it was corny to think it, but her mood was almost always sunny and bright, ever since Trey had become a permanent part of her world. Yes, she still experienced some black moments when she acutely missed Caddy. But that was only natural, and she'd learned to feel her grief, to move through it instead of fighting it.

For the most part, she felt like every day was a fresh new adventure. Life had taken on a golden sheen, and she owed it all to the dynamic, sexy . . . *brooding* man next to her.

What was *up* with him, anyway?

"Where are we going?" Eleanor wondered, straining to keep

up with him as they turned down Madison Avenue and walked toward the bridge. She was starting to get used to the amazing surprises life with Trey Riordan offered: jetting off to London or Paris for a work engagement that typically involved meeting amazing artists and watching them perform, or him surprising her with thoughtful gifts for no particular reason, like a rare first-edition copy of *Pride and Prejudice*, a beautiful gold and pearl necklace, and even—her favorite—a pair of genuine fur fans that Sally Rand herself had owned and used for her dances. They'd already put those to very good use.

"You'll see where we're going soon enough," Trey muttered, pulling her along. He led her down a flight of stairs.

"Isn't this the entrance to the water taxi? Are the water taxis even running yet?" she asked him.

"They technically don't start until tomorrow," he said. A bright yellow water taxi was pulled up next to the quay when they reached it. Eleanor looked at it in amazement.

"Wait . . . isn't this the one—"

"Yeah. It's the exact same one we took last November," Trey said. They approached an older, stocky man, and Trey shook his hand in greeting. "Eleanor, this is Reggie. Reggie, this is the lady I was telling you about."

"Pleasure to see you again, ma'am," the man said.

"You were our pilot last November," Eleanor said, smiling in disbelief and a little embarrassment.

Reggie's pale blue eyes sparkled beneath the cap he wore. "That's right. This time, Mr. Riordan is paying me not to go upstairs and oust you, though." Heat flushed her cheeks at the recollection of what Reggie had interrupted on their last trip. "Come on board. We're all set to go," he told Trey.

She followed Trey up to the enclosed deck. She saw with dawning amazement that a small table had been set up. On it was placed a basket, a vase of wildflowers, a bucket of chilling champagne and two flutes.

"You planned all this?" she asked him when he led her over to the exact same seats where they'd sat last November. She saw his small smile before he turned and began filling the flutes with champagne.

"It wasn't easy, hunting down our pilot and talking him into this," he said as he poured the champagne. "But at least because of the trouble we gave him, he remembered us," he added, humor glinting in his eyes as he handed her a champagne glass and sat down next to her. She laughed softly, feeling so full. So happy. The taxi left the quay, easing out on the river. The view rolled slowly past them, but she only had eyes for him.

"You know, for someone who claimed he didn't know the first thing about romance when we met, you sure are an expert at it now," she said, taking a sip of champagne.

He leaned back next to her, his blue eyes flashing with humor and heat. "You really think so?"

She glanced out at the stunning scenery, and the flowers, and the champagne . . . and him, her heart in her eyes.

"Here's to miracles happening, then," he said, leaning close so that she inhaled his delicious scent. He kissed her, his mouth coaxing and firm. Bold. Sweet. Her eyelids fluttered closed. She'd never get tired of his kisses. They melted her every time.

He lifted his mouth a moment later, but she kept her eyes closed, still pleasantly warm and dizzy from his kiss. Something cool and hard pressed against her mouth. She lifted heavy eyelids.

Her heart jumped in disbelief. The hair on her forearms stood on end. He was stroking her lower lip softly with a diamond ring. His eyes gleamed with heat as he looked down at her.

"You're the only woman who could turn me into a romantic,

Eleanor. I was a hopeless case before you came along. I can't ever let you go. It'd be the ruin of me, romantically speaking. Well, pretty much all around, come to think of it."

Her mouth trembled beneath the large, caressing diamond. Her eyes stung.

"Do you know that every day when I wake up since you've come into my life, I feel like I'm the luckiest woman alive?" she asked softly. "When I first saw you, you were this unbelievable, unobtainable fantasy."

"And now the fantasy is wearing thin?" he asked dryly.

"No. It's gotten even more wonderful. You really are my fantasy man. It's just that the fantasy is exponentially better in reality. I love you, Trey."

"I love you too. So much. I still can't believe it, but it keeps growing stronger. Deeper."

"I know," she agreed.

"Does this mean you'll marry me?" he asked her gruffly.

"Well I can't have you ruined. Romantically speaking or otherwise. Can I?" she asked him quietly.

She saw his quick, flashing smile. She felt the cool metal slip against her finger, and then Trey was kissing her. The water taxi's horn pealed and it echoed off the tunnel of the skyscrapers. To Eleanor, it sounded like the joyful shout of her heart.

There was something about the Tahoe air that made everything clear and luminous. Not just physical things either, Harper McFadden thought as she jogged down a stretch of beach, the cerulean lake glittering to the left of her. Her perception felt sharper in her new home. She felt a little lighter. The brilliant sun and pure air seemed to penetrate even the murkiest, saddest places of her spirit.

Alive.

That was it. She felt more alive here than she had since her parents' tragic death last year. Hopefully she was slowly—finally—leaving the shadows of grief behind.

She tensed and pulled up short in her run when a large, dark red dog with white markings began to charge her. She staggered back, dreading the imminent crash. The slashing teeth. *"Stay calm around them. Keep your fear boxed up tight. It'll only make them more aggressive if they sense it."*

The big dog pulled up at the last minute. He started to spin in excited, dopey circles in front of her.

She gave a startled laugh.

"You're not so scary, are you?" she murmured, reaching down cautiously to pet behind floppy ears. The dog immediately stopped dancing around and lifted his head, eyelids drooping and tongue lolling. Harper laughed and rubbed harder. "No, you're just a big pushover, aren't you?"

The dog whimpered blissfully.

Clearly, this particular dog was a cuddly pup with the appearance of a bear. Even so, her limbs still felt a little tingly from anxiety. This was one of the few things she *wasn't* so fond of in her new town. People adored their dogs here, to the point that they brought them inside the local stores and even the post office, and no one complained. She'd also noticed Tahoe Shores canines tended to be of the enormous variety. Unlike her former home in the Nob Hill neighborhood of San Francisco, leash laws were largely ignored here.

A figure cast a shadow over her and the dog.

"Sorry about that. He's like a two-year-old kid with the body of an ox. He doesn't know his own weight."

Harper didn't glance up immediately when the man approached. The thought struck her fleetingly that while his dog was a hyper, quivering beast, his owner's voice sounded mellow and smooth. Unhurried.

She dropped her hand from the enraptured dog and straightened. His head and shoulders rose above the background of the Sierra Nevada mountains and the setting sun. His dark shadow was cast in a reddish-gold corona. She held up her hand to shield her eyes and squinted. He came into focus. Her hand fell heedlessly to her side.

He was wearing a pair of dark blue swim trunks and nothing else. He'd just come out of the water. The way the trunks molded his body shredded her thoughts. Water gleamed on a lean, powerful torso, gilding him even more than the sun and his bronzed tan already did. His short wet hair was slicked back from a narrow, handsome face. Like her, he squinted as he examined her, even though he was turned away from the sun.

"It was a little intimidating, to be honest," she managed, gathering herself. He was gorgeous, sure, but she was still a little irritated that he let his gigantic dog roam free. Not everyone thought it was fun to be run down by a hundred-and-fifty-pound animal. People around here really needed to watch over their dogs better. "He was coming at me like a locomotive," she added.

"This is a private beach. It belongs to a friend of mine."

Harper blinked at the sudden coolness. It wasn't just his clipped tone, either. His narrow-eyed gaze was somehow . . . *cutting* as it moved over her face. It was like being scanned by a laser beam. The thought struck her that whoever this guy was, he regularly left people feeling tongue-tied and about six inches tall.

"I'm sorry," she said stiffly, standing tall to diminish the shrinking effect of his stare. "I was told by my Realtor that a Tahoe Shores resident could walk or run along the entire lakeshore within the town's city limits." She started to walk away from him.

"You misunderstood me."

"What?" She halted, looking over her shoulder.

Something crossed over his features, there and then gone. Was it frustration?

"You're right, technically speaking. The beach directly next to the lake is the town's property, even if we *are* on my friend's property at the moment," he said dryly, nodding at the distance between where they stood and the lake forty or so feet away.

"I'll get closer to the water, then."

"No, that's not what I meant. I wasn't calling you out for crossing my friend's beach. He'd be fine with it. You're welcome anytime."

"Oh." She gave a small shrug of bewilderment. She glanced uneasily at the lovely, sprawling, ultramodern mansion to the left of her, the one that must belong to his friend.

"I was just giving you fair warning. You might have another run in with Charger, or some other dog. Here, Charger." He calmly held out a large, outspread hand and the dog bounded over to him.

She spun fully to face him, unable to hide her smile at the vision of the rambunctious dog hopping up to reach his master's touch.

"I guess you knew him pretty well when you named him," she said.

"Yeah. I imagine he even charged out of the womb."

Charger frisked around a pair of long, strong-looking legs. He was a tall one. Six foot three or four? Her gaze stuck on his crotch. The wet trunks were revealing. *Very.* Heat flared in her cheeks.

"He interrupted your pace," he said.

She jerked her gaze guiltily up to his face. He waved at her jogging attire.

"Oh. It's okay. I never go that fast, anyway. And I'd just gotten started," she assured, her breathlessness at odds with her reply. "What breed is he?" Harper asked, nodding at the dog, hoping to distract him from her face. With her coloring, her blushes were annoyingly obvious.

"A Lab-pointer mix. I *think*, anyway. He didn't come with any papers. I got him from the local shelter."

"The Tahoe Shores Animal Shelter is close to the offices of my new job. It's huge. I heard it was the largest in Nevada." *Maybe that's why everyone is so dog-crazy around here.*

"You work at the *Sierra Tahoe Gazette*?" he asked. He noticed her surprised glance. He gave a small shrug. Harper experienced a stirring deep inside her, and realized it came from that small, sexy . . . yet somehow shy smile. But that couldn't be right. How could a man as cold and imperious as he'd seemed just seconds ago come off as *shy*?

"This is a small town. The *Gazette*'s office is the only building close to the shelter . . . besides the North Shore Fire Department." His gaze dropped over her slowly, and that flickering of her body swelled to a steady, pleasurable flame. "Although you *are* in good shape. Are you a firefighter?"

She laughed. No, he *definitely* wasn't shy. "You were right the first time." She stuck out her hand. "Harper McFadden. I started last week as the news editor at the *Gazette*."

He stepped closer. His hand felt damp and warm. It enfolded hers completely. She tried to make out the color of his narrowed eyes and saw shards of green, brown, and amber. Her heart gave a little jump.

Agate eyes.

"You left your job at the *San Francisco Chronicle* as a reporter."

Her mouth dropped open. "What?" she asked hollowly, almost certain she'd misheard him. Did his godlike attributes go beyond his phenomenal looks and aloofness? Was he omniscient as well?

She pulled on her hand, discombobulated, and he slowly released it from his grasp.

"I've read your articles in the *Chronicle*. I have offices in San Francisco. That piece you did on San Francisco's homeless children was top notch."

"Thank you," she managed, still knocked a little off balance.

He nodded and took a step back, as if he'd realized his unsettling effect on her. He did unsteady her, just not in the way he probably thought.

"You don't plan to write anymore?" Her spine stiffened a little. Force of habit. She'd been hearing that question a lot lately, usually accompanied by disappointment or bewilderment. Had she heard a hint of disapproval in this man's tone, or was it her own lack of confidence in her recent career change tainting her interpretation? *The latter, of course.* Why would a stranger care enough to be condemning?

"I wouldn't say that. I just wanted to experience a different side of the newspaper business," she replied neutrally.

"I love Tahoe Shores as much as the next resident, but . . . aren't we a far cry from San Francisco?" He reached down to distractedly scratch Charger, but his gaze on her remained sharp.

The easy richness of his voice beguiled her, but it was his calmness, his absolute, easy confidence that truly nudged her to let down her guard. There was a grace to him that one didn't usually see in such a masculine, virile man. It was that intangible quality that had called a walking god to mind.

She kept her gaze on his face, but it was just as distracting. He wore a thin, well-trimmed goatee that highlighted a sensual mouth. The hair on his face, chest, and head was wet at the moment, but appeared to be brown. Harper couldn't stop staring at his firm, well-shaped lips. She forced her gaze away and found herself watching his long fingers rubbing the dog's neck instead. It didn't help matters any.

"Sorry," he said after a short pause. "That's none of my business, is it?"

"No, it's not that. I just needed to get away from the grind." She tossed up her hands and glanced out at the aquamarine alpine lake, clear blue skies, and surrounding pine-covered mountains. "I wanted to try editing, and there was an opportunity here."

"Might be a shortage of actual *news* for a news editor, though," he said with a half smile. She saw the sharp gleam of curiosity in his hazel eyes.

"Maybe. But I could use the slow pace. The peace." His eyebrows arched. "For a little while, anyway," she added.

He nodded, and she had the fleeting, illogical thought that he understood. Maybe he really did. He had said he'd read her articles. Harper threw herself into her stories wholesale. Each one consumed her. Every one took a bit of her with it.

"Where are you staying?" he asked, looking down at Charger and gently squeezing a floppy ear. The dog quivered in pleasure.

Harper shifted her feet restlessly as another frisson of sensual awareness passed through her.

She really needed to snap out of it.

"I just moved in last Monday. Back there. Sierra Shores." She waved behind her to the beachside complex of townhomes. He nodded, his face striking her again as solemn and beautiful. His gaze flickered distractedly out toward the sparkling lake. He was losing interest in their conversation.

"You're from the south," she said impulsively.

His shadowed gaze zipped to her face. Why did he look so stiff? "Your accent," she said by way of explanation. "I didn't notice it at first, but it's definitely there." *Like a hint of rich, smooth dark chocolate.*

"Yeah. Most people don't catch that. South Carolina, born and bred," he said after a pause.

"I grew up in DC—Georgetown, actually. DC is a melting pot—so I have some experience with teasing out accents."

A silence descended, punctuated only by the hushed, rhythmic sound of the soft surf caressing the beach. He ran his hand distractedly across his damp, taut abdomen, the action scattering her thoughts. "Well . . ." he said after a pause, waving vaguely in the direction behind her. "We should let you get on with your jog. Sorry again for the interruption."

"I'm sorry for trespassing. I did it unknowingly."

"Like I said. You're welcome here."

She wondered what his friend thought of him handing out free passes to his property, but then dismissed the thought as quickly as she'd had it. He seemed the type of man to have friends who wouldn't argue with his proclamations.

"I hope you find what you're looking for here. The peace, I mean," he said.

Her heart fluttered. There it was again: a glimpse of unexpected sweetness, something that tugged at her and was in direct opposition to his potent masculinity and epic, effortless confidence.

Her strange musings evaporated in almost an instant when without another word he sauntered away from her, calling to Charger with that deep, mellow voice. After a moment, he lifted his arms to a casual boxer stance and broke into an easy jog. Charger bound into a gallop to follow him, barking ebulliently up at his master. Harper blinked, realizing she was entranced watching the rippling muscles of his gleaming back, hard, rounded biceps . . . and an incredible ass.

It took her a dazed half minute of resuming her jog in the opposite direction to realize he'd never told her his name.

It was all for the best, anyway. Harper was a little wary of men as good-looking as he'd been. She was *way* too prone to getting herself mixed up with self-involved narcissists. At age thirty-two, she'd finally learned the difficult lesson that what she wanted sexually—a powerful, confident male—was highly at odds with what she wanted emotionally—a smart, stimulating companion whom she respected, someone who really cared, a guy who *occasionally* thought enough of her to sacrifice his own needs in order to fulfill hers. Not all the time, of course. She wasn't needy and cherished her independence. But damn . . . *once* in a while? Was that really too much for a woman to ask?

Apparently so.

At any rate, she'd resolved to break her dysfunctional pattern. Each and every one of her past lovers had shone brilliantly in the beginning, and then proved himself to be gold-painted crap by the time she broke things off.

Don't kid yourself. None of your old boyfriends shone like he had just now.

Dangerous, a voice in her head insisted.

That was another habit Harper was trying to break: the fact

that when it came to her heart, she found potentially risky, powerful men fascinating, and yet . . . she feared them, as well. It seemed her head and her sexual appetites did constant battle.

Not that it mattered, she discounted, inhaling the pristine air to cleanse herself of thoughts of the man and the strangely charged moment. She settled into a comfortable jog. She had way more important things to consider than men and sex. Like her new life here, for instance. Her new job. A whole new future.

And it's not like he'd seemed remotely interested, anyway.

It was time for her to face up to the fact that she was alone in the world. Maybe she should consider getting a dog . . .

She imagined her parents' incredulous expressions if she ever told them she had a dog. She resisted an urge to laugh, but then almost immediately, that familiar hole opened up in her chest.

It'd never happen again, that she'd tell them about some new, exciting addition to her life.

As a teenager, Harper had suffered from debilitating anxiety. Her father had been a psychiatrist. Philip McFadden had spent a great deal of time and effort years ago to cure his daughter of several phobias and associated panic attacks. One of her phobias had been for dogs. Her mom and dad might have been stunned if they'd known she was considering a dog as a pet, but they would have been proud, too.

She'd come a long way from being that anxious, sad little girl. She'd never really thanked her parents for that.

Sheldon Sangar, the *Gazette*'s editor in chief, waved Harper in from across the newsroom. Or at least he beckoned her as best he could while clutching several bottles of water and a carton holding what looked like two strawberry smoothies from Lettie's Place, the local coffeehouse a couple of blocks away. In Harper's previous jobs, the typical fuel of the newsroom was adrenaline, caffeine, and junk food. At the *Sierra Tahoe Gazette*, the employees preferred salads, bottled water, and jogs on their lunch hour. Sheldon Sangar was no exception to this easygoing, health-conscious company attitude. It was strange to have an editor in chief who could have passed as a hippie if it weren't for his neat, short gray hair and newsroom badge.

"Do you have something for me?" Harper asked Sangar eagerly as she approached.

"Do you want a smoothie? I got one for Denise, but she had to take off early to take her daughter to the doctor for an infected spider bite," Sangar said, holding out the carton.

Harper briefly tried to picture her former bulldog-like editor-in-chief, Frazier Sorrenson, letting his assistant, Roberta, leave early because of a sick child. She failed in her imaginings. Roberta was lucky to get out of the newsroom every day by eight p.m. Harper doubted Frazier would let her go home early if her baby came down with typhoid.

"No, I mean . . . do you have a story for me? Things are pretty slow. I've already finished my edits and layouts." *By ten o'clock this morning.*

Sangar gave her a knowing glance over the frame of his glasses. "Sorry, no page-burners at the moment. I told you things could be pretty slow at the end of August. A lot of vacationers have cleared out now that school is starting, crime is at a standstill, and we haven't even got much to say about the Tahoe Shores football team yet. You *did* tell me you wanted an easy pace."

"I know. I'm not complaining," Harper assured.

And she wasn't, really. It was just hard to adjust her brain and body to the snail-like pace of a small town. It'd take some practice.

Sangar blinked as if he'd just thought of something and glanced down at the bottles of waters he clutched. "I *do* have something for you. Almost forgot. Denise told me to give it to you when I walked in. Came special delivery." He extended his thumb and forefinger, and Harper realized for the first time he held a white linen envelope. She took it, curious. Her name and the office address for the *Gazette* were written in elegant cursive on the front.

"Looks fancy. Like a wedding invitation or something," Sangar said, readjusting the bottles of water against his body. He turned and loped in the direction of his office.

"Yeah, except I don't know anybody around here who would ask me to . . ."

She trailed off when she realized Sangar was out of earshot. She started toward her office, tearing open the envelope. The stationery was a plain white linen card with the exception of some bold dark blue and gold lettering at the top: *Jacob R. Latimer, 935-939 Lakeview Boulevard, Tahoe Shores, NV, 89717.*

"Jacob Latimer?" she mumbled, her feet slowing. The name sounded familiar, but she couldn't pin down why exactly.

"What about Latimer?" a woman asked sharply.

Harper glanced up and saw that Ruth Dannen, their features, society, and entertainment editor, had halted in front of her. She was in her midfifties and had been pleasant enough to Harper since starting her new job, if a little gruff. Ruth was a polished, thin woman who gave off an air of hard-nosed sophistication and always being in the know about Tahoe people and events.

"It's an invitation," Harper said, puzzled. She reread the handwritten message inside out loud. "'Mr. Jacob Latimer requests the honor of your presence at a cocktail party tonight at his home. Please bring your invitation and present it to the security guard at the entry gate at 935 Lakeview Boulevard. Our apologies for the inconvenience in advance, but for security reasons, identification will be required and there will be a brief search of your car and person. No additional guests, please.'"

The note was signed by an Elizabeth Shields.

She glanced up when Ruth gave a low whistle.

"Well how do you rate?" Ruth wondered, giving Harper a sharp, incredulous once-over.

"What do you mean? Who's Latimer?"

"Only the richest of all the rich bastards who congregate around this lake. You've never heard of Latimer? The software mogul? Came out of nowhere when he was still practically a kid, making his first millions in the Clint Jefferies insider trading pharmaceutical scandal? No one could ever pin anything on him, of course. Jefferies was actually the focus of the Securities and Exchange Commission's investigation, which was eventually dropped for lack of evidence. They always go after the one with the money, not the small potatoes, like Latimer was at the time. If there *was* insider trading going on, both Latimer and Jefferies got away with it. By the time the scandal faded, Latimer was serving in army intelligence. He's a brilliant programmer. The military snapped him up in a New York minute from MIT to create anti-hacker software. I hear they gave him huge bonuses every time he managed to get into the government's high-security files, and then gave him even more money to utilize the knowledge for creating programs that kept criminals from doing the exact same thing he'd just done. He parlayed all he learned from serving in army intelligence—and all the money he made in the Jefferies pharmaceutical windfall—into—"

"Lattice," Harper finished, realization hitting her. Lattice was a well-known software giant. Of course. That's why she'd heard the name Jacob Latimer. Harper didn't know much about big business or technology movers and shakers, but she'd heard of Lattice. Even though Latimer's company had begun based on an antivirus security program for the military, it'd quickly moved on to public sector applications for human resources, and most recently to antivirus software for personal computers and devices.

"What does the owner of Lattice want with me?" Harper wondered.

Ruth just arched her plucked, dark blond eyebrows and dropped her gaze over Harper speculatively. "Maybe hair the color of copper and a girlish figure has more mileage than I'd thought these days. Latimer loves women. Rumor is, he has some unusual tastes in that arena."

Harper opened her mouth to tell the older woman that was ridiculous. And Harper's looks weren't *unusual*, thank you very much. She'd been referred to as the girl next door more than once in her life, much to her irritation.

"I don't see how he'd know anything about my existence, let alone my hair color. Seriously, what do you think this is about?"

Ruth held out her hand. Harper gave her the invitation. Ruth examined the contents, frowning slightly.

"It's genuine. I recognize Elizabeth's handwriting. She's his primary personal assistant. I think he has several, but she's his main one for the Tahoe compound. You have *no* idea why you're getting this? You don't know Latimer or any of his staff? His acquaintances? Never met him while you were in San Francisco?"

"No. I didn't even recognize his name at first."

"Well," Ruth said, giving the card back with a flick of her thin wrist, "that's an invite that almost everyone in the country would kill for, including me. Latimer keeps to himself in that lakeside compound of his. He's paranoid. Some people say it's because he's got plenty to hide. Lots of rumors have flown around about him over the years. Is he still involved with the U.S. military? Does he pull strings to move players on the chessboard of international relations? Is he a spy? He's definitely a big philanthropist— probably to gloss over the gaping holes in his respectability as far as his rise to power. Who knows, really? That's the question when it comes to Latimer, and I suspect the answer is: only Latimer himself. And possibly Clint Jefferies."

"Who's Clint Jefferies?"

"The pharmaceutical and real estate tycoon? Owns Markham Pharmaceuticals? Worth billions. Nice looking, but a bit of a douche if you ask me," Ruth replied with a sniff.

Harper definitely recognized the company name Markham. It was one of the top six pharmaceutical companies worldwide. "Right," Harper mused. "So how are Jefferies and Latimer related again?"

"Nowadays, they *aren't*, because that's the way Latimer wants it. Jefferies was his mentor a long time ago. But Latimer has held him at arm's length ever since the Markham insider trading scandal. That whole affair has been shrouded in mystery for years, just like Latimer himself. He's a reporter's dream and nightmare at once. *Someone* has done a good job of brushing the trail of his history clean," Ruth said with a pointed glance. "My bet is that the main trail sweeper is Latimer himself, with a little help from his buddies in military intelligence. I've been invited to a few charity events Latimer has sponsored at a local hotel. He only attends once in a while, and when he does, he's like a ghost. No one ever gets a good look at him, let alone talk to him. Rumor has it, he even has his women imported from other parts of the world. His deliberate avoidance of the women around here only adds to his mystique and allure. *And* to local females' frustration. You *have* to tell me every detail about the cocktail party."

"You mean you think I should go?"

Ruth looked scandalized. "Aren't you listening to what I'm saying? That's a golden ticket you're holding right there. His staff guards him like Fort Knox, both here and in San Francisco. Even if Latimer does his ghost act at this cocktail party, though, just getting behind those gates is a major coup. I've never been invited to the compound."

"But—"

"You *will* go," Ruth said with a glare. Harper gave her a dry *don't even think you can push me around* look. Ruth seemed to realize her harshness and laughed. "Jesus, how to explain to a peasant that you don't turn down an invitation from the king?" Harper opened her mouth to defend herself. "Oh, calm down," Ruth said, cutting her off with a wave of her hand and the air of someone who had more important things to consider than soothing a frayed ego. She took Harper by the arm and urged her toward her office. "I'm not being difficult, Harper. Honestly. It's just you don't *get* Tahoe Shores yet. Sure, we're a little Podunk town, but at the same time, we host some of the biggest movers and shakers in the world on that lakeshore. The Silicon Valley elite flock to the Nevada Tahoe shores for the tax breaks and the incredible views, and Jacob Latimer is one of the biggest of them all." Ruth stepped back in front of Harper's desk, letting go of her arm. "Now. Are you a newswoman, or not?"

Harper stilled at the challenge, eyes narrowing. "Of course."

"Then you're going to that damn party because this is the best bit of news this pitiful newspaper has had in ages. Who knows, maybe you'll get some dirt on Latimer in that close of proximity."

"I'm an editor now, not a reporter. Let alone an undercover one."

"I don't care if you're Ben freaking Bradlee, you're *going.*" Ruth pointed at Harper's chair. "Now sit down, and I'll try to prepare you for what you're about to get into. As best I can, anyway, since I only have my imagination to go on as far as what happens behind those gates."

Harper gave a bark of disbelieving laughter, but started around her desk, nevertheless. Some people might have been offended by Ruth's manner, but plainspoken bossiness was familiar to her. Ruth was the closest thing to a savvy newspaperwoman Harper had run into at the *Gazette*. The truth was, she wouldn't let Ruth boss her around if she wasn't curious herself about the invitation.

"You make a cocktail party sound like it's life altering," Harper said, plopping into her chair.

"You never know," Ruth replied drolly. "We're talking Jacob Latimer here. He's made it a business to alter lives. Maybe his own, most of all. He made a giant of himself out of nothing but shadows and whispers, after all. *That's* the potential story, if you ask me."

ABOUT THE AUTHOR

Beth Kery is the *New York Times* and *USA Today* bestselling author of more than thirty novels, including *Glow, Glimmer, The Affair, Since I Saw You, Because We Belong* and *When I'm With You*. She lives in Chicago with her family. Visit her online at bethkery.com.